Butterflies

MICHELLE SMART

This book is entirely a work of fiction. The names, characters and incidents portrayed in it are the product of the author's imagination or are used fictitiously. Any resemblance to actual persons, living or dead, events or localities, is entirely coincidental.

Copyright © 2024 by Michelle Smart

All rights reserved.

No part of this publication may be reproduced in any form or by any electronic or mechanical means, including information storage and retrieval systems, without written permission from the author, except for the use of brief quotations in a book review.

Any unauthorised use of this publication to train generative artificial intelligence (AI) technologies is expressly prohibited.

For information regarding subsidiary rights, please contact the author.

michelle@michellesmart.co.uk

Part One

NOW

Alex

There's a mechanical clunking in my head. I prise my eyes open and lift my neck to get a fix on where I am, but a shooting pain in my brain stops me in my tracks. I cry out. All that comes from my arid mouth is a muffled 'nya' sound. There's a funny taste on my tongue, far worse than the old morning-after taste of too much booze and too many cigarettes.

What the hell was I drinking last night…? The moment I wonder this, a shrapnel of panic fires through me, gaining speed and force as I realise that not only have my memories of the previous night fallen into a black void but all my memories. Everything.

I need to get off this bed. I try to move my limbs but my bones are too weighted. Something is compressing them. All I can do is part my lips and try to suck enough air in to keep the nausea churning in my stomach from ejecting and choking me.

Have I been drugged? Poisoned in a case of mistaken identity by a Russian KGB agent seeking to silence another old spy?

I'm not a spy. I know that. I'm not Russian.

So, who am I?

Where am I?

I close my eyes and concentrate on breathing.

Alex!

A sliver of the terror abides. That's my name. Alex. Alex Hammond. I strain for more facts but it's like groping through treacle.

How can I know what treacle is, what a Russian is, but not know anything more than my name?

More deep, regular breaths. The clunking in my brain has reduced a notch. One more deep breath and then I cautiously turn my head. The pain is a little less sharp.

I fix on an unfamiliar wall and blink to clear the cloud in my vision. A digital clock sits on the bedside table. It reads 07:18. The clock reminds me of the one I got for my fifteenth birthday...

I sit bolt upright. The pants of my breaths and thuds of my heart echo loudly in my ears and I stare open-mouthed at the unfamiliar black wardrobe and overflowing laundry basket at the foot of my unfamiliar bed. Unfamiliar and yet... I know them.

The clock blinks and as I watch the time change to 07:19, everything clicks into place in one mad gust that has me clutching at my throat to stifle a scream.

I'm hardly aware of the tears pouring down my face or know if it's horror or jubilation causing them to flow.

It worked. It fucking worked! I've travelled back thirty-three years.

And then I curl into a ball and sob until my ribs are bruised and my pillow's drenched.

Melody.

She was alive. Is alive.

Here, in this time, Melody is alive.

Now all I have to do is wait five years to start our lives together again.

Thursday 13th June 1996

BEFORE

Melody

The Merry Thief, a regular lunchtime spot for local office workers and passing tradesmen, and a good evening spot for Brocklehurst's underage drinkers, is a convenient ten-minute walk from the house I rent a room in, so how I've come to be late for my shift is a mystery. I mean, I set off in excellent time, giving myself two minutes to spare – after all, you never know who you're going to bump into and stop to chat with – but, despite walking directly from front door to pub door, I've still managed to be four minutes late. The scowl on Graham's face tells me my tardiness hasn't gone unnoticed. Oh well, he'll live. Which other sucker would he be able to pay a crummy five pounds an hour to?

Lorna, owner of my rented room, is one such sucker and I do an exaggerated double-take to see her at the table by the quiz machine.

Ignoring Graham's glowering, I head over to her.

"What are you doing here?" I haven't seen her all day. Admittedly, I've spent most of it sleeping off my hangover while she's been busy working through hers at her day job. She's not on the rota to work that night but Graham is such a knob of a boss that if you make the mistake of popping in for a drink with friends, he'll expect you to help out if it gets busy or cover for him if he wants to slope off to watch one of the soap-operas he's addicted to. The knobhead always forgets to pay you for it too. The last time he pulled that stunt, I helped myself to a pint of Stella and downed it in one, slamming the glass on the counter with a flourish while his face went beetroot. Along with tardiness, Graham also has an issue with women drinking pints. Naturally, I've taken to drinking pints just to annoy him. It's a shame I can only manage two in a row. The last time I drank three pints, Lorna and Megs had to drag me home and navigate strategic places for me to puke and wee as needed en route.

"I'm here with Alex." She nods at the bar.

A rowdy group of lads are crowded around it. As soon as I clock Matt amongst them, I quickly move my attention back to Lorna. "Since when have you been seeing someone?"

I've known Lorna for three years. If she's had a boyfriend or even a date in that time, she's kept it secret. If you ask her type, she brushes it off and says she's choosy. I bloody wish I was. I wouldn't have to spend the next however long avoiding Matt the Twat.

"I'm not seeing him, he's an old friend." She plucks a cigarette from the pack she's been twirling in her hands. "We met up after work for a catch-up. He's just moved back to Brocklehurst."

"And you brought him here? Are you mad?"

"I must be. Or all the vodka last night killed what's left of my brain cells."

I cackle. "Still up for tonight?"

She laughs. "Might as well try and kill my liver off too."

"Mel!"

Graham's shout reminds me I'm supposed to be working. I don't want to antagonise him too much in case he decides to rota me onto kitchen duties. The Merry Thief must be the only pub in the country that doesn't have a dishwasher in its kitchen.

I've taken only two steps when I come face-to-chest with a body carrying two pints that slosh over the owner's giant hands. I quickly jump back and wave my hands in the air. "Sorry, sorry, didn't see you there."

"Don't worry about it," comes an impossibly deep reply.

I look up at the head attached to the body and find myself gazing at possibly the most handsome face I've seen in my life. My eyes lock onto the most gorgeous shade of green, just long enough for a bolt of recognition to shoot through me and a huge smile to form unbidden on my face.

But there's no time for me to wonder where I know this hunk from as Graham's shouting at me over the noise of the growing crowd to move my backside.

I look at the hunk one more time then hurry to hang my jacket on the peg, lift the hatch and step behind the bar.

"Right," I say, sticking the newest Now album in the CD player. "Let's get some life in this place." I skip Queen's 'Too Much Love Will Kill You' (too depressing) and go straight to Oasis's 'Don't Look Back in Anger'.

I turn to the crowd around the bar and say, "Who's next?" At least six men wave their money at me.

Alex

"Who's that?" I ask of the pocket-dynamo hurtling behind the bar in knee-high Dr Marten's painted with tiny butterflies who'd looked at me as if I were the best Christmas present she'd ever received. I dry my beer-soaked hands on my jeans and sit back on the manky fitted seat next to Lorna. I don't worry about the spillage on the carpet; it'll soak in with the rest of the crap it's been gorging on over the years. I don't think The Merry Thief has been cleaned since we came for our first illegal drink here ten years ago when we were sixteen.

Before Lorna can answer, Oasis suddenly booms out of the speaker directly above, making us both jump and my ears ring.

"Melody," she answers before taking a small sip of her beer. "She's the one who beat you to my spare room."

Lorna was born sensible. She's had a steady job working at a bank on Watling Street since she left school and was the first of our old gang to actually buy a property, a narrow Victorian house, also on Watling Street. Cannily, she rents her two spare rooms out *and* she works a couple of shifts a week in this dive. If she hasn't got a stash of money squirreled away, I'm an aardvark.

I look again at the pocket-dynamo, now with her back to the bar adding a measure of clear spirit into a glass, and admire her hair. It falls to the base of her spine like wild black corkscrews. When she turns around, her gaze rests briefly on me before she places the glass on the bar.

"Reckon she'll let me share it?" I joke.

"Knowing Mel, yes. But only for a few days. She bores quickly."

"A few days would suit me." I grin. After the crap with Rachel, another relationship is the last thing I want. I raise my glass. "Cheers."

She clinks it and takes another small sip before placing her glass back on the sticky table. "So, where are you living? Did you go back to your dad's?"

Not a chance. I love my dad but he's a stickler for house rules. I'd be expected to be tucked up in bed by ten-o-clock every night. Everything has to be done his way, a trait that's worsened since mum died four years ago. She brought the fun side out of him. She brought the fun side out of everyone.

"I moved into Kermit's box room."

Kermit's real name is Paul but he's been known as Kermit since we were ten and he ate a handful of worms for a dare. The shade of green he turned was the single funniest moment of my childhood.

Lorna rolls her eyes. "God, the two of you living together... Bet it's like Men Behaving Badly come to life."

Considering that in the two weeks I've been living in Kermit's spare room most evenings have been spent drinking cans of beer and discussing the merits of Kylie Minogue's bottom, that isn't far off the mark. If his girlfriend cares, she doesn't show it. Ellie's evenings are spent stoned on Kermit's living-room floor feeding her addiction to Mario Kart.

"Go on," Lorna says. "Tell me what happened with Rachel."

"She decided she wanted a richer man."

"Really?"

"Well, richer than me. She went on one of those team building weekends and did the clichéd thing of screwing her boss. Came home and told me we were over. Moved out the same night."

She whistles. Then she looks at me slyly. "What's it like getting a taste of your own medicine?"

I wince. I should never have confessed to sleeping with a client when Rachel kicked me out that time. Lorn let me crash in her spare room for a couple of nights before Rachel took me back.

"It only happened the once," I defend myself. "And it was before we got engaged." There is no way I'm going to admit to the drunken one-night stand I had a few months ago. No one has ever found out, and Lorna doesn't need more ammunition to weaponise against me. I've no idea why I like her so much.

"Oh, that makes it all right then, does it?" she asks innocently.

"Give me a break, Lorn," I plead. "Trust me, Rachel had my balls in a vice for months after that." I only got her to unlock them by maxing my credit card on a diamond ring for her. I can still remember the way she raised her eyebrow in disappointment at it.

"I'll just bet she did." Her tone reminds me that Lorna never liked Rachel. The feeling was mutual. "Why did you move back here?"

"Couldn't afford the rent on my own. London prices are a bitch." And my work as a mosaic craftsman is specialised but sporadic. Feast or famine. One job can tide me and Jimmy over for months. Other months I'm scavenging the back of sofas for loose change to buy cigarettes. Rachel often liked to sneer that I'd bring in a better income if I changed to tiling as a trade. Everyone would need their bathrooms or kitchens tiled at some point. Only a handful would ever want a bespoke mosaic to walk on or look at.

"Rachel's the bitch," Lorna mutters. "I'm sorry, mate."

"Don't be." I dig my elbow into her ribs. "Life's a bitch but at least I dodged a bullet and didn't marry one."

She laughs and punches my arm. "There's a lot more bitches to choose from in this town, that's for sure. Mind you, you've already shagged most of them."

I look again at her new lodger. In a sea of familiar faces, hers is one of the few I don't recognise. The crowd around the bar has dispersed and she's chatting to Graham, the grumpy landlord who barred me weeks before I turned twenty-two when I got so drunk I damaged the pool table. This is the first time I've been back since. I assume he's forgotten about it as he didn't mention it; merely poured my pint with the usual scowl he bestows on everyone. At this moment his face has struck an extremely unnatural pose. A smile.

"Is *she* a bitch?" I ask.

Lorna follows my gaze. "Mel?" She ponders this then shakes her head. "No. She's as mad as a box of frogs and as incapable of being faithful as you are, but she's nice. Funny."

As if she can feel our attention on her, the pocket-dynamo looks our way. Her eyes linger on me for a moment, just long enough for a tingling sensation to run up my spine.

Melody

It's Alex! The hunk I walked into is Alex! I can't believe it!

The Thief is heaving, the bar a constant flow of thirsty customers and, though I go through the motions of serving them and give the usual banter, I'm wholly aware that Alex is here. In this pub. Sitting with one of my best friends.

The beats of my heart are erratic and when he gets to his feet and approaches the bar, they accelerate into a canter. Typical of my luck, Graham decides to pull his finger out and actually serve a customer, and it has to be Alex he chooses, leaving me to deal with Matt the Twat.

"Nine pounds thirty," I say after I pour his round, trying not to meet his eye.

He hands me a tenner and makes a point of pressing it into my hand. "Are you doing anything after work?"

"Sleeping," I reply kindly. Not quite a lie. I'm sure I'll fall asleep at some point. Just not with him. No way. Never again. The thought actually makes me feel quite sick.

Mercifully, a couple approaches the bar and I scoot over to serve them. While I pour their drinks, I catch Alex's eye again. There's interest but no recognition in his stare.

As soon as I finish serving them, I grab Graham before he can hide upstairs in his flat.

"I'm going to have a quick break before you go off to watch EastEnders," I tell him. If I phrase it as a question, he'll say no. Then, in case he's still inclined to say no, I open the bar hatch and hurry over to Lorna and Alex, pretending not to see Matt still trying to catch my eye.

When would he take the bloody *hint*?

"Can I join you?" I ask when I reach their table, speaking loudly to make myself heard over the music.

"Course," Lorna says. "Mel, this is Alex, Alex this is Melody."

I smile widely, drop onto the chair facing them and pull my

cigarettes from my cardigan pocket. I flip the lid and wave the packet at them. "Nice to meet you again."

His head tilts, face creased in confusion. When we met, he was clean shaven, his dark brown hair cropped short. Now, dressed in jeans and a black t-shirt, he has a goatee beard and his hair is chin length and keeps flopping over his gorgeous face.

Beautiful green eyes lock onto mine. I remember thinking *he* was beautiful. Now, he's far too rugged to be called beautiful but, deary me, the ruggedness only makes him sexier.

He plucks a cigarette from the packet. "We've met?"

"Don't you remember?" I put a cancer stick between my lips. I will quit one day. I'm quite sure it will be easy.

"No." Alex holds his lighter out for me. I accept the flame.

I admit to feeling a little crushed. Okay, a lot crushed. I haven't changed that much physically in the past five years, not like he has.

"Your parents own the fishing lakes near Hestcote, right?"

He lights his own cigarette and passes the light to Lorna. "Right..."

"See!" I'm triumphant. "A load of us went camping there five years ago. We might have forgotten to ask permission..." There was no 'might' about it. "We got a little noisy and some of the fishermen complained about us. I think we were scaring the fish or something. Anyway, you came down with your dad, I think to kick us off your land or something, but you ended up talking him into letting us stay the night so long as we stopped making such a racket." I stare into those gorgeous green eyes as I speak, waiting for the penny to drop for him too. There's still zero recognition. "You ended up hanging around with us. You and I spoke for *hours*. Do you really not remember?"

The shake of his head this time is much slower. His face inches a little closer to mine. "Trust me, if I'd spent hours talking to you, I would remember."

A frisson of something races up my spine and, despite the

crushing disappointment that the night that changed the course of my life left no impact on him at all, I smile.

"Warning," Lorna mutters. "Matt the Twat's coming over."

I barely have time to cover my exasperation before he's hovering awkwardly by my side, hands rammed in the pockets of his jeans.

"We're going to the Oak to watch the footy," he says. His gang of friends are bouncing noisily by the door. I pretend not to hear their catcalls.

"Okay... Have fun."

"Want me to come back when you finish and walk you home?"

"I'll walk back with Lorna, but thanks for the offer."

"Another time?"

I catch Alex's eye.

"We'll see." Why can't I just tell Matt to get lost? I don't want to spell it out and hurt his feelings, that's why. But really, why can't he just take the hint?

What is it with men? You sleep with one and think maybe (big maybe) you'd like a repeat performance but they blow you off, but when you sleep with one, regret it immediately and want to blow *them* off (no *double entendre* there thank you very much), they get it in their heads that you're now a couple and hang around like a bad smell. Sometimes I want to scream, 'We had sex. It was rubbish. Move on. Find someone else to have sex with and maybe the chemistry will be there to want to do it again.'

Problem is, some men thought the chemistry was there the first shit time.

Problem is, I hate hurting people's feelings. Even twats like Matt. I wish I could find the words to let him down gently. Make it crystal clear I'm not interested without hurting him.

One of Matt's mates bounds over and puts him in a headlock. "Come on, short arse. We're going to miss kick-off."

"Melody!"

I don't have to look to know it's Graham shouting at me.

"Back to the grindstone," I mutter, and take one last drag of my cigarette.

In the few minutes I've been away from the bar, the place has emptied, no doubt all the punters fleeing to the Oak to watch the group game. Graham couldn't give two hoots. He hates football. He's only agreed to show the England games of the Euro 96 tournament as all us bar-staff said we'd go on strike if he didn't. Any savings he'd make on our wages would be undermined by him having to do some actual work himself.

Still, at least his refusal to show the non-England games means I don't have to put up with Matt tonight.

Alex strolls over and leans on the bar.

My heart races. "What can I get you?"

His eyes gleam. "A pint of Stella, half for Lorn and whatever you're having."

I beam. "I'll have a half too, thank you, but I can't drink it 'til my shift finishes." I really hope he'll still be there for that.

It's funny how well I remember him from that night. A group of us had gone camping for no other reason than to get drunk and make-out. We all told our parents we were having sleepovers at each-other's houses, pooled our money together and brought the cheapest drinks we could find with the highest alcohol content. By the time Alex and his angry dad turned up, we were all pretty plastered. And yet I remember everything that followed so well. We talked for hours. I felt so special that this gorgeous older man – I'm pretty sure he said he was twenty-one at the time – was showing such interest in me. He asked me tons of questions, about my exams, my plans for the future, the music I was into, the books I liked to read. Everything.

I know I must sound awful for admitting this, what with me being there with my boyfriend and everything, but I was disappointed when Alex left without trying to kiss me or even asking if he could see me again. Unsurprisingly, Danny dumped me the next day. I didn't blame him.

It's mortifying to remember but for weeks after, I constantly played that Bryan Adams' song 'Everything I Do' in my bedroom and daydreamed about Alex like a lovesick schoolgirl. Which I suppose I had been.

And here he is, five years later, right here, right now. Right in front of me. Buying me a drink. Eyes sparkling with the same interest I'd seen back then.

When I've poured the drinks and taken his money, I print the receipt off and hunt for a pen. I hand the receipt to him. "Can you initial it please?"

"Why?"

"Graham won't believe me otherwise."

"He's always been a trusting soul."

I laugh. "He's from the same village as me. My mum grew up there too. She says when they were at school he would make the other kids sign a receipt for borrowing a pencil."

"What village is that?"

"Collingswood."

"One of the kids from my school came from Collingswood."

"Mark Wilcox?"

"You know him?"

I try not to laugh at this replay of a five-year-old conversation. That Alex had gone to school with Mark Wilcox was one of the only pieces of information I was able to prise out of him. "I don't know him well. He's six years older than me." If I wasn't from such a small village, I wouldn't know him at all. That he'd been the only person in the entire village to sport a bona fide Mohican helped identify him too.

He has a drink of his beer. "You're twenty-one?"

"Just turned."

"When?"

"Two weeks ago."

"Happy birthday."

"Thanks. You can buy me a drink if you want to make up for missing it and for forgetting my existence."

Lorna appears carrying her jacket and handbag. "Thanks for abandoning me."

He looks chagrined. "Sorry, Lorn."

She shakes her head and hauls herself onto a bar stool. "Do you remember her yet?" she asks Alex, flipping her cigarette packet open and offering them around.

He shakes his head and looks straight at me. "Was I on drugs that night? That's the only thing I can think of to explain it."

"You told us off for smoking dope."

"Did I? That doesn't sound like me."

"No, it really doesn't," Lorna agrees.

"Shut up, Lorn."

"No, don't shut up," I interject, laughing. "Tell me all his dirty secrets." I want to know them. All of them.

"There's not enough hours left in the day."

"That's okay, you can carry it on when we get to the Summer Gardens."

Alex chokes on his beer. "*You're* going to the Summer Gardens?" he says to Lorna. Summer Gardens is a modern complex six miles away in the city that has a number of bars and a nightclub in it. "*You?*"

She puts on her prim face. "Yes. And?"

"You? Clubbing? And on a school night?"

"Yes. And?"

"You've changed."

Her lips twitch. "It's Mel's fault. She's a terrible influence."

He looks at me.

I widen my eyes in mock innocence.

"You don't look like a clubber."

An astute observation considering I'm wearing black jeans, black t-shirt, an oversized black cardigan and my faithful Dr Martens.

"Thursday's indie and rock night," I explain.

"Am I invited?"

I meet Lorna's eye. She must have read the plea in mine for

her lips twitch and she nods. "But I warn you now, I will not play gooseberry. Got it?"

Alex

I don't trust the girls' assurance that there's no dress code on a Thursday night at the Summer Gardens, not until the doorman, who knows Melody by name, waves us in. I don't believe it's student night either, not until we fight the crowd to the front of the bar and get a shot for a pound each.

We clink our glasses together and down them. I've never seen Lorna have a shot before. Her idea of letting her hair down is to nurse two halves a lager over an entire night. I've only seen her drunk once, the night of my mother's funeral. It's a night we never speak of.

"Another!" Melody insists joyously, and I understand in an instant what Lorna means about her being a terrible influence. Except, I would call her a superb influence. I've never known Lorna smile so much and laugh, properly laugh, as much as she has tonight, and I can see it's being in Melody's orbit causing it. She might be top to toe in black but I've never met anyone who exudes sunshine like she does.

I've learned a lot about Melody Aldridge tonight. A virtually empty pub gave me time to learn that she's recently completed a history degree and that she managed a week back in the family home before her baby sister – a 'surprise' for her parents – waking her at five am every day got too much to cope with, hence her moving into Lorna's spare room. The two have been friends since Melody started working at The Merry Thief during her university holidays three years ago. She has a big interview in a few weeks for the role of assistant curator at Hampton Court Palace (funnily enough, I'm starting a job next week in Richmond, just a few miles from the palace). When I said I imagined her doing a more sociable job, she laughed. She laughs a lot.

Thankfully, Lorna hasn't spilled too many of my secrets. I'll have to pull her aside later and beg her not to give Melody the full lowdown of what a shit I've been.

After the third shot, Melody drags us onto the dancefloor. It's packed, forcing us to dance closely together. Which suits me just fine. What suits me even more is when Lorna starts dancing with a group of women and turns her back to us with a wink.

Melody is so short she barely reaches my shoulder. Diminutive size or not, there is no ignoring her, not with her hands waving all over the place and her black corkscrews flying in all directions as she belts out the words to 'Common People'. I notice a couple of lads on the edge of the dancefloor watching her.

I take a chance and put a hand on her hip. I can feel the heat of her body through it. She closes the gap between us.

"Do you want a drink?" I ask.

She cups her ear.

I lean down and manage a good inhale of her warm skin. "Drink?"

She rests a hand lightly on my shoulder and steps onto her tiptoes. "Yes please."

I've no idea who slips whose hand into whose but we leave the dancefloor with them clasped together. I only just remember to look out for Lorna so I can indicate where we're going. She sticks a thumb up and carries on dancing.

Grinning at each other, we have another couple of shots and then back to the dancefloor. As soon as we find a space, Melody's hands wind around my neck and she's gazing up at me, big black eyes holding me as tightly as her body as she moves to the music.

Melody Aldridge, I decide, is the sexiest creature I've ever met.

Friday 8th March 1991

NOW

Alex

I open my wardrobe door and am hit with scents of the past. For a long moment I'm incapable of doing anything but holding myself upright. I rifle through the limited offerings with nausea swirling thickly in my stomach, and select a pair of jeans. Even in my heavy-headed state, I know there's no way they're going to fit my thirty-six-inch waist. Very soon, I realise nothing's going to fit and don the grey polystyrene dressing gown hanging on the bedroom door. After counting to ten, I open the door and gingerly poke my head out. I listen carefully over the weighty beats of my heart. Someone's downstairs.

My bones are jellified. The nausea is getting worse. Saliva fills my mouth...

My body takes control and propels me over the threshold to the bathroom next door. I barely have time to register the old familiar scent of pine before I'm spewing my guts up into the toilet.

God alone knows – and for the first time, I wonder about that old man in the cemetery – how long I kneel there with my face in the loo and sweat pouring off me, too ill to even care that the puke expelling from me is black. Even when my stomach is emptied, I keep my face where it is, dry-heaving grey bile.

And then all that's left are crippling cramps. I put the lid down, flush, and haul myself to my feet then drag them the two steps to the sink. I splash water over my clammy face and then, as I'm patting myself dry, I see the reflection in the mirror and stagger back in fright.

I have to force air into my bruised lungs. With blood whooshing loudly in my head, I tip-toe back to the mirror, squinting with the same fear I had as a small boy when I needed the toilet at night and was terrified of seeing my reflection.

My second glance in the mirror is no less frightening. The man staring back at me... he's a *boy*. I peer closer. It's like looking at Ollie's son, James.

The room starts to swim around me.

James is seventeen. People have often said how much he looks like me and now, for the first time, I see it.

Tentatively, I touch the face. *My* face. My green eyes are bloodshot but the bags that have been permanent fixtures beneath them for at least a decade have disappeared. The lines on my forehead have disappeared, as have the folds of skin that have been steadily deepening in my cheeks. My lips are fuller. Darker. I have only one chin.

This is the face I last looked at thirty-three years ago.

My heart skips and more of the tension in me loosens.

Melody is here, in this world.

Where is she? What is she doing?

Melody

I throw my duvet off then immediately hug it back. My bedroom's *freezing*! Bloody radiator. How am I supposed to get dressed in this without my nipples getting frostbite? I bet it's warmer in the artic. Or arctic. Or whatever it's bloody called.

The stairs creak.

"I'm up!" I screech.

"You'd better be," Mum shouts back. "You've got five minutes, missy, or your breakfast goes in the bin."

"I *said*, I'm up!"

I jump out of bed and, shivering, grab my uniform off the floor and hide back under the duvet with it. God, I hate my life. Is it my fault my bed's so cosy? Is it my fault the heating in this house is a pile of crap? It's all right for *her*, she's got old skin. She's used to it.

Once I'm dressed, I quickly brush my teeth and wet my hair in the bathroom sink, run downstairs and throw myself onto my chair at the kitchen table.

"Nice of you to join us," Mum says in that sarcastic voice she greets me with every morning.

I smile at her.

'Don't look at me like that," she snaps. "Eat your breakfast. If you miss the coach, you'll have to walk. And don't even think of asking your dad."

Dad peers over his newspaper and gives me an apologetic shrug. I scowl back at the traitor.

"And why have you wet your hair?" she demands to know without so much as a pause for breath. It's a talent she has. "Are you trying to catch pneumonia?"

Dad kicks me under the table. It's his warning for me to shut up. As I don't particularly fancy being grounded for longer, I decide to obey, and take a huge bite of my toast to stop my mouth speaking for me. My Fat Mouth, as Mum calls it.

I shove more toast down my throat. Mum blames me for everything. It's not as if I deliberately miss the coach and it's not as if I miss it that often. I mean, I've only missed it twice this week. She just looks for any excuse to have a go at me. She hates me.

Toast finished, I deliberately, noisily, slurp my tea down then stomp out of the kitchen. Shoes and coat on, I throw my schoolbag over my shoulder.

"Bye," I shout. The front door slams behind me. It wasn't deliberate. Honest.

The second I'm round the corner, I unzip my coat and roll the top of my skirt up, then crouch down and take my secret stash of makeup out of my bag and quickly apply some mascara and lipstick.

There. Now I'm ready.

Alex

The clothes fit. Who'd have thought a black wine gum could make a man lose thirty-three years of age and three stone in weight overnight?

I'm not convinced that I'm not in the midst of a vivid dream. There's a surreal quality to everything. I'm having trouble focusing my eyes and my movements are sluggish.

But if I am in the middle of a dream, why am I frightened to go downstairs?

Gripping the bannister tightly, I tread down the stairs, my feet connecting with thin, fading patterned carpet that was replaced a good twenty years ago. Framed photos line the wallpapered stair walls. Me and Ollie, posing for our annual school photos. I soak them in. You can see the dimming of our smiles as each year passes, ranging from full beams when we were tiny to barely a grimace as we stride into adolescence.

"I can hear you, you know? Stop skulking and come and have your breakfast."

The words turn my veins to ice. The world spins with such violence that I hold onto the bannister for dear life. I cover my mouth, frightened I'm going to vomit again.

"Al?"

Feeling like a ghost – maybe I *am* a ghost? – I shuffle to the kitchen.

Terry Wogan's dulcet brogue fills my ears. The aroma of bacon and frying eggs fills my nose.

She's at the cooker, her back to me. She's wearing the tight jeans and loose jumper combination she always favoured.

"Pour us a cup of tea will you, love?" she asks, picking up a plate with a slice of toast on it.

I'm incapable of movement. My pounding heart is in my throat.

She expertly transfers the eggs from the frying pan onto the toast, then pinches two rashers of cooked bacon from the griddle, adds them to the plate, and turns round.

Her rapid, practised movements come to a sudden halt. Her perfectly plucked eyebrows draw together. "What's wrong?"

I'm crying. No, I'm bawling. Sobbing like a baby.

She hastily puts the plate on the table, then guides me to a chair, wraps her arms around me and holds me tight.

I cling to her, howling, overwhelmed as my senses are overloaded with the scent and touch of the mother I've grieved for over thirty years.

Melody

The bus stop that should be crowded with all the village kids taking the coach to school is empty.

Bugger.

Alex

"Eat something, it'll make you feel better," Mum says, patting my back and kissing the top of my head.

I blow my nose on the kitchen roll she's shoved in my hand.

When I look at her again, she's wearing the stern face I remember so well.

"Right, you," she says, sliding into her seat and pouring the tea. "I know you're hurting but we need to talk about last night."

I don't have the faintest idea what she's talking about.

"We've let you mope for a week but now it's time to man-up. It's not on for you to stay out until three in the morning on a work night and then make all that racket when you get in. You might be young and able to get away with four hours sleep, but your dad can't. He's nearly fifty, Al. I know that seems ancient to you but... Why are you smiling?"

I shake my head and take her hand. How can I tell her that I'm older than Dad? She'd have me committed.

She gives me another of her looks then shakes her head. "You look awful. What on earth were you drinking last night?"

I shrug by way of an answer. I've no idea where she thinks I was last night, or what she thinks I was doing.

My empty stomach rumbles and I finally look at the first plate of food my mum's cooked for me in three decades. The ache in my heart is acute but the intensity has shifted. Become sweeter.

When I took the black wine gum, my only thought was Melody. It never crossed my mind that going back in time would take me back to Mum too.

I remember when she died. All my regrets. All the things I wished I'd told her. How the grief and my guilt derailed me.

I kiss her knuckles. "I'm sorry."

Her eyes widen in shock.

"It won't happen again," I promise.

She snorts her disbelief but has a drink of her tea with a pleased smile.

I start to eat. My stomach gurgles, but I'm not sure if it's in protest or pleasure.

Mum rolls two cigarettes, puts one beside my mug and lights the other.

"Rose phoned last night," she says while my mouth is full of egg and bacon.

That jolts me.

I don't think I've thought of Rose in... must be decades.

"I think she wants you back." She has a drag of her rollup, looks at me through narrowed eyes, then smiles as she exhales. "You really do look like poo."

The gurgling in my stomach's definitely a protest. I push my half-empty plate to one side and light the rollup she made me. Melody and I quit years ago, but right now, smoking straight after a meal feels natural. If there's a chance I'm going to wake up in 2024 at any moment, I'm going to make the most of the here and now. Even if it's only a dream.

"Will you go back to her?" She stubs her rollup in the half-full ashtray.

"Who?"

She leans over and smacks me on the head. "Rose!"

A swell of happiness rushes up inside me, from low in my abdomen, rising through my chest and throat and expelling in a burst of laughter.

"No," I confirm when I catch my breath. "I won't go back to Rose."

I'm here for Melody.

"Good. She's a stuck-up madam."

I laugh again and lean over to kiss her cheek. As my lips make contact with her skin, a loud honk sounds through the kitchen from outside.

She looks at me expectantly.

"What?" I ask.

"Aren't you going to work?"

"Not today." Today, I'm going to get my bearings, let my stomach settle and then I'm going to find Melody.

She gives me her stern face again. "Then you can go outside and tell Jimmy you've decided to skive for the day."

My heart makes another jolt. "Jimmy?"

Jimmy, Mum's brother, died eight years ago.

The uncle who taught me my craft, who kept the business going on his own but still insisted on paying me while we went through the worst months of Mel's recovery after the hit and run, the man who was like a second father to me... He's alive too!

I jump up from the table just in time to dodge another smack on the head from Mum and rush outside.

Friday 14th June 1996

BEFORE

Melody

After fighting with the door lock, we stumble into the house giggling.

Lorna hiccups loudly. "Goin' bed," she slurs. "Got work shoon."

Alex and I have fits of laughter watching her crawl up the stairs. When she's safely at the top, I tug his hand. "Come on you." Oh dear. My voice is all blurry slurry too. "Bed."

Standing behind me, he wraps his arms around my waist and somehow we manage to stagger up the stairs.

The house is spinning, and when Becky opens her door I see three of her. No, four.

"Will you bloody well keep the noise down?" she snaps. "It's three-o-clock."

"Shorry." I prop myself against the wall to stop my legs from going under me. I'm going to pay for this tomorrow.

There's a loud bang from Lorna's room.

I think Becky glares at me. She definitely mutters, "For fuck's sake," and stomps over to Lorna's room and practically kicks the door open.

I look at Alex... well, try to look at him. He's become very blurry.

* * *

I wake to find myself thirsty, crammed in my single bed naked, next to a naked body.

Alex!

The night comes flooding back and, face pressed against his chest, I happily close my eyes to relive it. We danced and downed shots until the club closed. It was the best night. *The* best. We ate greasy burgers from the van while we waited at the taxi-rank. I don't remember inviting Alex back. In fact, I'm pretty sure I didn't give him any choice in the matter. Not that I remember him arguing the toss.

And I don't remember getting into bed. Or taking my clothes off. Or even entering my bedroom. Had we...?

I really need a drink.

Carefully disentangling myself, I edge off the bed, wincing at the pounding in my head. From the light filtering through my thin curtain, I guess it's early morning, maybe only six-o-clock or so.

As soon as I get to my feet, the room begins to spin. Somehow, I manage to put my dressing gown on and convince my jelly legs to carry me downstairs to the kitchen. I down a pint of water with two paracetamols, refill the glass and attempt the return journey.

Alex's eyes are open. He smiles at me. I swear my heart sighs.

"Water?" I whisper, perching myself next to him.

"Please."

He lifts himself onto an elbow and takes the glass along with the paracetamols I brought up with me. His hand isn't much steadier than mine.

Done, he lays back down. He hasn't taken his eyes off me the whole time.

"Sorry," he says.

"For what?"

"Passing out. Didn't realise how drunk I was." He winces. "Think I'm still drunk."

"I'm definitely still drunk."

With a smile, he lifts the duvet, inviting me back. I take a moment to drift my eyes over his naked body. My heart gives a definite sigh. Even in my part-drunk, part-hungover state, I can appreciate that his body is as gorgeous as his face.

I slip my dressing gown off. The moment I stretch out beside him, he envelopes me into his arms.

I don't think my heart has ever beat so hard, and when he kisses me, the heat that fills me is like nothing I've felt before.

When I finally drift back to sleep, my last thought is that sex with Alex is the opposite of shit. All I can do is hope he'll still be there when I next wake up.

Alex

I've never been so reluctant to leave a bed before, and it has nothing to do with my pounding head or the need for another five hours sleep.

I can't drag my gaze from Melody's sleeping face. I study the pale skin with the smattering of freckles over the cute nose with a chest so full it's a struggle to breathe.

Her eyes open and fix onto mine. I gaze into the dark, almost black, pools. See the tiny flecks of gold in them.

I can't stop the smile spreading over my face. She smiles back and presses her fingers to my cheek.

It is with deep reluctance that I say, "I have to go."

Her smile fades.

"I've an appointment in Buckingham in a couple of hours. For a potential job."

Her pretty lips pull in together but she nods.

"Are you working today?"

She shakes her head. "Not until six."

"Any plans until then?"

Another shake of her head.

"Shall I come back when I'm done?"

The smile returns. Her hand slides around my neck.

My plans to leave are delayed a little longer.

Wednesday 13th March 1991

NOW

Alex

Mum lets me borrow her car again. I hadn't appreciated how advanced cars in the twenty-first century had become until forced to drive a 1980 Ford Cortina. The radio crackles, and I have to keep fiddling with the tuning button, the heater works in fits and spurts, the driver's window keeps sticking and there's a loud clunk every time I change gear.

I'm nearly – nearly – certain that what's happening to me is real. I have travelled through time and taken possession of my twenty-one year old body. It's terrifying and exhilarating, a huge adventure where you know how the story unfolds but the details of the journey have faded through time.

I park in the school drop-off bay with a good view of the coaches. The nauseous churning in my stomach's returned but this time more from nerves than time-travel sickness. I had the same churn on Saturday when I parked across the road from Melody's house in Collingswood. I spent an hour there hoping for a glimpse of her, but all I saw were shadows in the windows. I would have stayed longer if a grumpy neighbour I didn't recognise hadn't banged on the window and told me to fuck off. It was probably for the best. God knows what I'd have done if I had seen her.

I'm still trying to get a handle on everything. Trust me, there's a lot to get a handle on. Everything. The dead who've come back to life. My dad with a straight back and a full head of hair. My brother, young, single, and reckless. Being older than my parents. Not being in pain – I hadn't realised how worn and achy my body had become until I was given this shiny new one. Old friends calling the house landline, many of whom I've lost touch with over the years.

I've pleaded sickness and, other than the stalking visit to Melody's house under the pretext of needing to visit the chemist, have stayed inside hiding from the world. Jimmy agreed with Mum that I looked like a bag of shit and has given me the week off to recover. That I puked in front of him and splattered his work boots helped convince him of this.

Another thing I need to get a handle on is my loss of independence. I don't have a car. I've only been able to borrow Mum's Cortina today as she has Wednesday afternoons off from her job at Brocklehurst post office.

The first students trickle through the school's main doors. The bottom of my stomach drops. The trickle turns into a deluge. Unable to see properly, I get out of the car and, lungs tightened into a ball, do my best to stick to my original plan of only scanning the faces heading to the coaches. I want to search every single face.

I almost miss her. So rarely does Melody tie her hair back that I'm focussed on using her black corkscrews as a marker. My gaze skips over her before registering the bouncy mass of hair sticking out of the back of her head in a ponytail.

She's with a couple of other girls, all with identical bags over their shoulders. They're huddled together like penguins, whether from the cold or because they're deep in animated conversation or both, I don't know. I can't even see her face. I just know that it's her, that she *is* here and that in this moment in time, she's got her whole life ahead of her.

When she disappears into the coach, I find I'm breathing properly for the first time since I woke up in my childhood bed.

Saturday 15th June 1996

BEFORE

Melody

I leave Alex sleeping while I run to work, arriving in a record four minutes, and just seven minutes late. Graham's familiar scowl greets me. He's only slightly mollified when, after fighting my way through the heaving crowd and the thick haze of cigarette smoke, I plant an impulsive kiss to his grumpy cheek. Not mollified enough not to send me to the kitchen as punishment though.

I'm too happy to care. I don't care either, when I walk in the kitchen and find a tower of crockery and pots and pans that need washing.

Gav and Carly are too busy fighting their way through the remaining food orders and snapping at each other to do much more than give me exhausted smiles of thanks. Bless them, they genuinely think I've volunteered to trash my hands on kitchen-cleaning duties. Graham's too tight to buy marigolds, never mind the dishwasher he's been promising all the three years I've worked here.

I turn the radio on – no wonder it's so tense in here without any kind of background to daydream to – and get stuck in.

"Why are you so happy?"

I look up from the foaming water to Carly's suspicious face. I hadn't noticed she'd made a start on the drying-up for me. "Hmm?"

"You're singing."

"Sorry." I've inherited my mother's non-dulcet tones.

She stares at my face a bit longer then nudges me. "Who is he?"

I grin. "Alex Hammond."

She pulls a face that pulls the smile from mine.

"You know him?"

"Yep."

"What's wrong with him?"

"He's a tart."

I don't know how to respond to that. I mean, Lorna has intimated as much about him. I'm pretty sure she's said the same about me too.

"It's very early days," I mumble, and am mortified to feel my face heat with a blush. Early days or not, since Alex returned from his appointment in Buckingham we've only left my bed for food and my evening shift, which he propped up the bar for the entirety of.

Carly scrutinises me for so long I feel another blush form. "Just be careful. I know his ex. He cheated on her. And the one before her..."

"Doesn't that make him a good match for Mel, then?" Gav calls from the other side of the kitchen with an evil cackle.

"I've never cheated," I protest.

"You cheated on Damian."

"Not intentionally! I didn't know he thought we were a couple."

"What about Simon?"

"We weren't together long enough for me to cheat."

Carly suddenly elbows me again. I follow her twitching gaze to find Matt the Twat standing in the kitchen doorway.

"Hi Mel." He raises his hand in a wave. "Graham said you were in here. Can I speak to you in private?"

"I'm really busy. Is it important?"

"I just wondered if you fancy going out for a drink when you finish your shift?"

"Erm... I'm really sorry but I've already made plans."

"Tomorrow?"

I brace myself. "Look, Matt, I'm really sorry but I, err, I'm kind of seeing someone."

His face falls. "But I thought you weren't looking for anything?"

If you thought that then why do you keep bloody hassling me two weeks after we spent one sodding night together? Instead of shouting this at him, I fix the kindest smile I can to my face. "It isn't really anything," I lie, "But I don't want to string you along." Stringing him along wouldn't be an issue if he'd taken the bloody hint in the first place.

Seriously, Men, when a girl tells you she's really busy and doesn't have time for a relationship *after* you've slept with her, then that means she doesn't want to take it any further.

He shuffles backwards then his crestfallen face glimmers. "Mate, I wasn't asking for marriage. I was just after a good time with a sure thing. See you around."

Carly's cackle of laughter breaks the stunned silence left in Matt's wake. She picks up the pile of clean plates into her meaty arms. "What a twat."

"Told you Alex is a good match for her," Gav shouts.

I laugh along with them but inside I burn with humiliation.

I should never have slept with Matt in the first place. The worst of it is, I didn't fancy him in the slightest. I was drunk. It was a party at the house he shares with Chris and Gav (not The Merry Thief chef Gav). I don't remember much about it and as far as I'm concerned those memories can stay locked away forever. I remember the sex being terrible but, mercifully, other than the flashing image of his horrible tattoo – a topless woman on his right bicep – not the details. Bad enough remembering how sick I felt when I woke up with his gurning face next to mine. I've never left a bed so fast in my life.

The only thing that stops my happy mood plummeting fully to dark is the thought of seeing Alex again. He's promised to be at the pub in time for kick-off and is bringing Kermit with him. He wants me to meet him.

Because this is the thing. It *is* something. This thing with Alex. And I have a horrible feeling that if he stands me up, it will really hurt.

Wednesday 29th May 1991

NOW

Melody

It's my birthday!

I bound out of bed and hurtle down the stairs.

Mum and Dad are in the kitchen drinking tea at the table. There's three gift-wrapped boxes and a pile of cards next to the teapot.

Mum's on her feet first. She gives me a tight hug that makes me feel all squidgy. "Happy birthday, sweetie."

Dad's hug's a little looser but his smile is just as warm as Mum's. "Happy birthday, Melody."

Mum pours me a cup of tea while I get down to the most important part of the day. The present opening.

I open Grandma Alison's first. It's a makeup set and, oh my God, it's so cool! There's eight eyeshadows, two blushers, four squares of lipstick, an eyeliner and a mascara. I rip the plastic film off it and lift the lid and inhale the delicious scent. I love the smell of makeup. It's my favourite scent in the whole world.

"I'll give you some lessons on how to use it all before we go out, if you like?" Mum says.

She's taking me to the city for lunch. I'm so lucky to be on exam leave from school! I'm hoping she's going to buy me a pair of Converses and another pair of jeans to replace the pair I accidentally ruined when I tried to cut my own rips into them. I really want a pair of Levi's. "Yes please."

Her smile is so wide I feel a little guilty about my secret makeup stash. It's not my fault that Hayley's mum's an Avon rep and gets tons of free samples and that Hayley gives me handfuls at a time. Hayley's mum's so cool. Hayley's been allowed to wear makeup since we were twelve. I have to keep my stash hidden or Mum will go spare.

I move on to the next present. It's from Aunty Jackie and Uncle Steve. Oh my God! It's a White Musk gift set! White Musk is my favourite scent in the whole world!

I nearly wet myself when I open the biggest present, from Mum and Dad. It's a new HiFi! And it has a CD player in it! Oh my God, it's soooooooooo cool!

I rip into the cards. Cash from Aunty Allie and Uncle Stelios, a cheque from Aunty Debs and a postal order from Grandpa Bob. Enough for me to buy three CDs!

Dad has to go to work but promises he'll set the HiFi up as soon as he gets back. I kiss him goodbye then rush upstairs to get dressed.

Alex

I get off the bus opposite Collingswood's village shop, zip my denim jacket against the slight chill, and start walking. I've learned that if I don't look purposeful, people get suspicious. It's not like 2024 when people are often too wary to confront loiterers.

Of all the things I've struggled to adjust to, that's been the hardest for me. Forget mobile phones the size of bricks morphing into sleek smartphones that fit in the palm of your hand and can bring up any information you want at the press of a button, it's attitudes that have changed at a faster pace than anything. In the last few years of my life with Mel, I often found myself censoring my words depending on the company (Alice) as it wasn't worth the self-righteous bollocking I'd get for it. There's no need to censor yourself here. If you offend someone, they either call you a twat or punch you in the face. Then it's forgotten.

It's freeing too, not being contactable twenty-four-seven. I get shivers to imagine Rose with a mobile phone. She's turned into quite the pest. I remember getting back with her a few times before I decided the sex wasn't worth the hassle of an uptight, control-freak girlfriend who wanted to police your every move and sulked for England if you went on a night out with your mates. But I can't do that this time round. I belong to Mel even if she doesn't yet belong to me.

The problem with Mel's house is that it's in a cul-de-sac. That makes it difficult to watch without being noticed. I've started a routine, a routine I appreciate must make me sound like a stalker. I defy anyone in my shoes not to do the same. Every Saturday morning, I take the bus to Brocklehurst and from there, the bus to Collingswood. That gives me an hour to walk past Melody's house, cut through the alleyway that runs alongside it, arrive at the pub for opening, sink a pint, then walk the reverse route back to the bus stop for the return journey home. I've done that for eight weeks. Walked past her house sixteen times. Haven't seen her once.

I've booked today off work to make the same journey as today is Melody's sixteenth birthday.

Just as I'm thinking how badly I long to see her, I turn into her cul-de-sac and there she is, getting into the front passenger seat of her mum's Escort. A swish of black corkscrews and she closes the door.

I force my feet to keep moving. I'm getting closer to her. The beats of my heart are drumming in my ears.

Patty comes out of the house. She's opening the driver's door as I get level with the front of the car. She meets my eye. Smiles in that open way I've always adored about her and inclines her head before disappearing into the car beside her daughter.

All I can see of Melody is her head hunched forward, examining something on her lap. She doesn't see me.

Saturday 22nd June 1996

BEFORE

Melody

I've just turned the kettle on when Lorna pounces. "Mel, a quick word?"

"Of course. Tea?"

"Yes, please. Look... I'm not saying I've got a problem with Alex staying here occasionally, but if he's going to be here all the time, he needs to start paying rent."

"We've only been seeing each other for a week." Nine days.

"Yeah, and he's been here the whole of that time."

"He's gone to work." Not much. He's not got much on until he starts his big job in Richmond next week, but he's helped his uncle on one of his jobs in London, and he's had a couple of appointments with potential new clients. And he's been at the pub for my shifts. And he paid a visit to his flat for clean clothes and stuff.

"Can't you spend time at his flat too? It'd give my ears a break. And while we're on the subject, you might want to think about getting a new bed. Those springs sound like they're about to go kaput."

I tighten the sash of my dressing gown not knowing whether

to laugh or hang my head in embarrassment. And we thought we'd been quiet when the girls were in the house... Oops.

"I'm sorry, Lorn." I pour hot water into the mugs. "I promise we'll be... err... quieter."

"Thank you."

"And I'll speak to him about stopping at his."

"Good. Let Kermit put up with the pair of you."

"All right, all right," I laugh. "I think you've embarrassed me enough for one morning."

She punches me lightly on the shoulder to show there are no hard feelings.

* * *

Alex is exactly where I left him in bed, except he's thrown the duvet off and is sporting a huge erection which he points to as I put our drinks on the bedside table.

"Lorna says we're being too noisy," I tell him, shrugging my dressing gown off.

He raises a seductive eyebrow and trails a finger down my belly.

"And she says we need to spend some nights at yours."

He pulls a face of mock horror before putting his mouth to my abdomen and blowing a raspberry.

I giggle.

"Shh," he says sternly, then budges over to make room for me. The bed creaks. As soon as I'm flat beside him, he rolls on top of me. The bed creaks again. "We're being too noisy are we?"

"Yes." I wrap my legs around his waist. "And apparently the bed creaks."

"Hmm... Then we should practice doing it quietly."

I grab hold of a butt cheek. "Practice makes perfect."

He kisses me. "*You're* perfect."

The bed creaks.

* * *

Graham might hate football but I'm willing to bet he won't hate the profit that comes from showing England's quarter-final against Spain. Our little corner of England is suffering a definite case of football fever and The Merry Thief is rammed. I don't remember it ever being this busy before, not even on New Year's Eve. When David Seaman saves the final Spanish penalty to put England through to the semi-final, a large crowd by the pool table throw themselves into a spontaneous pile-on. I pity whoever's squished at the bottom of it, right until Alex shakes himself out and grins at me. He turned up before kick-off with a group of his friends. I'd been rushed off my feet so there had only been the briefest of introductions.

Alex's friends leave soon after the final whistle to carry on the celebrations at Alex and Kermit's flat, but Alex waits for my shift to finish. We stop at the off-licence opposite the pub and then walk to his flat above the town's laundrette. I've never been someone who gets nervous about going to new places but when he opens the door, I have a severe case of butterflies in my belly. I hold his hand tightly as we climb the stairs, closing in on the drunken voices belting along to Fat Les's 'Vindaloo.'

My first impression of the place is of chaos. Honestly, it's like someone has detonated a bomb in it. The kitchen surfaces are crammed with dirty crockery and discarded food tins and packets, the floor strewn with overflowing bin bags and other detritus. And I thought *I* was messy!

Kermit greets me like an old friend. An infrequent drinker at the pub, his was a face that, until a week ago, I'd never known a name to put to. Only a little taller than me, he's as skinny as a rake and clearly hammered, and when he spots the wine bottle in my hand, makes it his mission to find a corkscrew. Drawers are thrown open and more stuff goes flying onto the floor.

"Found it!" he finally shouts from the previously overflowing kitchen table, and waves it at me.

"Cheers," I say. "I don't suppose you've got any glasses?"

He has to think about this. It looks like it takes much effort. "We've got mugs?"

"That'll do... Any clean ones?" I'm not hopeful.

He opens a cupboard. It has one clean item in it – a plastic Teenage Mutant Ninja Turtles beaker. Giggling, I pour my red wine into it and, staying close to Alex, join the party in the small living room, which has the same high level of disorder as the kitchen. The far wall has an impressive number of beer cans piled almost to the ceiling in a display of something that could, if you were myopic, be described as modern art.

Alex steps over the bodies splayed on the floor and wedges himself on the sofa, forcing the two blokes already sat on it playing Mario Kart to budge over. He pulls me onto his lap and wraps an arm around my waist. I do a quick head count. Twelve people. Of these, I know only three of them; Alex, Grace and Decker (no idea what his real name is). I've already forgotten most of the others' names from Alex's brief introductions earlier at the pub.

Secure on Alex's lap, I sip my wine and enjoy giving my aching feet a rest. The atmosphere is raucous. Joyful.

Kermit, fat spliff in his skinny fingers, props himself on the edge of the sofa next to us and is soon holding court with stories that get more and more outrageous and incrementally funnier. It takes about five minutes for me to decide I adore him. I know one of the two women squashed together on the single sofa is his girlfriend but can't work out which one. I hope it's the blonde. The brunette would be pretty were it not for her expression of someone chewing a wasp. When I meet her eye and smile, she gives me a look of such loathing my skin chills.

Alex

When half the guests have left and the other half are showing signs of passing out, I decide it's time to claim my bedroom before someone decides to bed down in it for the night. Considering the amount I've drunk, I should be as plastered as the rest of them but my brain and body are only a little woozy.

Melody's first words when we walk into it are a quiet, "You've got a double bed."

Unsure of the tone of her voice, I shrug. She's been in a strange mood this evening. Much less chatty and lively than normal. She had a few tokes of the joints being shared around but nothing more, and has only drunk half her bottle of wine.

She hugs her arms loosely around her belly, her gaze continuing to drift around the room. "It seems strange that we've spent the last nine days fighting for space in my single bed when you've got this."

Needing to touch her – I *always* needed to touch her – I unfold her arms and pull them behind my back. "There's more order at yours." Kermit made Mel, who left a trail of debris wherever she went, seem like someone with OCD.

"Your room's tidy." She doesn't tighten her arms around me like she usually does. Or press herself against me.

"I've not been here long enough to make it messy." I don't add that I popped over after she left for work that morning to have a quick tidy and change the bed sheets.

She steps out of my hold and turns her back to stare out of the window. I don't know what kind of view she expects. The flat's a two-minute walk from her house, set on a one-way street and backs onto The Sun & Star's tiny concrete beer garden. When I press myself against her and wrap my arms around her, she shrugs me off.

"What's wrong?"

"Nothing."

Why do women do that? They make a big show of acting upset or pissed off but when you ask them about it they always come back with that pathetic answer of, "nothing." Rachel was a nightmare for it. Usually, it never fails to piss me off but as my spidey-senses have been telling me for the last few hours that something's off with Mel, all I feel is a huge dose of trepidation.

She keeps her back to me when she breaks the silence. "That girl... the brunette who's friends with Kermit's girlfriend..."

Uh oh.

"Sophie?"

Her shoulders rise. "Why does she hate me?"

Bollocks.

"How can she hate you? She doesn't know you."

"That's what I thought. To start with. I thought I was imagining it but she definitely hates me. She was giving me daggers all night and when the pizza arrived and she was handing everyone's out, she left mine on the table. And I was the only person she didn't offer her cigarettes to. And she kept refusing mine."

Fuckity fuck fuck fuck. "She's a grumpy cow. Ignore her."

She twists round. For someone so short, she can stand tall when she puts her mind to it. Her black eyes scrutinise me, the light I'm used to seeing in them dulled. "Is she one of your exes?"

I could deny it but it would take one conversation with Kermit or Lorna for her to learn the truth.

Nausea roiling in my stomach, I nod.

"Did it end badly?"

"Something like that," I mutter.

"Then why was I on the receiving end of her daggers and not you?"

"I don't know."

Her eyes narrow in clear disbelief before she turns her back on me again and puts her hands on the windowsill. "Either you tell me what happened between you or I'm going home."

"Mel..."

She spins back round. To my shock, her eyes have filled with tears. Her throat moves a number of times before she says, "Look, this thing we've got... Al, I really like you. Okay? *Really* like you, but I've heard so many stories from so many different people about how you treat women..." Her chest rises sharply and she swallows. "I can't ignore it anymore."

On the defensive, I retort with, "I've heard stories about you too." How she slept around. Strung men along. Hadn't that been the first thing Lorna told me about her? How Mel bored easily?

She sucks a breath in but doesn't drop her stare. "What do you feel for me?"

Unprepared for the question, I just stare at her.

Her hands are making fists with her black and grey checked shirt. "If it's only sex then say so. I'm a big girl. I can take it. We haven't made any promises. But if it's more than sex... if we're going to take this any further... I need to know I can trust you. And I guess you need to know you can trust me too. But that's only if you want to take it further. If you don't see me as anything more than someone to have sex with then I'm really sorry but this is as far as it goes."

My legs feel shaky and for once it has nothing to do with all the alcohol I've consumed. I slump onto the bed and hang my head.

I don't know what she wants me to say. I don't know what I can truthfully say that won't scare her off. Because the truth is, I'm a shit.

The stillness between us is broken when Melody suddenly edges round the bed to the door.

"I'm going home," she says with what can only be described as dignity. "I'll see you around."

Something a lot like panic shoots through my chest. "Me and Sophie went out for a few months about two years ago. Before I got together with Rachel. I never ended it. Not properly. Just stopped calling her."

She freezes mid-stride.

"I cheated on her. I cheated on Rachel too." My panicking tongue has loosened as never before. "I've cheated in every relationship I've had. I slept with Sophie a few times after I moved in with Kermit but tonight's the first time I've seen her since I met you. I didn't bring you here before because she hangs around like a bad smell. She's Ellie's sister. I knew things would be awkward tonight when she saw me with you but I didn't think she'd take it out on you, I swear." And I wished I'd noticed. I'd been so relieved that she didn't throw a drink in my face that I thought she was cool and had moved on.

"Wow," Melody whispers, backing against the wall. "I don't think I was prepared for that level of honesty."

I hadn't been prepared for it either.

"So, she thinks you're a couple and that I'm the bitch stealing her man?"

"I don't know what she's thinking but I swear, I never said or did anything to make her think that." I made that mistake the first time. "I like sex. You know that. And she was offering."

Mel looks like she's going to be sick. My efforts at honesty are making things worse.

"I'm a shit. I treat women like shit. I lie and I cheat and..." I dig the pads of my fingers into my skull. "I don't know what it is about you, but you do something to me." It's like that shitty Paul Weller song. "Whatever it is, it's more than just sex. When I think of the future, all I see is you."

I hold my breath, suddenly certain this is the moment that will define the rest of my life. I feel it deep in my bones, a feeling I would have laughed my head off if any of my mates were to spout it.

Until the words started pouring out, I'd been too busy enjoying the intoxicating Melody ride to actually think about what was happening between us. But every word was the truth. In a few short weeks, my life has changed. *I've* changed.

I think I changed from that first night together.

A long time passes before she creeps from the wall and sits beside me. She rests her hand on my fist and gives the lightest of squeezes. I turn my hand so our palms press together. There's a loosening in my chest when she allows my fingers to thread through hers.

"Have you been with anyone else since we started seeing each other?"

"*No*." How can she ask that when we've spent every available minute together since the moment we met?

"I'd guessed from Sophie's daggers that something had happened between you," she admits quietly. "And the worst of it is, I knew it all happened before we met and I know I have no right to feel jealous, but I've never felt like this before. It scares me. Really scares me. I'm scared I'm in over my head. I don't know what stories you've heard about me but I can imagine, and I'm not going to lie about it. I've been with a lot of men, and I think the reason I've bounced from one to another is because I've been waiting to feel like this. How I feel for you. I think..." She takes a deep breath and turns her face to me.

Her dark, dark eyes are swirling.

"... I've been waiting for you."

My heart thumps.

Suddenly, she pulls a face and laughs lowly. "God, that sounds ridiculous, doesn't it?"

"No." It should. I know that. But it doesn't. It sounds right. True. Because, "I think I've been waiting for you too."

Her shoulders rise sharply. Her eyes glisten. She places her palm against my cheek. "Can I ask a promise of you?"

"Anything."

Her lips twitch with the ghost of a smile. "What we're feeling now... who knows how long it's going to last. With our track records it could all change tomorrow. I want you to promise me that as soon as you start having feelings for someone else... please tell me first. Don't act on it until you've ended it with me."

"Mel..."

"Promise me. Look me in the eye and promise." Another ghostly smile. "And I'll promise to try and believe it."

I wind a finger through one of her black corkscrews and rub my thumb over her cheek. "I promise."

Her eyes hold mine for the longest time. "Thank you."

Saturday 3rd August 1991

NOW

Melody

Hayley's mum drops us outside the cinema.

We climb out of the car, look at the queue, look at each other, then rush to join it.

"That boy's looking at me," Hayley whispers, tugging at the sleeve of my denim jacket.

I follow her gaze to the group of boys queueing a few feet in front of us. They're around our age. Surprise, surprise, one of them *is* looking at her, and he looks just like Keanu Reeves. The best-looking boys always fancy her.

She tugs her white vest-top down, sucks her belly in and sticks her tits out, then throws her blonde hair back and laughs, and suddenly she's transformed into the most entertaining and beautiful girl in the queue. As we inch our way forwards, the boys keep looking at us. Well, looking at Hayley. I keep catching the eye of the moody-looking blonde one. He's pretty cute but not as cute as the Keanu one.

When we get to the entrance, we've completed half the queue and can see the boards with all the timings. There's still tickets! And the boys are still looking at us.

"What do you thinking they're watching?" Hayley asks once they've bought their tickets and are in the popcorn queue.

"*Edward Scissorhands*, I hope."

"Dare you to ask."

"*You* ask."

She pinches my arm, hard. "Dared you first."

I rub my smarting arm and look at the boys again. The moody one's looking at his feet. Keanu's looking at Hayley.

I give a dramatic sigh then duck under the rope barrier and speed-walk to the popcorn queue.

Keanu goes bright red. So do his ears. Up close, he doesn't look a bit like Keanu Reeves.

"What you watching?" I ask.

"*Backdraft*."

"Okay." I speed walk back to Hayley, who's practically jumping with excitement. "*Backdraft*," I tell her.

We both look at the boards above the ticket sellers. *Backdraft*'s now sold out. As we're both sighing our disappointment, the dreaded sold-out notification appears next to *Edward Scissorhands* too. We're next to be served.

"*Robin Hood*?" Hayley suggests in desperation.

I pull a face. Kevin Costner is no Johnny Depp, but everything else is either sold out or an 18 rating or French. *Robin Hood*'s only got tickets left coz it's so popular they've got three screens showing it. "Okay." I sigh again. I hate popular things.

Alex

"I can't believe what a natural you are at this," Mum says. We're in the garden weeding. Last week's heavy rain has turned the garden into a sea of green. I wonder if it will last. I don't remember much about this August from the last time I experienced it. This was the month Ollie and I spent every weekend partying in the city.

"Must get it from you," I say with a grin. How can I tell her Melody and I learned to garden together? When we bought our house on Juniper Crescent five years after our wedding, we had huge plans for our little garden and, our first spring there, spent a fortune at the garden centre. By the end of that summer, all the plants and flowers were either dead or begging to be put out of their misery. It was a long learning curve. Eventually we got the hang of it and every summer our garden would be filled with sunflowers and all the other colourful flowers Melody loved so much.

Dad comes out carrying three bottles of lager. When I take mine, I catch the puzzled look in his eyes again. Mum thinks the hangover from hell back in March that forced me to take a week off work is the reason for the change in my party-loving ways. She thinks her youngest son grew up overnight. Ollie thinks I've been temporarily possessed in *Invasion of the Body Snatchers* fashion. Dad's the only one who senses the real, fundamental change in me.

We all drink thirstily then get back to the job in hand. If the weather holds, we're going to have a barbeque. If it doesn't hold, Mum'll bung the burgers and sausages in the oven.

She's pulling clumps of weeds out beneath the cherry tree when I notice her blanche and put a hand to her abdomen.

"You okay? I ask.

When she looks at me, her face has lost its colour.

Melody

Hayley whispers another snide comment about the film. I laugh quietly so she doesn't get upset, but secretly I wish she would SHUT UP. My eyes are glued to the screen.

"You crying?" She nudges me with her elbow to make sure I'm listening to her.

Ashamed of such uncool behaviour, I brazen it out. "I'm bored to tears."

She cackles.

But I'm not bored. I'm... I don't *know*! When Robin saved Maid Marion from the bastard Sheriff of Nottingham I thought my heart was going to choke me. And now they're getting married, and that song, and... oh, everything!

I hope I feel love like that one day. I hope someone loves me as much as Robin loves Marion.

"That was rubbish," Hayley says as we file out.

I pretend not to hear her.

Thursday 4th July 1996

BEFORE

Melody

Traffic on the drive to Richmond in Alex's van is heavier than expected but neither of us care. The longer we're stationary, the more we can hold hands.

I've never felt such a greedy need to touch someone. It's quite scary to think we've only known each other for twenty-one days (that night five years ago doesn't count, especially as Alex doesn't remember it). So I don't think about it. Problem solved!

I've got my job interview later this morning. By a wonderful coincidence, Alex's current job is in Richmond. The family who owns the house are in Tuscany. I'm really excited to see what he does for a living and excited for the interview. Of all the graduate jobs I've applied for, this is the one I really want. Hampton Court Palace is one of my favourite places.

The worst of the traffic has cleared when we drive into Richmond and it isn't long before Alex pulls in front of a set of electric gates. He opens the window, sticks his arm out, and puts a code into a box.

The gates open. So does my mouth.

"*This* is where you're working?"

He grins. "Nice, isn't it?"

"You never said it was a mansion," I accuse.

"Didn't I?" he says innocently before giving a loud rumble of laughter. "I wanted it to be a surprise for you. It's actually a converted chapel. It dates from the nineteenth century."

"It's beautiful," I say with all the reverence a sympathetically converted chapel deserves.

The long driveway cuts through a large manicured front garden filled with an abundance of colourful flowers. To the side of the mansion I spot a child's wooden play set with a swing and a slide and monkey-bars. I would have killed to have had that when I was a kid.

Inside, the vaulted ceilings are so high our voices echo, and I find myself whispering, "Is there staff here?"

"Only when the family's here. They've a gardener who lives locally but he doesn't come in the house." His eyes glitter. "We have the place all to ourselves."

I wrap my arms around his neck, rise onto my tiptoes and kiss him. "How unfortunate."

Alex

After straightening our clothes, I take Melody's hand and lead her up the cantilevered stairs and down the wide corridor to the bathroom I'm working in.

She's silent for the longest time, her eyes wide as she soaks it all in. "*You* did this?" she eventually says.

A swell of pride fills my chest. I always take before and after photos of my work, but Mel's the first person I've brought to a job in the four years since Jimmy considered my apprenticeship over and let me loose to work on my own.

"Can I touch it?" she asks.

"Sure."

She gently runs her fingers over the tiny tiles that currently fills a third of the feature wall.

"This is amazing." She shakes her head and looks at me with a bemused expression. "How on earth can your giant fingers do such intricate work?"

"Very carefully," I laugh.

"Did you design it?"

"I followed the brief I was given."

"But you designed it?"

I shrug. "I guess."

"You are so talented. I'm in awe."

I am struck with the urge to go straight out and buy Melody a house just so I can create a mosaic feature wall for her.

"Imagine having a bath surrounded by the Little Mermaid and all her friends," she murmurs, her attention back on the wall.

"You do know it's for a six-year-old girl?"

"Shut the front door!"

"Yep. She's a sweet thing but spoilt rotten."

"A six-year-old with a bathroom that's bigger than my bedroom?" She shakes her head again. "How the other half live."

"The parents have their own bathrooms too, even bigger than this."

She laughs. "I think I need to start playing the Lottery. That's the only way I'm going to afford a house like this."

"If you could have your own mosaic wall, what design would you have?"

"I'd have to think about it."

I put my hands on her hips and pull her to me. I can hardly believe how badly and how often I want her. At this rate, my cock's going to fall off. "When you've thought about it, let me know and I'll do it for you."

"I couldn't afford you."

"Marry me, and there's no cost."

She stills. Her dark eyes widen. "What did you say?"

I gaze into those beautiful eyes and something warm spreads through my chest and veins and limbs. A sense of rightness.

I capture one of her ebony curls and press my nose to hers. "I love you, Melody Aldridge. Marry me. Please."

My heart beats so hard and so fast while I wait for her answer that I fear it'll burst through my ribs.

The beaming smile I've fallen in love with spreads over her face and she loops her arms tightly around my neck.

"Yes," she says before kissing me. "Yes, yes, yes."

Melody

I'm floating so high on happiness that I can barely bring myself to care that I've blown my dream job. I know I've blown it. I could see it in their eyes. Arriving half-an-hour late was the first black mark against me. That I then, in my embarrassment for being late and high on the excitement of Alex's proposal, chattered through the interview like a woodpecker on speed, was the second cross against my name.

There's guilt in Alex's eyes when I get back in the van. It isn't his fault. We both got carried away celebrating and lost track of time. If I ever tag along on another job, I'll wear a chastity belt.

"Well?" he asks tentatively.

I lean in for a kiss. "If it's meant to be, it'll be."

Alex and I are meant to be. I love him and he loves me. That matters more than any job.

We spend the drive back to Brocklehurst holding hands and imagining the converted chapel we will one day own and all the mosaics Alex will create in it.

Monday 5th August 1991

NOW

Melody

"What are you doing up?" Mum asks, eyes wide in mock horror, her piece of toast hovering inches from her lips. From the expression on her face, anyone would think it's unheard of for me to be up at eight a.m. in the school holidays.

"Can I have a lift to Brocklehurst?" I've counted every penny I own and I only have enough to make my purchase and pay for the bus one-way. I would ask Dad for the money but he's already gone to work.

"Can I have a lift to Brocklehurst...?"

"Please?"

"What for?"

"I want to go to HMV."

"For what?"

I shrug. Mum still likes to embarrass me about my ancient New Kids on the Block obsession. I tore my Jordan Knight posters down a year ago! If she tells Hayley I'm buying that soppy Bryan Adams song, Hayley will call me a sell-out and tell everyone.

Mum gives me The Look.

"A want to buy a single," I mumble.//
"You've got the money?"
"Yes."
"You going to see anyone?"
"No."
"How are you getting home?"
"Bus."
"Got the money for that too?"
"Yes."

"If you don't, you'll have to walk or wait for me to finish." Mum's a nurse at Brocklehurst Medical Centre. She doesn't finish until six on Mondays.

"I've got bus money."

She looks me up and down then smiles. "Go on then. But get a move on – I need to leave in ten."

I hotfoot it to my bedroom and throw some clothes on.

Alex

The plumber who's installing our client's new bathroom has cocked up. The mosaic wall we're supposed to be starting today is delayed, giving me an unexpected day off. The Alex of old would have rubbed his hands, pegged it to the pub, and spent the day getting bladdered.

I can't remember the last time I got drunk. It gets to the stage when the three-day hangover takes all the fun out of it. I pat my hard, flat stomach and grin. *This* body is in its prime. A thumping headache that's clear by lunch is the worst hangover this body suffers from.

I grab my jacket and wallet and am hunting my house keys in the living room when Mum walks in.

"You're back..." *early*, I nearly say before the word cuts itself off from my lips. Mum looks like death warmed up. "You're not well?"

She shakes her head and sinks onto the nearest sofa. "I think my IBS is playing up. Janice sent me home."

I accepted her explanation of the cramps she suffered over the weekend as Women's Problems without question, but the mention of her IBS sets alarm bells ringing. A wave of cold dread sweeps through me.

A very hazy memory tugs at me. Christmas. Mum avoiding the cheese board, saying she was eliminating certain foods to see what the likely culprits triggering her debilitating IBS were.

It must be the Christmas coming up.

"You should go and see the doctor," I say with a calmness I do not feel.

"Don't be silly. It's just my IBS."

The IBS diagnosed to explain the bloating and onset of pains in her belly.

It's the wrong diagnosis.

"Mum, your stomach's been hurting you a lot lately." I choose my words carefully. I don't want to scare her, but *I'm* scared. I know the future. I've lived it. "I'm going to call the medical centre."

"No, Al," she protests. "I don't want to make a fuss."

It's the not wanting to make a fuss that killed you, I want to shout. But I can't. What I can do is play my one trump card. "Let me make an appointment for you. Please? For my peace of mind?"

Her eyes search mine. Then they close and she gives a short nod. "Okay. For you. But when they tell me off for wasting their time, I'll hold you responsible."

I've already lifted the receiver.

Melody

"This is so unfair," I say, folding my arms across my chest.

Mum takes a bite from her sandwich and chews slowly.

"Mum, *please*."

She swallows her bite. "I warned you. You said you had the money to get home."

"I *did*. It's not my fault that old git driver wouldn't believe I'm a junior."

"You're not a junior," she points out. "You're sixteen. You have to pay full rate."

"But I'm still at school!"

"I don't make the rules. I've already told you I don't have any cash on me. You're welcome to check my purse if you want. Either you wait for me to finish or you walk. The choice is yours."

"You don't finish for six hours!"

She shrugs. "Then best you get walking." She has another bite of her rapidly disappearing sandwich. My belly rumbles. I'm starving.

"What if I get kidnapped?"

"They'll soon give you back."

I scowl. "What if I get run over? Or die of hunger? Or thirst?"

"Stick to the paths and you won't get run over." She pops the last bit of her sandwich into her mouth.

God, I hate walking. It's the worst thing ever. Apart from playing hockey. I really, really, really hate hockey.

I'm debating whether or not to make myself cry when she suddenly thrusts the sandwich packet at me. There's half a sandwich in it. "Here," she says, "This'll stop you starving. You've got a pound on you – buy yourself some water. Got your house key?"

I nod.

"Show me."

I root around in my backpack and pull the key out.

"Call me when you get in. And don't slam the door on your way out."

I have no idea why I kiss her cheek before leaving.

Alex

The sound of a door slamming has me looking up from the 1987 car magazine I'm reading to pass the time. The culprit is so unexpected that I do one of those double takes you see from hammy actors.

It's Melody.

Mouth open in shock, I watch her stomp through the medical centre waiting room dressed in the early-nineties grunge uniform popular with everyone who doesn't want to conform. She has a sullen expression on her face I can only describe as Pure Teenager. When she reaches the reception desk, one of the receptionists calls out, "Bye, Melody," and, just like that, the sullenness disappears.

Melody raises her hand in a wave and cheerily calls back, "Bye, Mrs Emmins. See you soon."

It's the first time I've heard her voice in eight months and the force of it has tears stabbing the back of my eyes.

I'm on my feet, ready to chase after her, when Dr Faraday pokes his head out of his office and calls Mum's name.

Melody

I've walked only two of the six stupid miles back to Collingswood when the batteries of my Walkman die.

God, can life get any more unfair?

Saturday 30th August 1997

BEFORE

Melody

I wake to find Alice, not even two years old, fast asleep beside me. I'd warned Mum the little ratbag had learned to climb out of her cot but she didn't believe me. I've told her numerous times that Alice is incredibly advanced for her age, but she never believes that either. I have a feeling the plans to move Alice from the box-room nursery into this, my childhood bedroom, will now be accelerated. Somehow, I doubt they'll keep the walls the dark grey colour I insisted they be painted when I was fifteen. Under certain sunlight, you can still see traces of My Little Pony wallpaper.

There's a light rap on the door and then Mum's head appears. "Oh good, you're awake," she says, and then the rest of her emerges into the room, holding a cup of tea.

This is one of the many things I love about my mum. She brings me a cup of tea in bed when I stay over. This is the first time I've stayed over on my own in over a year. It will certainly be the last time I stay overnight here on my own.

Not until she leans over to place the cup on my bedside table does she notice Alice.

"How did she...?"

I raise an eyebrow in an 'I told you so,' fashion, and sit up.

Careful not to sit on Alice's feet, Mum climbs on the bed and stares at us both with the strangest smile on her face.

"You okay?" I ask.

She looks from me to Alice and back to me. "It doesn't feel real. That you're getting married. It feels like only yesterday that you were her age and breaking out of your cot."

"You're not going to cry are you?" Grandma Alison, Mum's mum, died last October. Mum is a stoical, pick-yourself-up-and-stop-whining type of woman but Grandma's death has affected her badly. The last few years have been one life-changing event after another for her. Two years after I flew the nest for university she found herself pregnant for the second time.

My surprise sister could easily have been a devastating blow. After all, Mum and Dad were only twenty when they had me and had been looking forward to enjoying their lives without the responsibility of a child, but they embraced the surprise. Alice is their little treasure and, as they explained, things were easier for them the second time round. They had more money, their mortgage was virtually paid off, and they had a readymade babysitter to dump their surprise on when they wanted a romantic weekend away, aka, me.

For all their positivity about their situation, it doesn't change the fact that the future they'd envisaged for themselves radically changed. It doesn't change the fact that Grandma's death has left my mum bereft, and I know she'll be feeling her loss keenly today. I feel it too, but it isn't a fraction of what Mum and her sisters are going through.

She shakes her head and ruffles my hair. "No tears. I promise. Did you bring your waterproof mascara for me?"

"Yep."

"Good... So, how are you feeling? Nervous?"

"Nope."

She peers closer, trying to see if I'm lying. "I was a bag of nerves when I married your dad."

"I've got butterflies," I admit. "But they're happy. *I'm* happy." Happier than I ever dreamed I could be. Today I'm going to marry Alex. Nothing has ever felt so right in my life.

"Good. You've picked yourself a good one there."

I smile. "I know."

Not that Alex is perfect. No way. Considering he was the one *really* renowned for cheating, I've not felt an ounce of jealousy or distrust since he made his promise to me. He, however, has developed an acute case of Being A Jealous Twat. Because of his newfound BAJT tendencies we've had some humdingers of arguments, real screaming rows, usually over something as innocuous as me having the temerity to talk to or mention another man. The only men exempt from his BAJT are male family members (both sides) and Kermit. Alex gets all arsey and possessive, which in turn puts my back up at the ridiculousness of it. As I screamed at him once, he needs to stop judging everyone, including me, against his own stupidly low standards. Just because he's cheated dozens of times doesn't mean everyone else is at it.

He doesn't like this side of himself any more than I do, and if I wasn't as possessive of him as he is of me (but without the jealousy, go figure), it would be much harder to cope with. The thing is, we both hate ourselves in the aftermath and both know his jealousy and my over-the-top reactions to it have the potential to destroy us. As a result, he's getting better at controlling it, and I'm getting better at diffusing it. When I sense he's about to turn into a BAJT on a night out, I pinch his bottom and whisper in his ear something along the lines of, 'If you want any chance of a blowjob tonight, smile or I'll use my teeth.'

A solitary tear trickles down Mum's cheek but she returns my smile. "Come on, time to get up. Your dad's making breakfast."

"I'm not hungry," I say at the same moment Alice opens her eyes and yawns widely. Then her beautiful blue eyes lock onto mine and she gives a smile as wide as her yawn. "'Ello Smelly."

* * *

Dad's head appears from the connecting door to the garage. He's wearing the furtive expression I know so well. "Where's your mum?" he hisses.

"Pinning Alice down so she can have her hair done." And I'm enjoying a few minutes to myself before Mum wedges me into my dress.

"Come here then."

"Why?" The hairdresser only finished doing my hair ten minutes ago and my nails are still drying. The last place I want to go is the cobwebby garage. It doesn't surprise me in the least that Dad hasn't acknowledged my hair, or that he's still wearing the old jeans and egg-stained t-shirt he walked the dog in. He can only concentrate on one thing at a time.

The tendons of his neck extend in exasperation. "Quick."

Dad's garage is a typical man-cave. Every wall is lined with shelves crammed with all sorts of tools and, what look to my untrained eyes, torture equipment, along with old paint pots, varnishes, and lots of random bits and pieces. On the concrete floor in the centre are four old motorbikes he's been doing-up since I was Alice's age. He might finish one of them one day. There's also the faint whiff of stale cigarette smoke. Dad's excellent at quitting smoking. He's done it many times.

"Close the door," he orders.

I obey, telling him, "You need to have a shower." And shave. His jaw is currently far more effective than the random bits of sandpaper littering the place.

"Plenty of time for that." I'm grateful he doesn't ask what he needs to shower for. Then he grins and opens a toolbox. Inside is a bottle of vodka and two shot glasses. "Thought you might need something for your nerves."

"I haven't got any nerves," I say for the umpteenth time that morning, although all these reminders that I should have nerves is having the effect of *making* me nervous.

"Well, I do." He fills both glasses and hands me one. "Don't tell your mum."

Figuring it would be rude not to, I clink my glass to his and down it. He refills them both and we do the same again.

"Another?" he asks hopefully.

"I don't think Mum will be happy if we stagger down the aisle, do you?"

He actually thinks about this.

On impulse, I plant a kiss on his cheek. "Love you."

"Love you too." And then the twat ruffles my hair.

Alex

Graham puts two pints down on the bar in front of us. "On the house," he says without the hint of a smile.

"Cheers, mate," I say, taken aback at this most uncharacteristic act of generosity.

He nods and side-steps away from us. Graham does not subscribe to the pub landlord creed of actually talking to your punters.

I meet Kermit's eye. He looks as stunned as I feel.

"Have the body-snatchers been in Brocklehurst?" he mutters under his breath.

"Must have... Cheers."

No sooner have we finished them than Ollie arrives and buys us a round. We would have stopped there but Melody's godfather Richard, who's staying at The Merry Thief, appears and insists on buying us another too. The pints are poured before his wife, wide-brimmed hat threatening to knock the head off anyone who gets within a foot of her, joins us.

"Aren't you supposed to be getting married in half-an-hour?" she scolds, tapping her watch.

Our quick drink has gone on a little longer than we'd planned. Oh well.

"Neck them?" Ollie suggests.

Kermit and I don't need any further persuasion and neither does Richard. Twenty seconds later the pints are drained and we're heading out of the pub with shouts of 'Good luck' ringing in our ears.

I grin. I don't need luck. I'm marrying Melody. I'm taking my lifetime quota of luck in one sitting.

Melody

The chauffeur pulls up outside the church. Dad reaches into the inside pocket of his morning suit jacket and produces a hipflask.

He notices the look I give him and juts his shaven chin defensively. "My nerves are shot."

I giggle and snatch it from his hand.

"Oi!"

I take a long drink and hand it back. "Don't tell Mum."

Alex

I know all brides are supposed to look beautiful on their wedding day but the moment Melody appears in the church doorway, I'm certain my heart is going to burst out of my chest. I've rarely seen her wear anything but black, have never seen her in a dress, and never seen her feet clad in anything but Dr Martens, so the impact of seeing her in an elegant strapless white dress and white stilettos is quadrupley effective. Even her wild black corkscrews have been tamed, piled artfully on her head and topped with a pretty tiara.

Roy holds her right arm and walks her to me with the face of a man who's just been told he's won the lottery. Alice clings to her left hand, totally ignoring Lorna's efforts to make her walk behind like a good bridesmaid should. When they reach me, the whole congregation is in fits of laughter at Alice's absolute refusal to leave Melody's side.

"Want Smelly!" she screams when Patty tries to prise her hand from Mel's. In the end, my dad, who for some reason Alice has taken a shine to, scoops her up and pins her to his lap. She kicks his shin a couple of times with the back of her heel, then sticks her thumb in her mouth and settles down.

And so it was with the church infused with absurdity and laughter that Melody and I pledged our lives together.

Melody

"Ladies and gentlemen, I give you, the bride and groom!"

Applause and catcalls follow us onto the dancefloor. I pretend not to notice mum's mock-scowling face at my abandonment of the ridiculous shoes she made me wear for the ceremony and wedding breakfast in favour of my trusty Dr Martens (I only agreed to the stupid shoes because it was *the* condition for her and Dad to hand over the cheque that paid for most of this wedding. She literally waved it in my face then held it out of reach until I promised), and throw my arms around Alex's neck. My cheeks ache from all the smiling I've done that day, but I can't stop the latest one forming.

"Everything I do...," my husband sings through lips that have widened into a smile to match my own.

I'm a married woman! Who'd have thought it?

If you'd told me eighteen months ago that I would get married on this day, I would have laughed in your face and told you to see a shrink.

I didn't know I was waiting for Alex.

I've thought about it a lot and I think I fell in love with him that night when I was sixteen but, other than those pathetic lovelorn schoolgirl weeks immediately after, didn't know it. That's why I did all the bouncing. None of the other men felt right. My body never responded as it should because none of them had been him.

A dark-haired mini tornado in a dusky pink bridesmaid dress breaks ranks from the side-lines and pelts to us, squealing, "Smelly, Smelly." Alex laughs, kisses me, and scoops Alice into his arms. Everyone else takes this as their cue and moments later the dancefloor is filled with all the people we love. Only Graham remains seated. When the track changes to 'Boom Shack-A-Lak', Lorna, my other bridesmaid, who's sworn to never forgive me for making her wear pink, takes pity on him and grabs his hand to drag him on the floor too.

By the time we make it to the hotel's honeymoon suite we're too exhausted and drunk to even attempt sex. We throw all the sweet wrappers, confetti, cigarette butts and other crap that's been hidden under the duvet – probably Kermit and Ollie's doing – and pass out, fully dressed, in each other's arms.

We have the rest of our lives to make up for it.

Saturday 6th April 2002

BEFORE

Melody

Juniper Crescent is a pretty little curved street in a quiet part of Brocklehurst. Number twenty-eight, which Alex and I are standing at the front gate of, is a small semi-detached house with a postage stamp of overgrown grass and weeds as a front garden. The door and the windowsills all look in need of a good lick of paint. Yet, despite this inauspicious start, my heart is racing.

We've finally saved enough money to put down a deposit for a home of our own. This is the first viewing we've been to where my spidey-senses haven't been shouting 'NO' before we even reach the front door.

My hand snug in Alex's, I open the gate, which almost comes off its hinges, and knock on the door.

The estate agent invites us in. Voices echo from within. I've barely wiped my boots and I'm already wishing I'd brought a stink-bomb to scare off the other viewers.

Alex and I drift through a small living room and into a cosy kitchen. I peer out of the window into the much more generously sized overgrown back garden and, though the sum total of my gardening skills consists of mowing the lawn under sufferance when I was still living at home, there's a zing in my veins to imagine ripping out all the weeds and replacing them with colourful flowers.

By the time we've explored a boxroom that isn't big enough to swing a cat, another bedroom, not much bigger than the boxroom but at least big enough to swing a cat; two at a stretch, a bathroom with the same delightful avocado coloured bath, sink and toilet that Grandma Alison had when I was little, and are looking out of the window in the master bedroom, I know this is it. One look at Alex's face is all I need to know he's feeling the same.

We've found our home.

Saturday 10th August 1991

NOW

Alex

Roy's mowing the front lawn when I walk past. He lifts a hand and nods an acknowledgement. I nod in return and continue walking.

I wish so hard that I could stop and talk to him. Have him invite me into his garage. Have him lift the lid of his toolbox to remove whatever booze he's not-so-secretly stashed in there (the Aldridge women humour him) and offer me a nip before earnestly asking my opinion on whatever it is about the female sex that's vexing him at that particular time. Right from the start, he reminded me of a mad professor. It makes my chest hurt to remember how Mel's death broke him.

Don't worry, Roy, I vow. I'll save her. *This time, it will be different. I promise.*

Saturday 13th December 2003

BEFORE

Melody

Alex lifts Alice so she can put the fairy on the top of the tree.

"Ready?" Dad asks.

"Ready," Mum agrees.

A moment later all the lights on the Christmas tree flash, along with all the other fairy lights Dad's strewn around the living room. It's so bright I almost have to shield my eyes.

Dad makes a celebratory Tim Henman style fist pump then rubs his hands together. "I think that calls for another drink. Alex?"

"Thanks but need to get Mel back as she's off out with Lorna tonight."

Dad harumphs. This is entirely for Alex. As far as Dad's concerned (and Mum and Alice), the sun shines out of my husband's arse. If we were to ever split up, they'd ask for custody of Alex ha ha.

"Dinner for one tomorrow?" I check with Mum as I kiss her goodbye. It's a rare Sunday we don't spend with my family. Quite frankly, Mum's Sunday roast is the one decent meal we get each week, the one event we always make sure to drag ourselves out of bed for.

"Yep. Send my love to Lorna."

"Will do."

We leave the Santa's Grotto that my family's home's been transformed into and get into Alex's work van. Jeez, it's bloody freezing!

While we wait for the heating to kick in and the condensation on the windscreen to clear, my phone makes a noise. A text message from Lorna.

Sorry, Mel, but really tired so need to cancel tonight. Will get together again properly soon.

I send her a quick message back.

No worries. Hope all's okay. Catch up soon. Love you x

"Who's that?" Alex asks.

"Lorna. She's cancelled on me." I meet his eye and grin. "So, what shall we do? Go back in for a drink with my dad?"

He pretends to think about this before squeezing the top of my thigh and leaning in for a delicious, biting kiss.

He only just keeps to the speed limit on the journey back home for yet another of our favourite early nights.

Saturday 24th August 1991

NOW

Alex

"Come on, Al, it's been ages since we went on a night out together."

Ollie's been on at me since I got back from my weekly stalk to Collingswood. There was no sign of Melody or her parents today.

"Sorry, Ols, I'm not in the mood." Ollie wants to go to Solaris. I have a vague remembrance of us going there my first time here. Vague because I got hammered and screwed a woman whose face I don't remember in the ladies loo. It's a night I have no wish to live again.

"You're never in the mood. What going on with you? You've been like this for months. Everyone's noticed."

I play for time but heavy nausea is swirling in my stomach again. "Noticed what?"

"How much you've fucking changed," he explodes, punching the wall with his fury. For the first time, I recognise it *as* fury. "You used to be a right laugh but now you're as fucking boring as Dad."

"Language!" Mum shouts from the living room.

Ollie's face contorts. "Fuck this," he mutters, then looks me right in the eye. "And fuck you."

Melody

I hold my backpack and kiss Dad on his cheek. "See you in the morning."

"Call me when you want collecting, and remember, don't do anything I wouldn't." He wriggles his shoulders as he always does whenever he says this to me. Which is most days.

"I won't." I'm too relieved that he's saved me a walk to Hayley's house for sarcasm. She lives right at the other end of the village, which is at *least* a ten-minute walk.

Dad waits until Hayley's mum opens the door before driving off.

Hayley's packed and ready.

"What time will you two be back?" her mum asks.

We look at each other.

"Ten?" Hayley says as if it's a question.

Her mum winks. "If I'm not up, don't wake me."

We set off. If her mum's watching, she'll see us turn right onto the High Street but instead of crossing over as we should to reach Georgina's house, we continue on our path until we reach Becket Close and take a sharp right. Georgina and Karen are already outside Danny's house. So too are Danny, Sam and Toby and the large backpack of booze we've pooled our money together to buy. Danny hurries to us and kisses me on the mouth. His lips are dry, but I don't mind. He's gorgeous! And popular! When he asked me out I was convinced he was asking me to ask Hayley out for him, but no, it was me he wanted. I was so shocked that – after consulting with Hayley first as I'm not stupid enough to forget that she fancied him last year – I said yes.

He grins – he really is gorgeous! – then bangs on the front door of his house.

His brother appears. He's really tall. I wonder if Danny will grow as tall as him? If so, he'd better get a move on.

Jonathan looks at all of us, grunts, and stands beside the small white (well, it would be if it was ever cleaned) van on the driveway. He's so cool! He holds his hand out. When we all stare at him blankly, he sighs and rubs his fingers and thumb together.

Dutifully, we all hand over the two one-pound coins we've each agreed to pay him. Satisfied with his loot, Jonathan unlocks the passenger door and the double doors at the back, and chucks in the two tents. "Right, squirts, in. Two up front, rest of you in the back.

Alex

I'm settled on the sofa watching television – I'd forgotten how hilarious Saturday evening TV in the 90's was – trying to forget Ollie's cold "fuck you," when there's a loud banging on the door. Mum and I let Dad answer it. It's bound to be an angler with a gripe. Mum's not been allowed to deal with any complaints since she laughed in the face of one complaining the fish didn't like the sweetcorn he was using as bait.

Dad's face is puce when he comes back in the living room. "Group of bloody kids set up camp at the bottom lake. Making a right racket and scaring the fish away."

Our lakes are on the edge of Hestcote village, only two miles from Brocklehurst. Local teenagers often sneak to the lakes to make-out. A couple of times a year, groups of them descend with the intention of partying, mistakenly thinking no-one will know they're there. I often wonder what colour Dad's face would turn if I told him they're still doing it in 2024.

I help myself to a biscuit and stretch my legs out.

"Jane, where's my keys?" Dad calls from the kitchen.

"In the fruit bowl where you left them." She doesn't take her eyes from the television. This is something else I'd forgotten – the art of watching television in the twentieth century. It requires total concentration. You can't pause a programme to deal with a grumpy husband or rewind bits you don't hear properly.

Dad's footsteps clump down the hallway. I would pity the teenagers about to get a tongue-lashing from him but teenagers are morons and deserve it, and as I think this, the whisper of a three decades-old conversation comes back to me and I sit up sharply.

"Hold on, Dad," I yell. "I'll come with you."

Mum looks at me as if I've just offered to clean his backside.

I can offer no explanation for this uncharacteristic selfless act that won't have her commit me to the nearest lunatic asylum.

Thursday 1st January 2004

BEFORE

Melody

Little fingers have a grip on one of my curls and are pulling it. The fingers let go. I keep my eyes closed and clamp my lips together, even when Alice boings my hair a second and then a third time. When she goes for it a fourth time, I grab her wrist and pin her down to blow a raspberry on her neck. She giggles.

"You hungry?" I whisper, although I have a feeling Alex has woken too. He'll probably feign sleep for another hour or so.

"Can we have pancakes?" she whispers back.

"Come on then."

She shoots off the bed and waits for me to follow suit. Alex and I long ago learned to wear nightclothes when Alice stayed over. One of the first things we (Alex! Turns out I'm rubbish at decoration and DIY) did when we bought our house two years ago was turn the smaller of the spare rooms into a bedroom for her. It's made zero difference to her habit of sneaking into our bed. My baby sister loves staying with us, and we love having her. Not that she's a baby anymore.

I remember when mum told me she was pregnant. I was

excited but when I look back, I can see how detached I really was about it, too busy having the time of my life at university to realise what a momentous thing was happening to my little family. When Alice was born, I thought she was cute but in that same detached manner. When I finished university and moved back home, I quickly moved into Lorna's – oh, the *pain* that claws me just to think of her – because I couldn't cope with a screaming baby alongside the screaming hangovers' I put myself through in those days.

It wasn't until Alice's third birthday party, when she got a Malteser stuck in her throat and my blood turned cold in terror, that I understood the depths of my feelings for her. Sometimes, I look at her and my heart hurts from all the love I feel. My adoration of her is entirely reciprocated.

In the kitchen, she hauls herself onto a breakfast bar stool. The black curly hair she inherited like me from our father stands on end, and she chatters ten-to-the-dozen while I make the batter. I'm reminded of Lorna's wry observation that Alice and I are so alike we could be Babushka dolls.

I suck a deep breath in and squeeze my eyes shut in an attempt to drive out the acute ache in my chest.

I asked for Alice to stay over because looking after her is the only distraction strong enough to stop me from falling apart.

I don't think either Alex or I would have got through last night without her here. We should have been out celebrating the New Year with Lorna like we've done every year since we got together. Instead, we're preparing ourselves for her funeral.

I was too young to go to Katie's funeral. A part of me wishes I was too young to go to Lorna's. I have no idea how I'm going to bear it.

"What's wrong, Smelly?"

I blink the hot tears pooling behind my eyes away and poke my tongue out at her. Now eight year's old, Alice still insists on calling me that.

"Just thinking of Lorna," I say. God, it hurts to even say her name. "What do you want on your pancakes?"

* * *

When we get back from our traditional New Year's Day dinner at Mum and Dad's (no idea how Mum managed to cook it with that hangover), Alex and I settle down to watch Coronation Street. I stretch out on the sofa, feet on his lap and a rapidly diminishing packet of chocolate digestives between us.

I find my attention wandering. It's wandered a lot that day.

I wait until it's finished before turning the sound down.

"Al..."

He turns bleary green eyes to me. Alex and my dad demolished three bottles of red wine between them over dinner.

"I've been thinking."

"Dangerous," he observes with a faint smile.

I kick his lap.

He leans into me and squeezes my sides. Then he kisses the tip of my nose. "Go on, tell me."

I run my fingers through his hair. "I want a baby."

There's a moment of stillness.

I hold my breath.

Alex and I discussed having babies when we married. I was honest about my reasons for not wanting them then; I was too selfish, I liked my sleep and, more than anything, I wanted to enjoy what we had. He was happy to wait, told me to let him know when I was ready. Bless him, I don't think he expected it to take over six years.

His eyes bore into mine. "Are you sure?"

Lorna's face floats before me.

Is she a butterfly now, like Katie?

Oh Lorna, why did you do it? Why didn't you talk to me? Or Alex? You've broken our hearts.

I wipe a tear away and nod.

Life is short. Life is precious. No one knows what's coming for them so why waste time?

I want Alex and I to make a family.

I nod again.

The first real smile I've seen in nearly a fortnight breaks over his face and he jumps off me and grabs hold of my hand. "Let's go make a baby."

Saturday 24th August 1991

NOW

Alex

I stride out of the house into the warm evening air and jump in Dad's pickup truck.

He gives me another of his puzzled 'what's happened to my son?' looks.

"Thought you might appreciate some back-up," I say.

He stares a little longer, blinks, nods to himself, and turns the engine on.

The bottom lake is only a ten-minute drive from the house and accessed through a private road that cuts through our woods and leads to a small car park.

Dad and I chat aimlessly about the new football season, something neither of us have much interest in. It's easier than talking about the subjects I sense he's too frightened to discuss: what's wrong with mum and is it serious, and what's wrong with me and is it serious. I wish I could put his mind at ease about either subject.

Sensing his fears helps me keep a grip on the nerves making mincemeat of my guts. I'm very likely wrong. Very likely. How is it possible that I'm right?

The odds of Melody being amongst this group are small. There must be hundreds, possibly thousands, of teenagers living within a ten-mile radius of the lakes and itching for a night of unsupervised fun.

The carpark is unsurprisingly full. It's a beautiful weekend.

We hear their music as soon as we open our doors. Definitely loud enough to scare the fish away.

The revellers are out of sight but easy to find by following the noise. They're camped in a clearing in an enclosed section of the woods about twenty yards from the edge of the lake. Two tents have been put up in a half-arsed fashion that would see them blown away by a minor gust of wind. There's seven of them. Four girls are drunk dancing and singing along to 'Groove Is in the Heart.'

A groove forms and stutters in *my* heart. It's a song Melody always asked the DJ to play when we went for a night out.

The setting sun and canopy of trees makes it hard to distinguish faces from the distance we're approaching, but another stutter of my heart tells me the identity of one of the drunk dancing girls.

My feet root to the ground. Disbelief and wonder fills me. It's not possible. It shouldn't be possible.

How is it possible for the future and the past to collide?

But then, how is it possible that I'm here at all?

I've barely time to pull myself together into the here and now when Dad goes steaming in and thumps their portable stereo off.

"Right, you trespassing buggers, what do you think you're playing at?" This is a question that does not require an answer. "This is private land. Pack your stuff together and get lost."

I'm too stunned at what's happening and at being within ten feet of Melody, who's wisely hiding behind one of the boys, to notice a brave but stupid boy take a step forward until he belligerently says, "We're not doing anything wrong."

My dad's the kind of bloke who thinks society will break down without a rigid adherence to rules. Telling him you're not doing anything wrong when you clearly are is a short cut to a thick ear. But only if you're his son. This brave, stupid lad is not his son so is only subject to a tongue lashing. From past experience, I'd say the thick ear is less painful.

The tongue lashing he subjects the boy to makes them all cringe.

Once Dad's diatribe is over, he points at the tents and snaps. "Well? Get on with it. Get them down or I'll do it myself."

It's Melody who finds some bravery this time. The smallest of them all, my pocket-dynamo, steps out of her hiding place behind the taller boy and meekly approaches Dad.

"We're really sorry." She hangs her head with such contrition I find myself fighting the unexpected urge to laugh. "We really didn't mean to scare the fish or upset the other people. I promise it won't happen again."

Dad looks slightly mollified. "I should hope not."

"Would it be okay for us to stay if we promise to be quiet? Only, our lift isn't coming for us 'til the morning."

"What time's your lift coming for you?" I ask, stepping in before Dad can explode with outrage and insist they walk like he's made all the others do over the years.

For the first time since the day I lost her, Melody's gaze locks onto me.

Her eyes widen. The beat that passes stretches and makes my heart balloon.

Then she blinks and answers. "Nine-o-clock."

I reluctantly tear my gaze from her and say to Dad, "How about I stay with them?"

Now he's the one to stare as if I've offered to clean his backside.

"Look at them," I say, thinking and speaking quickly. Isn't this how Melody explained this night to me? "They're just kids. It's getting dark. Anything could happen to them. I'll stay and keep an eye on them until their lift comes... unless you want to give them a lift in the truck?" The latter is something I know he absolutely will not want to do.

His lips pucker in the way that means he's thinking. Eventually he jerks his head. "Okay, then. But I tell you little buggers now, you give Alex any trouble and I'll hunt you down and tell your parents what you've been up to." He taps his temple. "I've got an excellent memory for faces. Got it?"

He hasn't. His memory for faces is useless. But they don't know that and they all solemnly nod their heads.

He turns back to me. I can't work out his expression. "I'll fetch you the camping gear."

I pat my backside. "And my cigarettes?" I cast a quick glance at the litter already strewn everywhere. "And a bin bag?"

His lips make the tiniest curve before he turns on his heel and returns to the carpark.

I wait until he's out of sight before facing the silent teenagers. Only one of them looks unafraid. Melody. She's staring at me with what can only be described as wonder.

Melody

Oh my God, Alex is *gorgeous*! He's the most beautiful man I've ever seen in my life. I know you're not supposed to say a man's beautiful but he is. He makes Keanu Reeves look ordinary. Actually, he looks a little like Keanu. I'm sure Keanu would kill to look like him!

He has such beautiful eyes. There's something about the way he looks at me that makes my belly go all squishy and my heart beat faster. Mum says I haven't got a shy bone in my body, but there's something about Alex that makes me feel shy.

I think he must make the others feel shy too, as things are pretty awkward until his dad comes back with a foldable chair and a bag of stuff for him. Alex pulls a bin bag from it and gives it to Danny.

We're very good and put all our litter in it. We're all to awestruck at this man who's saved us a five mile walk in the dark to argue. We wouldn't have left it though, honest... although, I'm not entirely sure any of us thought to bring a bag for the empties.

The sun's gone down now, and my bare arms are chilly.

Alex notices me rub them. "Have you brought a jumper with you?"

His voice is beautiful too. All deep and lovely.

"I've a jacket," I say, and go into our tent to get it.

I'm sharing with the girls but Danny's going to sneak in. It's because I wanted Danny to sneak into our tent that I came tonight. Mum won't let him in my bedroom, can you believe that? It's totally unfair. Hayley's allowed boys in her bedroom. I'm sixteen! I'm legal! But no, Mum says, 'Not under my roof,' and that's that. I can't see Danny when she's working as he's got a job working at the reclamation centre for his dad. I swear, I'm going to be a virgin forever.

When I come back out, Alex is explaining the exact kind of wood we need to build a fire. When he realises none of us thought to bring a torch, he shakes his head and pulls one out from his bag. He gives it to Toby and nods at Sam. "You two get the firewood. Stick to the path."

They trot off obediently.

Alex takes a small spade from his bag and starts digging a hole in a flat patch of ground. He keeps looking at me.

I'm trying to pluck up the courage to talk to him when Hayley sidles over. She folds her arms across her chest to push her tits up and make them look bigger.

"How old are you?" she asks him.

He looks at her briefly. "Twenty-one."

"When's your birthday?"

"Next month."

"What date?"

"The twenty fifth."

I sigh inwardly.

"Ooo, so you're a Libra?"
"If you say so."
"I'm a Gemini."

I'm taken with the urge to push her over. Preferably onto her face.

Alex

Melody is much quieter than I've ever known her be. I get the feeling she's not happy about her friend flirting with me. Hayley is a name that only rings the faintest bell. A name from Melody's past. She was never part of our lives together. I wonder how close they are. Hayley isn't Melody's usual kind of friend. She's too made-up. If she was a teenager in 2024, her career aspiration would be an Influencer.

I've got the campfire lit and its warmth is starting to penetrate. It makes me laugh to see them all huddle around it on the logs I encouraged them to find to sit on. This is why I firmly believe teenagers are morons. They get these great ideas in their heads but can't see any further to the practicalities needed to make them work. Their goal tonight was to stay somewhere free from prying adult eyes. They remembered to bring tents, booze, crisps and music. And that's it. See? Morons.

I was a moron like them once. The original Alex who possessed this body was a moron and a cheating dick until he met Melody. Anything good he ever did with his life was entirely down to her.

They're all in good spirits though. The awkwardness of earlier has lifted and they're back on the booze, cracking jokes and taking the piss out of each other. Except for Melody.

Danny squeezes into the space beside her, forcing one of the other girls to shift over. I feel nothing but pity for this scrawny teenager. He puts his arm around her. She tolerates it for a few minutes – I lived with Melody for twenty-eight years, I know when she's tolerating something – before she shrugs him off and gets to her feet. Her gaze darts to me then to Hayley, who's still blathering inanely into my ear. She assumes I find the subject of Madonna as fascinating as she does.

My heart contracts. *I miss you, Mel. I love you*.

After much shuffling, she finally reaches me and too-casually sits on the log on the other side of my chair to Hayley.

If she had any idea how much I long to wrap one of those curls in my fingers like I've done a thousand times...

She brings her knees up and hugs them.

This shyness is so unlike her that I feel compelled to break the ice. "You're Melody, right?"

She lifts her face to meet my stare and beams a smile so familiar and so missed a piece of my heart breaks off.

Melody

He knows my name! And I didn't even have to tell him it!

The way his eyes are holding mine... oh, it's like he's trying to read everything that's in my head (candyfloss, if Mum's right). No one has ever looked at me like that before.

"Is he your boyfriend?" he asks, nodding at Danny, who's looking very pinched.

I sigh. I want to say no but Hayley's listening. "Yeah."

"Been together long?"

"Two weeks and three days."

His lips pull together and release. They're beautiful lips. I bet they're not dry. I have a strong feeling he's trying not to laugh.

"Do you all go to school together?"

"Yeah. Well, we did. The boys have all left. Danny works for his dad. Toby's got an apprenticeship at a garage in Brocklehurst and Sam's got a job making phone calls or something. Me, Georgina and Karen are all going into sixth form. Hayley's going to college to do beauty." I notice his lips pull and release again at this.

"You're doing A' Levels?"

"Yeah. Do you work?"

"I do." He picks his cigarette packet up from the ground by his feet and puts one in his mouth.

"Can I have one?" I ask.

He raises an eyebrow.

"I've run out," I lie. Hayley, Danny and Toby smoke. I've tried it a few times. I've never really liked it but smoking's adult. I really, really want Alex to see me as an adult and not a schoolgirl. "Please? I'm old enough."

He hesitates some more before flicking the lid open. I pluck one out and put it between my lips. He flicks the lid of his zippo and I'm forced to lean close to him to catch the flame. I remember not to inhale too deeply so I don't have a coughing fit and prove myself a liar to him.

Hayley gets up and makes a big drama about walking over to Danny and offering him her cigarettes.

I catch Alex's eye again. There's an amused glint in it, but a softness too.

"What A' Levels are you going to do?" he asks, diving straight back to the subject I wanted to avoid, namely school.

"History, English Lit, and Art."

"Good choices. What do you want to do when you finish school?"

I shrug. I haven't got the faintest idea what I want to do.

Clamping his cigarette between his lips, he rifles through his huge rucksack and pulls out a bottle of rum. He unscrews it, takes a sip, and passes the bottle to me.

I put the bottle to my lips.

"Just have a nip," he warns. "It's potent stuff."

I do as he says, taking just enough to slosh over my tongue. It burns down my throat making me cough.

Alex laughs. "Smaller nip next time."

I nod, mostly because I can't speak. My eyes are streaming. He puts the bottle on the ground beside his cigarettes. He doesn't offer it to the others. It's like he doesn't see them. He only sees me.

My heart starts thrumming again. He likes me. This gorgeous man likes me.

Hayley stands up. She's got her sulky face on. "I'm bored. Can we put the music on?"

"Sure," Alex agrees, also standing, but not to sulk. He takes a log from the pile and puts it on the fire. "Just keep the sound down and no singing. My dad meant it about the noise – if he gets another complaint about you, he'll track you all down."

"He doesn't even know where we live," Danny sneers.

"How many sixteen-year-old Danny's live in Collingswood?" Alex asks pointedly.

Danny scowls and opens another can of cider.

My bum's getting numb. I wriggle it.

Alex goes into his rucksack again. This time he pulls out a compacted sleeping bag and indicates for me to get up. I obey. He pushes away his chair, the log I've been sitting on, and Hayley's abandoned one, unzips the sleeping bag and spreads it out on the ground. Then he sits on it, stretches his legs, looks at me hovering uselessly and pats the empty space beside him.

Butterflies are bashing their wings in my belly as I do my best to appear cool and sit on the opened sleeping bag next to him.

My insides are trembling.

"Are you cold?" he asks.

"A bit," I say, then hold my breath in hope he'll put an arm around me to warm me.

But no, he's back in the rucksack, this time producing a jumper which he hands to me.

"Are you sure?"

He grins. "I'm sure."

"Thank you." I take my thin jacket off and shrug his jumper over my head, making sure to have a good sniff as I pull it over my face. It smells of washing powder. It's so long I have to kneel to pull it over my bum and roll the sleeves three times. "How tall are you?"

"Six foot two."

"I wish I was tall."

His eyes lock on mine for the longest time. "You're perfect as you are."

My cheeks go red. I can feel the burn colouring my skin. It warms me as much as his jumper does.

No one has ever called me perfect before.

Alex

Melody's friends have gone into the tents. When Danny asked – although it seemed more of an order – if she was coming to bed, she didn't hesitate to shake her head and say, "Not yet."

I don't know how much making-out they intended to do but all I hear are drunken, stoned snores. When one of the lads produced a joint I wanted to laugh at the huge size and baggy amateurishness of it. It brought back so many memories of the first time I inhabited this body.

Melody was the only one who listened and refused the joint when I warned them it would rot their brain cells.

We're lying on our backs gazing up at the stars twinkling through the canopy of trees. I've folded my hands over my stomach as the temptation to take her hand is becoming torture.

I've spent the five months since I came back to 1991 longing to be with her again, to hold her, kiss her, touch her, make love to her, but while the 1991 Alex is physically thirty-three years younger than the 2024 version, the 1991 Melody is physically and emotionally thirty-three years younger than the Melody I buried.

I've never felt the age gap between us before. I hadn't appreciated the difference in emotional maturity between the Melody I fell in love with and the sixteen-year-old girl she was five years before we met. Saying that, neither of us were particularly mature when we got together. We matured and grew together.

She's so very young. In this here and now, she's younger than our child would have been had it lived.

"Do you really have no idea what you want to do when you leave school?" I've always thought Melody knew from a young age that she wanted to do something involving history.

"None at all. Mum keeps going on at me about university but that's coz she wants to get rid of me."

"Sure about that are you?"

"She hates me."

"She loves you." *And in less than a decade from now the two of you will be the best of friends.*

She snorts. "Can I have a cigarette?"

"I've not got many left so we'll have to go two's-up." That's a term I've not used in decades.

She rolls onto her belly and rests her cheek on her forearm to watch me while I scramble for the cigarettes. I know she's hoping I'll make a move on her. She has no idea how much her eyes and body-language are a giveaway for what she's thinking and feeling. It's one of the many things I love so much about her.

But I can't make the move we both long for. It would be wrong on too many levels.

"What does your dad think you should do?" I ask after I've lit the cigarette.

"He just wants me to be happy."

"I'm sure your mum does too."

"You don't know my mum. She's a bitch."

I smile at the petulance in her voice and pass the cigarette to her.

It's strange seeing Melody smoke after all these years, and it's strange seeing sixteen year olds smoke when I've become accustomed to the anti-smoking laws that are still long in the future. Here, in 1991, sixteen year olds are allowed to buy cigarettes and if they can find a pub landlord to serve them, to smoke them in pubs and anywhere else they fancy.

I remember when Melody quit for good, and it's this memory that's stopping me from refusing to share my cigarettes with her. I don't dare risk changing anything that will lead her to the same future point of quitting. The only butterfly effect I will risk is saving her from the accident. If I can do that, it will make her herculean effort to quit worth it forever.

"It gets better," I tell her. "I promise. She'll realise you're an adult soon and start treating you like one."

"You think?"

"Yep. And I also think you can't rule out university just because she wants you to go."

"What do you think I should do?"

I laugh. Oh, Melody, soon you'll have the courage of your own convictions. "Only you can decide that. What's your favourite subject at school?"

"History."

"What do you like about it?"

"I don't know."

"Yes you do."

She's silent while she smokes then she passes it back to me. I take it from her. Our fingers touch. She inches a tiny bit closer.

I'm struggling to breathe. I swallow hard and force my voice to remain steady. "Go on, tell me. What do you like about it?"

"Imagining how people lived," she finally answers. "It's like in medieval England, the people who lived in the cities would chuck their wee and poo onto the streets – everyone did that. Did they call out a warning? 'Poo Alert!' And if you were walking the streets, minding your own business, did you have to keep an eye out in case a bucket of crap was thrown on you, and did you have to pick your way through the streets so you didn't tread in it? And the *smell*...." Her nose wrinkles. "I mean, it must have been gross. And it wasn't just human poo."

I put the cigarette out and lay my cheek down, my heart

beating fast as her confidence in her subject grows and she becomes more and more animated.

She suddenly stops mid-flow and her forehead creases with anxiety. "Am I boring you?"

I want to smooth those creases with my thumb. "You could never bore me."

Her uncertainty disappears and she goes into full flow again.

The Melody I fell in love with is so close and yet so far I want to cry.

Thursday 3rd February 2005

BEFORE

Melody

I'm busy reading through page proofs when I get a text message from Alex on my Nokia. *Stuck in traffic on M25. You okay to get lift home? X*

I reply, *No problem. Will start dinner x,* then remember Hannah from the sales department who lives around the corner from us finished early. Never mind. I work with a great bunch of people. I'm sure I'll get a lift off someone.

"How are you getting on, Mel?" Steve, my editor, asks. It's deadline day for the next issue of *History Through Time* and the proofs need to be signed off this evening, however long it takes.

I'm eighteen weeks pregnant. Steve, a proud father of four children, has insisted I finish at normal time today rather than work late, citing that his wife was always exhausted in the early pregnancy stages. I'm technically way past the early stages, but come mid-afternoon, I still find myself flagging, so I gratefully accepted his kindness.

I stick a thumb up at him. "All good, thanks."

"Coffee?"

As I've already had two coffees that day, I decline, and so am delighted when, ten minutes later, he puts a plastic cup of hot chocolate on my desk and a packet of crisps. Crisps became something of an addiction to me from the moment I discovered I was pregnant. I'm perfectly aware I use them as a smoking substitute but I think my growing baby prefers smoky bacon to smoky nicotine.

I get stuck back into my work. I've the best job in the world. Sure, it's not the Hampton Court Palace job I once dreamed of but life has a way of working out for the best. Fortune has been serendipitous. A week after Alex proposed in that beautiful converted chapel and the excitement of it all resulted in me being late for the interview, I stumbled across an advert in our free local newspaper. The advert was for a writer to join the *History Through Time* (it's the magazine that's often advertised on TV with monthly freebies given to subscribers) editorial team. Not only was the publication based in Brocklehurst, something I'd no idea about, but the editor was willing to take a punt on me on the basis of my degree and me writing one article under his direction on Roman drinking habits in the time of Augustus. I've been here over eight years now and have loved every minute of it.

"Are you still here?"

I'm so immersed in the article I'm proof-reading that I blink to clear the grittiness in my eyes.

Steve looks pointedly at his watch. "It's six-o-clock. You should have gone by now."

I yawn widely, covering my mouth so as not to expose my tonsils, and inwardly curse. Unless any of the sales, marketing or accounts teams have dawdled, I'll be unlikely to cadge a lift off anyone. The rest of the editorial and graphics teams will be working late.

He rolls his eyes in the paternal fashion I've become used to. "Go on, you. Home."

"I don't mind staying."

"Go."

I mock salute and get to my feet.

Thinking I'll catch the bus, I grab my stuff, shout goodbye to everyone, walk down the narrow stairs and step into the dark evening. Blimey, it's *freezing*, and I quickly put my thick winter coat on. Just as I'm wrapping my scarf around me so it covers half my face as well as my neck, the bus I intended to catch pulls up. It's on the other side of the road and I wave to catch the driver's attention. He does a splendid job of ignoring me, despite my coat being fluorescent yellow (Alex bought it for me so no driver could ever fail to see me. Don't you just love irony?). By the time I'm able to cross safely, he's pulled out. Bastard.

The next bus isn't due for another half-hour so I call Alex in the hope he's fought through the traffic and is close by. It goes to voicemail. Doh. A part of me thinks about going back into the office and asking for a lift, but that really would be grossly selfish. None of them are likely to leave before ten p.m.

I'll just have to stop being lazy and walk. Our house is only a mile away, and I'm sure the midwife mentioned something about exercise being good for pregnant women. I just wish it wasn't so ruddy *cold*.

I could shave a few minutes of time by taking a shortcut but I don't like walking unlit paths when it's dark outside, so I walk the length of Brocklehurst's portion of Watling Street. I keep a brisk pace, hands in pockets, one holding onto my phone so I can answer immediately if Alex calls, and daydream about our baby.

Alice's face when we told her she was going to be an aunt was an absolute picture. She's only nine but adolescence is already clasping its first tendrils around her. One minute she's having screaming rows with Mum over wearing makeup (good luck there, Alice!), the next she's in bed cuddling her teddy-bears.

Mum was almost as thrilled as Alex at the pregnancy news. Dad scratched his head then disappeared into his garage, returning with a bottle of champagne he'd hidden, waiting for that very moment. He was flummoxed when I told him I wouldn't be drinking alcohol during the pregnancy.

Alex's dad sat there with a massive dappy grin on his face. He left the room to compose himself when Alex told him the baby would be called Jane if it was a girl. His eyes were red when he came back in, and gave us both a humungous hug.

Jane Lorna Hammond, to give her her full name. Lorna Jane has a better ring to it but we agreed without saying a word that our child should be named for his mum, a woman I never met but who raised two wonderful sons, one of whom is the love of my life.

We still haven't decided on a boy's name, and I'm running through possibilities when I reach the traffic lights I need to cross. The left lane is light with traffic for this time of day, especially compared with the busy right lane, and I wonder if there's been an accident further up and the police have stopped cars. I press the button and wait.

Alfred? Old names are coming back in fashion and I've taken a liking to the possible derivatives of that one.

The pedestrian walk sign flashes green and I step onto the road. Alfie? Bertie? Fred? Freddie –

The world goes black.

Alex

The moment I walk into the house I know something's wrong. Mel's distinctive yellow coat isn't hanging up. Her Dr Marten's and handbag aren't discarded on the floor for me to trip over. I'm already reaching for my mobile phone as I shout out her name. No answer. I call her mobile. Voicemail.

She should be home by now. I call her office. Her direct number goes to voicemail. I call it again. It's deadline day. If I keep calling her number, someone will pick up. I'm rewarded on the third try.

"Melody Hammond's phone," a female voice I don't recognise says.

"Hi, it's Alex, Melody's husband. Is she there?"

There's a beat of silence. "Melody left two hours ago."

Cold white noise whooshes in my head. I don't remember ending the call or trying Melody's mobile again. There's been two accidents on the portion of the A5 Watling Street that forms our town's main road. I had to divert around both of them. One had been a couple of miles from town. The other had been on the high street itself, traffic closed to both directions. If not for the detours, I would have been home twenty minutes ago. If not for the gridlocked M25 I would have been back in time to pick her up.

It's as all these thoughts zoom through my head that her mobile phone is finally answered.

It isn't Melody's voice on the other end.

Friday 4th February 2005

BEFORE

Alex

If not for her black hair, Melody would be indistinguishable from the white bedsheets. I've pulled the visitor's chair as close as I can get without disturbing all the tubes and things keeping her alive. I hold her hand. Sometimes I forget how tiny her hands are. How tiny *she* is. I've never thought of her as vulnerable before. Not my Melody. Not the woman who brims with life and vitality. My pocket-dynamo.

The only life in this room is the machine beeping with her vital statistics.

The doctors are hopeful she'll pull through. I try hard to cling to that. I know that's what *she* would do. She would look at the positives and hug them so tight that negativity wouldn't get a foot in the door.

The only positivity I can find is that she's still here. Clinging to life.

Stay with me, Mel. Please. Don't leave me. Don't leave me. I love you.

There's a tap on the door. Her parents. The hospital is being strict about enforcing the two visitors per patient rule. Her mum said only an hour ago that we should only start worrying if they agree to lift it. It was such a Mel thing to say. Try to find the light in the darkness.

My heart's too scared to let light in.

I kiss her cheek. "I love you, Mel," I whisper, praying with everything I have that she can hear me. "Fight. Stay with me."

Melody

It hurts to open my eyes. The brightness pierces straight through them.

Since when has our bedroom light been so bright?

A small torch is flashed in my eyes. Murmured voices.

I try to speak but I can't move my throat.

Suddenly, I'm terrified.

Saturday 5th February 2005

BEFORE

Melody

I know I'm in a hospital but for how long and, more importantly, *why*, I don't know. I know it's Alex holding my hand. I also know I'm capable of speaking and asking all the questions.

I'm frightened of the answers. Really frightened.

"Mel?"

I open my eyes and immediately wish I hadn't. Alex looks as if he hasn't slept in a month. Tears are falling down his cheeks.

I've never seen him cry before.

I manage one word. "Baby?"

He shakes his head.

Sunday 6th February 2005

BEFORE

Alex

The second visiting hours are open, I'm in the ward Melody was moved to overnight, trying to hold back my fury. As Melody was out of danger, they refused to let me sleep on the visitor's chair again and kicked me out. Then they moved her without informing me. When I arrived at nine a.m. they refused me entry altogether. Bastards, the lot of them. I thought the intensive care nurses had Hitler tendencies but they have nothing on the ones running this ward. What did they expect me to do? Pace the house worrying about how she was coping? Because that's exactly what I've spent the past five hours doing.

She doesn't quite blend in with the bedsheets anymore and she smiles to see me. It's a wan smile but still a smile. A Melody smile. She lifts an arm out to me. I kiss her gently and smooth her hair from her forehead.

"Do I look like shit?" Her voice is croaky.

"You look beautiful." I hope she doesn't have access to a mirror.

Her smile widens a little. "Liar."

I pull the chair over to her and envelope her hand, kissing it before hugging it to my chest.

Her smile falters. Falls. Tears spill down her cheeks. I brush away my own tears.

"What happened?" she asks.

"What do you remember?"

"Missing the bus. And the cold. That's it."

The police have pieced it together through witness statements. I explain it as best I can. "You were hit by a car at the traffic lights. The ones by the Indian."

She swallows a number of times. "Was it my fault?"

"No." I squeeze her hand and shake my head for emphasis. "No. All the witnesses said you waited for the green man. The car... it came from nowhere. They think he or she was distracted and didn't notice the lights go red."

Her eyes widen. "He or she? They didn't stop?"

"No. The thinking is they panicked." Whoever hit my wife had been speeding. The injuries she sustained were too extensive for them to have been obeying the speed limit. The driver had likely been stuck in the same traffic jam a couple of miles from town that I'd got stuck in and been impatient to get home. Their impatience killed our baby and killed any chance of us having one in the future. Melody suffered severe internal injuries that resulted in broken ribs, a broken pelvis and the doctors performing an emergency caesarean, a hysterectomy and a splenectomy. If not for the intravenous drugs being pumped into her, she would be ravaged with pain.

The drugs can only help her physical pain though. Emotionally, she's in a world of it.

Sunday 24th August 1991

NOW

Melody

Hayley doesn't say goodbye. She didn't want me to go back to her house. The only thing that stopped her refusing was that her mum would have asked questions. Her mum thinks we spent the night at Georgina's. Her mum knows I'm lazy and that my dad's collecting me.

I get in the car. Dad wrinkles his nose. "Have you been smoking?"

"Hayley has." I'm not saying anything he doesn't already know.

He leans over and sniffs my hair. "You smell like a bonfire."

I shrug.

His hands are on the steering wheel but he doesn't turn the engine on. "Where were you last night?"

"At Hayley's."

"If I go and ask her mum, she'll say the same will she?"

I burst into tears. For once, I'm not faking it, but the effect is the same. Dad really can't handle female tears. He pats my back ineffectually and waits for me to stop crying.

"We went camping at the fishing lakes," I confess.

"Camping? *You*?" I guess he's remembering the camping holiday we went on when I was twelve. It was not a success. Dad hasn't dared suggest a repeat. Any time something camping-related comes on the TV, Mum and I both shudder. "Who did you go with?"

"Hayley, Georgina and Karen." Even Dad would kill me if he thought boys were involved. "It was Hayley's idea. We just wanted to have some fun but –"

"How did you get there?" he interrupts, eyes narrowed.

"We walked." I see my lie has only made him more suspicious, so I quickly continue. "It was awful. We all fell out. Hayley was horrible. She –"

"Were you drinking?"

"Yes." I'm busted anyway. He'll forgive alcohol much quicker than he'll forgive boys, and admitting to alcohol makes him much less likely to interrogate me about the walking part. "I'm so sorry. It was a stupid idea and I promise I'll never do it again. I *swear*."

"Hmm." He turns the engine on and reverses out of Hayley's driveway.

"Are you going to tell Mum?" I ask in a small voice.

He sighs loudly. "I should. Honestly, Melody, what were you thinking? Four young girls camping alone on a fishing lake? Did you not think of the danger you were putting yourselves in?"

Relief escapes me but I make sure to keep my voice meek. "I promise I'll never do anything like it again. I'll accept any punishment you give me. I'll keep my room tidy forever..."

He snorts.

"... and do the dishes every night and clean your car every week for the next year and –"

He covers my hand and gives a quick squeeze before putting his back on the steering wheel. "I'm not going to lie for you. If your mum smells the bonfire you'll have to tell the truth and accept the consequences."

* * *

Mum doesn't smell the bonfire. Grandma Alison's coming for dinner and Mum's too busy weighing ingredients for the cherry almond tart she's making to do more than ask if I had a good time.

Later, after I've showered and shampooed the smell out of my hair, I wait until she's outside having a cigarette before shoving all my stinky clothes in the washing machine. I feel a real pang when I put Alex's jumper in with it.

Back in the privacy of my bedroom, I lay on my bed and recall every glorious moment spent with him.

Saturday 30th May 2015

BEFORE

Alex

I shout up the stairs for the third time. "Are you ready? The taxi will be here in a minute."

"One sec!" she shouts back for the third time.

Kermit and Ellie, dressed as a pair of American cheerleaders, pour themselves another shot of vodka each. Kermit passes his joint to me before downing his. I take a toke and pass it back. It isn't often they go out for a night. They had a surprise a few years back, a son born the year their youngest daughter started secondary school. With a young son, two teenage girls, the eldest of whom is preparing to go to university in September, money is extremely tight for them, so when they do go out, they like to pretend they're still in their twenties and not the same age of forty-six as I am.

Heavy footsteps plod down the stairs and then Melody appears in the kitchen.

"You look sick," Ellie enthuses. Melody laughs, although whether at the compliment or Ellie's slang is open to debate.

She does look 'sick' though. Spectacular. For this, her fortieth birthday party, she's decided to go as Morticia Addams and she's pulled it off to a T. Black hair (which has come courtesy of a bottle in recent years) straightened, dramatic makeup and an angular black dress. She's even had her nails extended and painted blood red to match her lipstick.

She extends a hand to me and gives me a seductive look. "Are we ready to party, Mr Addams?"

Yes, she's talked me into forgoing my plan of dressing up as Miss Whiplash and going as Gomez Addams instead, including talking me into growing a moustache for the occasion, which she painted with mascara earlier after she attacked my greying hair with Just for Men.

After another shot of vodka each, Melody grabs her walking stick which she's painted black for the night and we troop outside to the waiting taxi.

Melody

It's nights like this that I count my good fortune. Here, in the same hotel we celebrated our wedding, over a hundred of us are partying. A few of my friends blanched at the idea of celebrating turning forty and refused to acknowledge their own milestone. My attitude is different. I'm lucky to be here. Every birthday is a blessing.

I dance for a couple of tunes then sit to watch the madness. Unfortunately, my body tires easily, but that doesn't stop me enjoying myself or taking pleasure from others enjoying themselves. My parents, dressed at my insistence as Lurch and Granny, are bopping on the dancefloor with Alex's dad Mark, who's come with his new wife Kathy as Uncle Fester and Cousin It. Surrounding them are Batman and Robin, The Spice Girls, various ninjas and geishas, gangsters and a huge assortment of other disguises, some more imaginative than others. Graham, propped against the bar, has come as a pub landlord.

My nineteen-year-old sister bounds over to me with two small glasses in her hand.

"Jagerbomb!" she announces, handing me one. As usual, she looks stunning, even dressed as Wednesday Addams. Craig, her boyfriend who's probably outside with the other lepers smoking, has come as Pugsley.

Together, we throw the Jagerbombs down our necks. Before we've slammed our glasses on the table, her best friend Annalise (who used to spend her school lunch breaks with Alice at my house) appears with her girlfriend Lily and more Jagerbombs. On the count of three, the four of us down them.

Alice beams. Truly, she's beautiful. At her age I'd been pretty, but Alice is so much more than I've ever been. Three inches taller than me (she's inherited some of Dad's height), her skin has a creamy luminescence I would have killed for and her blue eyes are so big it isn't unusual for men to get lost in them when talking to her. She's far cleverer than me too and has almost completed her first year of a physics degree. She's mused about going into astrophysics, but I have no idea if that means she'll have to do another degree or if it would be a continuation of what she's already doing. All I know for certain about my little sister is that she and her friends live in a time where they can be anything they want and can love whomever they want to love without fear or prejudice.

"Are you thinking of Lorna?" Alice asks.

Amazed at her mindreading abilities, I gape.

She laughs but there's sadness to it. "You always get a funny look on your face when you're thinking of her."

I take her hand. "She loved you."

If only Lorna had lived long enough to see the little girl she doted on all grown up, part of a generation embracing their sexuality and thriving.

If only I'd recognised and understood the torment Lorna had been living with. But I hadn't. I'd been blind to it.

I will take those regrets to my grave.

Matt the Twat, dressed as a schoolgirl – he never fails to live up to his moniker – plonks a glass of red in front of me. "Happy birthday, Mel," he says, then plasters a wet kiss to my cheek.

I smile (I hope it doesn't look like a grimace) and resist wiping my cheek. I saw a different side to him after the accident that always makes me feel guilty about my natural aversion to him. He brought me flowers to the hospital and after I was discharged often popped over to check I was okay. Alex and I were even invited to his wedding three years ago. Alas, the marriage ended in divorce only eight months later when his wife discovered that he was, indeed, a twat. "Thanks, Matt."

"Great party," he enthuses.

"Thanks."

"Thanks for inviting me." And with that, Smash Mouth's 'All Star' comes on and he runs off to the dancefloor.

The party goes on. So many drinks are put in front of me I fear the table will collapse under the weight. Luckily Alex, Alice, Craig, Annalise and Lily make it their mission to help me drink them and by the time it comes for me to blow out the candles on my cake, we're all well on the way to being plastered.

I feel a real twinge of sadness when the DJ starts playing the slower, lovey-dovey songs. It means the night is almost over. I dance with my dad, whose Lurch headpiece has come off, and then Alex takes me in his arms for the final dance. It's Bryan Adams.

I sag into Alex's welcoming strength.

"You okay?" he whispers in my ear.

I nod into his chest. It never matters how tired I get. Alex is always there to hold me up. The few secret fears I had in the weeks and months after the accident, fears that he would fall out of love with me, fears that his yearning for a child would see him find another woman, fears that he wouldn't see me as *me* anymore, were all unfounded. Whenever I need him, whatever I need him for, he's always there, always loving me with the same strength that I love him.

Truly, I am blessed.

Saturday 31st August 1991

NOW

Alex

I finish my pint in The Collingswood Arms and then start the walk back to the bus stop. It's the last time I'll be doing this walk.

I said goodbye to Melody knowing it would be five years until we next meet.

Spending that night in the open air with her has put a lot of things in perspective. I can't interrupt her life again. It isn't fair on her. Melody needs her future to unfold the way it's supposed to. She needs to enjoy the experiences that turn her into the woman I fell in love with and, however desperately I want to hold her to me, I can't take that away from her.

I keep thinking, too, about the butterfly effect the old man – God? – warned me about in the cemetery. I've messed around with it enough, and now I need to choose wisely and tread carefully. I've got nearly five years to get things in shape so when Melody and I meet as we're supposed to, I can give her the life she always deserved but which we could never afford.

It will also give me the space to be there for Mum as I should have been the first time round. She's got her biopsy tomorrow, six months sooner than she had it the first time. I doubt it will make any difference to the long-term outlook – ovarian cancer survival rates are horrendous – but diagnosing it earlier might buy her more time. I know what's needed too, to help give her remaining months or years a better quality.

I will not drown myself in alcohol to block out what's happening to her. I will not allow my eyes to blur when I look at her so I don't see the pain ravaging her face. I will not ignore the phone ringing with the news that the end is near and that I should get straight to the hospital if I want to say goodbye. I will already be with her, holding her hand with Dad and Ollie.

When I get to Melody's house, I pause for one last look. One of the bedroom windows upstairs is open. It's Melody's room. I crane my ears and listen hard to the faint music seeping out, and then I smile.

It's Bryan Adams 'Everything I do'.

Melody

I can't stop crying. I don't know why. All week I've hugged that night with Alex close to me, replaying our conversations over and over, dreaming about him knocking on our front door and asking me out, imagining how it will feel when he kisses me, but today I feel sick, a bit like the time Snoop, our old dog, went missing and we looked everywhere for him for hours and hours but couldn't find him (a neighbour found him in her back garden the next day. He was fine. Lived another two happy years). A bit like that but much, much worse.

My door opens.

I close my eyes and pretend to be asleep.

Mum's not fooled. She turns my music down and sits on the edge of my bed. She strokes my hair. "Do you want to talk about it, sweetie?"

I shake my head but then the tears fall again and I shuffle over until my head is on her lap and I'm sobbing like a baby.

"Oh, Sweetie," she whispers. "I didn't realise it had got this bad."

I don't contradict her. I do feel bad that Hayley and I have gone from best friends to worst enemies, but it's more of a social thing than a friendship thing. I don't care about the end of our friendship half as much as I thought I would. Her outrage about Danny has nothing to do with the way I treated him – and that I really *do* feel awful about. How could I have been so cruel? I really, really didn't mean to hurt him and I don't blame him at all for hating me – but because she's jealous. Jealous that Danny fancied me and not her. I only said yes to him because she swore she didn't fancy him anymore and that she didn't mind if I said yes, and now she says I betrayed her! But I don't even believe that.

She's jealous because Alex only had eyes for me.

He's not here now though, is he? And now I can't shake the feeling I'll never see him again, and that hurts much more than all the rest of it. Really hurts.

Mum's rubbing my back. It feels really nice. "Look, you're starting sixth form in a few days," she says. "Hayley won't be there. It'll be a fresh start for you."

"Georgina and Karen will be," I sniff. They've both totally taken Hayley's side.

"But Hayley won't. She'll be off with a new gang of sycophants."

I've never heard the word sycophants before but I can guess what it means. It means Mum never liked Hayley. She thinks Hayley and I fell out over Danny. Which is kind-of true, in a kind-of way.

"Georgina and Karen are nice girls," she continues. "Without Hayley to suck-up to, they'll leave you alone or be your friend again. And don't forget all the other friends you've got. Think of all the Christmas cards you got. People like you, Mel, much more than they like her."

"Hayley's the prettiest girl in the school and the most popular."

"*Was* the prettiest girl in the school – you've blossomed, sweetie. Look in the mirror. You're much prettier than she is and you've got so much more going for you than looks. Hayley's popularity was a false one, and now she's left school, you wait, everyone will forget about her. Now, why don't you dry your eyes and come down and watch telly with us? I'll make some hot chocolate."

I hug her tighter. I wish I could tell her about Alex. I long to talk to someone about him and all these feelings inside me. I wish Katie was still here. We could talk about anything and there was no judging. We were more like sisters than best friends and now more tears leak out as I remember I will never see her or speak to her again. Bloody leukaemia.

Mum kisses the top of my head but then, as she sits back up, pulls my comfort jumper out from under my pillow. "Whose is this?"

I have just enough wits about me to lie. "Hayley's."

"Doesn't look like something she'd wear."

"That's why she gave it to me." Thank God I shrank it. I was so upset about that. How was I supposed to know wool shouldn't be tumble-dried?

She smooths my hair. "I'll make the hot chocolate."

Once she's closed my door, I hug Alex's jumper tight to me.

I wish it was him I was hugging.

Alex

There's a truism about misery loving company.

Mum and Dad have gone out for the night, and I was all settled on the sofa, ready for an evening alone with two four-packs of Bud for company, when Ollie casually mentioned he was going on the lash with some mates in Brocklehurst and just as casually asked if I wanted to join them.

My instinct was to say no, but then I caught the tightness in his features and the tension in his body. And I saw the hurt he was trying to hide.

I've refused every night out with him since I came back.

From Ollie's perspective, our brotherly relationship has gone from spending our weekend evenings buddying up with our respective mates and girlfriends, getting Tontoed and pissing Dad off by staggering in and making a racket in the early hours, to passing the salt over dinner. I've turned from a party animal into the most domesticated, boring twenty-one-year-old on the planet. And in Ollie's eyes it happened overnight.

So I said yes.

And now, crossing the road from The Oak to The Merry Thief, already pissed, I'm bloody glad I came. Six months spent stalking my teenage wife and with the doom of what's happening to mum bashing me, it feels fantastic to drink my cares away for one night.

The Merry Thief is heaving when we enter. Ollie and the others go straight to the pool table to put money on it while I get the drinks in.

"Alright, mate?" I shout to Graham when he scowls and raises his brow; his method of asking what he can get me. "Long time no see."

His brow rises further at my familiarity and he looks at me like I've curled one on his bar.

I'd forgotten that he doesn't know me. Not properly. Not the way he will in the decades Melody and I are together. One day, he will even – don't laugh – smile at me.

Biting my cheek to hold back my amusement, I order four pints and four chasers, then carry them over to Ollie, Stu and Pete, who've joined a group of girls sat near the pool table.

My heart sinks when I recognise Rachel amongst them.

Her eyes meet mine. She straightens on her stool and flicks her blonde hair over her shoulder.

I slept with her a number of times over a number of years before we got together. A number of those number of times, I had different girlfriends. Though our time together is nothing but a particularly sour blur in my memories, I think the only reason we did get together properly was because we were both looking to move to London. I'd completed my apprenticeship and, as the bulk of our commissions are in London and the suburbs, thought it'd be easier living there for the travelling (hint, it isn't. Not when you've got a van.). Also, I loved London's nightlife. Living there meant I could enjoy it every night. Rachel had a job in London too and though the commute wasn't too bad for her, she wanted to be where it was all happening. So we moved in together in a poky central London flat and made each other thoroughly miserable.

But none of that has happened yet and nor will it. This time, I watch the unfolding game of pool and pretend not to feel her watching me.

Undeterred, she sidles up to me. "You're friends with Lorna Garrard, aren't you?" she says.

"Yeah." I drink half my pint.

"She not out with you tonight?"

"No."

"Shame. I like Lorna."

As I choke on the mouthful of beer I'm about to swallow, the Shakespear's Sister song 'You're History' blasts out through the speakers.

I laugh. Rachel stares at me, no doubt wondering if I'm laughing at her. Which I am, in a way.

God, I wish I could share this moment with Melody. She would piss herself. I remember her telling me she bought this exact song and played it so much it got chewed up in her tape player.

"Lorna's a great girl. One in a million," I say when I finally catch my breath. I smile at her. Poor Rachel. She didn't deserve me. I definitely deserved her though. "Excuse me, but I'm up."

I leave her standing there and join Ollie at the pool table.

The unwritten rule for playing pool in The Merry Thief is

that, when there's a crowd, you play doubles and the winners stay on. Melody is a pool shark. Everyone underestimates her. Tonight, I'm doubled up with Ollie, who no-one underestimates. He can sink eight pints and still clear the table from the break. Tonight, we're both on form and when it's our turn to play, we win four games in a row and down the same number of beers and chasers while doing it. By our fifth game, I'm seeing two... no three... of each ball. Ollie wins the game for us.

Our sixth game and everything's blurred. When it's my turn to cue, Ollie shouts, "Stripes, Al, stripes! Not spots!"

I put the cue between my bridged fingers and aim. The first I know that I've fucked up is when I hear a smash.

Through all the raucous yet surprisingly distant laughter, I can vaguely see the picture frame the white ball's smashed into, and burst out laughing. I'm still laughing when I squint to focus on the green of the table and see the huge rip my terrible cuing has made in it. I'm quite sure, hammered though I am, that it's the exact same rip I made in this table the first time around.

I'm still laughing when Graham frogmarches me out of the pub.

I'm still laughing when I puke over Ollie's trainers.

"What you laughing at?" my pissed pissed-off brother asks. "You've just got us all barred."

"Butterfly effect," I explain. "Equilibrium of the ripples."

"You what?"

"Ols?"

"What?"

"I love you."

"Fuck off."

Friday 25th December 2020

BEFORE

Melody

Alice is in excellent form. While Mum cooks up a storm, she sits at the kitchen dining table regaling us with tales of all the micro-aggressions she's recently suffered at the hands of the men she works with and the ways she's dealt with them. Pity the poor fool who stupidly judges Alice on her appearance.

I've never worked in a heavily male-dominated industry like she does. The one time I suffered sexism at work happened a couple of years before my accident when I discovered a male colleague who did exactly the same work as me earned five grand a year more. I mentioned it to my editor. He spoke to HR for me and the situation was rectified. Sorted. I once made the mistake of saying this to Alice and was on the receiving end of a lecture that went on for so long I fell asleep. My weak and feeble body comes in useful sometimes as she couldn't tell me off for it, ha ha.

To be honest, I find a lot of her talk about micro-aggressions and identity politics exhausting. I have to accept that though we're sisters, she's of a different generation to me. I'm from the generation of ladettes where the girls played the boys at their own games and had a huge dollop of fun with it. And liver problems.

And, for all that Alice is welcoming and accepting of everyone's sexuality and abhors closeminded people, I wouldn't dare share some of the sexual experiences I had from the days before Alex with her. I'm quite sure she'd be enraged on my behalf. And maybe, in some of the cases, she would have a point. But still, what happened to having fun?

What happened to *Alice* having fun?

All the same, her pithy put-downs to her misogynistic (her word) colleagues and the way she relates them to us are gems, and it sure beats talking about Covid. None of us would be surprised if this is the last time we'll be allowed to see each other for a long while, not with the way case numbers are rising again. Still, with me being on the shielding list, they've all kept themselves isolated for the last week so I can safely join them today, and I will forgive Alice anything for that alone.

If she ever gets fed up with astrophysics, she could have a career as a stand-up. Even Mum, who frequently rolls her eyes at Alice's tales, is in fits of laughter. Poor Dad hides in the garage with Alex until certain it's all over. He finds the modern world baffling. I've no idea if Tristan, Alice's current boyfriend, wants to join the men. I don't think he'd dare ask! The pair are forced out of their hideaway when Christmas dinner is served. I notice Alex pour a larger measure of gin than usual into Alice's glass, giving me a sly wink as he passes it to her.

Once we're all crammed around the table and Mum's turned the radio up, she decrees it the end of all political and micro-aggression talk and we tuck in. Mum's cooking is as heavenly as ever. Even Tristan, who's normally too terrified of saying the wrong thing in front of Alice to speak, asks for second helpings of turkey. Honestly, that man needs to grow a spine. Mercifully for him, Alice is now so tiddled she forgets to lecture him about the evils of the poultry industry. Mercifully for the rest of us, she forgets to lecture us for the rest of the day too and, for a blissful few hours, it's like we've got the old Alice back.

It's almost midnight when Alex and I finally hug them all

goodbye and get into the car for home. I put the automatic into drive and wave frantically at the four of them huddled in the doorway.

Tuesday 20th July 1993

NOW

Alex

The rain that's lashed us all morning finally lets up. For a brief but glorious moment, the sun shines down and bounces off the hard wood of the coffin as Mum's lowered into the ground.

She would have liked that.

* * *

I'm sat on a table in the Red Lion beer garden, ineffectually sheltering alone from the rain under a parasol, smoking. I'm about to stub it out when Dad comes out carrying two pints.

"Bit much, isn't it?" he says as he climbs up to sit beside me.

I nod. "She would have loved it though."

He has a long drink of his pint and rocks his head in agreement.

Mum was always a sociable, much-loved woman but, going through her funeral a second time, it's still a shock to acknowledge the sheer number of people who've come to pay their last respects to her.

He offers me a cigarette.

We sit in silence for a long time, staring at the wall of water pouring around us.

Dad's the one to break it. "Thank you."

"For what?"

"Being there for her."

I punch him lightly on the arm.

His laugh turns into a drawn-out sigh and then he turns his head to look at me. He opens his mouth, hesitates, then quietly says, "You knew, didn't you?"

I gaze into the green eyes I inherited with a tightening chest and throat. This conversation has been a long time coming.

I keep my answer simple. "Yes."

His mouth pulls together and he nods. "How much longer did you give her?"

"A year."

He closes his eyes and breathes deeply. "Thank you."

Another companionable silence passes.

"Should I ask how?" he says.

"Depends how much you want to hear the answer."

He lights another cigarette, passes it to me, then lights one for himself. Eventually, he says, "There's a lot I don't understand about this world. A lot of it, I don't need to know. I just accept that it is." He has a long drag then exhales and holds the cigarette out at arm's length, examining it curiously. "How long for me?"

I'm glad this is a question I can't answer. "I don't know the answer to that. But you might want to encourage Jimmy to quit."

He looks at me sharply. Holds the stare. Then his mouth lilts into a half smile. "If there's anything important you think I should, err, know about, you will, err...?"

I lean my head on his shoulder. He stiffens. Physical father-son affection ended when I was in primary school.

"I will," I promise.

I feel a loosening of his tension and a tentative tilt of his head against mine before he punches me in the arm.

Laughing, we pick up our pints, say cheers, then down them.

As we're walking back inside, I casually say, "I'm looking at investing in some up-and-coming companies. Fancy coming in on it with me?"

He pretends to mull it over. "I could be tempted."

* * *

Buggy and Kermit punch me goodbye. We make arrangements to meet at the weekend for a beer. Lorna, who's divided her time between them and her parents during the wake, sits alone waiting for me. A strong sense of déjà vu strikes me. I get that a lot.

She smiles wanly as I take the seat next to her.

"How you holding up?" she asks.

I push the half pint I've bought her to rest beside the others she's got lined up. "Surprisingly well."

It's the truth. Grief sits in me like a deep, pitiless well, but it's a clean grief. No regrets to chew on my conscience.

The extra year of time gave Mum so much. She took the trip to Canada she always dreamed of and felt the spray of Niagara Falls on her face. She enjoyed a last Christmas with all of us there, not just there but present. She witnessed Ollie fall in love with one of the Macmillan nurses (the same nurse as the first time round but occurring a year later, so God knows what effect the butterfly will have for them). Best of all, her passing was peaceful. She took her last breath in a hospice staffed by the most compassionate people in the world, being held by the three people she loved most in the world.

Lorna picks the nearest glass to hand and raises it to me. "To your mum."

I clink my pint to it. "Mum." May she rest in peace.

We chat about nothing in particular, mostly about the house she's recently bought in Brocklehurst. Our families are old friends. We've grown up together, went through our school years together. There's always that comforting familiarity when I'm with her.

When the pub starts filling with its evening regulars and she asks if I want to pop over and see her new house, the most natural thing would be to agree.

The Alex who inhabited this body the first time round agreed. We bought a cheap bottle of whisky to share from the off-licence. In the morning we woke to find the bottle empty and ourselves naked in her bed.

In those years before Melody, I ruined many platonic female friendships by sleeping with them. Sleeping together never ruined mine and Lorna's. We both treated it – genuinely – as a drunken blip brought on by grief. After she died though, I came to wonder if that drunken blip was the reason I never saw the truth and the reason she couldn't come to me when she so desperately needed help.

This time, I wrap my arms tightly around her and kiss the top of her head. "I should be with Dad tonight. Another time, 'eh?"

She tilts her head and kisses me on the lips. "Okay." Then she smacks me on the back of the head and grins. "Call me if you need me."

Saturday 5th August 2023

BEFORE

Melody

This is the day I've been dreading for practically the whole of this year.

When Alice first mentioned she'd applied for a job at the European Southern Observatory, it took a while for the penny to drop that the observatory was actually in Chile and not somewhere nice and close like Switzerland. It was bad enough imagining her a two hour flight away never mind learning it took fourteen and a half hours to fly to Chile.

Despite all my dreams of sabotage, there was never any doubt in my mind that Alice would get the job. I'm not the only person in the world to recognise her brilliance, and now she's going to spend the next three years over fourteen hours away from me. I suffered enough when she was at university and that was only an hour away!

Despite feeling as sick as I've ever felt, I'm determined to project happiness for her, and I open the door with a wide smile that I hold for exactly one second before bursting into tears.

"I'm going to miss you," I sob, throwing my arms around her.

She hugs me back with one arm until Alex takes the cat cage from her, and then my baby sister is squishing me tightly. Knowing it's likely the last time she'll squish me for three years only makes me cry harder.

If Dotty the cat, released from her prison, hadn't swiped at my leg in her usual impervious fashion, I doubt I'd have let Alice go. But I did let her go, and ten minutes later Alex and I are on the street outside frantically waving her goodbye and I'm praying Dad stops blubbing pronto, before he crashes the car and makes Alice late for her flight...

On second thoughts, Dad, keep crying!

Tuesday 2nd January 2024

BEFORE

Alex

4 a.m.

After downing a strong coffee, I go up to our room. I leave the bedroom light off so as not to fully wake her.

"I'm off now," I whisper.

She mumbles before shuffling and groping for me. I take her hand and squeeze it. It's very warm from the cocoon she's made for herself with the duvet.

"Let me know when you get there," she murmurs sleepily.

"I will." I kiss her forehead. Is it my imagination or does it feel warmer than usual, even taking into account her duvet burrowing? "Are you okay?"

"Just tired."

"You sure? I don't have to go." But I know even as I say it that she'll refuse. The job I'm quoting for today is in Scotland, the client a member of the aristocracy. Mel is desperate for me to get it as the job's so big and the money correspondingly so lucrative that we'll have the spare cash to book flights to Chile to visit Alice.

I want the job – and it's a ninety per cent certainty that I'm going to get it – because the client's said he'll put me up in a cottage on the estate for the duration and that Mel can come with me. Be nice to have a break from the bloody cat. It's a right vicious thing, hiding behind doors to swipe at your leg at every available opportunity. Mel dotes on it and is completely uncaring that she currently looks as if she self-harms. In fairness, the cat dotes on Mel too when it's not clawing her, and is currently curled up on my side of the bed snoozing beside her.

"Don't be silly." Her words sound slurry but then, it is the middle of the night in Mel's world. "Drive safely."

"I promise." I kiss her again. "I love you."

"Love you too."

I lock the front door behind me.

Melody

11.a.m.

I can't believe how much effort it takes to reply to Alex's message. In the end, all I can manage are three kisses.

I'm just so tired and now all my muscles hurt too. I'm sure I've caught the flu. If I had the energy, I'd get out of bed and open the window as I'm all hot. Should have done that earlier when I dragged myself downstairs to feed Dotty. She must know I'm not well as she didn't even try to swipe her claws into my skin. The gauge she put in my calf the other day is still throbbing.

I manage to kick the duvet off and go back to sleep.

Alex

6 p.m.

"Hi, Ols, it's me. Can you do me a favour?"

"If I can. What's up?"

"Can you pop over to the house and check on Mel for me? She's not answering her phone."

I called with the good news that the job was mine and she sounded half asleep. Scrap the half. Rather than staying for lunch with the client, I decided to head straight home. Traffic has been a nightmare, and when I stopped at the first services, she didn't answer her phone. I'm now at the second set of services and she's still not answering and hasn't replied to the text I sent.

"Sorry, mate, we're still in the Lake District."

Fuck.

"What about her parents?"

"Still in Chile with Alice."

"Dad?"

"Gone to Kathy's daughter's. I'll try the neighbours."

"Okay. Let me know how she is."

"Will do. Cheers, bud."

I'm getting a real sense of déjà vu here but I bite it down, and bite down the angst in my stomach that Ollie's genuine worry added to, and wonder who else I can call because, thinking about it, I don't have the number for any of our neighbours.

Fuck.

I turn the engine back on and floor it.

***

9 p.m.

Even though I know to expect it, the ambulance outside our house still comes as a punch in the heart.

Thank fuck for Matt the Twat, the only person in my contacts able to answer my SOS. Who the fuck knew so many people went away to celebrate the New Year? The living room window's smashed from the brick I gave him permission to break it with, with a, "Just fucking do it."

The front door's open. A figure all in green fills the space, and as I throw myself out of my van and run to them, the paramedics carry Melody out of the house.

One look at her is enough for my punched heart to freeze. Her skin is white and yet patchy. Mottled.

She sees me and lifts her fingers to me. If she tries to speak, I can't hear her through the surgical mask covering her face.

I take her hand. Where this morning she was too warm, now she is too cold.

Wednesday 3rd January 2024

BEFORE

Alex

My phone buzzes in my hand. It's from Roy. It's the second text he's ever sent me.

Chin up. Our girls a fighter.

I smile to imagine him sweating over this simple message but then the words before me blur. He's as frightened as I am and he's still over seven thousand miles away. Their flight's due to take off in an hour.

Another message buzzes. And then another. And another. And another. Dad. Ollie. Kermit. Graham. Mel's old boss Steve. Annalise. Matt the Twat. Even Sophie. All replying to my latest update (although I never added fucking Sophie to the list): *Septic shock. If you pray then please pray*. All passing their love and best wishes to Mel. All knowing the danger she's in. All knowing how vulnerable her severely weakened body and the loss of her spleen from that accident all those years ago makes her – there's a reason Mel was put on the original Covid shielding list – and as I slump in my chair by her bed and silent tears roll down my face, the truth I've been batting away hits me like a punch in the gut.

For the second time in our twenty-eight years together, Melody is fighting for her life.

Saturday 11th September 1993

NOW

Melody

Mum and Dad squeeze the life out of me with their goodbye hugs. Mum 'had something in her eye,' the entire hour drive here and now I can't believe Dad looks like he's about to cry too! It's not as if I'm going away forever. We've already arranged for me to come home for a weekend next month and, as I've reminded them a billion times, Christmas will be here before we know it and I'll be home for weeks and weeks. Maybe that's what he's crying about, ha ha!

"Are you sure you don't want us to wait until your new friends arrive?" Dad asks.

I love that he's confident I'm going to make friends with the complete strangers I'll be sharing accommodation with for the next year. Maybe I will! Maybe we'll all want to rent a house together when we get kicked out of the halls of residence and be lifelong friends!

And maybe we'll hate the sight of each of other and spend our time resisting the urge to spit in each other's drinks. Who knows? My immediate future is a brand-new chapter in the Melody Aldridge Book of Life, and I'm about to turn the page and let it reveal itself to me. It's the most exciting feeling imaginable.

In the end, I practically have to force them out of the door.

Alone in my new bedroom, I sit on the bed which Mum insisted on making up for me with the brand-new bedding she bought, washed, and ironed for me, and open the one box I steered them away from helping me unpack. There's not much in it. A couple of childhood teddy bears. An old, framed photo of me and Katie, faces pressed together, beaming toothlessly at the camera when we were seven. A newer framed photo of me, Mum and Dad. A book of fairy tales Grandma Alison gave me for Christmas when I was little; it's my go-to comfort read. And Alex's much washed, shrunken jumper. I hug it to myself and smile. This jumper has become my talisman.

Every time I doubt myself, all I have to do is touch this jumper and I'm suffused with such warmth and happiness that I could sing from the top of my lungs. Alex's face has blurred in my memories but how he made me feel hasn't. This man, who'd never met me before in my life, saw something in me that made him certain I could accomplish anything I set my mind to.

I'm at peace with never seeing him again but this jumper is the only thing that stops me thinking that whole night was a dream.

I hear the main door open. I fold the jumper, kiss it, and shove it in a drawer. Then I bound out of my room and into the shared living quarters where a skinny lad with straggly blonde hair and fear in his eyes stands, flanked by equally terrified looking parents.

I give my widest smile and introduce myself.

Wowee, he's *gorgeous*!

Saturday 6th January 2024

BEFORE

Alex

"Ready?" the nurse asks.

Unable to speak, I jerk a nod.

We all file in. I hang back a little so Roy, Patty and Alice can say their goodbyes first. I don't know how long they take, barely feel the warmth of their hands as they squeeze mine and move to the back of the room, still there, still a presence, but giving a tiny illusion of privacy.

I sit on the closest visitor's chair with another strong sense of déjà vu, and take Melody's cool, limp hand into mine. The mask has been removed and there are vivid red lines etched in her face where it bit into it. The rest of her skin has a blueish tinge that makes me want to weep.

No weeping. Not now. Not here.

The silence with all the monitors and alarms now turned off is striking. Painful.

I clear my arid throat and lean my face close to hers to whisper, "Hiya, Mel. I'm back."

There's no response.

I stroke her shrunken cheek and gently pick a tress of her hair. Her curls have been brushed out, turning it into a black cloud.

She takes a breath. It's the first she's taken since I sat down. It sounds shallow. Too shallow.

I clear my throat again. "They say you can probably hear me. That you'll know I'm here..." There's a stinging in my eyes. I blink it away. This is the last time I'll ever speak to her. I have to swallow the lancing fist that has replaced my heart and get it right. I don't need to be a doctor to know it's close. Very close.

"I love you, Mel. So, so much. You brought the sun into my life and made it richer than I could have dreamed possible."

She takes another, shallower, breath.

There's a lump like a boulder in my throat and it takes several attempts to clear it enough to speak again.

Melody

I'm playing in a field with my best friend Katie. Or is it called a meadow? I think that's what Mummy calls it. There's lots and lots of pretty flowers around us and lots and lots of butterflies and it smells so fresh and flowery and beautiful. Katie's teaching me how to make daisy-chains.

"So, so much..."

I look up at the clear blue sky where the strange but familiar voice came from. The sun's warm on my face. It soaks into my skin.

I pull out another daisy. The stem's too small for me to put my nail through. Katie's finished hers. She's brilliant at making them.

"Than I could have dreamed possible..."

I look up again. My heart feels funny.

Katie smiles at me and leans over to put her daisy-chain on my head like a crown. She says something but I can't hear her words. Other words are echoing in my ears, the strange but familiar voice, pulling me, calling me, pulling me...

I'm not in the meadow anymore.

I feel a spasm of panic. Where am I? Where have the flowers gone?

Then I hear the voice again. It's very faint. I strain hard to hear.

"...not a single second that I've regretted marrying you. You saved me, Mel. If I could live my life again, I would do it all again. I would marry you again, in a heartbeat. I would stop this from happening." The voice chokes. "Oh, Mel, what am I going to do without you? I wish I had the words to tell you how special you are. You are everything to me. My whole life."

I try my hardest to reach him, but I can smell the flowers again. His hand feels so warm on mine. So precious.

The meadow's coming back into focus. I see a little girl with pigtails skipping happily through the dandelions. There's a butterfly on her shoulder.

I focus harder than I've ever focused before, gather the very last of my strength and open my eyes.

For one startlingly bright moment, I see his face clearly. The green eyes holding mine, brimming with so many emotions they pierce my slowing heart. The unshaven jaw flecked with grey. The firm lips tightly compressed. The dimpled chin, wobbling. The weather-beaten face that I fell in love with when I was sixteen years old and have loved every day of my life since, soaked with tears. The man who made me happier than I ever dreamed I could be.

I try to lift my head, to get closer to him. I breathe his name. "*Alex...*"

And then his face fades away, and I'm skipping after Katie in the meadow with the sun on my face and the heady perfume of flowers filling my lungs.

Wednesday 6th March 2024

BEFORE

Alex

I sweep the crap on the coffee table onto the floor with one swipe of my forearm and then tip the pills onto it. I take another swig from the bottle and begin to count. Seven antibiotics. Fourteen paracetamols. Six ibuprofens. I take another swig. Is this enough? Too much? Will it kill me like it did Lorna, or will I wake with multiple organ failure and have to extend my pathetic existence?

I never understood what drove Lorna to do what she did. I understand it now.

I look up at the hole where the ceiling light had been. Fucking useless thing. The noose would have worked if the fucking light fitting hadn't broken away.

I stagger to my feet and crunch over the crap on the floor to the kitchen, swigging from my friend Jim Beam.

This room was Melody's domain, her Queendom since she was forced to give up work after the accident. Boredom saw her discover a love of and talent for cooking, and over the years our small, basic kitchen transformed into a chef's paradise. I remodelled it myself ensuring she could prop herself on a stool whatever she was doing. Being at home for three months with her during the first Covid lockdown gave me an even greater appreciation of her culinary talents and the effort she put into it, all paced so as not to over-exert herself. She hated getting so tired that she had to go to bed before me.

We loved that first lockdown. We were ideally suited for all the Covid restrictions. Right from the day we met, we've never been happier than when we're together, and now I'm supposed to spend the rest of my life without her and think of her in the past and not the present. Fuck that.

I pull the largest knife from the block.

Where did she keep the knife sharpener? I root through the disorganised drawers (Mel always knew *exactly* where things were) until I find it. I put the knife between my teeth and stagger back to the living room with Jim and the sharpener in my hands, ignoring the cat who's kept a wary distance from me over the last two months. Only Mel's love of the vicious thing has stopped me wringing its neck for killing her. She would never forgive me for hurting the thing and so I have gone through the motions of feeding and watering it and keeping its litter tray clean. I'll let the family fight over who doesn't get to keep it once I'm gone.

Once satisfied the knife's sharp enough to cut through bone, I place it next to the pile of pills, pull my van keys out of my back pocket and add it to the row.

I drain the last of Jim and consider my options. Pills or knife? Both? Take the pills in one go then use the knife before the effects kick in? An insurance policy. The wrists are a non-starter. Bleeding out took too long. The neck? A possibility.

On the floor by my feet is Jim's identically named twin brother. I unscrew it and have a large drink while staring at the van keys. The easiest thing would be to go out in it, put my foot down (the turbo works like a dream) and smash it headfirst into a wall. So long as I don't put my seatbelt on, it's the most certain method to grant me oblivion. But it's the method most certain to make Melody angry. Too many risks. Other cars. Pedestrians...

I snap up the keys and throw them on the floor, disgusted

with myself for even contemplating that route. The speeding bastard who hit Mel didn't just ruin her life, kill our baby and kill our chances of ever having a child of our own, but killed *her,* more so than even the vicious cat with its bacteria riddled claws.

So many times I've wanted to hunt the speeding bastard down. I've dreamed about it. Revenge burns in my blood.

Melody refused to hate him. She could never hate anyone, was incapable of holding a grudge. She said whoever hit her would spend the rest of his or her (she refused too, to assume it was a man) life with it gnawing on their conscience. Eventually, I learned to keep my thirst for revenge to myself. My talk of it distressed her too much.

Her death certificate might have Sepsis listed on it, but there's not a single doubt in my mind that if that long-ago hit and run hadn't happened, Melody would still be here, whole and with her infection-fighting spleen intact.

But she isn't here. She's dead. Gone. Passed. Whatever fucking term you want to call it, she is gone.

And so am I.

I swallow another large swig with a grimace and make a snap decision. Pills followed by knife to the throat.

I study the bottle in my hand. Was there enough left to swallow the pills with it? I'll buy another bottle to be sure. In the morning. After I've said goodbye to Melody one last time.

Decision made, I stretch myself out and close my eyes for my last sleep.

Thursday 7th March 2024

BEFORE

Alex

The flowers that cover the mound of earth over Melody's body have long decayed but, miraculously, the wreaths have held their own against time and the atrocious weather. Let them bloom as long as they can. It's a colourful display she would love.

I pull out the frame from my inside pocket and crouch down to place it by the simple cross that will signify her life until the ordered headstone is finished. I've left enough space for my name to be added beneath hers.

"What a lovely photo."

The unexpected voice makes me jump, and I put a hand to the sodden grass to steady myself. I hadn't seen or sensed anyone approach me.

The man who's joined me crouches beside me to peer more closely at it. "Your wedding photo?"

I don't have the energy to respond sarcastically, so I nod and stretch upright. What other kind of photo had a woman in white lace and a man in a morning suit with their faces pressed together and a posy in their joined hands?

"She was a beautiful woman, your Melody."

"She was," I agree, wishing he would just fuck off and let me spend these last precious moments alone with her. But then I look at him more closely.

He's tiny. He has a shock of thick white hair and a round face that doesn't fit with his skinny body. He's wearing a thick blue checked overcoat, bright red chinos and on his feet are a pair of yellow wellington boots.

As comical as his appearance is, something about him makes my throat and mouth run dry. It's made worse that I can't determine his age. My eyes can't focus on anything of his face but his ice-blue eyes. He could be fifty. A hundred.

I swallow a number of times. "Do I know you?"

He looks up and smiles. "No."

"You knew Melody?"

"No."

"Then..." I swallow again. The palms of my hands have gone clammy. My heart is thrashing hard beneath my ribs. "How do you know her name?"

There's nothing on her grave with her name on it. I took the written tributes home weeks ago. Most are now in a box with a request they be buried with me. The rest are in an envelope for her parents and sister.

I hope Mel's right and that heaven exists, but if it doesn't and oblivion is all I have to look forward to, then I will take that.

His smile doesn't falter. "I know many things, Alex."

He stands up.

I take an instinctive step back.

The man's even shorter than I thought, shorter even than Mel's diddy height, but my insides liquidise like they would if I were being confronted by a rugby scrumhalf.

He holds up a hand. "Peace, my friend."

"I'm not your friend."

"No. But I am yours." He shoves his hands into his pockets and hunches his shoulders. "I don't know why the cold always takes me by surprise."

"What?"

"Where I come from, the sun shines all year round."

I try to take another step back, but my leaden legs won't obey. They *can't* obey. My feet have been glued to the ground.

I experience a very sudden and very real need to release my bladder.

He smiles again. "You have nothing to fear, Alex."

"What...?" I swallow again. I can't get any moisture into my throat. "What do you want from me?"

"Nothing. I am here to present you with an opportunity."

"For what?"

"To see Melody again."

If he hadn't spoken with such sincerity, I would have laughed. Not that I'm capable of laughing. All I'm capable of doing is staring at him, and I mean this literally. I can no longer work my mouth any more than I can work my feet.

The longer I look, the less blurred his face becomes. Features are emerging and, while they're far from being in focus, I imagine something similar to an aged Bilbo Baggins. My racing pulses slow a little.

He hunches his shoulders against the chill again. "Forgive me," he says kindly. "It has been a long time."

I rub the back of my neck. At least my hands and arms are still working, small comfort when a living hobbit has cast a spell on my legs and mouth, and as I think this, I realise what's happening.

I'm dreaming. A very lucid dream to be true, but when you've sunk as much Jim Beam as I have recently, hardly surprising.

"Okay, Alex, I'll go along with that and let you think this is a dream. It isn't," he adds, his thick white brows dancing mischievously, "But I appreciate that what you're experiencing is discomfiting."

He even sounds like Bilbo Baggins.

"I've been compared to him before," he muses, "but I can

assure you, my toes are far from hairy. Still, it's far too cold to waste any more time, so let's forego further pleasantries and get down to business. I have in my pocket a pill that will get you to Melody in a far less painful fashion than the paraphernalia you've got waiting for you at home."

My jaw drops.

This old man has been spying on me? But how? X-ray vision? Spyware in my home?

"Oh, nothing sinister like that, I assure you," he says, continuing to read my thoughts. "But I've been keeping a kindly eye on you since Melody's death." His nose scrunches. "I've been concerned for your state of mind and considering what you've got planned for yourself when you get home, I was right to be. I quite understand it," he continues in his soft, kindly manner. "Your Melody is a very special person, and if you hadn't recognised that and been so true to her then I wouldn't be standing here."

Let's not pretend I'm still staring at him. I'm gawping.

"It's a rare person who fights the human malice in them. She wasn't an angel of course – luckily for you or I wouldn't be standing here; isn't serendipity marvellous? – and she made some dubious choices in adolescence, but who doesn't? She always *tried* to be kind, and that counts for a great deal. People's intentions."

He pulls his right hand out of his pocket and extends it to me. Cupped in his palm is something that looks like a round black wine gum.

"You can have your wish, Alex. Take this before you go to sleep and when you awake it will be precisely thirty-three years ago. You can have your time with her again."

I think my eyes might have popped out.

He gives a slight, disapproving tut. "Is that not what you said to Melody on her deathbed? *If I could live my life again, I would do it all again. I would marry you again, in a heartbeat*? This pill will give you that." His nose scrunches again. "I'm afraid it will take you back a few years early but that can't be helped. It is what it is. A thirty-three year reset. If you require the science for this specific number then I suggest you watch the German show *Dark* on Netflix. It explains it very well, much better than I can. You can watch it now or save it for another thirty-three years – if you take the pill, all you will take back with you are your memories. Here, take it."

I try to resist, but my hand reaches for it. My fingers pluck it out of his hand.

"There is no obligation for you to ingest it. Throw it in the bin or flush it in the lavatory if you distrust it. But if you do take it, you can live your life with her again, and with all the knowledge you've gained in this life. Just be aware of the butterfly effect. I'm sure you're familiar with that term?"

I nod. The pill is enclosed in my hand. It's weighty, like holding a piece of lead.

He smiles and raises his hand. "Then I bid you farewell. Good luck in whatever you decide."

For such an aged man he moves surprisingly swiftly, and when I attempt a step of my own, I find my legs unlocked.

"What if it kills me?" I shout.

He looks over his shoulder and laughs without malice. "Is that not what you intended for yourself anyway?"

* * *

I'm back on the sofa, exactly where I sat last night. The cat is sat on the arm of the chair beside me, watching me with interest. Spread over the coffee table before me are the same pile of pills, the same carving knife, and the same letters of apology I've written to my dad and brother and Melody's family. Next to them is the large black pill. In my hand, my trusty friend Jim.

I've given up thinking that what happened at the cemetery was a dream. It happened. The black pill proves it.

I've studied it extensively. Physically, it looks like a wine gum, but it's harder to the touch. Solid. I practically stuck it up my nose trying to get a whiff of its scent but there's nothing to smell. Whatever properties it consists of, I imagine the greatest risk will be it getting stuck in my windpipe. Death by choking. Hadn't considered that method.

Fuck it. What do I have to lose? Nothing. Either I die (job done), wake up in 1991 (look, there's a flying pig) or wake up on the sofa. If the latter, then that pile of pills and carving knife will still be there waiting for me.

I lean over and stroke the cat's head. "You've got enough food and water to keep you going until they find me," I tell it. Tell her. "Whoever agrees to home you next, be nice to them, okay?"

She nuzzles into my hand with a purr.

I put the black pill in my mouth, down it with a quarter of the bottle, and wipe the back of my mouth.

Thursday June 13th / Friday 14th June 1996

NOW

Melody

The Merry Thief, a regular lunchtime spot for local office workers and passing tradesmen, and a good evening spot for Brocklehurst's underage drinkers, is a convenient ten-minute walk from the house I rent a room in, so how I've come to be late for my shift is a mystery. I mean, I set off in excellent time, giving myself two minutes to spare – after all, you never know who you're going to bump into and stop to chat with – but, despite walking directly from front door to pub door, I've still managed to be four minutes late. The scowl on Graham's face tells me my tardiness hasn't gone unnoticed. Oh well, he'll live. Which other sucker would he be able to pay a crummy five pounds an hour to?

Pretending not to see Matt the Twat amongst the crowd waiting to be served, I hurry to hang my jacket on the peg, lift the hatch and step behind the bar.

"Right," I say, sticking the newest Now album in the CD player. "Let's get some life in this place." I skip Queen's 'Too Much Love Will Kill You' (too depressing) and go straight to Oasis's 'Don't Look Back in Anger'.

I turn to the crowd around the bar and say, "Who's next?" At least six men wave their money at me.

It's busy this early evening, which is great for me as it makes the time go quicker. The only blip comes when Matt the Twat approaches the bar. Typical Graham decides to pull his finger out and actually serve a customer but does he deal with Matt the Twat? No, he leaves him for me.

"Nine pounds thirty," I say after I pour his round, trying not to meet his eye.

He hands me a tenner and makes a point of pressing it into my hand. "Are you doing anything after work?"

"Sleeping," I reply kindly. Not quite a lie. I'm sure I'll fall asleep at some point. Just not with him. No way. Never again. The thought actually makes me feel quite sick.

Mercifully, a couple approaches the bar and I scoot over to serve them.

Soon, the pub starts to empty and Graham buggers off to his flat upstairs to watch EastEnders. I get busy clearing and wiping tables, avoiding the area Matt's in, obviously. Hopefully he'll scarper soon too. I've loaded the bar dishwasher and am emptying the beer trays when Lorna walks in.

"How's the head?" I ask when she reaches the bar.

She scowls then sniggers. "Better now, no thanks to you. Did you enjoy your lie-in?"

"Yes, thank you very much." Poor Lorna started work at nine-o-clock. She's got an excellent job in a bank up the road so why she does the odd shift in this crummy place beats me. It's not as if she needs the money, not with me and Becky renting her two spare rooms. When I first met her three years ago, I thought she was nice but a bit boring, but actually, she's *really* nice (if you can cope with her dry sarcasm) and a right laugh. I love her to bits. "What are you doing here?"

"I tried calling but no-one answered, so thought I'd time coming over for EastEnders."

We both snigger. Graham always does a vanishing act when it's Soap Opera Time.

"I've booked us a taxi for when you finish," she adds.

"You're still up for the Summer Gardens?" I ask, delighted.

Thursdays is student night at the Summer Gardens and it's all indie and rock music. Best of all, it's a pound a shot for the whole night. As someone who's currently skint, a pound a shot is not to be sniffed at. Honestly, my student debt is ridiculous despite taking every shift I could in this dive in all my university holidays. Plus the music there's great. Watching Lorna get tiddled is an added bonus.

She pulls a face but I can see the smile she's trying to suppress. "You're a terrible influence."

I poke my tongue at her.

"Warning," she suddenly mutters. "Matt the Twat's coming over."

I barely have time to cover my exasperation before he's hovering awkwardly in front me, hands rammed in the pockets of his jeans.

"We're going to the Oak to watch the footy," he says. His gang of friends are bouncing noisily by the door. I pretend not to hear their catcalls.

"Okay... Have fun."

"Want me to come back when you finish and walk you home?"

"I'll walk back with Lorna, but thanks for the offer." No way am I telling him we're going to the Summer Gardens. By an amazing coincidence, he'll probably be planning to go there too.

"Another time?"

I catch Lorna's eye. Her face is bright red.

"We'll see." Why can't I just tell Matt to get lost? I don't want to spell it out and hurt his feelings, that's why. But really, why can't he just take the hint?

What is it with men? You sleep with one and think maybe

(big maybe) you'd like a repeat performance but they blow you off, but when you sleep with one, regret it immediately and want to blow *them* off (no *double entendre* there thank you very much), they get it in their heads that you're now a couple and hang around like a bad smell. Sometimes I want to scream, 'We had sex. It was rubbish. Move on. Find someone else to have sex with and maybe the chemistry will be there to want to do it again.'

Problem is, some men thought the chemistry was there the first shit time.

Problem is, I hate hurting people's feelings. Even twats like Matt. I wish I could find the words to let him down gently. Make it crystal clear I'm not interested without hurting him.

One of Matt's mates bounds over and puts him in a headlock. "Come on, short arse. We're going to miss kick-off."

Lorna waits until he's left the pub before she bursts into peals of laughter. "He's got it bad."

"Don't," I moan.

Still laughing, she lifts herself onto the bar and plants a kiss on my cheek. "I'm going to grab something to eat. I'll be back in a couple of hours."

I can still hear her laughter when the door closes behind her.

* * *

One good thing about going clubbing after an evening shift is not having to queue for long. My old mate Richie's on the door tonight and waves us to the front. I love Richie. In sixth form, we used to share cigarettes behind the sports hall. He was always a weedy-looking thing but the September we returned to the upper sixth, Richie returned a foot taller and a foot wider than the boy who'd finished the lower sixth.

"Find me when you're on your break," I say as we go through the door.

He sticks his thumb up.

The Summer Gardens is heaving. I grab Lorna's hand. We

barge our way to the front of the bar, sink a couple of shots each and then hit the crowded dancefloor.

There's a lot of familiar faces tonight and we join a group of girls we've buddied up with before. So many great tunes are playing that time flies as we dance our boots off. I wait until 'Boys and Girls' has finished – I *love* Blur, have a vague plan in my head to stalk Alex James and make him fall for me – then make a drink signal to Lorna.

She's giving our order when someone gropes my bum.

"Pack it in," I yell over the noise, swatting the hand.

There's a rumble of laughter in my ear and when I turn my head, I sigh internally to see the bloke wedging himself next to me.

I should have guessed. It's Mr Gropey-Hands. He's a regular here. All the females know him. He's the short twat who takes advantage of the packed dance floor to press himself against the women (but only the short ones – if he was to press himself against anyone over five foot three, he'd be jabbing their thigh). I've had his erection pressed against my buttocks twice before. I've accidentally trodden on his foot twice too.

"You have a lovely bum," Mr Gropey-Hands says with what I'm sure he believes is a dazzling smile but is more of a drunken gargoyle look.

"My boyfriend thinks so too," I lie sweetly before immediately turning away. He's plastered.

He taps me on the shoulder.

I clench my teeth and face him again. "Yes?"

He hiccups. "Buy you drink to say sorry?" It comes out as *shay shorry*.

"No, thank you."

"I inshisht."

Lorna and I look at each other and shrug. A free drink's a free drink.

"Okay, but touch me again and you're a dead man."

He grins sheepishly, then leans across me and shouts at the bargirl to get me and Lorna another shot each.

Mr Gropey-Hands raises his shot glass. We clink ours to it and down them in unison with him, then down the two Lorna's just paid for.

"Thanks for the drink," I say to Mr Gropey-Hands.

Pretending not to notice his lecherous wink, Lorna and I peg it back to the dancefloor. Mr Gropey-Hands follows us. After a couple of sharp elbows in his belly, he gives up trying to grope me and just drunk dances with us instead. When we head back to the bar for another couple of shots each, we buy him one too, then manage to shake him off.

The dancefloor's now so packed we're jammed like sardines, but with 'Smells Like Teen Spirit' to headbang to, no one cares. Tonight, the atmosphere is pumping and I'm quite sure we'll be here until kicking out time. I love dancing with Lorna. There's something exhilarating about watching someone so prim and proper by day really let their short hair down by night. I especially love it when she sings along. She always mangles the words, ha ha.

When 'Wonderwall' comes on, Lorna shouts that she's going to the loo. As she wonders off, Mr Gropey-Hands decides to try his luck again and rubs himself against me like a horny dog. He's so drunk, he doesn't even flinch when my boot connects with his ankle.

I back away from him as much as I can so he's got less room to grope, and spot a couple of lads I recognise dancing close to us. I throw my arms around the nearest one.

"Can you pretend to be my boyfriend for five minutes?" I shout cheekily. It's a tried and trusted method of ridding yourself of a drunken sex-pest.

"Only if you buy me a drink," he shouts back, already sliding an arm around my back.

"Done!"

He's not bad looking and it's no effort at all to gyrate into him. By the time Lorna's back, Mr Gropey-Hands has a new victim.

I forget all about my promise of buying my pretend boyfriend a drink until Lorna and I are at the bar downing shots and he taps me on the shoulder. I think I might have had enough by now as I can see two of him, but I'm not so far gone that I can't order another round. When he sticks his tongue down my throat after we've downed them, I'm happy to respond in kind until Lorna tugs at my top and I abandon him mid-Frenchie to stagger back to the dancefloor, only to then find Lorna dragging me by the hand in the other direction.

"Where we going?" I ask.

"Home."

'But s'not over yet."

"Remember what you made me promise the other week? That I had to take you home if you started snogging random men again?"

"Don't 'member that."

"Yes you do, and you've just snogged a random man."

"Have I?" And then I remember my pretend boyfriend and giggle. "Oh yesh. I 'member. Shorry, Lorny-bops."

Outside, clean air replacing *eau de sweaty bodies*, we get in the taxi queue and I prop my backside against a boulder to keep myself upright. Yep. Am definitely drunk.

I let go of Lorna's hand to light a cigarette. She plucks it out of my mouth and turns it the right way round for me.

I giggle again and lean in for the light she's offering, but before I can catch the flame, something slams into my back. I throw my hands out to break my fall but I've barely thudded onto the concrete when there's a sharp pain in my skull and my head's yanked back.

A blurry woman's face comes before mine. "Get your own fucking boyfriend, bitch, and leave mine alone." Another sharp pain, this time in my side, and then she lets go of my hair. Her legs walk away from me.

A different face appears. Lorna. She's speaking but I can't hear her. The thrashing of my heartbeat in my ears is deafening.

Ice has formed in my chest, so solid I can't speak or breathe through it.

Lorna helps me to my feet. Only her arm wrapped tightly around my waist stops my shaking legs tumbling me back to the ground.

There's a crowd around us.

"I want to go home," I whisper, but they're all too busy talking amongst themselves about what to do to hear me.

Richie's face swims before me. I make out words like ambulance and police.

I cling to Lorna and shake my head. "I'm fine."

"Mel..."

"I said I'm *fine*."

I manage to hold back the tears until Lorna and I are safely cocooned in the taxi.

She holds my hands tightly all the way home.

Friday 14th June 1996

NOW

Alex

I check my appearance one final time. I've spent the past year growing my hair out so it's chin length and flops over my face. My goatee beard is, I think, trimmed as it was the first time. I'm certain these are the same clothes I was wearing. If not the very same ones, they're identical. My aftershave's the same – that was easy to remember as I only wore Davidoff until Melody bought me a new scent for my thirtieth.

I feel sick. The closer this date's drawn, the deeper the nausea has lodged.

I say goodbye to Kermit and Ellie, light a cigarette, and get walking. Lorna finishes at five-thirty. I'm outside the bank with ten minutes to spare.

At thirty-five minutes past five, the bank staff leave from the staff exit at the side, Lorna amongst them. She spots me straight away and her face lights with the same smile I remember from all those years ago.

This is that time. *This* is all those years ago.

Finally, it's here.

"Alex!" she says as if she hasn't seen me in decades when it's only been a year and we last spoke a couple of weeks ago when I called to ask about her spare room. "What are you doing here?"

I've been careful to keep things the same. As much as I can, anyway. The most important things. Continuing with my job, taking the same commissions. Living in London – although not with Rachel – for two years and moving in with Kermit on the same date as before.

"No work today," I say in an almost verbatim repeat of the first time. "Thought I'd see if you fancied a drink and a catch-up."

Her face falls. "Oh, that's a lovely idea but I can't."

That's not part of the script. What she's supposed to say is, "That sounds lovely!" and then we choose The Merry Thief because it reminds us of our teenage years and we want to see if I'm still barred and because it's the closest pub to the bank.

I clear my suddenly dry throat. "Why not?"

"It's Kelly's birthday – Kelly from work. It's her thirtieth. She's having a party at the Marriot in the City."

A wave of coldness washes over me, freezing my veins and bones.

No, no, no, no...

My heart is hammering so hard I can barely hear myself think to say, "Have you got time for a quick one before you go?"

"I can't. Marie's giving me a lift." She tugs at the large canvas bag on her shoulder. "I'm getting changed in her room at the hotel."

A small, red car swerves in the space by the kerb in front of us. The car behind honks its horn in anger at it.

"How about tomorrow?" Lorna suggests as she opens the passenger door. "I'm working the lunch shift at The Merry Thief but I'm free from three?"

"Great." My voice sounds faint to my own ears. "I'll meet you when you finish."

She jumps in the car. Seconds later, it pulls into the traffic.

I watch it disappear into the distance.

The freezing of my bones has lessened. Now they feel like jelly.

After all that planning...

I can scarcely believe it. I've got the wrong fucking day.

I'm a day late.

Melody

My legs feel like lead as I drag them down Watling Street. I feel sick to the pit of my stomach. My head hurts. Really hurts. I wish I was still in bed. I wish I'd never gone to the Summer Gardens.

I just want to go back and hide under my duvet and cry. The only thing that got me out of bed was knowing Lorna would skip her work party if I didn't.

Poor Lorna. She checked on me before she went to work and called during her lunchbreak and again when she finished. Her voice was too gentle. It was like she was speaking to a poorly child. I made my own voice sound cheerful. Told her I was absolutely fine.

I don't want her worrying about me. It wasn't her fault.

As The Merry Thief looms closer, I straighten my back and lift my chin.

I'll be fine. Work is the best place for me. Keep busy. Don't give myself time to think.

At the door, I swallow hard before fixing a smile to my face and breezing in.

Alex

She's here. My beautiful pocket-dynamo, my Melody, is here. I whisper a silent prayer of thanks that I'm not too late.

She walks past my table without seeing me.

"Melody!" I call her name before I can stop myself.

She pauses mid-step and turns to the sound of my voice.

I jump to my feet and in three quick strides I'm right before her, gazing straight into her beautiful dark eyes.

"Oh, Mel," I whisper.

The last four years and ten months have been the most difficult, horrendous years of my life. Keeping my silent promise, to let her live her life and enjoy all the moments that turn her into my Melody, has been torture. The only thing that's kept me going is the thought of this moment, and I can't contain my joy a moment longer. I pull her into my arms and hold her tight.

My senses fill with her familiar Melody scent and I want to weep.

But in my joy, I'm holding her too tightly. She's too stiff. I loosen my embrace. She disentangles her arms and wriggles free.

"What the *fuck* do you think you're doing?"

I put my hand to my cheek, unable to comprehend the stinging to it any more than I can comprehend her venomous words.

In all our twenty-eight years together, Melody never raised her hand to me or anyone.

The woman who deplores violence has just slapped me. Worse, she looks like she's about to burst into tears.

"Mel?" I clear my throat, horrified to have scared her so badly. "It's me. Alex. Don't you remember me? We –"

She holds her palm out and steps back. "I don't care who you are. You don't get to touch me. Do you hear me? You don't get to *ever* touch me."

"Is this man bothering you?"

I don't hear Graham approach. I'm not aware of anything apart from Melody and the disintegration of the moment I've spent so many years dreaming of, not until he puts his bulk between me and Melody and stares at me as if I'm something dirty he's trodden on.

She's crying now. Openly.

"Mel, I'm so sorry," I say, but that only makes her cry harder and cower into Graham, whose face contorts.

'I remember you," he says with quiet menace. "And I remember you're barred. Now get out. You're not welcome here."

"Please," I beseech. "I didn't mean to scare her." I try to get past him, to her, to make her understand I would rather die than do anything to hurt her. "Mel, I swear I didn't mean to –"

A punch in my gut cuts me short, doubling me over. I have no time to catch my breath before Graham's grabs the scruff of my jacket and t-shirt and unceremoniously drags me out of the pub. At the door, he pushes me, sending me sprawling onto my arse.

He looms over me. "Step foot in here again and I call the police. Bother Melody again and I won't bother with the police. Understand?"

Part Two

NOW

Sunday 16th June 1996

Alex

I take a deep breath to brace myself and knock on the door.

Becky answers. It's the first time I've seen her in decades. She moved out of Lorna's a few months after Melody and I got together and I don't remember seeing much of her after that. The last I heard, she'd emigrated to New Zealand.

"Yes?" She stares at me with that slightly aggressive expression I remember, and I remember she's never met me before.

"Is Lorna in?"

She looks me up and down again, then calls out to her.

Footsteps thud down the stairs and Lorna appears. "You must be psychic. I was about to give you a ring."

My heart racing, I follow her into the narrow Victorian terrace.

"Tea? Coffee?" she asks.

"Tea, cheers."

I last visited this house a year ago. I turned up on Lorna's doorstep and stayed for a couple of nights in her spare room, the one now occupied by Becky, just as I did my first time around. The difference this time had been that I hadn't been kicked out of my home by Rachel. This time there was no me and Rachel. This time it was a spontaneous visit to an old friend.

As we go through to the kitchen, adrenaline pounds through me. Any second now, Melody will appear. She'll hear the voices and her insatiable curiosity will compel her to bound down the stairs and see who's here. Lorna will introduce us and whatever it was that scared her about me the other day will be dispelled.

"I thought you were going to meet me at the pub," Lorna says as she lobs t-bags into two mugs.

"Hangover from hell." It's the truth. After the disaster of mine and Melody's reunion, I went to The Oak for a pint and chaser to calm myself. I lost count after the fifth pint. I woke spreadeagled on my bed at Kermit's, fully dressed and with the worst hangover I've had in decades.

She grins. "I thought you looked like shit."

I grunt. She should have seen me yesterday.

Yesterday was a day of torture. The moment I came back to consciousness all I could see were Melody's tears and her stricken face.

I forced myself to stay inside. If I'd left the flat, I wouldn't have been able to resist seeking her out and that would have made things worse. Melody's incapable of holding onto anger or upset for longer than twenty-four hours but also incapable of seeing reason within that timeframe. She needs time to calm down.

Thank God for Kermit. He left me alone only long enough to stock up on lager from the off-licence. Instead of watching England play the Auld Enemy of Scotland, we spent the day drinking, getting stoned and playing Mario Kart. Kermit kept up an inane level of bonkers chatter and recycled all his old jokes. For a stoner, he's got a superb emotion radar.

Becky pokes her head into the kitchen. "I'm going to Josh's now. See ya later."

Once she's gone, the house feels quiet. Too quiet. "Where's your other housemate?" I ask casually.

Melody doesn't just leave a trail of mess wherever she goes;

she leaves a trail of noise. It's impossible for her to enter a room without turning the radio or television on.

"She's gone to her mum's for some TLC. Sugar?"

"No thanks. What does she need TLC for?"

Lorna passes my tea to me. "She was assaulted the other night at... Bloody hell, Al, you okay?"

Hot tea has sloshed over my hand.

The room feels like it's spinning around me. I grip the kitchen worktop and force air into my lungs.

"Alex?"

Lorna's concerned face floats before me.

"You okay?" she repeats.

I nod.

"Let's get water on that," she says.

I let her drag me to the sink.

"What happened to her?" I ask. My voice is hoarse.

She holds my hand firmly under the tap. Cold running water pours over the scald. "We went clubbing at the Summer Gardens. Mel got pissed and snogged some bloke. His girlfriend attacked Mel for it. It was horrible."

I close my eyes. "Was she hurt?"

"More shaken than hurt. We were waiting for a taxi when the girlfriend appeared from nowhere and sent her flying. It all happened really quickly, was over in seconds, but poor Mel was really shaken by it."

Lorna turns the tap off, pats my hand dry with a tea-towel and examines the wound. "You'll live," she decides.

By the time we're sat in her small living room my stomach is churning. I can't stop thinking of Melody's tears and the way she cowered into Graham for protection from me. I should have known there was something wrong from that reaction alone. Melody's not someone who scares easily. She takes basic personal safety measures, like never walking on her own late at night, but she doesn't see danger at every turn. She doesn't expect the worst of people. She always assumes the best. To be assaulted, no matter how fleeting it might have been, would have distressed her terribly.

"When did this all happen?" Drum beats are smashing loudly in my head. I already know the answer but need to hear it.

"Thursday night."

I cradle my head and dig the tips of my fingers hard into my pounding skull. There's a good chance I'm going to vomit.

It's all my fault. Melody's assault.

My fault.

I should have been there.

Fingers touch my cheek.

Lorna's crouched in front of me. There's concern on her face. "Al?"

"I know her." I don't mean to say that. It just comes out.

"Melody?"

I pinch the bridge of my nose and nod.

Her expression is astounded. "Really?"

"We met a long time ago. She... made an impression."

She studies me a little longer then taps my cheek in a light slap. "Don't worry about her. She's not someone to mope. She'll be fine."

Melody

Mum's dressing gown is lovely and soft and fluffy. I don't want to take it off but she's insisting I have a bath. She says I stink.

I turn the taps and pour some of Alice's bubble bath in. I don't know what it is about baby bubble bath that I like so much but as the scented steam from the pouring water rises, the tightness in my lungs loosen.

I take the dressing gown and nightshirt off, and tentatively sniff an armpit. Yuck.

And then I catch sight of my naked figure in the bathroom mirror. The woman caught me with the toe of her boot right above my left hip. The bruise is huge and vivid. I look away and get in the bath.

Submerged in the hot water, I close my eyes. Tears leak from them. This time I let them fall.

I don't want to think of that night but I can't help it. It's played on a loop in my head since I woke on Friday. The worst of it is, I don't remember much about it. I remember kissing someone but I wouldn't put money on recognising him in a line-up.

I remember her though. The hatred in her eyes. The stench of alcohol on her breath. The way her spittle landed on my face.

Alex's face drifts in front of me. I close my eyes and push him away.

I haven't washed my hair since Wednesday. It stinks worse than any ashtray.

Pinching my nose, I slowly slide my head under. I don't stop when the water sluices over the wound on the back of my scalp. I'm just grateful it's stopped throbbing. Now it's just a sharp sting. Hair wet, I carefully lather Alice's baby shampoo into it. Once I've rinsed, lumpy scabs float in the water.

I haven't dared look at it or get anyone else to look. I don't want to know how much of my hair she ripped out.

* * *

I'm playing with Alice in the living room. Mum's cooking Sunday dinner. Dad's mowing the garden. I'm a lot less stinky now.

It's amazing the mess an eight-month baby can make. She's definitely my sister! I've put her play mat on the floor and she's on her belly sucking the fabric, her little plump body rocking backwards and forwards.

While she's busy sucking, I figure I should clear up some of the mess, and shuffle to the other side of the room to gather together the building blocks she's lobbed everywhere. I'm putting them in one of her many toy boxes when I see she's lifted her head and is looking at me.

I spread my legs, pat the space between them, and call her to me.

Her face screws up and her one tooth, cut through only a week ago, gleams under the sunlight pouring into the room as she gives me the cheekiest smile I've ever seen.

Her arms move forward. And then her body follows suit. She's moved around a foot when the penny drops.

Alice is crawling.

"Mum!" I yell, not taking my eyes off my baby sister.

I tap the space between my legs again. "That's it, Alice. Come to Melody."

She obeys. My God! Look at her go! Working commando-style, Alice crosses the living room floor to me. When she reaches my feet, I lean forward and scoop her up.

"You clever girl!" I tell her, holding her high above me. Her plump legs kick out in excitement.

I look at Mum, who's answered my call and is standing at the threshold of the door watching us with the strangest expression.

My excitement dims. "Are you okay?"

The widest smile spreads over her face. Hurrying over to us, she sits on the floor beside me, plants a kiss on both our cheeks and then takes Alice from me. Alice immediately starts to cry.

Laughing, Mum gives her back. Alice immediately stops crying.

"Dinner won't be long," Mum says, getting back to her feet. When she reaches the door, she looks back at me. "If you want to move back, you can, you know that, right? This will always be your home, for as long as you want or need it to be."

* * *

We're all watching Wednesday's episode of *Coronation Street*, which mum recorded. Mum's cuddled up next to Dad. Alice is cuddled in my arms, pulling my hair. She's normally in bed by now. Her eyes are getting heavy. I kiss her button nose.

The television blurs as my thoughts drift back to Alex. I know I over-reacted but until he lunged at me on Friday, I hadn't given him more than a passing thought since I started university.

I keep trying to work out what it was about him that scared me so much. When I think of all that time I believed myself in love with him, you'd think I'd have been thrilled to see him.

Was it because I was so raw from Thursday night? I suppose that must play a part in it. He caught me off-guard like that woman did, but it was more than that. He looked at me and acted like he *knew* me. Properly knew me. Like I meant something special to him and not someone he spent one night talking to five years ago. The way he lunged at me still makes my heart race to think about. The way he squeezed all the air from me.

It was like my being there had made his whole damn life, and now guilt stabs at me for the way I reacted.

I wait until the adverts before getting up. Intending to put Alice to bed, I surprise myself by saying, "Did you mean it about me moving back?"

They both straighten. Their faces turn to me like a pair of synchronised meerkats.

"Of course," Mum says.

"Is tomorrow too soon?"

Monday 17th June 1996

Alex

For the second day in row, I knock on Lorna's front door.

A figure appears behind the frosted glass. The handle turns. The door opens a couple of inches. Part of Melody's face appears. She keeps the internal chain locked.

"Yes?" she says. Then she recognises me, and the eye I can see in the crack widens.

"Oh, hi Melody," I say as if I'm mildly surprised to see her, as if I hadn't scared the life out of her the other day. "Lorna said you were living with her. Is she in?"

I know she isn't. I've picked my time carefully. Four pm. Lorna's at her day job. Melody never worked afternoon shifts on a weekday.

She doesn't answer. I sense her suspicion, but the fact she hasn't slammed the door in my face is encouraging.

"We're old friends," I explain.

"You and Lorna?"

"Yes. We grew up together, went to school together... Our parents are friends."

I sense a slight relaxation. "She's at work."

"Never mind, I just popped over on the off-chance – I finished early. But I'm glad you're in. I was hoping I'd see you so I could say sorry for scaring you like I did the other day. I'd had a bit too much to drink and when I saw you and recognised you, the alcohol got the better of me."

My pre-scripted words are rewarded with her undoing the chain and opening the door. She's wearing the exact clothes she wore the day we met.

"I'm sorry too." She hugs her arms around her chest. "I was feeling a bit fragile that day." She's still fragile. There's deep, purple circles under her eyes. Melody hasn't been sleeping. "You caught me off-guard."

"I noticed," I say, trying to make light of it, and this time I'm rewarded with a partial Melody smile. "So, how's life? Been up to much the last five years?"

She raises her shoulders and pulls her neck down in the way she always does when asked a question impossible to answer in one punchy sentence. "A bit. You?"

"A bit."

Her smile widens. The need to touch her is close to overwhelming. To pull her to me and hold her. And probably scare her again.

"I'd better go," I say.

I've got to take this slowly. I can't recreate the day we met. The circumstances and atmosphere of that ship have sailed. "It's good to see you."

"And you."

"See you around."

She nods.

As I turn to walk away, she says, "I'll tell Lorna you called round."

"Cheers."

"And I'll ask Graham to lift your ban."

Our eyes meet. My heart wrenches.

I love you, Mel.

I smile, nod, and leave.

Melody

I go back to my room to continue packing, but instead of tackling the piles of clothes and books I've dumped on my bed, I peer out of the window. My bedroom faces the street. Alex has crossed the road. His hands are jammed in his jacket pockets, shoulders rolled forwards as if he's upset about something.

There's an inexplicable lump in my chest.

Lorna's mentioned an Alex a few times but until he turned up, I had no idea her Alex was the man my sixteen-year-old-self thought of as *my* Alex. I don't usually give much truck to coincidence but what a wonderful coincidence that he chose to pop over to see her while I was in and that I had the chance to say sorry for my overreaction. He didn't mean any harm when he lunged at me. The way my pulses raced when he stared in my eyes and made his apology for scaring me...

Oh, but it's the way they raced that night!

I came so close to inviting him in. It was right there on the tip of my tongue.

I only realise he's stopped walking when he turns his head and looks directly at my window.

I slide onto my bottom and put a hand to my chest to temper my thumping heart.

* * *

"What are you going to do with my room?" I ask Lorna. We're having a cup of tea while I wait for Dad to collect me. "Do you know anyone who'll want it?"

I gave her cash for two weeks extra rent to make up for leaving her in the lurch but she shoved it straight back into my handbag. She refused to listen to my arguments as to why she should have it.

I wish she'd take it.

I don't know who feels the most guilt between us: Lorna, for failing to help me on Friday night, or me for abandoning her.

Neither of us should feel guilt. There was nothing Lorna could have done to stop the attack, and it was over with too quickly for her to react. We have no tenancy contract, just a loose verbal agreement, so I shouldn't feel awful for upping sticks and leaving with only a day's notice. But I do. And she does.

She pulls a face. "My old mate Alex was looking to rent somewhere – you beat him to your room by a couple of days. I'll give him first refusal."

Just the mention of his name makes my heart jolt. I've thought about little but him since he turned up on the doorstep earlier. I lean forwards. "Alex?"

"Yeah. That reminds me, he came over yesterday. Said he knew you."

The racing of my heart comes to an instant halt. Ice coils up my spine.

"Alex Hammond?" she says, looking at me closely in the silence. "Tall bloke. Dark hair. Gorgeous looking. Ring any bells?"

I manage to nod and clear my throat. "Alex was here *yesterday*?" I clarify.

"Yeah. He moved to London a few years ago but it got too expensive or something so he moved back last month. He came over for a catch-up – we're old mates." Her eyes narrow a fraction. "Why? What's wrong?"

My throat has run dry. "He came to see you today too."

"Did he?" She looks flummoxed.

"This afternoon. He specifically asked for you."

"That's strange, he knew I'd be at work," she says.

The doorbell rings.

Yes, I think, as she goes off to answer the door. He knew.

Alex lied. He didn't come over to see Lorna. He came to see me.

The coincidence of him turning up here three days after pouncing on me in the pub was no coincidence at all.

Tuesday 18th June 1996

Alex

I clamber over the piles of rubbish strewn over the kitchen floor and grab the phone before it rings off. "Hello?"

"Al?"

"Yes."

"It's Lorna."

"Hi, Lorn. What you up to?"

"Not a lot. Just calling to let you know Mel's moved out so my spare room's going again if you still want it?"

"She's moved out?"

"Yeah. Last night. Moved back with her parents."

When Melody and I first got together she would have preferred to live in a cardboard box than move back with her parents.

The old man's warning about the butterfly effect echoes through the static playing in my ears.

"Al? You still there?"

I clear my throat. "Yeah. Just thinking."

I look at the chaos surrounding me. I think of Ellie's sister Sophie, whose efforts at getting me into bed are becoming more blatant by the day. Remembering how nasty she was to Melody makes it an effort for me to be civil to her. She either doesn't notice my borderline rudeness or doesn't care.

I think quickly. The butterfly effect is speeding up, but if I act quickly, its ripples don't have to change everything. Melody and Lorna are close friends. I'll have more opportunity to meet up with her naturally living with Lorna.

"This weekend suit you?" I ask.

"Perfect."

Saturday 22nd June 1996

Alex

Despite him being the colour of his name, Kermit helps me carry the few boxes and suitcases into the back of my van. This is another good reason for me to move out. Getting stoned and drinking heavily is a way of life for Kermit, and will be until the birth of his first child in a few years. The child him and Ellie are both currently adamant they don't ever want. I'm in a young man's body so can take the abuse but the fun of it left me over a decade ago.

He hands me the joint. I have a toke and pass it back.

"Cheers for putting me up," I say.

"Can't believe you're abandoning me to these two." He grins and looks over his shoulder before adding in an undertone, "Can't you take Sophie with you?"

"Fuck off."

"I'll pay her rent for you. Not that she pays me any fucking rent."

"Charge her."

"Ellie won't let me." He looks over his shoulder again and shudders. "I swear their cycles are in sync."

"If you need rescuing when it's that time of the month, just shout."

"What, so you can laugh at me?"

I punch his arm. "That's what mates are for. Smell you later."

He punches me back. "Don't be a stranger."

* * *

I sit on the bed and lean back against the wall. Memories are flooding me. This is the bed Mel and I first shagged in. We never called it *making love*. Not out loud. Too sappy.

We shared this single bed for six months before Mel heard about the flat for rent above the chip shop and we got our deposit down before the other interested parties. This pine wardrobe is the one Mel created space in to fit my clothes with her own. It was so crammed inside the pressure used to make the doors fly open. These bookshelves are the ones that were once piled with her favourite books and CDs.

There's nothing of her left in here apart from memories. Give Melody her due, she might be a messy bugger, but when she puts her mind to cleaning something, she really goes for it. Not even a stray sock stuck in the corner under the bed. The small dressing table that used to have piles of makeup, hair products, perfume, loose change and random bits and pieces, all coated with a fine layer of dust, is spotless and polished.

I can feel her in here though, closer to me than she's been since the night at the fishing lake.

"Al?" Lorna's voice calls from the other side of the door.

I snap myself out of my reverie and invite her in.

She casts a quick gaze around the room and grins. "How long can you keep it tidy for?"

"Longer than Mel," I laugh.

She looks at me strangely.

"She comes across as messy," I quickly say, then even more quickly add, "but I bet she's not as messy as Kermit."

She laughs. "I'm always surprised Kermit remembers to brush his teeth so that's a bet I won't take. Anyway, I'm off to work."

"Thought you said you had the weekend off?"

"I did but Mel's quit and the cover Graham had for her shift today has pulled a sickie, so I'm going in."

For fucks sake!

"When did she quit?"

"Wednesday. She's got herself a job in her village shop – more sociable hours and she doesn't have to deal with drunken twats."

Twat. Melody's favourite word.

"Anyway, I'm off. I'll be back around seven."

"Join you when you've finished?" I suggest.

"You're barred, remember, so it'll have to be in the Oak."

"I'm *still* barred?"

"Oh, I assumed you knew. Graham updated the barred list and added your name to it."

"When?"

"This week. First I saw of it was last night. Assumed you knew – thought he must have seen you around and remembered what you did to the pool table. I would have asked but he was in a foul mood so I left it. And speaking of him being in a foul mood, I'd better go before I'm late."

Alone, I take a number of deep breaths and try to clear my head.

Melody must have forgotten to tell Graham to take my name off the barred list. That's understandable after the week she's had. It doesn't mean anything and I shouldn't worry that it does. I shouldn't worry that she's quit her job at the pub either. She would have quit soon anyway, when she gets the job at *History Through Time*.

I have to accept that my fuck-up has upended everything, and even if I hadn't fucked the date up, the path we took the first time can't be recreated in a linear line because I'm not the same man I was then. The only thing that's the same is my love for Melody and her love for me.

How many times did she tell me that she fell in love with me when she was sixteen and that she'd spent the years until we next met subconsciously waiting for me? For fucks sake, she was playing *our* song a week after the night by the fishing lake! I remember planning our wedding and trying to decide what the first song should be. I've never seen her blush so hard as when she said she wanted Bryan Adams' 'Everything I Do'. I'd always thought it was naff but because it was Mel, I agreed.

Days after, we went out drinking. She got pissed and confessed that it was the song she'd fallen in love with around the time she'd fallen in love with me, and that she could never hear it without thinking of me.

She does love me. I just need patience and to stop panicking when, every time I put the pieces into play to move myself in her orbit, she makes a move that pulls her further out of it.

Friday 28th June 1996

Alex

The drive back from my quote in Abingdon goes much smoother than I expected and I'm on the A5 towards Brocklehurst by three-thirty. The turning to Collingswood is fast approaching and I flick my indicators on before I'm even conscious of what I'm doing.

By the time I pull up outside Collingswood's village shop, my heart is thumping.

A group of noisy school kids go inside. I follow them in before I can change my mind and almost trip over a schoolbag. The kids have decided that pooling their money right by the door is a great idea.

It's been many years since I was last in this shop. In a decade or so it will have a major refurbishment, but for now it's a cramped space with newspapers to the left of the door, sweets and crisps lining the wall to the right and a central aisle selling Happy Shopper crap that no-one buys unless they're desperate and which hides the counter from view. At the far end is a narrow walkway that leads to the dingy post office. The refurb will open it up and make it much harder for the kids to nick stuff. I join the queue snaking around the aisle.

The woman serving behind the counter is about thirty years older and five stone heavier than Melody.

I buy my cigarettes and leave.

Melody

I'm hiding in the post-office pretending to tidy-up the greeting cards and praying he doesn't need stamps or a birthday card or a packet of biros.

I'm not convinced he didn't see me. I'd just finished stacking a box of Polos onto the sweet stand when I spotted the tall figure walk in and practically trip over the kids loitering in the doorway. I pegged it straight into the post office, moving so quickly I impressed myself.

I give it five minutes and take a peek. The top of his head is visible. He's being served. I duck back out of view.

What's he doing here? Collingswood's out in the sticks. There's no through-road here. No one uses us as a shortcut or anything. The only people who use our shop are the people who live here.

The next time I poke my head out, he's gone. I expel a long breath and walk to the counter.

"That bloke who was just in here," I casually say to my boss who's owned the shop longer than I've been alive. "Do you know his name?"

"The tall one?" Mary pulls a face at my nod. "No. Never seen him before. Why?"

"No reason. Just thought I recognised him but couldn't figure out where from." I smile to reassure her then go back to the stock room to hunt for a box of Mars Bars.

Thursday 4th July 1996

Melody

I kiss Dad's cheek and open the car door.

"Any problems, call me," he yells as I get out.

"Will do," I yell back, and join the early-morning throng into the train station.

Dad bought himself a mobile phone at the weekend and I think he would wee himself if I actually called him on it. Honestly, I don't see the point in mobile phones. Who wants to be contactable all the time? Mind you, anyone stupid enough to buy one round here (sorry Dad!) is safe from being contacted as there's no signal to receive any calls. Dad spent half of Sunday calling the house phone for the fun of it, but had to stand on a chair in the bathroom to get the only soupcon of signal within the brick walls. Still, it was fun watching him attempt to write a text message to Uncle Stelios (he popped over a fortnight ago to show off his new mobile phone and Dad immediately coveted one for himself). Watching Dad try to text was like watching a small child learn to read their first words. After twenty minutes of sweat, the message wouldn't send. No signal, ha ha. I'm quite sure the pain he suffered will stop him ever sending another one.

I've given myself plenty of time to get to Richmond but I can't help looking at my watch every five minutes. I've never had nerves like this before, and the closer the train takes us to London, the more they grow. When we arrive at Euston, the second leg of my journey begins with an underground ride to Vauxhall and then an overground one to Hampton Court train station. From there, it's a short walk.

When I arrive at the palace, I check my watch and see it's taken me exactly two hours and twenty-five minutes travelling time from home to palace. It's less than an hour to drive but seeing as I don't have a driving licence, that's an option I can't consider if I get the job. I did mention to Dad the other day about having driving lessons with him again but he suddenly developed an extremely acute case of deafness.

I stare again at the giant courtyard. The nerves in my stomach have turned into huge flapping butterflies. I've got three more interviews lined up but to paraphrase the brilliant Spice Girls song, this is the one *I really, really want*. I remember coming here as a little girl but my only real memory of it is getting lost in the maze. Mum and Dad brought me back for my seventeenth birthday and regaled me with family gossip of a great aunt on Mum's side who, with zero evidence, believed the family to be descendants of Anne Boleyn. Maybe this bonkers story played its part but, whatever, I fell in love with the place and spent the whole day soaking it in, trying to imagine it all as a real, working palace filled with courtiers and butt tons of staff.

To spend my working life here, enclosed in the walls where Henry VIII and his succession of wives feasted, hunted, jousted and generally made merry for weeks if not months at a time, each stay marking another deterioration in the king's health and a growth in his tyranny, the full spectrum of emotions that must have been lived here in a world that's utterly alien to us and yet so humanly familiar... It would be a dream come true.

Now all I have to do is find the interview room and not muck it up.

Eek.

Alex

I'm standing by the pillars with the statues of lions on them that lead to the palace's grand main entrance, rehearsing what I'm going to say to Melody. The best I've come up with is, 'Lorna mentioned you had an interview here today. I'm only working round the corner so thought I'd pop over and see if you fancied some lunch.'

My stomach is churning its agitation. I know I've got the date right. How could I forget the day Melody agreed to marry me?

Yes, yes, yes.

To play safe with the timings, I got here an hour ago. Crowds of people have swept past me on this working day, mostly pensioners and groups of noisy school children from an array of nationalities. Nobody has paid me the blindest bit of attention. Just wait twenty-eight years. No way a single man loitering around the entrance of a tourist attraction filled with school kids will pass unnoticed then.

I light my fourth cigarette in an hour. I don't even want it. The first three have dried my throat out but I don't dare leave my spot to find a shop or anything selling water. The date itself might have imprinted in my mind but the timings are vaguer. I'm sure the interview was around lunchtime-ish because we stopped at a petrol station on the drive home for sandwiches and I used the ring-pull of my coke can as a makeshift engagement ring.

A mass of curly black hair catches my attention.

My breath catches in my throat.

It's her.

Melody

Oh, I could cartwheel the length of the palace's magnificent driveway! I could hop and skip to the group of primary school kids picnicking on the grass to my left and steal all their fizzy drinks and biscuits. I could climb that pillar, balance myself on the lion's head and shout, 'Hurrah!'

The interview went well. Really, really well. They liked me, I'm sure of it. I'm one step closer to making the job mine –

What the actual...?

I stop walking.

The tall man standing beneath the pillar I've just imagined myself scaling is staring at me. From this distance, he looks just like Alex.

The heated rush of blood zipping through me tells me it *is* Alex.

For a long moment I gaze back, my feet not moving, not until my rushing blood whooshes to my head and my legs propel me to him in strides much longer and quicker than my lazy bones usually take.

"What are you doing here?" I demand when I career to a halt in front of him.

The surprise on his face only feeds my anger. The fucker was obviously expecting a happy greeting.

If that night at the Summer Gardens taught me anything, it's to keep your wits about you at all times and trust your instincts. I was too drunk to have any instincts or wits that night. I will never put myself in that position again, and Alex Hammond has proved he's not to be trusted and that I should have trusted my instincts when the lunge he made at me frightened me.

"Cat got your tongue?"

His throat moves before he says, "Lorna mentioned –"

"Let me guess, she happened to tell you I had an interview here today?"

"Mel –"

"Don't *Mel* me, you creep."

He grabs at his hair. "I'm working round the corner –"

"Of course you are! You just happen to be working in Richmond the day I've got an interview here, just like you were only dropping by on the off-chance Lorna was home when you bloody well knew she was at work, and like you just *happened* to come into the shop I work in which is stuck in the middle of bloody nowhere."

His face pales.

"Yes," I hiss. "I saw you. I don't know what weird little fantasies you've got going on in your head about me but you can scrub them right the fuck out and keep the fuck away from me. Come near me again and I'll report you to the police for harassment."

Unable to look at his ashen face a moment longer, I storm past him.

"Melody, I'm sorry!" he calls. There's distress in his deep voice. Good. Let him be distressed. See how he likes it. "I'm not a stalker, I swear. Please, I just want –"

"I don't care what you want!" I scream over my shoulder, upping my pace. "Just leave me alone!" And then I break into a run, dodging pedestrians and traffic until I reach the train station and double over, my throat raw, a stitch in my stomach and tears streaming down my face.

Alex

Fuuuuuck!

Fuck, fuck, fuck, fuck, fuck.

* * *

I'm in the living room drinking my old friend Jim when Lorna gets home from work.

She stands in the doorway.

My cheeks refuse to greet her with a smile so I raise Jim to her instead.

Her features tighten. She disappears, returning some minutes later with a large glass of white wine, which she holds carefully as she curls up on the sofa next to me.

"Alex, we need to talk."

"'bout what?"

The phone rings before she can answer. With an impatient sigh, Lorna crosses the living room to answer it.

"Hello...? Yes, who shall I say is speaking...? Okay." She covers the mouthpiece. "It's for you. A Greg Rylance?"

I tilt my fuzzy head back. "Tell him to call me tomorrow."

She politely passes my message to Greg then listens a few moments before hanging up the phone. Her puzzled gaze rests on me. "He said to tell you they've sourced the required bricks and that the refurb can start next Monday."

I feel sick. A sickness like I've never felt. Worse than the effects that black wine gum had. Worse than any hangover. As wrenching as the sickness when I knew Melody was going to die but different. A different pain.

I have a swig of Jim in another effort to quell it.

"Cheers." I wipe my mouth with the back of my hand.

She sits back down and faces me. "What's that all about?"

I close my eyes. "Nothing important." Not now, in any case.

She's silent for a long time again. She's gearing up to bollock me about something.

"Melody called."

I should have guessed. I drink some more Jim.

"She called me at work," Lorna stresses, "because she didn't want to call the house. She didn't want to risk you answering it."

I have another swig.

"What's going on?"

I shrug.

"How did you know she had an interview at Hampton Court

today?" she persists. "I didn't know the date so I couldn't have told you." When I still don't answer, her voice rises. "How did you know?"

I raise Jim to my lips again but she snatches it out of my hand before it connects.

"Do you know what you're coming across as?" she says angrily. "One of those stalky blokes. My instinct was to defend you and tell her you're not like that, and now she's angry with me and I'm wondering if she was right about –"

"That won't last."

"What?"

"Her anger. It never does. She'll forgive you by Saturday." But she won't forgive me. I feel it in my bones. I've played this all wrong and scared her too much.

"How do you *know* that?"

"Because I know her."

She straightens sharply. "No you don't. You met her once, five years ago – she told me. How can you think you know her –"

"I was married to her for twenty-seven years."

Well that shuts her up.

Lorna's mouth drops open. Her eyes widen. She stares at me as if I've suddenly sprouted two heads and then her shoulders shake and she bursts out laughing.

I wait until her laughter quiets to snorts of mirth and she's licking the wine she's spilt off her hand to snatch Jim back off her.

I take an extra big swig then look her right in the eye.

"Melody and I got engaged thirty-three years ago today," I tell her baldly. "On that day, I drove her to Richmond for her interview because I was working round the corner from the palace, just as I was today. I showed her the bathroom I was working on and proposed to her and she said yes."

Yes, yes, yes.

"My proposal made her late for the interview and she didn't get the job. She got a job at *History Through Time* magazine instead, and worked there for nine years until some bastard ran his car into her, killed our unborn baby, and almost killed her."

All her amusement has vanished.

"We married on the thirtieth of August 1997. You were a bridesmaid. So was Mel's sister, Alice. Five years after the wedding, we bought a house on Juniper Crescent. We lived there until Mel died in January 2024. The car accident caused a lot of internal damage. They had to remove her spleen. It fucked her immune system. One of the scratches she got from Dotty the cat got infected. Led to Sepsis and then septic shock. After she died, I was given the chance to come back and start my life with her again, but I've fucked it up. She shouldn't have been assaulted the other week because I should have been at the Summer Gardens with you both, because that was the day Mel and I got together. I've been trying to put things right, but I've done it all wrong and now she's scared of me, and if you want to have me committed for all this, then be my guest. I don't give a shit."

I don't care if Lorna believes me. I don't care if she laughs at me. I don't care if she calls my dad and tells him to commit me to a mental asylum.

I don't care about anything anymore.

She raises her wine glass slowly to her mouth and has a small drink, then nods at Jim. "How much of that have you had?" she asks shakily.

I wave the bottle that's now barely a quarter full.

I drain half of what's left and take her hand. It's rigid in mine but she doesn't pull away and she doesn't drop her stare.

"You think I'm deluded or whatever. I don't blame you. I'd think the same, and I'm trying to think of what happened first time round that hasn't happened yet but will soon so you'll know I've not lost my marbles, but the only thing I can think of is Mel's Grandma Alison dying later this year. Patty used her share of the inheritance to pay for most of our wedding."

A low, frightened, mewing comes from Lorna's throat.

"Oh, and Princess Diana dies next year. It happened the day after our wedding."

The morning after our wedding, bleary eyed and hungover to our teeth yet ecstatically happy, we joined our families in the hotel restaurant for breakfast. Sombre doesn't begin to describe the atmosphere we walked into.

Now Lorna does snatch her hand from mine. She cowers into herself.

"Sorry, Lorn. She gets chased by paparazzi and crashes into a bridge or something in Paris. Think her driver was drunk. Oh, and she was with the old Harrods owner's son, Dodi something. He died too. I'll try and think of other things that happen sooner... Mel and I were too loved-up to pay much attention to the news back then."

The room's spinning. Jim has done his work. I finish the bottle to play safe.

"Going to bed. Night, mate."

She doesn't answer. I feel her frightened stare follow me out of the room.

Friday 5th July 1996

Alex

I drink two strong coffees with painkillers and escape the house without seeing Lorna. My head's throbbing and I take the drive to Richmond slowly and make it to the converted chapel without having to pull over and puke.

I gaze at the house. I don't want to go in. Never want to step foot in it again. The only thing stopping me from reversing and hightailing away is professional pride.

In the bathroom I study the work I've already completed. The happy ghosts of the past that have haunted my time here are silent today. Melody's voice has disappeared.

So has her smile.

Melody

"Present for you," Dad announces when he gets in from work. His excitement is so palpable that I know immediately what it is. He holds out the hand he's been hiding behind his back and, beaming, presents me with a boxed Nokia.

"Cheers, Dad!" No sooner is it in my hand than Alice, who's on my lap, grabs it.

"Look what Daddy's got for Alice." Dad produces a baby book not much bigger than his hand. Alice lets go of my Nokia and grabs the book. It goes straight in her mouth.

I only mentioned over dinner last night that I wanted to get one. Naturally, Dad assumed it was because I was as enthralled by his phone as he is. Even when I said it was because I thought it a good idea to have one for when travelling to and from work (if and when I get a job that involves travelling, that is – I don't want to jinx myself with the Hampton Court job) and he nodded his agreement, I could quite clearly see he thought I was making excuses to justify my own coveting of his wonderous gadget.

I didn't correct him. I don't want to frighten him like I've been frightened. My dad's no fighter but if I tell him I have a stalker, his protective instincts will come out and he'll track Alex down and probably be the one to get hurt in the process.

Dad takes the box from me. "This needs to be charged for ten hours before you can use it. Want me to set it up for you?"

It would be like stealing Alice's favourite teddy bear to say no. "Yes, please."

He's practically dancing a jig. "I'll give you a lesson on how to use it when it's ready to go."

"You're the expert."

He taps his nose. "Told you you'd want one too, didn't I? Eh? You wait. Your mum will be making excuses for one soon too."

"No I won't," she yells from the kitchen.

"How much do I owe you?" I pray it's not more than my weekly wage.

"For you, my angel, nothing."

"Don't be silly," I protest. "These things cost a fortune."

"Your safety is worth any expense."

"Don't I get consulted in this?" Mum yells again. Her ear-wigging skills are spectacular.

"I did consult you, my love," he calls back.

"*When?*"

"This morning. I said to you, shall we treat Melody to it seeing as her student debt is more than our mortgage, and you said that was a *fantastic* idea."

Mum's head appears around the door. "Roy?"

"Yes, my love?"

"That conversation happened in your head."

He looks flummoxed. "Did it?"

She rolls her eyes and disappears again, saying, "Come and help me fix dinner."

Dad gives me a sheepish grin. "Better do as I'm told."

Left alone again with Alice, I pull her new book out of her mouth.

"Melody read it?" I say when she goes to grab it again. It's a farmyard book, page after page of individual farm animals with their appropriate noises to recite and inappropriate textures for her to touch (go on, someone tell why the pig is textured with velvet). She loves it so much that when we're done, she shoves it in my face as a demand to make me read it again. I obey. Alice has me wrapped around her tiny little finger.

Moving back in with Mum and Dad is the best decision I've made in a long time. Probably since I went off to university. Living here means I get to be with Alice every day. This baby... oh, she's just wonderful. I adore her; am utterly ashamed at how annoying I once found her early morning cries. Of course she cries. She's a baby. It's her job to cry!

I don't know how long I'll stay but, for now, this is where I need to be. Somewhere safe. Somewhere where I have to temper my worst excesses. I can't go off drinking and clubbing at all hours with a baby to think of. I don't even want to go clubbing. The life I've been living...

It's too much. Jumping in and out of bed with random men, spending half my life avoiding the ones I've slept with and the other half wondering what's so wrong with me that they're avoiding me. I need to slow down. Take a breath. Save the alcohol abuse for the weekends.

There's a sharp pang as I realise I won't be able to crash at Lorna's like I used to in the university holidays anymore. Not while Alex is living with her.

I can't believe I feel guilty for telling her what he's done. Honestly, I'm pathetic. The man stalks me all the way to Richmond, frightens me enough that I think getting a mobile phone is a good idea, and I feel guilty for telling him to do one and for ratting him out to Lorna. See? Pathetic.

I need to stop thinking about him. The racing of my heart around him is just an echo of my old feelings and I absolutely should not trust them. Who in their right mind would trust the judgement of a sixteen-year-old who only agreed to go out with a boy because he was popular, and who'd only recently stopped thinking New Kids on the Block were musical geniuses?

All I need to trust is the truth, which is that Alex Hammond is a liar and a creep and a stalker.

Alex

The traffic back to Brocklehurst's a nightmare and it's late when I get home. Lorna's waiting up for me, just as I expected her to be.

"I know you want us to talk," I say, pre-empting her, "But let me take a shower first, okay?"

Clean and with fresh clothes on, I join her in the living room. She's made me a cup of tea, which I take to be a good sign.

She tightens the sash of her dressing gown around her waist and swallows hard before speaking. "What you told me last night... Do you remember?"

"I remember."

"Please tell me you were lying."

I hold her stare. As Melody would say, what's done is done. I can't un-tell her and what have I got left to lose? This is Lorna, the only female in my life I've never lied to. Even Melody doesn't get that honour, not if you count white lies like, 'No, your passport photo does not make you look like the Medusa.'

She blinks and looks away. "It's impossible, you know that, right?"

"Is it?"

"You *know* it is. I mean, *time travelling*? Either you're pulling some really cruel trick or you need to see a doctor."

"Lorn..."

She shakes her head violently. "No. I don't want to hear any more about it. As an excuse to justify harassment, it's just plain shit." She wipes away a tear. "It's only because you're my oldest friend and I love you that I'm not going to tell you to leave, but I love Melody too and you're putting me in a horrible position."

And just like that, her distress makes me wish I'd denied everything and blamed it on alcohol-induced psychosis.

But it's too late now.

Everything in my life is too fucking late.

"If you want me to go then I'll go, and I won't blame you or think badly of you for it."

"I don't want you to go, damn it!" She wipes another tear away.

"Look, Lorn, I'm not going to be here for much longer anyway."

A crease forms in her brow.

"I've bought a house. That's what the call yesterday from that Greg Rylance was about. The renovations will take three, four months and then I can move in."

"What house?" she asks, bewildered. "Where?"

"That converted chapel at the end of town. You know the one?"

"The huge place with the boarded-up windows?"

I nod.

Her bewilderment only grows and I know she's thinking of the money side of it. "But *how*?"

But she's scared enough as it without me adding to the impossible burden I've already loaded on her shoulders.

"I've been stashing money away over the years." Before she can question this, I continue. "How about I promise never to mention any of this again and we both pretend last night never happened, and any time you want to go out with Melody and have her stay over, I promise to stop at Kermit's or Dad's?"

She pulls a tissue out of her pocket and blows her nose noisily. Then she looks at me for the longest time. "Only if you promise you'll see someone about it? Please? For me?"

That's an easy thing to promise seeing as she hasn't specified who or what profession that someone should be. "I promise."

Saturday 28th September 1996

Melody

I hover at Lorna's front door. She notices. "Don't worry, he's already left. Won't be back until lunch tomorrow."

I wait for relief to flow through my tight chest but nothing happens. I step over the threshold anyway. It's the second time I've entered the house since I moved out. I didn't trust his word via Lorna that he would stay out all night the first time, so got Dad to pick me up at pumpkin-turning time. This time, I've packed an overnight bag.

Becky appears. "Peach schnapps?"

She shoves a shot of it in my hand before I can say no.

Oh well. It's been a good month since I last had a proper drink.

The three of us raise our glasses and down them.

A dozen or so mostly funny birthday cards are on display in the living room. Being nosy, I pick one of them up. Inside, it reads:

To Alex, Happy birthday you old fart, Kermit & Ellie

There is no reason on earth why a birthday card should make my heart pang so hard.

I hastily put it back and willingly take another shot from Becky, which I down even quicker than the first, then push Alex from my mind.

Pushing him from my mind is something I do on a regular basis.

Becky throws her handbag over her shoulder and decrees it time to go.

I've only been out with Becky once, last New Year's Eve. I was still a student, home for the Christmas holidays. Dad dropped me at the house (he really is a most excellent taxi driver) and Becky was moping because her boyfriend Josh had the flu. The invitation to join us at the house-party we were going to had left my lips before my eyes could register Lorna standing behind her waving her hands frantically and mouthing, 'NO!'

Thankfully, it was an experience we never had to repeat.

When I lived with them, I always felt compelled to invite Becky wherever we went because I can't imagine anything worse than feeling excluded from the people you live with. Mercifully, she always said no. I give her credit, her reasoning was always because her and Josh were saving for a deposit to buy their own home, and now they've done it and are moving to a flat in the city next week. This is our goodbye shindig for her.

The first pub we hit is The Fox & Hound, generally known as The Worst Pub in Town. It's a horrible dive of a pub, so horrible it makes The Merry Thief seem like The Ritz. But Becky has planned the route and we meekly obey, too fearful of having our ears sliced by her sharp tongue to complain.

Next is The Plough, and things improve massively. A handful of her work colleagues are waiting there for us (all looking as terrified as we feel), and by the time we make it to The Merry Thief, I'm feeling pretty tiddled.

"When are you coming back?" Graham demands to know while he's serving me.

"Never!" I blow him a kiss.

He nearly smiles. "How's the job going?"

"Really well, thanks."

I've worked at Hampton Court Palace for a month now. I love the job but the five hours a day of travelling is killing me. Dragging my lazy butt out of bed at five every morning is as hard as it was to drag myself out of bed for school. I've started looking into renting somewhere closer but Richmond prices are exorbitant compared to Brocklehurst prices, even for a single room in a shared house. Maybe I'll find someone with a nice shed to rent. Or a tent. Or a cardboard box.

"Seen any ghosts yet?" Graham considers himself an expert on ghosts. When I told him I'd applied to the palace he couldn't wait to tell me about all its reputed hauntings.

"Not yet but I'll let you know when I do."

"If it gets too scary, there's always a job here for you."

"Only if you up my wages."

"Piss off."

"I love you too."

Blowing him another kiss, I carry the tray of drinks to the table Becky's commandeered. It's not long before the pub's packed and we're joined by loads more people. Unfortunately one of them is Matt the Twat. I wedge myself between Lorna and Jasmin so he can't try and get into my knickers.

After two more drinks, Becky gets to her feet, claps her hands, and announces it's time to hit The Oak. I'm quite tempted to buy her a whistle so she can call us all to heel.

It's as we're walking out of The Merry Thief that I see him. He's getting out of the driver's side of a pick-up truck parked in the Market Square.

It's like he's got an internal radar or something. His eyes immediately connect with mine.

Even from this distance, I see him jolt.

My heart hammers into my suddenly dry throat.

He's joined by an older man, almost as tall as him.

His gaze stays connected to mine for another moment and then he turns and, together with the man who I guess is his dad, crosses the road. He turns back for one last look at me before they enter the Chinese takeaway.

Only when Lorna tugs at my arm do I realise my feet have rooted to the ground.

Alex

"You alright?" Dad asks as we queue.

I manage a nod. My heart's thumping too hard for speech.

It's the first time I've seen Melody since Richmond.

When we reach the front, our order, which Dad phoned in earlier, is ready for us.

"Fancy a quick pint before we head back?" he says as puts his change in his back pocket.

"No." I can't do that to Melody. I promised Lorna I would stay at Dad's until tomorrow lunchtime.

I knew I was dicing with danger just coming to collect the Chinese. I wouldn't have come if Dad hadn't decided to crack open the scotch and announce I would have to drive. He handed me the keys to his pick-up as if he were handing me the keys to the Crown Jewels.

I hope I haven't ruined her night.

Sunday 29th September 1996

Melody

I peer cautiously through one eye. Everything's blurry. There's a weight over my belly. It's an arm. I push it off and shuffle to the edge of the bed and, tangled in my duvet, fall straight onto someone lying on the floor.

Shit.

I'm not in a bed. I'm in Lorna's living room, along with a roomful of other comatose people.

In desperate need of a wee, water and pain killers, I crawl off the comatose person I've landed on and use the edge of the sofa to lever myself up, then fall straight back onto them.

My slowly focusing eyes make out who I've been sharing the sofa with. Matt the Twat.

I'm almost scared to pat myself down. Top and bra on... Check. Jeans and knickers on... Check.

Phew!

I crawl up the stairs to the bathroom but am too dizzy (drunk) to dare walk back down them, so shuffle down on my bottom and stagger to the kitchen. I fill the kettle and heap two spoonfuls of coffee into a mug. My throat feels as disgusting as my mouth tastes, but I pull a squashed cigarette out of the squashed packet in my back pocket and light it with my shaking hand.

Drinking coffee and smoking alone at the tiny kitchen table, I frantically search my alcohol-abused brain for memories of last night. The last thing I remember is Becky ordering us out of The Merry Thief. After that, nothing. Not a jot. Not a fragment. A total blank canvas.

Shit.

I'm on my third coffee when I hear the first sounds of life. The stairs creak and Lorna appears and mumbles a greeting. She opens the kitchen blind and daylight pools in, temporarily blinding me.

I light her a squashed cigarette and pass it to her while she makes herself a pint of tea.

Neither of us speaks until she sits opposite me and slumps over the table. "My head…" She groans, then lifts said head to peer at me. "How's yours?"

"Getting there."

Her face falls back onto her arms. Her voice is muffled. "Been up long?"

"'bout an hour."

"Surprised you're alive. You were hammered."

I finish my coffee, brace myself, then ask, "Did I do anything I should know about?"

She raises her head again. "You don't remember?"

Uh oh.

"I don't remember anything after The Merry Thief," I confess sheepishly.

"Not surprised. You were on a mission."

But *I'm* surprised. The only mission I remember being on was to let my hair down and have a good time, not drink so much I became blotto. I've hardly lived like a nun since that horrible night at the Summer Gardens, have been out drinking loads of times, but my newfound self-preservation means I've finally learned to respect my alcohol limits and I don't understand why I would breach them now. "Was I?"

She laughs. I think. Or it might be a grunt. "When we got to The Oak, you insisted we play that drinking game Fuzzy Duck."

That alarms me. "*I* insisted? Not Becky?"

Something like a smile lights her face. "You're very brave."

"I must have been if I went over her head."

The sound she makes this time is definitely a laugh. "You were plastered by the time we finished playing so I brought you home."

"Sorry."

"I thought it best – you were snogging Matt the Twat."

"*Noooo*." I cover my instantly flaming cheeks. Of everyone I could have snogged, why him? "Is that why he came back here?"

"He didn't. Only Grace and Liv came back and..." She sees something in my face and her eyes widen. "Becky came back later with a load of others but I was already in bed. Think they must have had a lock-in at The Red Lion. She didn't bring him back with them did she?"

"Must have done coz he was cuddled up to me on the sofa when I woke up. He's still in there."

"The sneaky *fucker*." She snatches my cigarettes, pulls one out, unsquashes it and lights up. When she looks at me, she's visibly calmer. "Still, it's not like he could have done anything is it?" She frames this as a hope. "You passed out as soon as we got in. You didn't even wake when we put Abba on."

"He cuddled up to me but he didn't do anything," I assure her, even while I'm wondering what in hell I was playing at snogging a man who makes my skin crawl.

How could I have let myself get into such a state?

A face I don't recognise staggers into the kitchen. Lorna doesn't recognise her either but is nice enough to make her a cup of tea. I use the interruption to call my dad and ask him to collect me.

I really want to get out of here before Matt wakes up. If I have to see his gurning face, all the coffee I've drunk to sober myself up is liable to upchuck over him.

Alex

Lorna's sprawled out under a duvet on the sofa when I get home. I take one look at her pale face and manage my first real smile in weeks. "You look like death."

"I feel like death," she mutters.

That'll teach her to try and keep up with Melody, a thought I keep to myself. She doesn't like me talking about her.

"Have you eaten?"

She shakes her head.

"Bacon sandwich?"

She shakes her head then nods then shakes it again.

I laugh. Lorna always has a hangover after a night out with Mel.

The kitchen is a tip. Someone's clearly abandoned their effort to clean up. I'm guessing Lorna. Becky has an allergy to housework far worse than Melody's. At least Melody tries. I won't miss Becky when she moves out.

I turn the grill on for the bacon and then get loading the new dishwasher Lorna's treated herself to.

When the sandwiches are made, I take them and two mugs of tea into the living room. I put one of the plates on Lorna's stomach.

"If you still don't want it, I'll have it," I tell her, then lift her feet up and park my backside next to her.

After a tentative first nibble, she demolishes it. I take the plate off her and replace it with the tea.

"Better?" I ask once she's drunk it.

She nods and smiles. "Thank you."

"Heavy night, I take it?"

"We played Fuzzy Duck."

"Ouch."

"Exactly."

I have to ask. Even at the risk of upsetting her. "How is she?"

Her face immediately pinches in on itself.

"Please, Lorn. I just want to know how she is, that's all."

She sighs and pulls out a cushion from beneath the duvet and throws it at me. "She's fine. Hungover but fine."

"Enjoying her job?" That's the only nugget Lorna has deigned to share with me. That Melody got the job at Hampton Court Palace.

"She loves it." She looks at me for a long time and sighs again. "I don't suppose there's any harm in telling you. She's looking to move to Richmond."

I didn't think it was possible for more pain to cut me but that does.

The only comfort I have is that Melody's close by. She's scared of me. She hates me. But she's close.

"Can't cope with the travelling?" I guess. Even before the hit and run, Melody was useless at getting out of bed. I've never known anyone hit a snooze button so many times. I'm sure she must hold the record for it.

There's a flickering in Lorna's eyes.

I've come to think that on some subconscious level, Lorna believes me but she's too much of a rationalist to allow herself to admit it. The implications are too fantastical and frightening for her. She was raised a strict Roman Catholic, but the beliefs she grew up with are beliefs she spurned in late adolescence. She has no truck with astrology or fortune telling, or anything else along those lines. She believes what her eyes and ears tell her.

"Will you do me a favour and apologise to her for me?" I ask. "Dad had a couple of drinks so I had to drive to get the Chinese last night."

There's another flicker in her eyes. "She saw you?"

"Didn't she say?"

"No."

"It was when you were all leaving The Merry Thief. We'd just parked on the Market Square. I didn't approach her or anything, but she did see me."

Lorna's jaw clenches then relaxes. "I'll tell her."

"Cheers, Lorn."

She smiles, but it's an uncertain smile.

Melody and I are not going to happen. I accept that. I accept too, that her life is taking her in the direction it would have gone if we hadn't met at all. Her happiness is the only thing I care about and she *is* happy. I saw that last night, before her eyes locked onto mine. She's still the sunny, vivacious person I fell in love with, my little pocket-dynamo, but to distress her any more by trying to force a relationship risks destroying that sunshine. I'd rather rip my heart out than see her cry again.

To know I was the reason for those tears kills me.

Monday 7th October 1996

Melody

Oh, wow. This house is beautiful.

House? What am I saying? It's not a house! It's a mansion! With its own electric gates too!

I don't know what I expected from the notice pinned on the staff board but it wasn't this. The notice read:

Room available in Richmond home for single female palace worker. Nominal rent in exchange for two evenings babysitting a week.

I checked with Julia that it wasn't some perve trying to lure young women into his lair and she assured me it's legitimate. The owners love having Hampton Court Palace on their doorstep, are aware of the expense many of the junior workers endure with their travelling and want to help in their own way. Two members of staff before me have lived in this particular home. Both were happy.

Someone could have told me it was a mansion!

Awed, I walk a humongously long driveway that cuts through a manicured front garden I can easily imagine bursting with floral colour in the spring and summer. I spot a child's wooden play set to the side of the mansion, with a swing and a slide and monkey bars. I would have killed to have had that when I was a kid.

Even before I reach the front door, I imagine having Alice here to visit. She turns one next week and is already walking (can you believe, her first steps were a run?) and talking. Okay, I exaggerate. She's hardly spouting Shakespeare but she's currently up to six individual words and, when she intersperses them with her babble, can hold a conversation. Obviously, you can't understand a word of it but she's proud as punch at making herself heard. Dad darkly says that this is an omen, ha ha. I just want her to get a move on and say my name. Is it wrong to be jealous that she can say dog but not Melody?

Kirsty, one half of the couple who owns the mansion, greets me. She's a tall, slim woman with the straightest, blondest hair I've seen that's not on the cover of a magazine. Her warm smile puts me at ease, and I follow her through to the orangery (who has an orangery?!) trying to stop my eyes from popping out.

This place is amazing! Honestly, I mean, I know I work in a palace, but this is an ordinary woman living in a home with *cantilevered stairs*.

"You look impressed," she observes. Her accent is pure East End.

"Your home is beautiful," I tell her.

"I know!" She laughs. "I still wake up most days and pinch myself that it's mine."

"I'd pinch myself too. Was it once a chapel?"

"Yep. Dates around mid-nineteenth century. We bought it when I was pregnant with Molly. Wanted to escape city life."

"How old's Molly now?"

"Six. She's at school." She looks at her watch. I'm betting it costs more than all my mum's jewellery put together. "She finishes in ten minutes."

"Oh. Do you need to collect her?"

"Greta's already left."

"Who's Greta?"

"The au pair. You'll meet them both soon, but while we have the house to ourselves..." She extends an arm into the orangery, which to my disappointment is really just an extra-large conservatory with a fancy name.

A cafetiere of coffee and two cups are already set out for us. Kirsty pours, and then we get down to business. She amiably fires what must be a hundred questions at me, which I don't blame her for. It's a risk inviting a stranger to live in your home.

Just to be invited inside feels like a lottery win. To be allowed to live here would be mind-blowing.

A door slams. Moments later, a small child with white-blonde hair appears.

"You must be Molly," I say with a smile.

She looks me up and down. "Yes. And who are you?"

I bite my cheek not to laugh. Her mum might be pure East End but this little girl is aristocratic posh.

"I'm Melody."

"Are you going to live with us?"

"That's up to your mummy."

Kirsty rises to her feet. "Why don't you show Melody her room?"

Molly holds her hand out to me. I take it. She smiles. Dimples appear in her cheek.

'My' room is as beautiful as the rest of the place. It has a double bed, a good-size wardrobe, a dressing table and its own adjoining bathroom.

"Would you like to see my bathroom?" Molly asks as I'm admiring the shower.

"You have your own bathroom?"

She giggles, and for the first time sounds exactly her age. She tugs at my hand. "Yes. Come and look. Mummy says I'm a very lucky girl to have it."

Expecting nothing more than a posh bathroom, what I find leaves me speechless.

Not only is it bigger than my parents' bedroom but one of

the walls is an intricate mosaic of the Little Mermaid and friends playing and swimming in the bottom of the deep blue sea.

It's stunning. Truly stunning. So stunning that not only am I speechless but there's a lump in my throat and I'm shaking.

"Don't you like it?" Molly asks.

"I like it very much." My voice is hoarse.

"Then why are you crying?"

I put a hand to my cheek. It's wet.

"I don't know," I whisper.

And I *don't* know. All I do know is that looking at this beautifully created mosaic makes me feel like my heart's breaking.

Saturday 19th October 1996

Alex

I unlock the door and step into my new home, feeling the precise opposite of how I expected to feel in this moment when I bought it.

"Well, we know who Dad's going to live with when he's old and infirm," Ollie says as he carries the last of the boxes past me. I say, 'last of,' as if I have a lorry full of possessions when all my stuff fits into four boxes and three suitcases.

I muster a laugh. "No way I'm cleaning his arse."

"If I need my arse cleaning, shoot me," Dad says. "Is that everything?"

"Yep."

"Then let's call the Chinese."

I bribed them into helping me with the promise of food and booze. I didn't need help – I've just explained the paucity of my possessions – but I wasn't ready to enter the house for the first time on my own.

This is the home I bought for me and Mel two years ago. I roamed the plentiful derelict rooms and imagined us and our future children filling them. I believed then that our dream of having children could come true this time round. I stood at the back door and surveyed the sprawling grounds, and imagined our future children and their friends running and laughing and exploring all the hidden spaces.

Tonight, I need company, because the knowledge none of those imaginings are going to happen is a cloud growing bigger and darker with each passing day.

Monday 21st October 1996

Melody

I'm holding a fractious Alice and supervising Dad's loading of my suitcases into the car. He's taken the day off work to drive me and my possessions to Richmond. Not all my stuff though. I'm keeping a load of it in my bedroom. I have Sundays and Mondays off so will come home on those days. No way I can go more than a week without my Alice fix!

Dad can't wait to see the converted chapel. Mum can't wait to see it either, but Alice is teething again, hence the fractiousness, so she's going to stay at home with her. Every meal together since I met Kirsty has been spent with them demanding ever more details about the place. They're fascinated. Their faces when I described the mosaic in Molly's bathroom was a picture. Both their jaws dropped in unison. Was hilarious!

"Where did you put the flask?" Dad asks as he shuts the boot. He won't travel any distance greater than ten miles without a coffee to hand.

"In the freezer."

"Ha bloody ha."

I snigger. "It's in the car."

'Car!" Alice suddenly yells. "Car! Car!" And then she pulls my hair.

In the house, the phone rings. The sound of it makes Dad pat his backside. "Where's my mobile?"

"Where you left it?"

"Ha bloody ha." His face screws up. "I had it a minute ago."

He's rummaging in the glovebox when Mum screams, "*Roy*!" We look at each other in alarm and run inside.

Thursday 24th October 1996

Alex

Early evening, a loud, rapid knock on my new front door wakes me from my doze. I drag myself off the sofa and open it to find Lorna bathed in the glow of the powerful night lights. There's a box at her feet.

"Hello, you!" My spirits lift a little to see her. She's not due for a visit until Saturday. "Come in."

She folds her arms tightly across her chest. Her eyes are red raw.

"You okay?"

Face turning the same shade as her eyes, she shakes her head. Tears spill down her cheeks.

Alarmed at her state, I go to put an arm around her and lead her inside but she shrinks away from me.

"How did you do it?"

I don't have a clue what she's talking about. "Do what?"

"Melody's nan. She's dead."

My heart plummets to my feet. "Grandma Alison?"

"Melody's aunt found her Monday morning. You said..." She takes a gulp of air and whispers, "You said she would die soon."

I grab at my hair. "Look, come inside. I'll make us a drink and we can talk."

Her voice rises. "What have you *done*? She was only sixty-three, there was nothing wrong with her."

"Lorn, it's heart failure. That's what the autopsy will find."

"How can you know that?" She's sobbing. "This is all shades of fucked up."

"I know."

"You don't! How can you? You *can't* have known this. You *can't*. It's impossible."

I'm trying not to cry myself. "You know how."

She shakes her head violently and taps the box with her toe. "These are the bits you left at mine." She's backing away from me. "Don't come back. I love you, Al, but you scare me. I don't want to see you again, okay? You need to keep out of my life, and for the love of God, keep away from Melody."

Then she turns and runs.

Tuesday 19th November 1996

Melody

Molly is as good as gold in the bath. She plays happily with her myriad of bath toys and when I tell her to get out, she obeys without question. Maybe it's because I've let her turn into a prune.

Her bathroom is such a soothing place to be. Sat on the corner chair, supervising to ensure she doesn't drown, I gaze at the mosaic with more peace in my heart than I've felt in a month. Maybe it's the change of scenery. My delayed move to Richmond finally happened this weekend. Mum and Alice came with us. They needed a change of scenery too. It has been a horrendous time for everyone, but especially for Mum.

It was so sudden. Scarily sudden. No warning. No chance to prepare.

Poor Mum. Her dad, my Grandpa Clive, died when she was thirteen. I can't imagine losing her or Dad. I don't want to imagine losing both of them.

I *won't* imagine it, so I look at the mosaic again to stop myself.

Once Molly's dry and in a clean nightdress, I put all the toys away and rinse the bath. Gathering her dirty clothes together, I stare again at the mosaic. There's so much of it to see. Every time I look, I find something new.

Kirsty, immaculately made up for her evening out, comes in. "We're off now. You've got my number stored?"

I nod. This is my first time babysitting Molly. Our agreement is I babysit her two nights a week when Greta, the au pair, has her days off.

"Great. Dunno what time we'll be back. You know how these things can drag on."

"Err…. No." Mick (or Michael as I've been instructed to call him if anyone visits or phones) is in banking. Don't ask me what he does in banking as when Kirsty tried to explain it to me, my brain glazed over. Basically, he's just as you'd imagine one of those eighties' yuppies all grown up to be. I don't like him half as much as I like Kirsty.

She cackles. "If you're lucky, you'll never find out."

Alex

I ignore the banging on the door and turn the volume of the telly up. Whoever it is can sod off. The only company I want is my old friend Jim. He's such good company that I've already started on his twin.

The banging on the front living room window startles twin-Jim out of my hand.

It takes three attempts for my hand to clasp onto it. Amber liquid has pooled over the hardwood floor.

I slide onto the floor, landing with a bump, and wipe it with my sleeve. Melody won't want warped floorboards.

Did I say that I've drafted my will? Saw the solicitor on Friday to sort it. Ollie, Dad, Kermit, Jimmy and Lorna all get specific shares each. Melody gets the rest, including the house. Going back to the solicitors on Thursday to sign it then I'll be all done.

"What the fuck is going on?"

I look in the direction of the voice. "Oh. Hello, Ols." It's a struggle to make my tongue and lips form words. "How'd you get in?"

"Kitchen door. You're bloody lucky I did – I was about to call the police."

"What for? Shomefing happen?"

I grab onto the sofa and haul myself up.

Should have stayed put. The room's spinning.

"You, you dick. You were supposed to come for dinner on Sunday. What's going on? You won't answer the door, you ignore everyone's calls, Jimmy says you haven't been to work in over a week and now I find you on a bender? Fuck's sake, Al, the state of you."

"I'm grand," I say in my best Irish accent. Father Ted's been on. Me and Mel used to laugh like drains at it.

"You're a mess. This place is a mess. You've spunked thousands in renovating the place and treat it like this? I take it from all the empties around the place that you're trying to kill yourself?"

I laugh.

He punches me in the mouth. "You selfish prick."

"Ow." I touch my mouth. It's wet. I think it might be blood.

"That hurt did it? *Grand.*" He crouches down to face level with me. I can see three of him.

The room is really spinning now. Feels like I'm on a Waltzer. I always hated Waltzers. They always made me sick.

I try to focus my eyes but the harder I try, the more they want to close.

Ollie's saying something. His mouth's moving, but his words are getting fainter and fainter...

* * *

The room's dusky when I open my eyes. A coffee table's been dragged over to within arm's reach. There's a pint of water on it and two painkillers. I throw them down my neck then push the blanket off and crawl to the nearest bathroom.

I need more water so drag my legs to the kitchen. I down another pint then sag onto a seat at the table by the bay window.

There's a pile of newspapers stacked on it with a note at the top. It reads: *Gone to get food. DO NOT try and kill yourself until I get back.*

Beside the note is a cigarette and a lighter.

While I smoke, I pull the top newspaper from the pile. It's the local rag. I squint at the date. It's from two weeks ago.

A spark ignites in the few brain cells Jim hasn't killed, and I turn to the obituaries. I scan the notices carefully until I find the one the spark told me to look for.

Alison Patricia Bennet, aged 63, from Collingswood, sadly passed away suddenly on the 21st October. Much loved mother of Jaqueline, Patricia and Allie, and a loving grandma to Stephen, James, Nikos, Melody and Alice. Alison's funeral will take place at...

The rest of the words blur as I'm thrown back to the time when Patty and her sisters, all white-faced and red-eyed, chose those words. Melody and I hovered with Roy and Stelios in the background, providing them with a steady flow of tea.

I remember too, sitting in my small living room with Patty, Roy, and Alice, trying to hold ourselves together while we decided on the words we would use for Melody's obituary.

I pinch the bridge of my nose. The back of my eyes are burning.

What the hell gives me the right feel sorry for myself when I've been given a chance millions of people would rip an arm off to be given?

The front door slams.

Ollie stomps in, a bulging paper bag in one hand, a cardboard tray with two large coffees in the other, scowling at me.

"I'm sorry," I say before he can speak. "You're right. I'm a selfish prick."

His scowl loosens. "Surprised you remember." He puts his goodies on the table. From it, he pulls out two bacon McMuffins and a hash-brown and passes them to me, then pulls out the same for himself.

My stomach growls. I can't remember the last time I ate. I dimly remember searching for food in the kitchen yesterday and giving up when I couldn't be arsed to clean any crockery or cutlery to eat it with.

Unless he hired some overnight cleaning fairies, Ollie did it for me.

When he's finished stuffing his face, he lights a cigarette and looks me square in the eye. "Going to tell me what's going on?"

All I can tell him is a version of the truth. "Sometimes the days seem very dark."

He continues staring at me. I hear his foot tapping against the stone tiles.

"I miss her too, you know," he says. "Every single fucking day."

He's talking about Mum.

"Amber reckons you're suffering delayed grief. I was a prick for the first year, did you know that?"

I shake my head. I thought Ollie had stopped being a prick when he met Amber.

"Took it all out on her. Made her life hell." He has a long drag and exhales slowly before a wry smile plays on his lips. "She's a Macmillan nurse so was prepared for it. She's said all along that you were handling it too well. She warned me and Dad that you were heading for a crash. Don't think she expected it to take three years."

How's Ollie to know I'd already grieved our mother and that every extra day with her was a blessing and a privilege that helped steady me for living her death a second time?

I really *am* a selfish prick.

But better they all think it's delayed grief about Mum than know the truth.

I've been grieving losing Melody again.

Nothing can steady or sweeten that.

Losing Lorna feels like I've lost the last link to her.

Reading Alison's obituary was the punch I needed to pull myself together. I can't let the darkness take me. I need to think of the things not yet lost.

In the here and now, both Melody and Lorna are alive and healthy. They're lost from me but not from life. Not yet.

I don't know if the butterfly effect will stop their deaths but if I pickle myself into a coffin, how can I try and save either of them if these particular paths continue as they did the first time?

Melody would want me to save Lorna too.

I've managed five years here without Mel in my life and though I know they'll be long years, I can manage another nine. For Melody's sake and the future she deserves, I can do that.

Sunday 4th May 1997

Melody

Mum, Dad and Alice arrive in Richmond early. Normally, I get the train and Dad collects me at the station, but today we're taking Alice for her first visit to the palace (yay, just where I want to spend my day off).

Kirsty abandons her morning meditation to say hello. She's met Mum and Dad a couple of times now, and generously insisted they park their car here for the day rather than fight the other tourists for a decent parking spot at the palace.

"We were thinking we could take Molly with us," Mum says to her while Dad's unloading the car, and without any consultation with me. "If you don't already have plans, that is?"

Kirsty's face lights up. "Great idea. She'd love that, thanks. She's at her horse-riding lesson but when she gets back, I'll get Lisa to call Mel and meet up with you there."

Lisa's the new au pair. She's the third one they've employed since I moved in.

"I don't get a strong signal at the palace," I warn her.

Kirsty's not in the least perturbed. "I'm sure she'll find you."

For a woman so generous with her money and hospitality,

Kirsty's amazingly frugal when it comes to spending time with her daughter. Mick's even worse. He spends more nights at their Bayswater flat than the family home.

Dad's struggling to open Alice's buggy. Kirsty sidles up to him and casually palms something that looks like a business card into his hand.

"Found this in the study," she tells him.

He abandons the buggy and peers closely at it. I'm guessing he's forgotten his reading glasses. Again.

After further close scrutiny, a beam spreads over his face, and he tucks the business card carefully into his wallet.

"What's that?" I ask.

He taps his nose and wiggles his eyebrows.

Friday 11th July 1997

Alex

I turn into the cul de sac, the blood rushing in my ears drowning out The Prodigy's 'Breathe' on the radio.

Jimmy called me early this morning. He's been up all night. He could have just told me he had food poisoning without going into detail. Upshot is, he's in no state to see a potential new client and needs me to do the quote for him on my way to my own job.

It makes no difference who does the quoting or the designs or the work itself. We're as skilled as each other.

Work has been my unexpected saviour. It gives me a reason to get out of bed. It gives me purpose. I became a mosaic craftsman for no other reason than Jimmy offered me an apprenticeship when I left school. I hated school. When I left, the only thing I knew for certain was what I didn't want, and that was to work in an office. Jimmy was the same when he left school. He recognised in me a kindred spirit and gave me a chance without knowing if I had the aptitude or talent for it. That I did have the aptitude and talent came as a surprise to us both.

I get out of the van and, work bag in hand, stare at the front door.

The ripples of the butterfly effect are spreading. I created a garden mosaic for the couple whose house I'm visiting the first time round, but it happened seven or eight years from now and I didn't charge them for it. Well, you can't charge your in-laws can you? Not when it's a gift from yourself for their thirtieth wedding anniversary.

Roy opens the door. He's carrying Alice. To see the pair of them...

God, my heart swells like a balloon.

"Mr Aldridge?" I say politely.

Before he can reply, Alice holds her arms out to me, hands making grabbing motions, and squeals, "Al, Al!"

Stunned, I lock onto her happy blue eyes.

Roy tries to keep a firm grip on her with one arm while holding the other out to me. "Call me Roy. You must be Jimmy."

My throat's gone dry. I shake his hand, swallowing first to get the words out. "Apologies but Jimmy's ill. I'm Alex, his business partner."

"Pleased to meet you."

"Al! Al!"

Roy chucks her under the chin. "Clever girl!" Then, his attention back on me, wryly says, "Never one to be left out, this is Alice."

"Al!" Her squeal has become a scream. "Al! Al!"

Clearly bemused, Roy says, "Yes, Alice, we know your name." Then he looks back at me. "Come in. The boss has put the kettle on."

It's been quite a few years since I've had that feeling of walking into the past and, though I was expecting it, it's still strong enough to stun my vocal chords. I use the time spent removing my work boots to get a grip of myself.

This is the carpet that was laid the first time Mel brought me here. That's the wallpaper. The comfortable sofas. The round, rarely used walnut dining table in the corner of the living room. Over the next two decades, everything will be replaced. Apart from the photographs. Their frames will be changed, their positions moved, other pictures will be added to the clusters, but the faces currently beaming out will stay. Melody's first primary school picture, her hair in bunches, black curls sticking out in right-angles either side of her face. Her graduation picture.

I take this all in with a sweep of an eye as I follow Roy into the extended kitchen that's Patty's domain.

While Roy puts a wriggling, furious Alice into the highchair and tries to pacify her with a yogurt, Patty greets me with the friendly smile I remember so well. "Hi Jimmy, I'm Patty. Nice to meet you. Tea or coffee?"

"Tea please, and sorry to disappoint you but I'm Alex, Jimmy's business partner. Unfortunately he's ill so I'll be doing the design and quote if that's alright with you?"

"Ah, the nephew!" she says. "Is he okay?"

"Food poisoning."

"Poor thing. Milk and sugar?"

"Just a splash of milk, please."

"Al! Al!"

"Say Alice," Patty scolds, stressing the iss.

Alice flings her yogurt across the room. A globule lands on Roy's head. He's entirely unperturbed.

Once the mess has been cleaned up, Roy says, "Ready to see the bathroom?"

"Not the garden?" I ask, confused, which then makes Patty and Roy confused.

"No, it's the bathroom we want doing," Patty says. "We're having a new suite put in and have decided to go the whole hog with it."

"But I love the idea of getting the garden done too," Roy pipes up.

"Apologies," I say. "I must have misheard Jimmy." That's a lie. I stopped listening as soon as he gave me the surname. "He wasn't able to talk for long," I add, feeling the need to explain my lack of professionalism.

Roy snorts, and leans over to take a calmer Alice out of the highchair. "Not surprised. Remember when I had food poisoning, Pats? Dodgy prawn sandwich. Sick as a dog for days. I spent more time on the–"

"I'm sure Alex doesn't want to hear about that," she interrupts, giving me a conspiratorial wink.

Roy holds Alice to his chest. Her cheek rests on his shoulder. She looks sleepy. Ollie's kids were the same when they were toddlers. Full of all the energy in the world one minute, fast asleep the next.

At the top of the stairs, Roy says, "I'll put this one down for a nap and join you in a mo."

As he turns, Alice's eyes flutter open and fix on me. "Al, where Smelly?"

The hairs on the nape of my neck lift.

It *can't* be…?

Fearing my eyes are going to pop out, I watch as her heavy eyes close again. She sticks her thumb in her mouth. Roy disappears with her into Alice's bedroom.

I have no idea how I drag my legs to the bathroom.

Working on autopilot, I put my work bag on the closed toilet lid and pull out my notepad, pen and tape-measure.

"We want the mosaic to cover the whole wall," Patty tells me with a sweep of an arm, indicating the bath wall.

Roy joins us, clever eyes alive with interest and excitement, bushy eyebrows wiggling. "What have I missed?"

"Nothing," Patty tells him.

"Oh good. We want the bath wall done."

It's patently obvious neither of them heard what Alice said.

Did I mishear her?

I must have done.

It's being in this house. Melody's essence is everywhere.

I clear my throat. "Do you have a design in mind?"

Roy rubs his chin. "We're thinking of a water scene, aren't we, Pats?"

She nods.

"Saw the mosaic you did for that family in Richmond," Roy tells me. "Sure it was you, not Jimmy that did it, so this is a stroke of luck, him being ill... not for your uncle, obviously," he hastens to add. "Bloody fantastic, wasn't it Pats? That mosaic? It's what gave us the idea. Our other daughter lodges there and was raving about it – did you know we've got another daughter?"

I'm glad I can respond with a shake of my head. My vocal chords have become paralysed again.

"We couldn't wait to have a look. Blew us away. Couldn't believe it when we found out you were local to us. Thought we'd never be able to afford one for ourselves but we've come into a bit of money recently and just thought, 'why not?'"

A shadow crosses Patty's face. I know in an instant where the money has come from. Her mother.

For the first time it occurs to me that the butterfly's ripples might not always work against me.

Roy sees the shadow too and takes Patty's hand. It's not a showy gesture, just a sweet, simple unspoken sign to show he understood.

"Which family in Richmond?" I manage to ask. But I know.

Of course I know.

Roy scratches his head. "You know, I can't bloody remember. Bloody great father I am not remembering the name of my daughter's landlords. What's their name, Pats? I know she's Kirsty and he's Mick..."

I lean against the wall and focus on nothing more than keeping my legs upright.

"Their surname's Philpot," Patty supplies. "You did a mosaic of –"

"The Little Mermaid," I finish.

Sunday 3rd August 1997

Melody

The middle-aged man in the seat opposite me gets off at the stop before mine, leaving his copy of The News of the World on the table. As someone who loves salacious tittle tattle, I quickly swipe it for myself and get stuck in. I've only read the first three pages when the train stops at my station, so I take it with me.

Lorna's in the pick-up place. She was recently promoted and is now managing a branch of her bank in the city. It took her a week to get sick of the unreliable bus network between Brocklehurst and the city. Last week, almost exactly ten years after she passed her driving test and almost exactly ten years since she was last behind a wheel, she became the proud owner of a second-hand VW Polo.

She's so busy concentrating and I'm so busy cowering that we don't make any conversation until we get to her house.

It's not long until we're reclined on loungers in the garden sunbathing with a bottle of white wine. Both of us are determined to spend our first whole day together in months doing nothing but eat, drink and catch-up.

"What's the latest with Martin?" she asks, diving straight in.

"It's over."

She turns onto her side to face me and lowers her sunglasses. "Go on, what happened? Spill."

Lorna already knows I was ready to end things with him.

To be honest, I only started seeing him because I woke one morning a couple of months ago and realised I was twenty-two and hadn't had sex in over a year and that at the rate I was going, I was going to wake up one day a dried-up old spinster. My next visit home, Mum and I went for a girlie drink in the local pub and bumped into Martin, an old school mate of mine. Well, I say 'mate,' but only in the loosest terms. I always thought he was a bit of a twat. I'm sure he spends more time in front of a mirror than any girl ever does.

But people change and when he asked me on a date, my shrivelled vagina came to mind and I said yes. Shrivelled vagina notwithstanding, I must be growing up because I refused to have sex with him on the first date. For the first time in my semblance of an adult life, I insisted on taking it slowly. Only being able to see him twice a week – I'm only home from Richmond on Sundays and Mondays – helped with this. But I couldn't put it off forever and two weeks ago, I finally consented to going back to his house with him.

The sex lived up to all my low expectations. He left me cold.

God, what is *wrong* with me? Martin is good looking, has a great body (and doesn't he just know it), a vaguely reasonable sense of humour... On paper, he's everything a girl who's not too fussy could want.

Why am I such a Fussy Fanny? And why have I suddenly *got* such a fussy fanny?

I light us both a cigarette and pass Lorna's over. She already knows about the shit sex. "Dad invited him over for a barbecue last Sunday."

"No way?"

"Yes way. He bumped into him in the village shop that morning and asked him. You know what my dad's like."

She nods her sympathy.

I came home all prepared to tell Martin that we were over only to have the poor sod thinking we must be moving up a stage to be invited to the parents' house.

"Anyway, turns out that Dad inviting him over was the best thing he could have done."

"How?"

"Alice."

"What about her?"

"The little madam was horrible to him. Honestly, Lorn, I've never seen her behave that way. You know what she's like – loves everyone. Not Martin. I've no idea why but she disliked him from the word go. Every time he tried to engage with her, she told him to go away and called him a poo poo, which was funny but she didn't say it in a funny way. She really meant it. Then, when he tried to pick her up and cuddle her into submission, she bit his arm."

Baby teeth are *very* sharp.

Lorna's completely agog. "*No?*"

"He was not amused and called her a little bitch. He said it quietly but Mum and I both heard."

"Oops."

"Oops indeed. Mum went mad – we both did. It was the *way* he said it. You know? Not jokey or playful." I have a drink of my wine to calm the anger I can feel brewing back in me.

It was Martin's own bloody fault that Alice bit him. She only knows a few words and used them to make it very clear she didn't like him and didn't want him near her, but he wouldn't listen or leave her alone. Thought he could charm her into liking him, then when she reacted, swore at her. The bastard swore at a toddler he'd provoked.

"So you dumped him there and then?"

"Dad did it for me. When he realised what we were all arguing about, he told Martin to get out and never come back." My dad is so laid back he could be a mattress but threaten the females in his life and he turns into a rottweiler. "He stalked out looking all injured and hard-done-by."

"Oh, gawd, does that mean you haven't actually told him he's dumped?" Lorna says, alarmed. "He's not going to still be thinking–?"

"Chill," I interrupt. "I sent him a text. He didn't reply."

"What did you say?"

"That taking everything into consideration, I thought it best we go back to being just friends."

She gives me a stern looks. "You're useless."

"I nearly sent him one saying, 'In case you didn't get the message, we're over,' but deleted it for being too mean."

"Too mean would have been, 'In case you didn't get the message, you're a wanker and you're dumped.'"

"At least I made sure he got the message," I defend myself.

She grins. "You've definitely improved on the dumping score."

I grin back. "Thank you. Anyway, that's enough talk about Martin. I've got a date lined up with someone else for Wednesday."

"Already?" she squeals.

I snigger happily. I've a much better feeling about Chris than I ever had for Martin. Chris is sweet.

"Tell me everything!"

"His name's Chris and he's recently started work at the palace with the conservation team. He lives in Richmond and I met him last week when I was on my lunch break and we got talking. He's a Tudor buff like me. We've met up for lunch a couple of times since, and honestly, we have such a laugh."

"Age? Looks? Height? Marital status?"

"I don't know his age but I'd say around mid-to-late-twenties. Looks-wise... he looks a bit like a cuddly Mikey from The Goonies. Height-wise, a few inches taller than me."

"A short arse then."

"Hilarious." But not wrong. "I'm hoping his marital status is single or it means he's a complete douchebag."

"Who asked who out?"

"I asked him. Honestly, Lorn, he's so funny and sweet and... *nice*," I finish lamely but truthfully. Chris is nice and not the least bit predatory.

"About time you dated someone who was nice." She sits up and raises her glass to me. "To a successful date."

"Let's face it, it can't be worse than the dates I had with Martin." And every other bloke I've ever dated.

We finish our drinks then Lorna goes in to refill our glasses. I lay back down, close my eyes and enjoy the feel of the sun soaking into my skin.

This is the first time I've been able to properly sunbathe this summer. Obviously, I can't enjoy the sun when I'm at work and it's difficult to catch the sun when you're hanging out with a toddler on your days off. Mum's gone back to work part time on Mondays and Tuesdays, and I look after Alice on Mondays for her, so the only thing I tend to catch in the garden is the sand she flings everywhere. Tomorrow, though, Mum's taking the day off, so I can sleep in as long as I like and it won't matter if I have a fuzzy head.

How long does it take to refill two wine glasses? Lorna's been gone ages. Thinking I should check on her, I toodle into the house and find her in the kitchen standing over the table.

"You okay?" I ask.

She spins round. The newspaper I swiped from the train is open on the table.

"I wondered why you were taking so long." I step beside her to see what's got her so riveted. It's just all the stuff about Princess Di and her new beau, the Harrods owner's son. "Ha! You like salacious gossip as much as I do."

Her smile seems weak. Forced.

"What's wrong?"

She shakes her head. "Nothing."

"You're sure?"

She nods vigorously. Too vigorously. "Fancy some cheese on toast to go with the wine?"

Figuring she's embarrassed at being caught sucking up the tittle-tattle she normally despises, and with a stomach that's now growling in anticipation of food, I let it go. "Sure. Thanks."

"Thought we could get a Chinese for dinner," she says, riffling through the fridge. It's barer than I've ever known it. Lorna's stopped having lodgers.

"Sounds great," I reply.

While she gets grilling, I sip my wine and read all about the budding Di and Dodi romance. I wonder if Mum's heard about it yet and if she's thinking about Grandma Alison. Grandma Alison thought the sun shone out of Princess Di's arse while mum thinks she's an attention-seeking hussy. Whenever they got onto the subject of her (which was often), Dad would escape into his garage. When they started shouting at each other over whose opinion was the right opinion, I would join him. We'd wait half-an-hour then Dad would make me poke my head back in to see if a cease-fire had been declared. Invariably, I'd find them both tiddled and laughing about something else entirely.

Cheese on toast done, we go back in the garden and eat, laugh, and laze the day away.

Monday 4th August 1997

Melody

My bedside clock reads 10:36.

I roll onto my back, yawn, stretch, then smile. *Beautiful lie-in, oh how I've missed you.*

This is the longest I've stayed in bed since Easter.

Needing the toilet, I go straight to Mum and Dad's en suite. The Great Bathroom Renovation started two weeks ago and I'm banned from the family bathroom until it's complete. Dad's got it in his head that he wants to do a big 'reveal' a la Changing Rooms. So long as he hasn't got Laurence Llewelyn-Bowen in as designer for it, everything will be grand. Honestly, you can see the fear in the eyes of the couples who learn Laurence is being let loose in their home, ha ha.

Mum and Alice are in the living room watching Teletubbies. Poor Mum. I've no idea what it is about this programme but Alice ruddy loves it. Dad's recorded all the episodes for her. Sticking it on is a sure-fire way to cut a temper-tantrum off at its head.

Alice clambers off the sofa and toddles to me.

"Tea?" Mum asks.

"Please." I pick Alice up and sit on the sofa with her on my lap. She shoves her thumb straight into her mouth. "Are we still going shopping?"

"Yep. If we aim to leave in an hour we can have lunch while we're out."

"Sounds like a plan."

A few minutes later Mum's back carrying three cups of tea. She puts two on the windowsill above my head then carries the other upstairs.

"How are they getting on?" I ask when she comes back down.

She beams and plonks herself next to us. "It looks amazing."

"Going to tell me what they're doing that's got you and Dad so excited?"

"All I can tell you is that there's only one tradesman in now and that to call him a tradesman is to do him a disservice."

"What does that mean?"

"I could tell you, but then I'd have to kill you."

"Oh, please let me look," I beg. "I won't tell Dad."

"He'll know by your reaction if you've seen it before it's finished."

"What if I accidentally open the door?"

"I've asked him to keep it locked to stop any little accidents like that from happening."

I pretend to pout. "That is so mean."

Her eyes are sparkling. "Do you know what's even meaner?"

"What?"

"The tradesman currently locked in the bathroom is something of a hunk."

That piques my interest and I straighten.

"Al, Smelly," Alice pipes up.

"Al*ice*," Mum corrects, ruffling her curly mop while dropping a wink at me. "But seeing as you're banned from going in there until it's all done, you'll just have to take my word for it and I'll have to be the one to keep supplying him with cups of tea."

Alice twists around, taps my cheek for attention and leans her cherubic face right into mine. "*Al*."

I catch her podgy hands and look back at Mum. "That is so unfair."

She cackles wickedly and reaches for her tea. 'I know."

"You're married."

"Your dad would understand."

"God, you're gross."

"Al!" Alice bellows this so loudly my ears ring.

"Don't shout," I scold her.

"Al ba'oom!"

"Ah, you want to see the bathroom too?" I tickle her ribs. "I'm going to have a shower but when I get back down we'll gang up on Mummy and force her to let us see it, okay?"

The little ratbag kicks me with both feet. "Al, Smelly! Al!"

I kiss her furious red cheek. "Okay, *Al*. Happy now?"

She looks at me as if she's actually contemplating if she's happy with my answer. Honestly, this child is going to be trouble when she's older. While she's contemplating, I pass her back to Mum. "She's all yours."

Alex

I recognise the footsteps bounding up the stairs. It's a sound that envelopes me with bittersweet memories.

When you live with someone for a long period of time, their particular rhythms and quirks as they go about daily life are things that seep into you. Generally, you barely notice. As an example of what I mean, Melody has a particular way of eating apples. She always starts by taking the biggest chunk out of it that she can manage which she then follows with dozens and dozens of mouselike bites. It wasn't until Jimmy and I paired up on a particularly big job and he ate an apple during a break that I realised I could be blindfolded in a room full of apple-munchers and identify Melody by sound alone. And now I find it's the same with her footsteps.

Before the accident, she would bound up a set of stairs in her own particular joyful rhythm. After, her steps were softer and slower. Cautious.

My face can't work out if it wants to smile widely or crumple and cry to hear the joyful bounds I last heard decades ago.

A door closes.

I will my shaking hand to steady.

I started work for Roy and Patty last Tuesday. I've never had to concentrate so hard on a job in my life but I had those four days to settle myself and get my head in the work-game. I was making good, steady progress. I expected to complete the job without seeing her.

I sensed her presence the moment Patty opened the door this morning, before I tripped over the butterfly-painted Dr Martens.

Patty had rolled her eyes as she apologised about her grown-up daughter's inability to throw off all her adolescent habits. I had to bite my cheek to stop myself telling her some adolescent habits would be with Melody for life.

Since then, I've been trying my hardest to focus, but it's bloody hard when you've got both ears attuned to every sound outside the room you've been told to lock yourself in. And it's even harder when your ears are attuned to the sound of your own wife. Harder still when your wife not only doesn't know she's your wife but hates your guts.

It will scare the life out of her if she sees me.

Footsteps bound past the bathroom. Another door closes. On the other side of the wall I'm mosaicking, a shower kicks in.

My chest tightens then expands in a burst.

Closing my eyes, I press my cheek to the wall dividing us and spread my palm and fingers against it.

Come back to me, Mel. Forgive me.

Melody

When I was a teenager, it infuriated me that Mum and Dad had their own power shower in their en suite. Actually, it infuriated me that they had an en suite.

God, I was a selfish, *horrible* teenager. If I ever have kids, I just know they're going to be spawns of Satan as a means of payback.

I thought it grossly unfair that I only had a full-size family bathroom pretty much to myself, mostly because the shower in said bathroom is crap, essentially an attachment hooked on the wall connected to the main bath tap. A plastic sheet thing on a rail traversing the bath allegedly stops the water spraying everywhere, but as the spray is more like the trickle given when a dog's bladder is empty but he still wants to leave his mark, that plastic sheet thing has yet to be properly tested.

Funnily enough, it's only since living in a Richmond mansion that I can appreciate our crappy family bathroom shower. I sincerely hope they've kept it in The Great Bathroom Renovation, just to remind me how lucky and blessed my life has been.

I think of little Molly and I want to weep. She's being raised in a home the teenage me would have killed to live in but the people doing the raising are the hired help. The au pair does all the ferrying around: school runs, playdates, ballet lessons, horse-riding lessons. She also bathes her, puts her to bed and reads her a bedtime story five nights a week. I bathe her, put her to bed and read her bedtime story the other two nights.

I can't remember a single night of my childhood when my mum or dad didn't tuck me into bed, lay down next to me, and read me a bedtime story.

I really wish I'd appreciated them more when I was younger but I didn't. I took their love and constant presence for granted. They worked hard to provide for me but they were always there too. Unlike poor Molly, who eats her meals with whoever the current au pair is or with me, I ate all my meals at home at the kitchen table with both of my parents. Molly hardly knows her dad. Which is probably for the best because Mick's a twat. So great a twat is he that he's pushed Matt the Twat down into second place in the list of biggest twats. I hope Kirsty sees sense and divorces his twattish arse.

I wouldn't trade my childhood for Molly's, not in a million years.

As the spray of Mum and Dad's shower pours over me, a wave of something... longing...? I don't know what it is, but it rolls and writhes in my stomach and for reasons I don't understand, I press my cheek to the tiled wall and close my eyes.

For a few, brief seconds that somehow stretch, the rolling and writhing pitch into a sharp pain that brings stabbing tears to the back of my eyes.

Alex

There's a knock on the bathroom door and then Roy's voice calls through. "Only me!"

I grin at his terrible Harry Enfield impression and unlock it.

He hands me a cup of tea, beams, looks over his shoulder, then steps inside, hurriedly closing the door behind him. He looks at the wall I'm working on. His beam gets even wider. "This is looking fantastic. *Fantastic.*"

This is the kind of customer reaction I live for. With Roy, I get it every day. He likes nothing more than joining me when he finishes work and chatting until I finish for the day.

"Thank you. All being well, I should be done on Friday."

He rubs his hands in glee, keen eyes soaking in every detail. "Fantastic," he repeats under his breath before rubbing his hands again. "Just thought I'd let you know, Pats has done you a plate of shepherd's pie to take home."

The aroma of Patty's cooking has made my belly rumble this past hour. Melody inherited her culinary skills from her.

"That's really kind of her," I say. I've never had customers insist on feeding me as much as the Aldridge's do. If I didn't love them already, I'd have fallen in love with them on this job alone.

"The hours you work, feeding you's the least we can do. Anyway, I'll say *au revoir* now – my daughter needs a lift to the train station so I'd best get going before she gives me earache about missing her train."

He says it with such affection that I can't help but smile.

My worry about bumping into Melody was groundless. The females of the house have spent most of the day shopping. They returned an hour ago.

I long to see her, *ache* to, but the last thing she needs is to bump into the man she's convinced is a stalker in her home.

"I'll see you in the morning then," I say.

A strange, shifty expression flits across Roy's face. "I suppose you'll be needing to make a move soon too?"

Unsure what his expression or tone are getting at or implying – I've been here since eight a.m. – I cautiously answer with, "Once I've got this water lily finished." By then, Melody will be gone and the danger of her seeing me will have passed.

He nods sagely. "I suppose you've got a wife..." His eyes dip to my left hand. "...or girlfriend to get home to?"

"No."

"Get off. Good looking, talented bloke like you?"

Now I'm really bemused. "I'm single."

"Good." He nods vigorously before quickly correcting himself and shaking his head. "I mean, that's a shame." He scratches beneath his ear. "Have you met my daughter Melody?"

The penny drops and so does my stomach. In my daze I manage a truthful, "Not today."

Before he can respond, footsteps bound up the stairs, a hand raps vigorously on the bathroom door and a voice bellows, "Dad! We've got to go!"

Roy presses his back against the door to stop her barging in. "Coming, my angel." His eyes roll humorously and he puts a hand to his mouth and lowers his voice. "Shall I introduce you?"

"Dad!"

"Best you get her to the train station," I advise.

"*Dad*!"

"Coming!" he shouts back.

Footsteps stomp back down the stairs.

Roy opens the bathroom door. "Next time, eh?"

"Next time," I agree.

The next time she's home, it'll be finished.

Melody

Traffic's light, which is just as well as when we're a mile from the station I remember I've left my phone charging in the kitchen.

Dad takes my screech of, "I've left my phone behind!" with his usual affability.

"Can't you put your foot down?" I beg two minutes later. Dad takes prides in being a safe, considerate driver, which basically translates as he drives like an old granny on a Sunday.

"What for? You're going to miss your train."

"But I'd like to not miss the next one too. You wouldn't want me hanging around on the platform alone when it's dark would you?"

That does the trick. He ups the speed by five whole miles an hour.

Back home, he stays behind the wheel with the engine running while I jump out to get my phone. I throw the door open and am about to hurl myself through the living room door when a tall figure coming down the stairs stops me in my tracks.

He clocks me and stops mid-stride.

Oh my *heart*. It thumps like a wild animal throwing itself at the bars of the cage it's been trapped in.

"Are you off now, Alex–?" Mum, appearing through the

living room door, cuts herself off as she spots me. "What are you doing back?"

I blink hard and shake my head in an effort to clear its roaring. All I can manage is a croaking, "My phone."

She gives me the exasperated smile I haven't seen in years. "And after all the grief you gave your dad about being late?" Then she looks up at Alex, who's still frozen on the stairs. "All done for the day?"

His throat moves. He clears it. "Yes. All done."

"I'll get your dinner for you. Oh, and this is my daughter, Melody. Melody, this is Alex, he's doing the work in our bathroom." She disappears into the living room, reappearing a nano-second later to add, "Alex, do *not* tell her what you're doing."

And then I'm trapped in the small landing between the front door and the stairs with Alex Hammond, and no matter how hard I strain my vocal chords to speak... shout... *scream*... they refuse to obey.

He doesn't seem much more capable of speech than I am.

A blast of the car's horn cuts through the silence and then Mum reappears with a plate wrapped in foil in one hand and my phone and charger in the other.

Alex takes the last two steps and takes the plate from her with a murmured, "Thanks."

"Al!"

Mum reacts to Alice's entry into the tight confines of the hallway with a shocked, "How on earth did you escape your highchair, young lady?"

Alice ignores her, toddling to Alex and making grabby hands at him.

He puts his plate on the stairs and picks her up.

Secure in his arms, she looks at me and earnestly says, "Al, Smelly. Al."

I feel my eyes widen at the same moment the front door flies open and the handle slams into my side.

"Are you coming or what?" Dad demands, unaware he's just maimed me.

Utterly discombobulated (and discombobulated that discombobulated is a word that springs into my mind), I nod, give mum another kiss on the cheek, then, holding my breath so as not to breathe in any Alex Hammond smell, lean in to kiss Alice.

Alice grabs hold of one of my curls and yanks it. "Al, Smelly," she repeats.

I look up and my eyes lock onto the most gorgeous shade of green I've ever seen in my life.

How had I not noticed them before?

But I had, I remember. When I was sixteen. I dreamt of those green eyes every night for two years.

When I was sixteen, naïve and stupid.

Alice practically headbutts me. "Al!"

I force my attention back to her and force a smile to my face. "Yes, Alice," I croak. "That's Alex."

I'm getting back in the car when Mum shouts, "Oi, candyfloss brain."

I take my phone from her with an embarrassed, "Thank you."

Sunday 10th August 1997

Melody

I can't stop staring at the mosaic.

"Mel?"

I clear my throat before calling back. "I'm in the bathroom."

"Still?"

I look at my watch and experience a frisson of surprise. I've been in here for ten minutes.

My gaze is drawn again to the intricate work of art on our bathroom wall.

The one in Molly's bathroom of The Little Mermaid and Friends has a magical, childlike quality to it. This one evokes the same feeling of wonder but that's where the similarity ends.

Two small children sit with their heads bowed on what could be a riverbank or a large pond, surrounded by grasses and reeds and water flowers. Their legs dangle in the water up to their knees. A butterfly hovers over the shoulder of the older child.

Those children are me and Alice. You can just make out our ever-so-slightly distorted faces in the water's reflection. The black curly hair would give it away in any case.

It blows my mind that I'm looking at a mosaic.

And it makes my heart hammer and stutter to know it was Alex who created this.

Who would have imagined a man like him had the sensitivity to produce something as beautiful as this? Five-hundred years ago, Henry VIII would have paid a fortune to have something like this in one of his palaces.

There's a tap on the door and then Mum comes in. "They'll be here soon."

I nod. Aunty Allie, Uncle Stelios and Nikos are coming over so Dad can show the bathroom off.

I spot a pair of discarded red wellies virtually hidden behind some waterlilies.

"I can't stop staring at it either," Mum says. "Must have spent an hour in here yesterday."

"Alex did this?" I whisper.

Her gaze turns sharply to me. "You know him?"

"He's friends with Lorna." And once stalked me, I nearly add.

It was over a year ago and he's behaved impeccably since Lorna warned him off, but he still frightens me... or is it the way I react to him that frightens me? I honestly don't know, but my feelings for him are so... *violent*, especially when considering that Matt the Twat's stalking of me elicits only mild revulsion, some irritation and the occasional urge to kick him.

"You never said."

"I never had the chance."

"He didn't mention it either."

I feel her curiosity, and all I can answer with is a shrug. If I tell her now, over a year after it all happened, she'll be angry and upset that I didn't tell her before. Worse, it will taint the mosaic they've invested so much money and emotion in for them.

Dad, Alice in his arms, joins us.

"*There* you are," he says in his usual jovial fashion. And then his attention is captured too. Even Alice is quiet.

"Still can't get over this," Dad says, breaking the silence.

"After seeing little Molly's mosaic, I knew it would be good but I never expected it to be *this* good."

"Alex did Molly's mosaic too?" I ask, startled.

Dad looks at me as if I've asked the dumbest question in the history of dumb questions, and I remember something.

"That's what that business card with Kirsty was about?"

"For such a clever girl, you can't half be dim at catching on to things," he says indulgently, then his eyes gleam with excitement. "Can't wait to see Stelios's reaction – he'll be *green*."

The doorbell rings.

Somehow Dad manages to rub his hands without dropping Alice. "That'll be him, Pats!"

He dashes out of the bathroom like an eager schoolboy about to show off his football sticker collection to his best mate.

Saturday 30th August 1997

Alex

I knock on the front door. My lungs don't seem to want to take in air.

Roy doesn't leave me waiting long. He opens the door and greets me with that big smile of his, a smile that widens to his ears when I hand over a bottle of Italian red he's partial to.

"My favourite wine!" he exclaims, ushering me inside.

I follow him through the living room and the kitchen, trying my best to listen to his enthusiastic chatter over Rod Stewart blaring out of the speakers. In two decades time, Roy will download every Rod Stewart album in existence and play it on shuffle for a bit of variety.

When Roy called the other day to invite me over for a barbecue, my primary emotion was relief.

Melody can't have told her parents about me stalking her, not if they're inviting me to a social thing.

Does that mean she no longer hates me? Or is it that she doesn't want to spoil the mosaic for them? If I know my kind-hearted Melody, it'll be the latter, but I can't help the nugget of hope that her feelings towards me have softened.

BUTTERFLIES

She didn't look scared when she saw me on the stairs. Shocked, absolutely. And angry. But she had stared at me without the fear that had rung from her eyes outside the palace.

That fear still makes me feel sick to remember. I don't want to push my luck or make her uncomfortable in her own home but the invitation was for a Saturday. Melody works on Saturdays.

All those thoughts, along with the invitation being for the one particular Saturday I had been dreading spending alone, sped through my head in the brief pause before I accepted Roy's invitation.

There's a crowd of people crammed around the rectangular garden table. I recognise all the faces except for one, a chubby round-faced man of roughly my age.

Roy claps his hands together. "The guest of honour is here!"

Everyone stops chattering and turns to me, welcoming smiles spreading. I don't need to concentrate on the names being thrown at me. All these people, apart from chubby cheeks, were at my wedding exactly thirty years ago.

That's Roy's pencil-thin sister Debs and her boyfriend Jason, who, if I'm remembering rightly, she dumps one Christmas Day soon when he makes the mistake of thinking an iron is a suitable gift for the woman letting you live rent-free in her home. And that's Patty's sister Allie and brother-in-law Stelios, Roy's best mate. And that's Allie and Stelios's son Nikos, the same age as Melody and built like a brick shithouse – Nikos is the cousin who decided to practice rugby tackling on Melody when they were fourteen and almost knocked her out. And that's Bob, Roy's dad, deaf as a post and as eccentric as his son, fated to go to sleep one afternoon about five or six years from now watching Escape to the Country and not wake up.

Alice, playing on the lawn with Debs' young skinny daughter Charlotte, spots me and comes tearing over.

I scoop her up. She beams.

Patty gives a wry smile and shakes her head. "You must give

off some kind of pheromone that children love. Alice is obsessed with you. Everything lately has been, 'Al, Al, Al.'"

I smile in response and prod Alice's snub nose. She giggles.

I would love to ask Alice what she knows about me and how she knows it but it would be pointless. I already know the answer in my gut and it's an answer she couldn't give even if she wasn't a toddler and unable to string a full sentence together. It's some kind of imprint. A residue from my first life here, like pollen from a flower, has lodged in her. That's the conclusion I've come to anyway. I'm probably wrong but seeing as there's no one I can debate it with, as an answer it will have to do.

"Smelly!" Alice suddenly shouts. "Smelly! Al!"

I'm so busy rearing my face out of the reach of her arms and hands flapping about in excitement that it takes a beat to register who's just stepped into the garden from the kitchen.

Another beat passes. Blood rushes to my head.

She's here.

I hold my breath.

"Smelly!" Alice shouts again.

Melody walks towards me but her stare is fixed on Alice. The beats of my heart increase.

And then she's in front of me. She's wearing the Dr Martens she wore the day we met. She wore them too, when I spun her around the dancefloor on our wedding night.

"Al, Smelly," Alice tells her.

She doesn't look at me. "Yes, Alice, Alex is here."

This pleases Alice, who now holds her arms out for Melody to take her.

Melody steps closer. I lower myself a little to make the passing of the toddler easier.

Melody's hand brushes against my stomach as she grips Alice's waist. A lock of her hair brushes against my cheek. I catch the lightest waft of White Musk.

The second Alice is secure in her arms, she hurries away and squeezes onto the seat next to chubby cheeks.

"I hear you know my Melody," Roy says. He hands me a can of lager.

My Melody.

My heart beats even harder.

I look at her. Her body is twisted so I'm out of her line of sight.

My Melody.

Melody here, on our wedding day, when she should be working.

I would love to think this is fate and the butterfly effect finally working in my favour but I'm not a fool.

I manage a smile at the man who should be my father-in-law. "Through Lorna," I say.

"*Love* Lorna," Roy enthuses. "Great girl."

"Roy, something's burning," Debs shouts.

"Great." He rubs his hands together and indicates for me to follow him. "Means the barbecue's ready."

My stomach's too tight for food.

Roy helps me wedge myself into a chair between him and his dad. The sociable crowd surrounding me pepper me with questions about my work. I answer as best I can.

Melody is the only one to ignore me. She still hasn't looked at me or acknowledged my existence.

Coming here was a mistake.

I should have discouraged Roy from joining me for mammoth chats every afternoon I worked in that bathroom. I should have refused all the food Patty plied me with. Most of all, I should have kept Alice at a distance.

All those things I should have done to stop myself falling in love with Melody's family again.

I'll stay for an hour out of politeness and then I'll make my excuses and leave.

Chubby cheeks is trying to engage with Alice, who's sat on Melody's lap. I'm not sure if I'm imagining it but she looks like she's deliberately ignoring him just like her sister is deliberately ignoring me. He leans over her to whisper into Melody's ear. She grins and bends her head to whisper into Alice's ear.

"Who's that?" I ask Roy, nodding at chubby cheeks.

"Ah, that's Chris, Mel's new 'friend.'" He winks at me, the most unsubtle winks in the history of unsubtle winks. "She's moving into his 'spare room'..." He gives another unsubtle wink. "...tomorrow."

It's like I've just swallowed a bucket of ice. "He's her boyfriend?"

"No, they're just '*friends*.'" This time he gives air quotes to accompany the wink.

The ice has spread to every inch of my body but I've had enough practice of acting normal while coping with utter shit happening inside me to casually ask, "What's he like?"

His face screws up. "First time I've met him but have to admit, first impressions are good." Then he elbows me and says in a much brighter tone, "Don't imagine it'll last though."

"Why not?"

"He's too...." His face screws up again. "... short."

I laugh along with him.

Melody

Alice has condescended to answer one of Chris's questions. Success!

She made him work for it though. And refused to look at him while she answered. But at least she answered.

Poor Chris. He has the patience of a saint.

What is it with my little sister and men? I mean, she *hated* Martin (justifiably, although we didn't realise that to begin with) and, though she's marginally less hostile to Chris, she still spent the first three hours he was here, before the family arrived, refusing to engage with him on any level. How can a toddler be so practiced in the art of snubbing someone?

He's worn her down though. I knew he would. But, unlike twat-face Martin, he didn't force it. If she was to bite Chris he'd probably scold her gently then ruffle her hair to show there was no hard feelings (I wouldn't ruffle her hair if she bit me, that's for sure. I'd let Mum deal with the little madam).

Her attitude to both Martin and Chris makes her utter adoration of Alex even more inexplicable. Dad's smitten too. The way he's been banging on about him, I'm surprised he hasn't kidnapped him and tied him up in the attic as a pet. Despite all this, it came as a shock when Mum mentioned they'd invited him over when we arrived this morning. I've been as jumpy as a girl with ants in her knickers ever since.

I happened to be in the living room by the window when his van pulled up. For some reason even more inexplicable than Alice and Dad's adoration, I pegged it upstairs and locked myself in the bathroom. Just for a few minutes. Just to catch my breath. And check my makeup hadn't smudged. Just to brace myself for being in his orbit.

I sense him staring at me and move closer to Chris, doing my best not to stare back.

"Not hungry?" Chris asks, eying my still-full plate.

"Not really," I admit.

"Can I have your burger?"

"Haven't you already had one?"

I don't say this because I think he's being greedy but because Dad's barbecuing skills are legendary. For being crap. He takes such joy in it though, that no one has the heart to tell him barbecuing and cremating are two separate things.

"I quite like the flavour of burnt," Chris says.

"Then knock yourself out."

He happily munches my burger then hoovers up my leftover potato salad before leaning over the table and stabbing another sausage that's more charcoal than pork onto his plate.

As well as being a human vacuum cleaner, Chris is also incredibly sociable. Once we've finished eating and Dad pops into the house, he murmurs, "Just going to say hello to Mosaic Man," and is off to plonk himself in Dad's chair before I can stop him.

Aunt Debs jumps into Chris's freshly vacated seat and offers me a cigarette. I wait until Alice has toddled off to Mum... no, she's bypassed Mum and is aiming for Alex. Him and Chris are deep in conversation and I don't think he's noticed her but, without breaking eye-contact with Chris, he leans down and picks her up. He holds her really securely. Has he got children or younger siblings of his own? Those are practiced moves.

"Oh, you've got it bad." Aunt Debs' raspy voice breaks through.

"Sorry?" I ask.

She nods at Alex and Chris. "Your new boyfriend. You can't take your eyes off him."

My cheeks burn hotter than her lit cigarette for her to think I've been staring at Chris, hotter still with embarrassment and disquiet that I was actually staring at Alex, and I quickly light the cigarette she's given me and inhale furiously. "He's not my boyfriend."

She leans into me and conspiratorially whispers, "Of course he isn't."

I grit my teeth. "We're just friends."

Why am I so angry? Normally I would just slap her playfully on the arm and stick my tongue out at her.

I blame Alex 'Stalker' Hammond.

But is he really a stalker? That's a question that's been playing over and over in my mind since I learned he did Molly's bathroom mosaic. I know it was done when the Philpotts were in Tuscany last year. When I had my interview at the palace. Ergo, Alex really was working around the corner from the palace that day.

But even if I accept he was in Richmond for legitimate reasons, that still doesn't explain how he knew *I* was there. Lorna was adamant she hadn't even mentioned it in passing to him.

So how did he know?

And why do I care? Stalker or not, Alex Hammond scares me.

His hair has flopped onto his face. He brushes it away then, still holding Alice, reaches over for his drink. His throat is very strong...

What a *weird* thing to notice. Almost as weird as noticing that his hands are massive and that his fingers are long and attractive.

From nowhere, a fizzy warmth spreads between my legs and I swear all my organs swell and push together... and then he turns his face towards me and I only just have the wits to whip my gaze back to Aunt Debs before our eyes can connect.

I down the rest of my wine and pretend to listen to Aunt Debs waffling when the truth is her voice is muffled over the roar in my ears.

I'm reaching for the bottle when I hear Alex's deep voice call out a goodbye.

There's a wave of protest from the others but I don't look at him. I don't dare.

And then he's gone and I'm trembling so hard I knock my glass over.

Alex

For fucks sake. Of all the shitty wanking bollocky bollocks.

Chris is a nice bloke. A proper nice bloke. The kind of bloke who treats women well. The kind of bloke who takes the rubbish out without having to be asked, who provides painkillers for period pain without having to be asked, and who cleans up after himself. The kind of bloke who is an extra considerate driver when he has a female passenger in his car.

Worse, he's a history buff. Worse still, he's a history buff for the Tudor period.

I was never able to satisfy that side of Melody. I would visit historical sites with her and happily listen to her enthuse about the subject, but I was never able to join in. I could only listen. Chris can join in and feed her enthusiasm rather than just go along with it like I did.

He's perfect for her. Worse, it's blindingly obvious that he adores her.

He's exactly the kind of man she deserves.

The track pumping out of the kitchen as I leave the house changes. Now it's Rod singing 'The First Cut is The Deepest'.

Very fucking apt.

Sunday 31st August 1997

Alex

The doorbell rings, immediately followed by the loud pounding of fist against timber. It takes me approximately ten steps to reach the door from the kitchen. The bell's ringing again before I get to it.

It's Lorna.

Her eyes are red raw, face blotchy, her short brown hair looking as if she's spent the day pulling at it.

She chews at her bottom lip before asking, "Can I come in?" Her voice sounds as raw as her eyes.

A part of me has been expecting this visit.

When we reach the kitchen, I see her taking everything in and remember this is the first time she's been inside my house.

"This is really nice," she says.

"Thank you. Get you a drink?"

"Tea?"

She sits down while I fill the kettle.

"You hungry?" She's lost weight. Her face is gaunt.

She shakes her head. "Can I smoke?"

"Go ahead."

The scent of cigarette smoke wafts over to me.

Tea made, I carry the mugs over to the table, light my own cigarette – I think I'm now the only smoker on the planet actively willing the chemicals to do their worse – and study my oldest friend. Her hands are shaking.

When she meets my eye, tears leak from hers.

I lean over and put my hand on hers. "It's okay, Lorn," I tell her.

She wipes her eyes with the back of her wrist and jerks her head.

I squeeze her hand for luck and lean back in my chair. I can only imagine what's going through her mind.

A long period of silence passes before she raises her stare back to mine. "I didn't want to believe you," she whispers.

I smile without any malice. I could never feel anything but love for this woman. "I'd have been the same in your shoes."

"I still don't want to believe it. I don't see how..." She raises her shoulders in a helpless fashion then tilts her head back and mutters, "Fuck," under her breath. "Diana and the Harrods son. That's what you told me."

"Dodi Al Fayed."

"What?"

"His name. Diana's boyfriend. Dodi Al Fayed." When I told Lorna all those months ago that they would die, his name had escaped me. Re-watching the coverage this morning – and it's coverage that will last for months – reminded me how upsetting Melody found it that Dodi was relegated to a footnote in Princess Diana's death when he had lost his life too.

She cradles her mug, her gaze now distant. "I got up early. Made a cup of tea. Turned the radio on. They were playing that Puff Daddy song, that 'Missing You'. I was carrying the cup to the table when the song finished and the first thing the DJ said was that she was dead. The cup fell out of my hand." Her eyes are wide when she looks back at me. "All day I've been trying to wake up, but I'm not dreaming am I?"

"No. I'm sorry."

She wipes her freshly leaking eyes. "How?"

"How did I travel back in time thirty-three years?"

She nods.

"Long or short version?"

"The whole version."

I get up. "In that case, I'd better get Jim. You're going to need him."

Melody

I can't stop crying. This is just awful. Awful. Mum, no fan of Princess Di, can't stop crying either. Dad keeps roaming the house scratching his head. Even Alice is subdued but I suppose she's just picking up on the atmosphere. The only adult vaguely with it is Chris, but even he's lost his sparkle. He's the one who woke us with the news. He slept on the sofa and switched the telly on when he woke. Rushed up the stairs and banged on my bedroom door to tell me.

Our plan to drive back to Richmond today and move my stuff into Chris's has been put on the backburner. We're still in our pyjamas.

Mum blows her nose really loudly, sniffs, and says, "I need to sort Alice's dinner out. Anyone else hungry? There's leftovers from yesterday we can have."

I shrug. I don't know if I'm hungry or not.

Silly, isn't it? To cry and lose my appetite over the death of someone I've never met.

Chris moves his arm from around me. "Why don't I feed Alice while you sort the rest out?"

Mum blows her nose again. "Would you?"

"Course." He bows his head to Alice, who's snuggled on my lap. "Shall we get your dinner?"

She contemplates him for a moment then holds her arms out to him.

I notice the delight flash in his eyes at her acceptance.

He really is the sweetest, loveliest man.

I just wish I could fall in love with him and that he could fall in love with me.

And I wish I hadn't dreamed of Alex last night.

Alex

Lorna's drunk about a quarter of the bottle of Jim. For a lightweight like her, that's the equivalent of a full bottle but there's no sign that she's drunk. If anything, she looks stone cold sober.

Over the last few hours, I've told her everything, from the night Melody and I got together, to our marriage, to the hit and run and its aftermath, to the pandemic and shielding Melody through it, all the way through to Melody contracting something else entirely that's equally deadly to those with shit immune systems. I told her how I'd planned to kill myself and my meeting with the man in cemetery and the wine gum shaped pill he gave me. I told her about the five years spent waiting for Melody to blossom from a teenage girl into the woman I first fell in love with. And I told her how I'd screwed everything up by being a day too late.

Throughout it, she's remained silent, eyes fixed on me, her only movements her hand moving her glass to her mouth and her throat swallowing the alcohol.

"So the night we went to the Summer Gardens, you were supposed to be there?" she asks. Her voice is croaky after all that silence.

I nod.

"She wasn't assaulted that night, when you were there?"

I shake my head. "My screw-up over the day changed everything."

She stretches her legs out and blows a long puff of air. "Mate, I'm sorry."

"Yeah."

She finishes the drizzle of Jim left in her glass, pours us both another, and lights us both a cigarette. Then she laughs and her shoulders finally relax. "You're a twat."

My shoulders jerk in an effort to laugh with her. "Yeah."

"I'll explain it all to her."

"No."

"She'll listen to me."

"Doesn't mean she'll believe you."

"Al..."

"No." On this I am clear in my mind. "Mel's built herself a different life. Telling her would be like throwing a bomb in it. She's happy. Her boyfriend seems like one of the good guys –"

"You've met Chris?" she interrupts.

"Yesterday." I explain briefly about Roy and Patty's commission, how it came about and how it's turned into a friendship of sorts. A friendship I have to put the breaks on.

Melody didn't want me at her house. That was clear. She wants nothing to do with me.

"This all means something," Lorna says. "You have to tell her."

"No. Put yourself in Mel's shoes. How would you feel if she told you someone you think of as Stalky McStalkface is in fact your spouse who's travelled back thirty-three years into the past?"

She considers this then sniggers. "Stalky McStalkface?"

My laugh sounds more like a grunt. "One day you'll hear about Boaty McBoatface and it'll make sense." Years from now, a new research vessel will be launched, the public asked to suggest names for it and then vote on them. Boaty McBoatface wins by a country mile. If I'm remembering rightly, those in charge refuse to give the vessel that name but right up until her death, Melody and I never lost an opportunity to play on it. If I was in a bad mood she'd call me Grumpy McGrumpface. When she cheated at cards she was Cheaty McCheatface.

"You can't tell her, Lorn."

"How can I *not* tell her?"

"By putting her first. She's living the life she would have led if she'd never met me and she's happy living it. She's moving in with that Chris."

"Is she?" She almost spills Jim from her glass. "Since when?"

"They're moving her stuff from the chapel into his flat today."

"But they've only been together a few weeks. Last time I spoke to her, nothing had happened between them, not even a kiss."

"I can count on two hands the number of nights Melody and I spent apart after we got together and they were the night before our wedding and the nights she was in hospital after the hit and run."

I don't count the nights she spent in hospital before she died. When the ambulance drove her away from our home, it drove her away from this earth.

"When she falls in love, that's it," I continue. "She falls quickly and hard. If their feelings for each other are as strong as ours were, I've got no chance. She's his now. And even if you're right and there's nothing sexual between them, it doesn't change the fact that she doesn't want me anywhere near her. If you'd seen her at the barbecue, you'd know what I mean. I might have been a ghost as far as she was concerned."

"Shit." She bows her head. "How can you be so calm about it?"

"The only thing that's stopped me going out of my mind today is you."

"Me?"

"I've spent the whole day hoping you would come. If you hadn't, I would have written a letter explaining everything to you.

Nothing's been easy since I came back but this is just..." I shake my head, unable to think of a word to describe the agony ripping me. "Mel's my world but I'm not hers, and I can't do this anymore."

Her head shoots back up. "What do you mean?"

"I need to get out of Brocklehurst. Get out of England."

Her eyes close. "For a minute I thought you meant something else."

"No." I am emphatic. I take her hand and wait until she's looking at me. "I wanted to kill myself when she died. I've thought about ending things a few times since I've been back but..." I take a deep breath. My next words might one day make all the difference. "When someone takes their own life, the people they leave behind, the people who loved them, are never the same. It rips them apart. They don't just suffer grief but guilt too. It haunts them. There are too many questions that can never be answered to give them peace."

If I choose to leave this life once I've stopped Lorna doing the unthinkable and prevented Melody's hit and run, I'll make damn sure it looks like an accident.

I *hate* the selfish bastard raw grief turned me into. I cannot believe I was prepared to put the people who love me through the same pain and turmoil Lorna's death put us all through.

Melody would never have forgiven me.

"Who are you talking about?" Lorna whispers.

"I'm not saying. My screw-up has changed so many things that I'm hoping it will change that too, but I'll still do everything I can to stop it happening. Just in case. But that's in the future. I'm going to speak to Jimmy tomorrow and tell him I'm quitting, work out what to do about the business and our outstanding contracts, and then once things are sorted, I'm going to get myself on the first available flight to Australia."

Her face is stricken. "You're going to *Australia*?"

"Yes." I have enough in the bank to be welcomed there with open arms.

I spent five years building a fortune for when Melody and I restarted our lives together. I dreamed of us travelling the world, going anywhere we fancied by whatever means we wanted.

If I can't enjoy that money with Mel, then at least I can use it to escape and give her the peace of mind and space she needs from me until it's time for me to come back and stop her and Lorna taking their fateful paths.

I'll see if Dad wants to come with me. I can make sure he comes back in time to meet Kathy. Or maybe he'll meet someone else. I have no control of the butterfly effect anymore.

I was a fool to ever think I did.

Sunday 14th September 1997

Melody

My second experience of being a passenger with Lorna as my taxi-driver is no less terrifying than the first. I've never known anyone drive with white knuckles, their back hunched over the steering wheel and their face practically touching the windscreen. I dread to think how many more near-misses there would be if she wasn't concentrating so hard. Still, we arrive in Brocklehurst with only severe palpitations so I'll take that as a win.

I dump my overnight bag at the bottom of the stairs and soon we're snuggled up at opposite ends of her new sofa, sipping wine and eating our weight in Wotsits.

"So what's new?" I ask.

She shrugs. "Not much. Same shit and all that."

"You've seemed really busy."

Lorna and I have hardly spoken in the last couple of weeks. I was starting to worry I'd done something to upset her – she seemed off or distracted every time I called her and always in a rush to get off the phone – but when I suggested coming to hers today and sleeping over, she sounded genuinely happy. I was so relieved that she wasn't pissed off with me that when she offered to collect me from the train station, I didn't have the heart to say I'd rather take my chances hitch-hiking.

"I've had a lot of things on my mind," she says.

"Like what?"

Her eyes hold mine. There's an intensity in them that has anticipation rising in me, a certainty she's about to reveal something important. Hopefully something juicy.

She looks away and disappoints me by answering, "Just work stuff. I'm applying for another promotion. Lots of swotting to do before the interview."

It sounds plausible. "Are you sure that's all it is? I was worried I'd done something to upset you."

A pained expression crosses her face and she pats my leg. "Not you, lovely. I'm sorry. It wasn't anything personal. The promotion's a lot more money but a lot more responsibility too."

"Will you have to work more hours?"

"Probably."

"Lorn, how are you ever going to find a nice man if you're always working? At least when you worked at The Thief you had the opportunity to meet people."

"Yeah, but those people were twats."

I try not to laugh as I've just taken a sip of my wine but it comes out anyway and chardonnay spurts out of my mouth and nose with it.

Lorna's lips twitch and in moments she's laughing too, and I'm so relieved I was imagining her distance with me – well, imagining that it was personal towards me – that I stretch my legs out over her lap the way I used to do when we lived together. My hogging of the sofa never failed to do her head in.

She slaps my feet with another laugh then relaxes. "How are things working out with Chris? Anything happened yet?"

"No. And it's not going to."

"Why not? Did you decide to give Chipolata Mick a try after all?"

"Very bloody funny."

I knew I shouldn't have told her how Mick 'accidentally' dropped his towel in front of me. It was like being flashed by a chipolata nestled in a pair of oversized brussels sprouts.

I don't need to fill Lorna in on how, between Mick's creepiness and both his and Kirsty's time-neglect of their daughter, I'd reached the end of my tether of living with them. Not just that, but I'd had enough of being a lodger and feeling as if I needed to confine myself to my bedroom (when I wasn't babysitting, of course. Those two nights of contractual babysitting duties were rigorously enforced, even if they had no plans).

I don't need to fill her in because we've already talked about it, just as I confided in Chris about it too. His subsequent offer for me to have his spare room and be his flat mate made me think that fate had decided to bestow kindness to me. The two weeks I've spent living with him has only reinforced that thought. We've already started arguing over what to watch on the telly.

Lorna's holding her glass to her mouth, her only movement the rubbing of the glass's rim over her lips. She's staring at me with the strangest expression. "So you don't think you and Chris will ever get together?"

I take her glass and top us both up. Then I hand hers back, look her in the eye and say, "Chris is gay."

She has the sudden stillness of a possum. Her eyes widen in a good impression of an owl. It takes a long time for her to respond. "Say that again?"

"He's gay. He told me on our second date. We were talking about exes and he just came out with it."

She looks confused. "So why did he go on a date with you?"

"Because he likes me. I told you, we really hit off, just like you and I did when we met. He wanted to be my friend."

"And it doesn't bother you?"

"Not in the slightest. I knew by the end of our first date that I didn't fancy him. If anything, it was a relief." Alex's gorgeous face floats into my mind again. I push it away. Again.

"I don't mean about that – I mean it doesn't bother you that he's..." She hesitates. "A gay?"

The reason I've waited to tell Lorna in person about Chris is because I have no idea what Lorna's thoughts are on homosexuality. I know her dad's homophobic. When I was living with her, he came over to fix the washing machine and a song by a gay singer came on the radio. Her dad called him names I knew were cruel when I was in primary school. I remember she looked uncomfortable about it but she didn't challenge him or anything, and after he'd gone we both seemed to make a point of not talking about it, so I really don't know if she's prejudiced too. I hope not. I really hope not.

"Of course it doesn't bother me." I can't help the confrontational edge in my voice. "Why should it?"

"It would bother a lot of people around here."

"That's because there's a lot of twats around here."

Her lips pull into something resembling a smile.

"Chris is the nicest man I've ever met and I adore him beyond words. Please don't judge him. He can't help how he's wired."

She breathes in deeply.

I watch her closely. Am I imagining that she looks like she's about to cry?

But then the moment passes and she attempts another smile. "I'm sorry. I wasn't judging him. You just took me by surprise. You totally deserve a flatmate you're happy and comfortable with and from what Alex told me, he sounds like a great bloke and –"

She cuts herself off. Eyes that so recently resembled owls squeeze themselves shut. "Sorry," she mutters. "I know you don't like me talking about him."

My heart's pumping but I manage to keep a grip of my voice. "He's been your friend longer than I have. Don't feel you have to check what you say around me."

"I don't... Okay, when it comes to Alex, I do."

"Then stop it. Please. I'm assuming you know of the work he's done for my parents?"

She nods.

"And obviously you know about the barbecue if he's spoken to you about Chris, so as you've probably gathered, my parents, Dad especially, thinks the sun shines out of his derriere. He can't stop banging on about him. Alice thinks he's the second coming or something, Chris spoke to him for five minutes and said he wished Alex was gay, and now I don't know if I've got him all wrong. Have I, Lorn? Have I got him wrong?"

My words have come out in a jumble, thoughts that have been swirling in whispers in my head since the barbecue unravelling in a splurge.

Lorna's lips draw together. She jerks a nod. "He can be a twat but he's one of the good guys. He never meant to frighten you. He was just..." She expels a long breath. "Happy to see you again."

I tip the last of my wine into my mouth. It takes effort to swallow it. "Did you know he did Molly's bathroom in Richmond too?"

She hesitates before giving another nod. "He told me the other week. The day Diana died."

A tear falls down her cheek.

Alarmed, I squeeze her hand. "What's wrong?"

The single tears turns into a waterfall.

Don't tell me she's still upset about Princess Diana? I mean, yes, I cried, but only on the day itself. And the day of the funeral. But seeing as everyone else cried, I'm not going to beat myself up about it. But to still be upset over it? Isn't that a bit excessive?

Once the waterfall runs empty, she scrambles in her pocket for a scrappy bit of tissue and honks her nose into it. After a couple of deep breaths to compose herself, she draws her knees to her chest. "He's moving to Australia."

The rush of blood to my head dizzies me. I have to blink to clear it and clear my throat to say, "Alex is?"

She dabs at her eyes with the snotty tissue and nods.

"When?"

"In a couple of weeks."

The rushing of blood turns into a roar.

"I'm sorry," I whisper.

"So am I." Lorna grimaces and pats my foot. "We need more wine. Fancy pizza?"

I will not cry.

There is no reason for me to *want* to cry. I should be celebrating!

"Is the Pope a Catholic?"

Tuesday 14th October 1997

Melody

My alarm goes off. I slap the snooze button without opening my eyes and snuggle deeper into my duvet.

Instead of going back to sleep like I usually do (I hit the snooze button on average four times before dragging myself out of bed), my brain has decided to go straight into wake mode. Very strange.

Rain is pelting against my window. Goody. Nothing I love more than a twenty-minute walk in the rain. Chris has the day off. Chris loves his lay ins as much as I do and has threatened me with a week of washing up if I wake him. Chris suggested I get a bicycle for his days off. Chris can ram it. Bicycles are evil. They make your thighs hurt more than walking does. Apparently this side-effect dies away once you've built your thigh muscles up. I will take his word for it.

The second time the alarm goes, I turn it off and sit up.

There's a horrible weighty feeling in my chest. It reminds me of the time I forged a letter from Mum to get out of games at school. My forgery skills were completely amateur and Mrs Pepper hauled me into her office to confront me. After the rollicking of all rollickings, she left me hanging over whether she was going to tell Mum. For days I felt sick and weighty with dread. At my next PE lesson, Mrs Pepper pulled me aside and said she'd decided, on this occasion, not to involve my parents, "in the mattery of your forgery." I could have kissed her! Believe me, any career aspirations as a criminal forger I might have had were killed on the spot.

There was a reason for that weighty dread when I was fourteen, but I haven't a clue why I'm feeling something similar to it now. Or why I'm crying.

Alex

The stewardesses finish their safety demonstration and disappear behind the curtains to take their seats.

I stare out of the window. The rain is tipping down. Very fitting.

Once we're in the air, I stare intently at the diminishing roads and streets below us.

I couldn't resist driving through Richmond on my way to the airport. Ollie, who is driving my car back, thought I'd lost my marbles. I lied and said I'd taken a wrong turn. Pathetic, I know, but I kept my eyes peeled to every figure walking the rain-lashed streets, even though I knew Melody would be burrowed under her duvet, probably fighting her alarm clock.

Is that Richmond disappearing below me?

And then we're in the clouds, and Melody and England are gone.

Part Three

Friday 5th April 2002

Alex

Walking the streets of Brocklehurst after four and a half years away is as surreal a feeling as I have known since I awoke over three decades in the past.

It was easy to assimilate in Australia, and Sydney is a great city for a young (on the outside), single man with cash to burn. It has a fantastic climate, beaches on the doorstep and a rhythm very different to the one I've spent both my lives in. It was everything I hoped it would be.

The bustle of Watling Street is a different kind of bustle to Sydney. The air feels different. It smells different too.

I've missed it a lot.

Hardly anything has changed but the few new shopfronts are enough for me to recognise the onset of changes coming to the town. Over the next two decades, Brocklehurst will become gentrified. Most of the shops and many of the pubs will be replaced with coffee shops and restaurants and niche boutiques. The grocer and one of the butchers have already gone, unable to compete with the new Waitrose that's opened.

The jeweller's that's been here all my life is still trading. It's

Dad's sixtieth tomorrow and the expensive garden statue I bought him on a trip to Japan didn't survive the flight home. I can't think of anything else to get him so have decided on a new watch.

The shopfront isn't promising. It doesn't look as if it's been cleaned since I left. Expecting the worst, I go in, and so am pleasantly surprised when the owner, who's at least ninety, brings out a tray of Rolexes for me.

Purchase made, I leave the shop and head towards the newsagent for a birthday card. As I'm passing one of the town's many estate agents, one of the properties advertised on the glass front stops me in my tracks.

I look closely at it. My heart is pounding.

It's the house on Juniper Crescent that Melody and I spent the majority of our married life in.

Saturday 6th April 2002

Melody

Juniper Crescent is a pretty little curved street in a quiet part of Brocklehurst. Number twenty-eight, which Alice and I are standing at the front gate of, is a small semi-detached house with a postage stamp of overgrown grass and weeds as a front garden. The door and the windowsills all look in need of a good lick of paint. Yet, despite this inauspicious start, my heart is racing.

Holding firmly to Alice's hand, I open the gate, which almost comes off its hinges, and knock on the door.

The estate agent invites us inside. Voices echo from within. I've barely wiped my boots and I'm already wishing I'd brought a stink-bomb to scare off the other viewers.

I guess I should back up a bit and explain that when I booked this week's holiday from work, it was to look after Alice so Mum and Dad could celebrate their wedding anniversary sightseeing *sans* kidlets in Florence. It was not with the intention of doing any house-hunting.

I haven't actually *done* any house-hunting, it's just that I was flicking through the free local paper the other night, idly looking in the property section, and for some reason this house caught my eye. A few pages on in the job section, I noticed Brocklehurst Manor advertising for a curator. I've never even heard of Brocklehurst Manor.

So here I am, viewing a house I'm not going to buy, and with a job interview lined up for Monday for a job I'm not going to take.

I would have asked Lorna to come with us today but she's buggered off on holiday (I know! Lorna's taken a holiday!) with her work friend Carrie to one of the Greek islands. No idea why she'd want to go on holiday this early in the season, but hey ho. A sun tan isn't everything. Quite frankly, I hope it rains. That'll teach her not to invite me along, ha ha.

Alice and I drift through the small living room and into the cosy kitchen. I peer out of the window into the much more generously sized overgrown back garden, and can't help wishing I'd saved more of my money over the years. What am I saying, wish I'd saved *more*? Wish I'd saved *any*! My savings are zero.

I can't afford to buy a house. I'm happy living in Richmond. I've got a great job, a fantastic flatmate and a heap of good friends there. Life is good. There's no reason for me to want to change any of it.

But this garden has the potential to be something beautiful. The whole house has the potential to be something special.

I must not think like this! And I must not think venomous thoughts at whoever's now knocking on the front door. Stupid open viewings.

At the top of the stairs is a boxroom that isn't big enough to swing a cat. Next to it is a bathroom with the same delightful avocado coloured bath, sink and toilet that Grandma Alison had when I was little. Next to the bathroom is another bedroom, not much bigger than the boxroom but at least big enough to swing a cat; two at a stretch. The third and final bedroom is much bigger, and when I walk into it I'm filled with such a powerful sense of déjà vu that my feet root to the floor.

Aware of people behind me, I pull myself together and head

to the window. As I take in the new perspective of the back garden, that déjà vu feeling hits me again and for a moment all I can see is this very same garden filled with giant sunflowers and other colourful flowers whose names I don't have a clue of. This is very strange considering I've never gardened in my life, nor had any inclination to.

Alice suddenly rips her hand from mine and screams, "Alex!"

I whip around to find her throwing herself at the legs of Alex Hammond.

Alex

I thought I'd hallucinated her.

I was convinced the memories flashing like a reel of all the years we spent under this roof, starting from the moment I touched that front gate, had conjured her up like a dessert mirage.

But it is her.

Alice holds my legs tightly, which is just as well as they've weakened so much they need all the support they can get. She beams up at me flashing her tiny white teeth.

"Hello, Alice," I manage to say, grateful for the moment addressing her gives me to compose myself before I have to acknowledge Melody.

Someone's trying to get into the room behind me – I wonder if they and the others here were the same viewers we bid against the first time around – so I walk to Mel with Alice hanging to my legs like a limpet.

She's wearing clothes I don't recognise: a short denim skirt over thick black tights, a black top and an oversized chunky maroon cardigan. I remember when her old chunky black cardigan finally gave up the ghost. We shopped for hours looking for a suitable replacement. She settled on another black one then.

Alice pipes up first, gleefully saying, "Look, Smelly, it's Alex!"

"I can see that," she says lightly. Then the almost black eyes make contact with mine.

There's apprehension in her stare but, for the first time since that day outside Hampton Court Palace, no fear, anger or hostility.

"I can't believe she remembers you. How long's it been?"

"Coming up to five years." Four years and eight months since we last saw each other.

It feels ten times that.

"I knew she was a child genius." Her lips tug into a smile that lands as a punch in my chest. "So how are you? I hear you're living in Australia."

She's making conversation with me?

I have no idea how I manage to make my voice conversational too.

"Yep, living the beach bum life – I run a bar near Sydney Harbour." I bought it once all the legalities of living in Australia were taken care of. I figured surrounding myself with people who want to have a good time would stave of my loneliness and help stave off the darkness. For the most part, it worked. For the most part.

"You're not doing your mosaics anymore?"

"Not that much of a call for it out there," I lie. I wouldn't know. I didn't try. I moved to Australia partly to find a way of living without her. Creating mosaics would have suffused me in too many memories.

"That's a real shame."

She means it.

My heart has swollen so hard it's pushing into my ribs.

"How about you?" I ask. "How have you been?"

"Good. All good." Her forehead furrows. It's a furrow that over the next two decades will turn into a groove to match the laughter-lines that will imbed around her eyes. "How come you're viewing this place?"

"Curiosity. I'm only home for my dad's birthday. It's his sixtieth. Heard there was an open-viewing and thought I'd have a look. I used to know a couple who lived here."

"You're not planning on moving back?"

"Not yet. One day, though."

She nods slowly then gives another smile. It's not the beaming Melody smile I remember so vividly, but it's genuine and it tightens my chest. "Lorna will be pleased. She misses you." She looks down at Alice, who's listening intently to our conversation, then back to me. "So the couple you know who lived here…"

My chest is so tight it's hurting to breathe. "That was a long time ago."

"Were they happy here?"

I ram my hand in my jacket pocket to stop it reaching for a curl. "Very."

I shuffle aside to give the estate agent space to pass us. He's showing the single man the built-in wardrobes that sit either side of the bed. Melody pleaded with me until I gave in and painted them a bright yellow.

The memories are flooding me now. The urge to touch her is becoming unbearable.

It didn't cross my mind that I would see her during my short visit back, never mind bump into her in our marital home.

It's overwhelming. The compulsion to entwine a curl around my finger is growing by the second.

I need to leave before I do something stupid.

"I have to go," I tell her.

I know the disappointment flashing in her eyes is wishful thinking on my part.

"We're having a birthday party for Dad tonight and I need to sort myself out for it," I explain. "Was good to see you."

"And you."

Does she mean that? Or is she just saying it to be polite? My senses are too overloaded for me to guess.

"Good luck with the house."

She pulls a face. "Bidding against this lot? Fat chance, not with what I can afford."

"Nothing ventured, nothing gained." I force my voice to remain neutral. "This house was made for you."

Her eyes widen.

I hold Alice by the waist and lift her so her legs are dangling and her face is level with mine, and plant a great big kiss on her gleeful cheek.

I flip my hand as a final goodbye and leave the room. I don't look back. I keep a steady pace until I reach the nearest newsagent and buy my first packet of cigarettes in four years.

Melody

"Why has Alex gone?" Alice asks.

"He needs to get ready for his dad's birthday party."

"Can we go?"

"We're not invited."

"Alex will invite you if you ask him."

I smile at my earnest little sister. I can't believe she recognised him. Last time she saw him, she was a toddler, not even two-years-old. "Maybe. But it's rude to invite yourself to a party, so you and I will stick to our date of *The Little Mermaid* and all the popcorn we can eat."

Alice is obsessed with *The Little Mermaid*. Her favourite items of clothing are her Ariel nightdress and Ariel knickers with the individual days of the week on. Her entire bedroom from wallpaper to curtains is *The Little Mermaid*. Every time I go in her bedroom (which used to be mine – we swapped a few years back so she could have the bigger room), my mind automatically turns to Alex and *The Little Mermaid* mosaic he created for Molly.

Every time I go in our family bathroom, the mosaic he created for us reminds me of him too.

My thoughts aren't any safer from him in Richmond. Every time I pass the pillars with the lion statues on them, I think of him. I pass those pillars at least twice a day, five days a week.

I haven't seen Alex in nearly five years but I've thought of him nearly every day.

Scrap the nearly.

I've dreamed of him too. Don't get me wrong, it's not a nightly thing or anything (that really would be worrying), has happened only a handful of times or so since he moved to Australia, but they're crazy dreams. Crazy dreams where I'm chasing him down a street screaming his name but he can't hear me. They stay with me for days.

They're unsettling.

What's more unsettling is the disappointment that slapped me when he had to go. Most unsettling still is that I'm feeling something like I did when my cousin Nikos rugby tackled me when we were kids and sent me flying. Winded.

Alex

Ollie hands me a beer.

"I need to ask you a favour," I shout over the music.

"Oh?"

"It involves cash and is probably illegal."

His eyebrows rise in interest. "Go on."

I explain what I need him to do. I'm flying back to Sydney on Monday and can't do the logistics myself.

When I finish and we've got fresh pints in hand, he says, "All sounds a bit B-List Movie, mate."

"Does that mean you'll do it?"

"Course. Bit of excitement isn't it?"

When Ollie sussed I had a knack of selecting the best fledging companies to invest in (mine and Dad's increased riches helped convince him that I wasn't full of bullshit), he decided to have a piece of the action. He quit his job last year and now spends his time working on his golf handicap rather than in an office. He gets bored.

"There is that," I agree.

"What if I get caught?"

"Don't get caught."

"*Is* it illegal?"

"Only if you get caught."

He looks me up and down and grins. "When you move back, we should set up business together."

"What you thinking?" I ask. "Something along the line of The Krays?"

He cracks up. "I can just imagine it. The Hammond Brothers. Who will we demand protection money from? The WI?"

"The darts club? And what about the am-dram group?"

"Perfect. Any idea when you think you'll be home for good? Just so I know when to perfect my knuckle-dusting and Chelsea smiles skills for."

"Next year."

His smile makes me laugh. Who'd have thought moving to the other side of the world would bring me and Ollie closer? Not me, that's for sure. Never thought I'd miss the arsy twat or him me, but there you go.

I will keep to my original plan but, bloody hell, after seeing Melody today, getting back on a plane and flying to the other side of the world will do me.

What were the chances she would be there, in *our* house? She's lived and worked in Richmond for five years and from everything Lorna's told me in our frequent chats, they've been happy years for her.

But she was there, in the house we made into a home, and the more I think about it, the more I think that fate might – just might – not be done with us yet.

I will not be the King of Wishful Thinking and read more into Mel's body-language than was there, but she wasn't unhappy to see me. For sure, she was apprehensive, but she was friendly. Far friendlier than I would have dared dream.

For someone determined not to be The King of Wishful Thinking, I'm doing a damned good impression of one.

One step at a time, and if I end up stuck on the first step of distant amiability with her, then I will take it. It's a whole load better than fear and hostility.

A hand slaps each of our backs. Ollie and I rock forward, spilling beer over our hands.

"What are you two up to?" Dad asks, speaking as if we're still good-for-nothing teenagers.

Ollie winks at me. "Alex is moving back home next year."

Dad's mouth opens in his best goldfish impression, and then he does something he hasn't done since I was a child. He embraces me.

"Best birthday present I could have asked for," he says gruffly, and slaps my back again.

The music changes to the B52's 'Love shack'. One of Melody's many favourite songs. And a favourite of Gloria's, who dashes to Dad's side and grabs his hand.

"Come and dance with me."

"I don't dance."

"You do now."

He pretends to look disgruntled but willingly follows Gloria onto the dancefloor. Dancing near them is Kathy. I wonder if she ever looks at Dad and feels a pang of anything?

The father who mourned my mum the first time around is different in this life. I often wonder if it's because they packed so much in during the time she had left this time round that he had few of the haunting regrets of the first time, enabling him to move on with his life quicker than he could before. Before, it took six years for him to even contemplate going on a date. This time, it took him four. That date was with Gloria, the bar manager of the golf club him and Ollie are members of. They're still together, although there's been no talk of marriage like there had been at this stage with Kathy.

The only relationship that formed after my dash through time and has worked out how it did the first time amongst my family and friends, is Ollie and Amber's. They met almost a year after they met the first time but are as happy as they were in their first incarnation. I'm glad for them. And relieved. Very relieved.

It's good to know all my fuckups haven't fucked up everything.

Sunday 7th April 2002

Melody

If there's anyone in the world who can cook a roast beef dinner better than my mum then I'm an aardvark. Today, for some stupid reason I can't begin to fathom, I'm too antsy to enjoy it. Her Yorkshire puddings taste like cardboard on my tongue.

I force it all down, then eat my share of the lemon-curd pavlova she's whipped up.

Once the clean-up's done, I'm about to plonk myself on the sofa next to Alice for a snooze in front of the telly, as per the Aldridge family tradition that's held us in good stead for twenty-seven years, when Dad clears his throat and beckons me back into the kitchen.

Seeing me do an about-turn, Alice slides off the sofa and follows.

"Do you want some crisps, Alice?" Mum asks. She holds up a packet of Alice's strictly rationed favourites.

"Yes!"

"Yes...?"

"Please?"

"Good girl." Mum opens the packet but before Alice can take it, tells her, "You have to eat them in the living room."

Any other child would snatch and run. Not Alice. Her little eyes narrow in suspicion. She knows when she's being got rid of.

Then Dad says the magic words, "You can watch *The Little Mermaid*," and, crisps in hand, she's off like a rocket.

Dad rubs his hands. "Right, we've only got a couple of minutes before she holds us hostage for more food, so let's make this quick. When your Grandma Alison died, we put a share of the money we inherited aside for you and your sister."

"We want you to use your share as a deposit for a house," Mum says.

I just stare at them.

"It doesn't have to be this house – I know it's out of your reach, although I do think it's worth taking a punt – but there's plenty of smaller properties around that would suit you."

Dad's looking at me expectantly but I'm (don't laugh) lost for words. He shakes his head in a disappointed fashion. "Don't you want to know how much your share's worth?"

Mum leans forwards. "Seven thousand pounds."

"It would have been more but we spent a bit more on the bathroom than we intended," Dad says sheepishly.

Mum gives a bark of laughter. "A *bit*?"

He grins. "Still, seven thousand pounds isn't to be sniffed at, is it?"

I shake my head. My head is reeling.

"We've been keeping it safe for when you get married or buy a house, whichever came first," Dad adds.

Marriage? Fat chance. It's been so long since I had a date that went anywhere that if a penis were to approach me, my shrivelled raisin of a vagina would need a complete refresher course in what to do.

"My God, you two know how to keep a secret. Seven thousand pounds? That's... incredible." I have absolutely no control of the laughter making my shoulders shake, and I'm still laughing when I give them both a huge, squishy hug. "Thank you, thank you. You're the best parents in the world."

"We know," Dad agrees modestly.

Wednesday 10th April 2002

Alex

The line to the UK is decent enough but my efforts to hold a conversation are hindered by the noisy, drunk students who've just staggered into my bar.

"Let me make sure I've understood you," I say, jamming a finger in my ear. "The highest bid was four grand over the asking price?"

"Yes. Four grand. Fourteen thousand pounds higher than the lady's bid. Do you still want to go ahead?"

I can hear the pound signs ringing in his head across the lands and oceans separating us.

"Definitely."

"And you'll still pay my legal fees?"

"Yes."

"And –"

Impatient, I cut him off. "And the five grand arrangement fee, yes. Everything stands. Twenty grand in cash, including legal fees, total. Have you still got my brother's number?"

"In my filo-fax."

"Call him first thing and he'll sort the money for you. You'll get the first half when the deal is confirmed – I want a copy of the estate agent's letter. Ollie will fax it to me. You'll get the other half on completion. Any problems, call Ollie immediately. He can always get hold of me."

"Will do."

"Think of a good story to explain it."

"To who?"

"The estate agent and your bank manager for a start."

Simon knows this is illegal. He's too greedy to care.

The twenty grand I'm paying him to accept Melody's offer on his dead mother's house is cash he might be questioned about if he tries to bank it. In 2024 he would definitely be questioned about it.

"I will."

"Good. And Simon?"

"Yes?"

"If you screw her over, I will hunt you down, okay?"

I hear his gulp. "I won't."

"Good. Nice doing business with you."

Feeling like a cross between Liam Neeson and Ronnie Kray, I hang up and face the pissed students waiting to be served.

Friday 5th July 2002

Melody

I unlock the door with the key given to me thirteen minutes ago. The excitement rushing through me is so strong I could easily be sick, and as I step over the threshold into my very first home and look at the faded swirling purple pattern on the threadbare carpet, I think it doesn't matter if I puke as no-one will be able to tell the difference.

Empty of furniture, the house looks even shabbier, something I wouldn't have believed possible, but I don't care.

I still have to pinch myself that my offer was accepted. Even with Mum and Dad's deposit and stretching myself to the outer limit of my bank's mortgage offer, I still came in ten grand under the asking price. I was so convinced the other bidders would go in higher than me that I almost didn't bother.

It was Alex's advice of nothing ventured, nothing gained that talked me into it. It kept going round and round in my head until I put the offer in to shut it up. You could have knocked me down with the feather of a blue tit when the estate agent said my offer had been accepted.

I've spent three months dreaming of all the bright colours

I'm going to paint the rooms and all the renovations I'm going to make. The kitchen and bathroom both need ripping out but I can make-do with a simple makeover until I have the money. Aunt Debs jazzed up her kitchen last year with a lick of paint over all the tiles and cupboard doors. I already know what colours I'm going to do mine – sunshine yellow for the cupboards and a pale blue for the tiles. I'm going to paint butterflies on the tiles too.

Oh, I could float on a cloud of the candyfloss Mum used to say had replaced my brain.

"Mel!"

Dad's shout pulls me out of my daydream. I rush back outside to find him and Uncle Stelios wrestling a sofa, donated by Uncle Stelios himself, out of Uncle Stelios's work van. Parked in front of them is Lorna, who's taken the day off work to help. Her car is piled with so much of my stuff that the bottom of it is practically skimming the road. There's twice the stuff I brought home from Richmond with me (I started at Brocklehurst Manor six weeks ago – yes, I got the job! Found out the same day my offer on this place was accepted – so moved back into Mum and Dad's while the legal stuff for the house move was sorted). I have no idea what's in half the boxes. Mum got Dad to take them out of the attic for me. Apparently it's stuff she's been looking after for me until I bought a home of my own.

A car beeps and Mum waves as she drives past in search of a parking space. Her car is also sagging under the weight of all my crap.

Only Alice and Chris are missing but Alice is at school and Chris couldn't get the day off work, so I forgive them. Chris is driving up tonight and is going to spend the weekend helping me set everything up. Alice is coming for a sleepover tomorrow too. She will no doubt try and convince me to paint everything in Ariel colours.

All these people who love me. All these people willingly giving up their time for me. Truly, I am blessed.

There is no reason for the ache in my heart that makes me feel like there's something missing.

Saturday 31st August 2002

Melody

When Alice grows up, she should definitely apply for a job as a despot somewhere. She's a natural for the role.

My intention to paint the larger of my spare rooms burnt orange was overridden by the sheer force of her will. She bullied me into decorating it Ariel colours and plastering *The Little Mermaid* stickers everywhere. Oh, and buying matching Ariel curtains and bedding for it too.

Typical of the little ratbag, she's yet to spend a whole night in it. She sleeps over most weekends and always sneaks into my bed. She's currently splayed like a starfish leaving me about an inch of bed to call my own.

Honestly, she's got me wrapped around her little finger.

The worst of it is, every time I go in her room (she made me paint her name on the door) or walk past it, so approximately a hundred times a day, I think of Alex Hammond.

Cheers, Despot Alice.

Thursday 6th November 2003

Melody

"Happy birthday!" I reach into the bag I carried the entire thirty-minute walk to work this morning and then the fifteen-minute walk from work to Lorna's house, and pull out a bottle of Baileys.

Lorna sighs but I can tell she's happy to see me. "Is that a birthday present, or has Christmas come early?"

"Part of your birthday present, Little Miss Sarky." I thrust it at her. "Pour us both a glass and I'll give you the other part." I take her gift-wrapped jumper from the bag, wave it in her face, then hide it behind my back and barge my way into her house.

While Lorna's sorting the drinks, I put her present on the coffee table and have a nose through her birthday cards.

"Where's Carrie?" I ask once she's got the drinks sorted. I've got used to her workmate Carrie always being around. She's been lodging at Lorna's since their Greek holiday. The poor thing's going through a really nasty divorce. Turns out her soon-to-be-ex owns the marital home in his sole name and is doing everything he can to stop her having any of the equity, even though she spent five years contributing to the mortgage and all the bills.

"The wanker's working late so she's popped over to the house to get her post. She'll be back soon. How's work for you?"

"Dead as a dodo."

Her expression is sympathetic. Lorna knows what a problem Brocklehurst Manor has attracting visitors. I'm in charge of a fantastical amount of treasure and wonders that no-one knows exists.

I accepted the job blissfully ignorant that finances for the manor were so perilous that, unless there's a major drive to increase visitor numbers by approximately a million percent within the next two years, the funds will run dry. Or so the Trustees told me last week when they asked me to come up with fundraising and visitor attraction ideas to save it.

It's amazing the ideas a girl can come up with when her job's under threat and she has a mortgage to pay. I will be presenting those ideas to the Trustees in a fortnight.

"Another?" Lorna asks when my glass is empty.

"No thanks. I've promised Graham I'll pop in The Thief for a birthday drink with him."

"It's a trap!"

I snigger. "Probably. Want to come?"

"And get suckered into cleaning tables for him again? No chance."

"He won't ask you to do anything – it's your birthday too." That Lorna shares her birthday with Graham is something that brings her great joy. Honest. "Come and celebrate."

"We're celebrating on Saturday."

"But your birthday's *today*."

"It's a school night."

"You're thirty-three, not ninety-three. One drink won't kill you."

"No."

"Go on."

"No."

"Go on, go on, go on, go on, go on."

Even my best Mrs Doyle impression (Lorna and I are huge Father Ted fans) can't persuade her.

"Carrie's bringing a curry home with her, so go on, go on, go on and sod off."

I stick my tongue out at her.

Her doorbell rings.

I grab my coat and bag and pretend to huff my way to the front door.

The spirit of Cousin Nikos rugby tackles me.

Standing there is the man Despot Alice has helped ensure I think of dozens of times a day. The same man my heart gave a giant leap for when Lorna told me he'd moved back to England. The man my eyes have searched for every time I've left the house since.

Alex

You'd think I would have braced myself for the possibility of seeing Melody at Lorna's wouldn't you?

I've been back in England for two months without catching a glimpse of her. This hasn't been helped by me living with Ollie and Amber in the city. A tenancy issue with the family renting my house in Brocklehurst means I've not been able to move into my own home. That's been rectified and I'm moving in next weekend, but in the meantime I'm determined not to be Stalky McStalkface again. Other than a few visits to Lorna and Kermit, I've avoided the town. It's safer that way.

But I have been preparing myself to see her when I move into my home. She won't be able to think of me as Stalky McStalkface then.

When Lorna told me Mel had taken a job at Brocklehurst Manor, the urge to get the first flight back to England and kick my tenants out was so strong that I drove to the airport with my passport and wallet before coming to my senses.

Mel's move to Brocklehurst and new job there are the latest effects of the butterfly's wings flapping. I've got to let the effects continue on their natural course.

And my priority has to be Lorna. She's the one who will need me soon. Very soon.

So, not expecting to see Mel, I stand at Lorna's door and stare at her like Gormless Gordon.

Lorna breaks the silence by punching my arm and saying, "What are you doing here?"

"What do you think?" I hand her the gift bag. "Happy birthday."

"I am popular today... Ooo, is that your new car?" She points to my Audi TT parked outside her house.

"Yep. Picked it up on Monday. Fancy a birthday spin?"

I originally selected a Jaguar but Ollie told me it was an old man's car. One day I'm going to tell him that I'm older than Dad, just to see his face.

"Can I drive it?"

"When you learn to drive."

She splutters with outrage.

Melody catches my eye and lets out a snigger. She's been in a car with Lorna behind the wheel too, then.

Warmth fills my chest.

"How are you doing?" I ask her, making sure to keep my tone casual.

"Grand," she says in an Irish accent that tells me she's either just binged her Father Ted videos or binged her Marian Keyes books. "You?"

"Grand."

"Enjoying life back in England?"

"Not the weather so much."

She looks up at the sky. "At least it's not raining."

"There's that," I agree.

"Stuff the weather and take me for a drive," Lorna says impatiently.

"Thought you were waiting for your takeaway?" Melody says in a good-humoured snide.

"Mel, this is an Audi TT." Lorna shakes her head despairingly, and I grin. It seems Melody's complete lack of interest in cars in our old life has followed her into this one.

Melody's nose wrinkles. "Are Audis the cars that come without indicators?"

I laugh. "You're thinking of BMWs."

Her sparkling eyes meet mine again. "I'll take your word for it."

"You're welcome to have a ride and see for yourself."

"I'm good thanks." She pulls a yellow hat out of her pocket and rams it onto her head. "I'll leave you two to enjoy your car-ride."

"Wish Graham a happy birthday for me," Lorna says, kissing her cheek.

"Will do."

"You still coming here first on Saturday?"

"Yep." Melody hesitates before looking back at me. "Are you coming too?"

"Coming where?"

"Birthday drinks for Lorna, Saturday night. A load of us are doing a pub crawl and force-feeding her shots."

I'm actually speechless.

Is Melody giving me the go-ahead to join her on a night out?

I dart a glance at Lorna, who's doing her best not to appear gobsmacked at this turn of events too. She actually said the other day about sounding Melody out about me joining them for her birthday drinks, but I told her not to. I will not impose myself on her. If I'm to climb up from the step of distant amiability with her, it has to come from Melody and not from Lorna trying to shoehorn us together.

Looks like I've been promoted to the second step of amiability without the distance. I'll grab it with both hands, thank you.

Not wanting to sound over-enthusiastic and pathetically grateful, and thus scare her off, I do my best John Travolta as Vincent Vega and play it cool. "Suppose it depends if Lorn wants me there."

Lorna pretends to think. "I suppose you can come."

"Don't sound too enthusiastic."

I know damn well she's playing it cool too.

"Does that mean you're coming?" Melody asks.

"Go on then."

The old mischievous look I haven't seen in years appears on her face. "In that case, I'd better tell Graham to take you off the barred list."

And I thought her invitation had made my chest light and yet full? That was *nothing* compared to what was happening inside it now.

"Thank you."

She smiles. "You're welcome. See you Saturday."

Melody

I can't believe I suggested Alex Hammond join us for Lorna's birthday drinks. It just came out, a bit like the time when my old science teacher told me off for talking in class, and I called her a cow in my head, not realising until she turned puce that I'd said it out loud. This time, I didn't even say it in my head.

The cold that froze my nose and earlobes on the walk to Lorna's isn't biting me anymore. I'm so warm and springy inside that I could whip my coat off and skip all the way down Watling Street.

Saturday 8th November 2003

Melody

Of all the days to wake up with the bloody flu.

Alex

She's got the bloody flu.

Friday 28th November 2003

Melody

For a historian, I was woefully ignorant of the history I grew up surrounded by. I blame my school. How could they not have arranged a day trip to the town's great manor house once owned by a member of the Rivers family? As in, the Rivers, Henry VIII's family on his mother's side? How could I have not known that Henry VIII and his Queen Katherine Howard once stayed at the manor on one of their progresses, or that Queen Elizabeth I stayed there too?

Originally built in 1455, a fire destroyed most of the manor at the turn of the sixteenth century and it was rebuilt in Tudor style with that characteristic black and white striped exterior I adore. It's my delight and pleasure to be tasked with curating the treasures within it. And my burden. Because, as a destination for visitors to spend their hard-earned money, it's shit, and in all honesty, I don't blame my school for not taking us there. We'd have been bored out of our tiny minds in minutes.

And so I came to the end of my presentation before the board of trustees last week with my younger, tiny-minded, candy-floss-brained self in mind, and hoped they would see that my vision for the place has at its heart that girl and all the other children and adults for whom history should come alive for in a place like this too.

I got the go-ahead yesterday, and now I look at my two part-time assistants (I'm the only paid full-time employee) and the handful of volunteers I'm relying on to help make my vision for this place a reality, and wait for the mass exodus.

After all, I'm only asking for help and ideas to raise a million pounds and so turn the stables into a café and gift shop, put what's left of the grounds back to its original splendour, turn the manor's original Tudor kitchen into a proper working kitchen so we can do demonstrations of how the Tudors and Elizabethans made and cooked food, and do the structural work needed to stop the buttery and servery from collapsing. Oh, and convert the old barn into a dedicated building to home all the Roman artifacts that have been dug up over the years in Brocklehurst (honestly, the town is a treasure-trove of history). Oh, and we need to get the money raised by the end of next year.

Easy!

Not.

Honestly, I can't believe the Trustees agreed to all this. I thought if I lobbed a load of ideas at them, they'd select a couple they thought most viable. Me and my big mouth. Turns out they agree with my thoughts that all the publicity we'd generate through the fundraising drive would bring visitors in to see what all the fuss was about.

Kelly, one of the volunteers, raises her hand.

I hold my breath.

"What about hosting a music festival on the grounds next summer? My brother's in a folk band. He knows loads of bands on the local folk scene. Half of them will turn up for free beer if it's a good cause."

"Are the grounds big enough?" I ask dubiously. The Trustees sold off most of the land as part of the deal when they sold the manor's old chapel fifty years ago. That sale had been to pay for the renovations of the great hall. Honestly, the manor is a veritable money pit.

Kelly nods enthusiastically, and says, "We can make it work but we can always ask the family who own the chapel if we can use their grounds too."

"What about an Easter treasure hunt?" Martha suggests. "We can ask to use the chapel's grounds for that too."

And then we're in the midst of a fundraising brainstorm that fills me with such pride I could snog the lot of them.

Friday 5th December 2003

Melody

I've never actually spoken to the family who live in the old chapel, but as they share a land boundary with the manor, I've seen them enough times for us to wave greetings at each other.

Oh well, nothing ventured, nothing gained, and I push open the iron gate at the bottom of their gravel drive.

The mum or dad have a new car, I note when I near the chapel itself. A sparkling blue thing that is surprisingly familiar. Surprising because I never notice cars.

While the manor is hidden away from the main road, there's a specific spot on Watling Street where, in the winter, you can see the chapel in the distance. I remember as a child it being this dilapidated building with boarded-up windows. The renovation it underwent in the last decade was beautifully done and I hope they invite me inside so I can have a nose at the interior.

I walk up the steps to the huge front door and ring the bell.

Alex

The last person I expect to see at my front door is Melody. From the way her eyes pop, the last person she expected to open the door is me. For a couple of seconds we simply gape at each other before I recover myself.

"Hello, you. This is a pleasant surprise."

She blinks the shock from her face. "Hello to you too. What are you doing here?"

"I live here."

"Do you? Since when?"

"Since the tenants moved out. Are you here to see them?"

That furrow appears in her brow. "Who?"

"The old tenants. The Holdens."

"Oh. Is that their name? Yes. I was."

"I can pass a message on if you like?" Realising I'm on the verge of blowing a superb opportunity that might never come again, I quickly add, "I was about to put the kettle on. Fancy a cuppa?"

She grazes her bottom lip with her teeth then smiles and nods. "Go on then."

I stand aside to admit her into the house I bought entirely for her, and hope she can't see the strength of my heartbeat pounding beneath my sweater.

Melody

The interior of the chapel is even better than the exterior and I can't help gawping.

"What do you think?" Alex asks as he leads me into a *humungous* kitchen. I'm quite sure my entire house would fit in this room.

"It's beautiful." I shake my head. I would be raving even more about it if it wasn't Alex leading me through, but it is him, and I'm having to concentrate really hard against the thuds of my heart not to show how thrilled I am to see him.

The first sight of him sent such a huge rush of joy through me that there's no other explanation for it.

I can't pinpoint when, exactly, my feelings for Alex morphed from fear and loathing to warmth and butterflies, but morphed they have.

I like Alex Hammond.

I like him a lot.

I even like the long stride of his legs in those faded jeans he's wearing. And the lumberjack shirt he's wearing with it.

"It reminds me of Kirsty and Mick's chapel conversion in Richmond but this is much nicer," I say. "Homelier. It's got a really nice vibe."

His eyes lock with mine.

It's the first time their names have been mentioned between us. I wonder why that is, and it's a shock to realise we've hardly spoken since that night at the fishing lake. Funny that. In my head, we've had lots of conversations, especially since I saw him at Lorna's on her birthday.

The man who's rarely been far from my mind all these years, for good and bad, has taken complete possession of it again. I've been daydreaming of him like I used to when I was a teenager with the time to daydream. I've imagined bumping into him a thousand times. The casual way I would act and my gracious acceptance of a drink.

I can't believe my daydreams have come to life and that this is happening.

"Tea or coffee?" he asks.

"Tea, please."

I run a hand over one of the many oak kitchen counters. It's wonderfully smooth beneath my skin. "Who's the chef here?"

"There isn't one. I do all the cooking."

"Then that makes *you* the chef," I point out.

He puts the kettle under the running tap. "Trust me, no one who has eaten my food would call me a chef."

"Same."

He turns his face to me. "You don't cook?"

"You sound surprised."

"You just strike me as someone who would enjoy cooking."

"The only thing I enjoy cooking is super-noodles."

That makes him laugh. He has a lovely laugh. Deep and rumbly.

Tea made, he carries the mugs to the round table by a bay window which overlooks the humungous garden I'm here to talk about.

He offers me a cigarette.

"No thank you, I've quit."

"When was that?"

"When I got the flu." I've managed twenty-eight days. I've broken my record by twenty-seven days. Being knocked out for five of those days with the flu greatly assisted this. If I'd known it was such a good stop-smoking device, I'd have snogged anyone who thought they were coming down with symptoms of it.

"Good for you." He closes the packet.

"Don't not smoke on my account," I tell him. "Lorna smoked in front of me the other day and I was fine." Apart from wanting to rip it out of her hand and smoke the entire thing in one long drag. I left when she lit her third.

His smile's rueful. "It's fine. I should quit too. So, what was the message you wanted me to pass to the Holdens?"

I take a sip of my tea and find it has been made in Goldilocks fashion. Just right.

Alex must be psychic – he didn't even ask how I like it!

"There's not much point now. I assumed they owned the place. I never spoke to them, but they looked like really nice people so I didn't feel awkward having to ask them, but it's a bit different if it's a faceless landlord and –"

"Mel," he interrupts. "This is *my* house."

"What? You own it?"

I assumed he was renting. I've been half-expecting other hirsute males to emerge, a group of mates pooling their money together to live the high life in the poshest bachelor pad in town.

"Yep."

"You are kidding, right?"

"Nope."

"Well, flabber my gast. You *own* this place? And there was me thinking last year that you were interested in bidding for my little house when all along you could afford something like this."

His face creases with amusement but there's something in his eyes that stops my laughter in its tracks.

"What's wrong?" I ask.

He pulls a rueful smile and shakes his head. "Nothing. How is the house?"

"Apart from all my DIY disasters... fine."

"What DIY disasters?"

"You don't want to hear it."

"Try me."

"Okay, but if you laugh, I'll have to kill you."

Alex

I cannot begin to describe what it feels like to have Melody here, in the home that's hers as much as mine, listening to her go into full lyrical flow for the first time since that night by the lake.

"I blame Changing Rooms," she says after describing the disaster of painting her kitchen cupboards without sanding them first. "It lulled me into a false sense of security and made me believe it's easy transform a room into a masterpiece over a weekend... so long as you don't have Laurence Llewelyn-Bowen calling the shots, ha ha! Honestly, you should have seen the kitchen floor – it was more yellow paint than lino, so I had the great idea of ripping it up and replacing it with some cheap laminate. *Big* mistake. Huge."

"What happened?"

"I hammered a nail through a waterpipe and flooded my kitchen. Worst thing is, there was no need for me to nail the flooring down but the recommended glue looked exactly the same as the crap PVA stuff we used in primary school, so I thought it practical to hammer nails in to be sure. I then made matters worse by pulling the nail out. Water everywhere. And then I *might* have made matters worse by flailing around like a headless chicken before seeking help."

She pauses for breath to light a cigarette. While she's been talking, she's pulled the packet of cigarettes over, pulled two out, passed one to me, picked up the lighter and held the flame to me.

I'm convinced she doesn't even realise she's doing it.

"I called Dad, Mum and Lorna but they were all busy at work, then I called my Uncle Stelios but I couldn't hear him over the background noise, so I called my cousin Nikos who bloody laughed at me and hung up. Honestly, I got so desperate that I even called Graham, but he was as much help as a cauliflower."

"Why didn't you call a plumber?"

"Because I'm a twat and didn't think of calling one until after I'd called everyone else." Her pretty teeth flash. "I finally got hold of one, and the first thing he asked was if I'd turned the stopcock off. I thought he was being a perv and hung up on him." She's laughing so hard the rest of her words are indistinguishable, and I'm laughing so hard I wouldn't be able to hear them if they were distinct. She finishes her story with, "Thank God for home insurance!"

"I'll have to give you my number so you've got another name to call for your next disaster," I tease.

"Don't or I'll take you up on it..." Her black eyes suddenly narrow with speculation.

"What?"

"Nothing."

"Don't tell fibs. You want to ask me something."

Her mouth drops open. "How do you know that?"

Because I lived the best years of my life with you. "I'm good at reading people. Go on, ask me."

"I was going to ask if you're any good at tiling but didn't want to insult you. You're an artist not a tiler."

Her easy compliment makes me wish I were a peacock so I could preen and shake my tailfeather.

"I'm excellent at tiling and would be happy to do any tiling you need."

"A whole bathroom? I've kind of pulled all the tiles off mine. Dad keeps threatening to put the new ones up but to be honest, I get my DIY skills from him. I would like to point out, though, that I'm *great* at painting walls and glossing now I've got the hang of it, so it's only the tiles I need doing, but only if you're absolutely sure."

"It would be my pleasure."

She beams and gets her phone out of her bag. "Let me have your number."

I recite it to her.

She keys it in then looks at me with those beautiful sparkling eyes. "I've sent you a text."

My phone pings.

"That was quick!"

"I live in about the only place in Brocklehurst with a decent signal. Now, are you hungry? Because I'm starving and that new Chinese next to The Plough delivers."

She looks at her watch and gives a bark of laughter. "My God, is that the time? I only popped over to ask a quick question."

I'm already on my feet and at the drawer with all the takeaway menus in. "You can ask it over Chinese. What shall we order?"

"I'm not fussy. You choose."

I make the call and when I get off, she's looking at me with fresh amazement.

"What now?" I ask lightly.

"You just chose my favourite dishes."

Our favourite dishes.

"Our tastebuds must be aligned."

Melody

I haven't had a drop of alcohol but I feel drunk. Happy drunk. *Really* happy drunk.

While we wait for the Chinese to be delivered, Alex gives me a tour of his home, and wow, it is amazing, not just the scale and proportions of the place but the decoration too. The bright, sunny colours of the rooms and the quirky furnishings are exactly what I would have chosen. He must have made a massive amount of money selling his bar in Sydney to buy something like this.

I keep seeing glimpses of his garden too, from all different vantage points. It's beautiful and has been designed with such care and attention that I don't see how he'd be okay with hordes of people trampling all over it on two separate occasions. I've already decided not to bother asking when he asks me again, while we're eating, what I came here for.

"That's a lot of fundraising you need to do," he says when I finish boring him with my sorry tale of the dilapidated manor.

"It is. I know we're biting off more than we can chew but basically, my attitude is go big or go home."

"That's the best attitude."

"Why, thank you, kind sir."

His eyes gleam. "You're most welcome, my lady."

My belly goes all squidgy.

"Have you thought about approaching local businesses for donations?" he asks. "They could do fundraisers too."

"Excellent idea."

"And get the local press in on it early too."

"Do you want to join the fundraising committee?" I'm only half joking.

"I'd rather put pins in my eyes."

"Bit drastic."

He grins.

God, I'm starting to love his smile.

"You never know," he says, "Donations from businesses might raise the whole lot for you but if they don't, and you want to use my garden, then it's all yours for whatever you need."

My mouth drops open. "Are you sure?"

"I'm sure."

"That's amazingly kind of you, thank you." I'm trying not to stare at his hands. They're huge. I wonder what he'd do if I put my hands to them to compare the size difference.

"I do have one condition."

Stop staring at his hands!

"Which is?"

"When the renovations start, you have to promise not to offer help in any shape or form. The whole manor might collapse."

* * *

I can't believe how quickly the evening has gone. Or how much I've enjoyed (loved) Alex's company. Or how reluctant I am to leave.

But leave I must. I have work in the morning.

Being a responsible adult can be very hard at times.

"I'll give you a lift home," he says when I (reluctantly) tell him I need to go.

"Are you sure? I don't mind walking."

His lips twitch as if he knows I've just told a huge fib, but his answer is firm. "I insist."

The interior of his car is spotless. It smells of leather, and when Alex closes his door, I catch the most delicious scent of fading aftershave. It's mouth-watering. I have to force my backside to stay firmly attached to the seat and not lean a little bit closer so I can inhale it a little more deeply.

The radio's tuned to Virgin, the station I listen to when I get bored with Radio One. I'm absurdly pleased at this latest similarity between us.

Honestly, our tastes are so similar. Food. Interior decoration. Radio station.

No Doubt's 'I'm Just a Girl' is playing.

"I love this song," I tell him.

He grins and turns the volume up, then turns the car round and heads down his long drive.

At the gate, he jumps out to open it.

I wait, tapping my foot. "What's my destiny, what I've succumbed..." I sing along at the exact moment Alex gets back in. I immediately shut up.

Amusement crinkles his eyes. "Go ahead, have a sing song."

"You've never heard my singing."

"Bad is it?" he asks lightly.

"Graham used to threaten the punters who wouldn't drink up after last orders with it."

His laughter fills the car.

I find myself staring at his hands again.

Gwen's excellent polemic against sexism comes to an end and the next song starts without any preamble. It's The Calling, 'Wherever You Will Go'.

Silence falls between us.

Alex navigates his way onto Watling Street.

I pretend to look ahead but really, I'm side-eying the hands that created those wonderful mosaics in Molly's and my parents' bathrooms. Honestly, they're fascinating, and now I find my gaze darting to the thighs separated from mine by a gear stick and find myself wondering about the appendage between them and if it matches the hands for size.

Oh my God, I'm imagining Alex Hammond's penis.

I honestly cannot remember the last time I even had a passing thought to a man's penis. I mean, the last one I saw was Chipolata Mick's and that was a fleeting 'accident.' Accident or not, it was enough to put me off penises for life. I defy any woman to look at that particular specimen and not want to join a nunnery.

Alex turns into Juniper Crescent and parks in front of my house.

The silence grows louder.

I clear my throat and keep my gaze fixed ahead. "Well... thank you for a lovely evening."

The best evening.

"My pleasure. Maybe we can do it again some time."

"I'd like that." Very much. Very, very much.

"Let me know when you want me to look at your bathroom."

"Will do." *Right now*? "I'm sure you'll take one look and run out screaming in horror."

"I'll try my best not to scream."

I look at him.

There's amusement on his face. And something else. Something that makes the spot between my legs pulse.

My heart is beating very hard.

I don't want to say goodbye.

I have to force my hands to open the door. "Goodnight. And thanks again."

His eyes are still on me. "Goodnight, Melody. Sleep tight."

I'm pretty sure I float rather than walk to my door.

I grope in my bag for my keys, all fingers and thumbs. Once I've unlocked it, I push the door open then turn for one last look.

He's still there, waiting for me to get safely inside.

I wave.

He waves back.

I close the door. When I go to the living room window to draw the curtains, he's gone.

Saturday 13th December 2003

Melody

Lorna looks awful. Really awful. Like she hasn't slept for a year or brushed her hair in all that time either. When I step past her, I get a whiff of stale sweat and stale cigarettes delightfully combined with alcohol seeping from pores.

Her voice is very dull. "Didn't you get my message?"

"No," I lie.

I got her message alright, and something smelt off with it. Lorna never bows out of a girly night at the last minute. And if she does, it's never by text message. And never with the excuse of being too tired.

My concern rises when I follow her into her usually spotless kitchen. It's in the same state as mine. Actually, I think it might be worse. "What's wrong, Lorn?"

Her answer is a terse, "Nothing. Tea or coffee?"

"Tea, thanks."

She puts the kettle on and takes the last two mugs from the cupboard. All the rest, along with a good dozen glasses and plates encrusted with the debris of meals, are lining the counter.

"Where's Carrie?" I ask.

"Moved out."

"You never said." I open the dishwasher. It's empty. The first mug I grab to put in it looks like it'll need to be disinfected and bleached, never mind washed. "When was that?"

"Last weekend. Gone back to the husband. They're making another go of it."

"Well consider me shocked." The second mug is in as bad a state as the first.

She turns sharply to me. "What are you doing?"

"Helping."

"I'm quite capable of loading my own fucking dishwasher."

Taken aback, I hold my hands up in the sign of peace and sidle over to the table.

Her back's to me, but I'm watching her closely enough to see her still and take a deep breath.

"I'm sorry," she mutters. "It's been a shit week at work and I had a shit night's sleep. I didn't mean to take it out on you."

"That's okay... Are you sure you're okay though? Apart from work being shit, I mean?"

She brings the mugs over. She's made coffee. I keep my mouth shut about it.

She lights a cigarette without offering me one. Her ashtray is so full, butts and ash have spilled onto the table. I don't dare empty it.

I think hard for a neutral subject. "Guess what happened at work yesterday?" I tried calling her about it last night but she didn't return my call. Knowing I'd be seeing her this evening, I wasn't concerned.

I should have been concerned.

Dull eyes meet mine for a nano-second, and she answers with another shrug.

I've been trying to cut down on my own smoking, limiting myself to only one an hour, but I take my packet out of my handbag and light up. "Well, you know we're planning to spend

2004 doing a mass fundraise for all the renovations and stuff we want to do?"

Her head moves in what I think is a nod.

"We were told by a solicitor on Friday that he has a client willing to donate the entire amount."

There's a mild flicker of interest on her pallid face.

"We couldn't believe it. I still can't believe it. Seriously, Lorn, there's someone out there who's donating a *million quid*. The whole shebang. The Trustees are meeting with the solicitor on Monday. It should be in the account by the end of the week. Isn't that amazing?"

She stubs her cigarette out. "That's great. I'm pleased for you."

"I can't believe the donor wants to stay anonymous. I mean, that's just mind blowing. Normally when people donate large sums of cash they want the whole world to know, but our benefactor insists on being anonymous."

Her gaze flickers to mine and this time doesn't immediately dart away. "Anonymous?" Her mouth forms the tiniest sneer. "Right."

She lights another cigarette.

I stand up. "Just going to use your loo."

Another shrug.

I run upstairs and lock the bathroom door. It's in the same state as the kitchen.

I put the toilet seat down and take my phone out of my handbag, and scroll to the number I've stared at a thousand times since I stored it in my contacts. Every incoming call and text has made my heart jump with hope that it's him.

I quickly write a message. *Hi Alex, it's Melody. Sorry to disturb you but v worried about Lorna. Something v wrong and need help to handle it. Understand if you're busy.*

I press send and wait for the meagre signal to do its job, then flush the loo.

When I open the door to go back downstairs, I notice

Carrie's bedroom door opposite is wide open. That her room is empty is no shock. What *is* a shock is the smashed dressing table mirror.

I cover my mouth. My heart is beating very fast. My brain is working hard too. Pieces of a jigsaw I hadn't realised were puzzle pieces are fitting together.

Other than moving hand to mouth to smoke, I don't think Lorna's moved an inch of her body since I went upstairs.

"Lorn?" I whisper.

Vacant eyes meet mine and suddenly, I *know* I'm right.

Oh poor, poor Lorna.

Alex

When Melody's name flashes on the small screen of my phone, I swear my heart explodes. I've spent the two weeks since our evening together determined not to harass her, waiting for her to make the first move, and here it is.

And then I read the message.

Oh shit.

It's started.

I make my excuses to Ollie and Amber, who are feeding me, Dad and Gloria curry, and run to my car.

Weaving my way through the traffic, I force myself to think clearly and remember events that happened so long ago.

Lorna's death four days before Christmas poleaxed us.

We never learned when, exactly, everything fell apart for her, but we never forgave ourselves for missing the signs. We'd taken her messages that she was too busy with work to meet up with us at face value.

Her overdose was a cry for help. She regretted it and called for an ambulance. She called them too fucking late. Multiple organ failure. Two days later, she was dead.

It was the most desperate cry for help because she

didn't know how to ask for it any other way. She didn't think she had anyone she could turn to. Didn't think any of us would understand. Was frightened we would condemn her.

I let myself into the house I'd planned to camp out in from tomorrow morning.

I find them in the living room. Lorna's curled up on Melody's lap sobbing her heart out.

Melody

I stroke Lorna's cheek, turn her bedside light off, and tiptoe out of the room.

Alex is in the kitchen loading the dishwasher. The moment he arrived, the knotty panic in my belly loosened. There's something very comforting about his presence here and I'm filled with the urge to wrap my arms around him.

"Is she asleep?" he asks.

"Yes." I sit at the table and rub my eyes. "Did you know?"

His shoulders rise. "Not officially."

"I didn't." What kind of self-absorbed, selfish person am I? How could I not know something so fundamental about my best friend?

I think the sound of Lorna's sobs broke off a piece of my heart.

My broken heart for her is nothing compared to what's happened to her own heart. It's been smashed to pieces.

After years of living in denial about her sexuality, hating that men left her cold but that women fascinated her, Lorna finally found love.

But it was a secret love. Secret through fear. Lorna was terrified of her dad's reaction. Carrie was terrified of what their colleagues and everyone else would say.

"I wanted to tell you," Lorna whispered to me. "I knew you

wouldn't judge. But she made me promise not to. She made me lie to you. She was ashamed, Mel."

Last week, Carrie decided she couldn't do it anymore and went back to her husband. Lorna has been living in a black hole ever since.

Alex drops into the chair opposite me. His gaze locks onto mine. "We're here for her now. That's what matters."

Monday 24th December 2003

Melody

"Is the popcorn ready?" asks Alice, who's just thumped her way down the stairs on her bottom dressed in her favourite Ariel nightie.

"Ask Mum."

"MUM, IS THE POPCORN READY?"

"TWO MINUTES. AND DON'T SHOUT!"

Alice jumps onto the sofa and snuggles up next to me. "What are we watching?"

"No idea. It's a surprise. Just remember, no whining. It's Dad's choice." And he *loves* keeping us in suspense about it.

It's that time of year in the Aldridge household when Mum makes popcorn and Dad chooses a video for us all to watch before we go to bed and wait for Father Christmas to break into the house and deliver our presents. This is the first time Alice has been deemed old enough to join in, and she's nearly as excited about it as she is for Christmas Day itself.

Soon, we've all got bowls of popcorn on our laps, drinks are on the coffee table (Alice has milk, the rest of us have our traditional glass of Christmas port), and Dad's shaking the remote control to get it to work so he can fast-forward the trailers. He's going to be in heaven tomorrow when he opens the DVD player Mum's bought for him. I've bought his favourite films for him to play in it: *Shrek* and *This Is Spinal Tap*.

I know within two seconds what the film is.

"Ouch."

"Sorry."

My fingers have tensed so much they've dug into Alice's arm.

I'm suddenly incapable of eating popcorn, glued to a film I watched so many times in my sixth form years that I know it word-for-word.

I'm glued in the same way I was when I watched it that first time with Hayley. Building in me are the same feelings I experienced then too, the same longing, and with them come memories, brighter and clearer than they've been in years, and it's no longer Kevin Costner's face my eyes are seeing but Alex's.

Alex is inextricably linked to this film and to the ache watching it that first time formed in me twelve years ago.

I sneak my phone out of my pocket and write him a message.

How is she?

After a moment of dithering, I add *x* to it and press send.

A message pings back within minutes.

Holding up x

I clutch the phone to my chest and watch the rest of the film.

Tuesday 25th December 2003

Alex

My phone pings.

Merry Christmas. Hope you have a lovely day x

I message her straight back.

Merry Christmas to you too x

"Is that Melody?" Lorna asks from her seat at my kitchen table.

"How did you guess?"

She smiles. It's the first real smile I've seen since Melody sent her frightened message to me. "The look on your face. What's going on with you two?"

"Nothing."

"You fat liar."

"It's just messages."

"Does she put kisses on them?"

"Mind your own business."

"You two are my business."

"Lorn…"

"Don't let my broken heart get in the way. Life's too short."

"Not for me."

She laughs. A real laugh. Lighting a cigarette, her laughter fades. "Thank you."

"For what?"

"You know what. If not for you and Mel..." She inhales deeply and exhales slowly. Her eyes fill with tears. "How long until it feels better?"

I wish I could wave a magic wand and make all the pain flee from her, but life doesn't work like that. Sometimes you just have to accept that pain is the reverse side of joy.

"It takes as long as it takes."

She closes her eyes and mumbles, "Great."

"But you will feel better one day," I assure her, challenging my inner Melody.

"I get now, why you wanted to top yourself when she died."

"Is that how you feel?" I ask carefully.

She shakes her head. "No. I've thought about it, I won't lie, not to you, but no, not now. Those feelings have gone."

That, I'm sure, is Melody's doing. Her guessing the truth, and the warmth and love she enveloped Lorna in made all the difference.

My plan had been to watch her like a hawk and physically stop her doing it by whatever means necessary. Melody simply gave her the love and understanding she needed.

Mel's close friendship with Chris, a friendship that never existed in our other life, gave her an insight into the prejudice that comes with loving people of your own sex and an understanding of how crippling it can be to come out of a closet no-one knows you've locked yourself in, even when your heart has been shredded and you're drowning in unbearable darkness. The last of it is something I do understand because I've lived it.

"It's never the answer," I tell her. "Just keep on doing what you're doing. Take one day at a time."

"If there's no end-date, does that mean you and Mel are going to keep babysitting me indefinitely?"

And we thought we'd been subtle in our plot to never leave Lorna alone.

I laugh. "We'll babysit you for as long as you need us to. We both love you."

She wipes a tear and sniffs. "I know. I love you both too and you love each other. Please, sort your shit out and make it happen."

"I'm not pushing her."

There's a song by the band Semisonic called 'Secret Smile'. When I first heard it a year or so after we married, it always brought to mind the look in Melody's eyes whenever she looked at me. It was a look only for me.

I saw that look the night she spent the evening in my home with me. I've seen it many times these last ten days too, when we've Lorna-sat together.

It's going to happen. I feel it. Awareness has been growing and swirling between us, but it will happen when she's ready. Melody isn't someone to throw caution to the wind and jump into bed with someone. Not this version of her. She's older and wiser than the young woman who fell straight into bed with me in our first incarnation.

I've waited almost thirteen years. I can wait however long she needs. That I'm even waiting rather than merely existing shows have far things have come for us.

"I get that. And you're right not to." Lorna stubs her cigarette out, and pushes her chair back. "Right, what do you need me to do?"

"Lay the table. They'll be here soon." Dad, Gloria, Ollie, Amber, their toddler Lauren, and Gloria's sister Gaynor – no, that isn't a joke – are joining us for Christmas dinner. We're all going to muck in and cook it together and, apparently, not kill each other while doing it.

"I can do that." She walks to the door and turns back to me. "When you two do get together, you need to tell her the truth. You know that, right?"

Wednesday 31st December 2003

Melody

The Merry Thief is heaving. So heaving that Graham has suckered me into helping out behind the bar. Lorna hid behind Alex so he couldn't see her and sucker her in too.

As I'm doing a good deed, I feel no obligation to wait until I finish working before I consume the many drinks I'm bought. It's amazing how generous people become on New Year's Eve. Free drinks? Bring it on.

"Do we have to have the music so loud?" Graham shouts at me between serving customers. "I can't hear myself think."

"If you don't want me to go on strike then yes. Anyway, the customers are enjoying it, so stop your whining."

He scowls but can't argue with me. Well, he can, but my threat to go on strike stops him.

A load of customers have rearranged the tables to create a dancefloor near the pool table. There's a good twenty people wagging fingers in each other's faces and singing along to The Black Eyed Peas' 'Shut Up'.

I'm too busy to do more than shake my tush while I pour pints, spirits and shots, but I never lose my awareness of what

Alex is doing. He's spent the evening playing pool with a crowd of his and Lorna's old mates, many of whom have become my friends over the years too.

I see him pass the pool cue to someone. I immediately tell Graham I'm taking a break and hurry away with my rum and coke before he can object.

I elbow my way through the makeshift dancefloor.

Lorna's deep in conversation with Jasmin, which is great to see. I've been really worried about my lovely Lorn but she really does seem to be over the worst of it. I don't know how much of it's for show but her smile's started meeting her eyes again, which I'm taking as a good sign. That she's here, voluntarily celebrating the New Year with us, is just wonderful, and I don't feel any guilt in winking an acknowledgement at her then carrying on past her to stand before Alex.

I beam a smile at him. I can't help it. There's something about this man that makes me happy just to be in his orbit.

Alex's smile for me more than meets his eyes. He gets off his stool and indicates that I have it.

I shake my head and shout, "If I rest my feet now, I won't want to get back behind the bar."

He places a hand lightly on my hip and puts his mouth to my ear. "Good. Then you'll have to stay here with me."

Ohmigod.

Right there in the middle of the heaving pub, I experience such a thrill of heat that it makes me feel quite weak.

He sits back on the stool. If I'd taken it, I'd have had to climb up.

Now both his hands are resting on my hips. I'm standing between his legs. Our bodies are almost touching. We're so close the heat of his body is permeating through my clothes.

His mouth goes to my ear again. "Are you going to tell Graham to do one by midnight?"

I lean closer, brushing my cheek to his. He smells divine. "Definitely."

His lips touch my lobe. "Good."

God, my skin is on fire. I can hardly breathe.

There's a tap on my shoulder.

It's Lorna.

"Jasmin's invited me round hers so I'm going to make a move," she shouts. "I'll see you Friday night, yeah?"

"Are we not invited?"

There's a shine in her eyes I don't think I've ever seen before. And a touch of apprehension. "Only I'm invited."

My stare shoots to Jasmin.

She meets my eye. A smile tugs on her lips but I sense fear.

I grin at her then hug Lorna. "Have fun," I whisper.

"If anyone asks, will you tell people you're joining us?" she whispers back.

"Of course. And if they ask if they can come too, I'll tell them to bugger off and host their own party."

She laughs. "Sure you will." Then she cups her hand around my ear and says, "Think it's time you and Alex had a private party for two as well."

I actually feel my cheeks turn the colour of beetroot.

She kisses my beetroot cheek. "Love ya, Mel."

"Love you too, Lorn."

They slip out through the back. Everyone's too busy dancing and chatting and laughing to notice.

Beyonce's on now. 'Crazy in Love'.

I twist back round to Alex, who must have caught the gist of what was being said between us considering I was trapped between his thighs the entire conversation.

His hands snake from my hips to rest on my lower back, bringing me even closer.

He gives me a look I swear makes my heart sigh.

His mouth finds its way back to my ear. "Can I walk you home later?"

The pulse between my legs is so strong I tighten my hold around his neck.

When did I even *put* my arms around his neck? I don't remember. It doesn't matter.

Holding Alex like this and him holding me like this feels right. The rightest I've felt in a long, long time.

I press my cheek back to his. "How about you walk me home now?"

He pulls his head back. His eyes are gleaming.

God, he is *sexy*.

Not bothering to say goodbye to anyone or tell Graham that I'm abandoning him, we dart out of the pub with Beyonce warbling about not being herself lately.

I know exactly what she means.

* * *

We hold hands the entire ten-minute walk back to mine. I don't think I've ever gone this long in someone's company without talking but I'm too busy keeping my feet walking rather than floating to speak.

I can hear my heartbeats. They're very fast. Frighteningly fast.

It's not until I open the front door that I remember the state I left the house in.

Alex looks neither perturbed nor surprised at it, simply follows my lead and steps over the discarded mugs, socks, magazines and books sprawled over the living room carpet.

"I've not got any booze in," I tell him. I'm proud I can actually form a complete sentence. My brain is a fuzzy mess, and my discombobulation is discombobulatingly discombobulating.

"Coffee's fine."

My hands are shaking so much that when I put the spoonful of instant into his mug, I miss and coffee granules scatter over the counter.

I wipe it up, taking the opportunity to wipe three days' worth of breadcrumbs off the counter too, then carry the mugs into the living room. Only by a miracle do I not slosh half the contents onto the carpet.

Fresh nerves have me rifling through my CD collection for music to listen to, but making a choice is impossible with Alex Hammond's eyes boring into me.

"Choose something," I order.

He stands beside me and flips through the collection.

His arm brushes against mine.

I'm struggling to breathe.

I need a cigarette.

His focus still on my CDs, he takes his cigarette packet and lighter out of his jacket pocket and hands them to me.

Did I actually speak my thought aloud?

His eyes meet mine. "Light one for me?"

I nod.

I don't think I can speak anymore.

He places my Coldplay CD into the player while I light the cigarettes. I pass his to him. Our fingers touch. My heart jolts.

I sit on the sofa. He sits at the other end. I put an ashtray on the floor between us.

Alex is the one to break the silence. "I like what you've done to the place."

"What, even the mess?"

"Especially the mess."

"Your house is so tidy." And clean. Much cleaner than mine.

He must think I'm a right slob. What was I thinking, inviting him in?

"There's only me and I'm pretty tidy."

"Don't marry me then. I'd turn it into a pigsty in days."

Oh shit, why did I say that? Who on earth mentions marriage before they've even gone to bed together?

The beats of my heart ramp up a notch.

I open my mouth to change the subject, but my brain's shut down.

I have never, in my entire life, been so aware of another person. It's actually quite terrifying.

More terrifying still, I can't think of anything to say.

I'm never short of something to say.

He interrupts my pathetic internal monologue with a soft, "Melody?"

I finally drag my stare from the carpet and look at him.

He's much closer than I'd realised. Close enough that I can see flecks in his green eyes. I notice a tiny, much faded scar on his chin.

I swallow and manage to croak, "Yes?"

He doesn't answer. Not with words. He's staring at me. Properly staring at me.

The tips of our knees touch.

I'm struggling to breathe again.

The tips of his fingers touch mine and then my cigarette is plucked from my trembling hand.

He puts it with his in the ashtray, then faces me again.

He presses a finger to my cheek.

His mouth is so close to mine his breath's whispering on my lips.

I close my eyes and breathe him in.

His lips brush against mine.

Alex

If this is a dream then don't you dare wake me up.

Melody

I have been kissed many times. Too many.

Never have I felt anything like this.

A dam bursts inside me releasing a flood of heat and without even knowing how I've got there, I'm half-on Alex's lap with our arms wrapped tightly around each other and our bodies crushed together.

This is the kiss I've been waiting my whole life for.

Alex

This is Melody. This is really Melody, sat on my lap, kissing me as if she's been hungering for me with the same agony in which I've hungered for her all these years.

The scent of her skin, the taste of her mouth, the softness of her breasts pressed against my chest...

It's all so familiar and yet all so new and all so damn intoxicating and overwhelming that I break the kiss with a wrench and cup her cheeks.

I stare into the dark eyes of the woman I have loved for longer than I have currently walked on this earth.

She's breathing as heavily as I am.

"I..." God, it's right there on the tip of my tongue, the compulsion to tell her that I love her, that I've loved her forever, that I will always love her. But it's too soon, and I draw her back to me and taste her kisses again. There's an urgency in them. It's as strong in her as it is in me.

Friday 2nd January 2004

Alex

I can't drag my gaze from Melody's sleeping face. There's just enough illumination coming into the room from the light we never got round to turning off downstairs for me to study the pale skin with the smattering of freckles over the cute nose. My chest is so full it's a struggle to breathe.

It's a struggle to believe that this is real.

All those years of misery without her, most of them with no hope of her coming back to me, and here I am. Here we are.

It's incredible.

Since we fell into bed, we've only left it for tea, toast, and super-noodles.

I know now that I should have kept my mindset on a Melody level. Never give up hope.

Her eyes open and fix onto mine. I gaze into the dark, almost black pools. See the tiny flecks of gold in them. It feels like I'm staring into them for the first time.

I can't stop the smile spreading over my face. She smiles back, presses her fingers to my cheek and raises her head to kiss me.

Melody

My alarm clock wakes me.

Without opening my eyes, I press a kiss to Alex's chest, disentangle an arm from his sleeping hold, and hit the snooze button.

The two nights we've just shared relive themselves in my mind as I doze back off.

The two best nights of my life.

Turns out my severely neglected, shrivelled raisin of a vagina works fine thank you very much.

When I finally get round to opening my eyes, the daylight tells me it's way past getting-out-of-bed time.

My alarm clock reads 08:14.

"Shit, shit, shit, shit, shit!"

I'm supposed to be at work in sixteen minutes. I must have turned the alarm clock off instead of hitting snooze.

It's one thing fobbing Mum and Dad off (I lied and told them I had too big a hangover to come over for New Year's dinner), but I can't skive off work.

I jump out of bed and pull my wardrobe doors open. I need a shower, but there isn't time. I quickly pull underwear and a jumper off the shelves and rescue my black jeans from the floor.

Alex is awake, a sleepy, sexy smile on his gorgeous face.

"I'm so sorry," I say, kicking the wardrobe doors shut. "I've overslept. I've got to go to work."

It occurs to me that I'm suffering zero shyness at him seeing me fully naked.

I can hardly reconcile all those years spent frightened of him. What wasted years they were.

He yawns and stretches an arm over his head.

God, his body is delicious. I have the most severe temptation to call in sick and jump back on him.

"My car's parked outside Lorn's. I can give you a lift from there."

I lean over and kiss him. Then kiss him again. And then I drop the clothes I've just gathered together and jump on him.

Alex

Watching Melody rush around after oversleeping brings back so many memories I could explode from the exhilaration of witnessing it again.

She emerges from the bathroom smelling of toothpaste, grabs a bottle of perfume off her dresser and drenches herself in it. I don't recognise the scent, but I happily inhale it.

I follow her downstairs.

She grabs her Dr Martens and shoves a foot in one of them. "Any plans today?" she asks, not looking at me.

"Catch up on sleep and wait for my favourite pocket-dynamo to finish work."

Her eyes lift to mine. A huge grin spreads over her face.

"I might get some food in too, to feed her something that isn't toast or super-noodles."

In one motion, she abandons her other boot and jumps up to fling her arms around my neck and kiss me.

God, we shagged only fifteen minutes ago, and I'm already hard again.

I would blame it on thirteen years of celibacy, but it's Melody causing it. My beautiful, sexy, pocket-dynamo.

My Melody.

My Melody.

Monday 15th March 2004

Melody

I'm tracing circles around Alex's nipple. He's pretending to be asleep. I know he's pretending because his cock is growing against my thigh.

I'm glad Chipolata Mick didn't manage to put me off men for life. Very glad.

Alex is the opposite to Chipolata Mick, if you know what I mean, ha ha.

Honestly, I feel like a lovesick schoolgirl around him. I never felt like this when I *was* a lovesick schoolgirl, in those years when I thought myself in love with him.

It's incredible to think that was almost thirteen years ago. It feels so distant now, like that night happened to someone else and I was just an observer to it.

If you'd told my sixteen-year-old self that one day she would fall into bed with Alex Hammond and then never leave it (metaphorically), she would have jumped up and down and squealed for joy.

We haven't spent a night apart. He takes me to work and collects me from work. We often drop in at Lorna's to check her heart's still mending (that thing with Jasmin was a short-lived rebound fling that served the purpose of proving to Lorna that there are other women than Carrie in the world. One day, when she's ready, she'll go out there and meet them). And then we go to bed. Sometimes at his house. Sometimes at mine. We're equally comfortable at both.

He stops pretending to be asleep and rolls me onto my back.

I smile, hook an arm around his neck and sigh. "I think I love you."

I didn't mean to say that. In fact, I have no idea where those words came from. But they are true. I know that as they fall from my lips.

I can't bear to be parted from him. Have to force myself to share my time with anyone else. I count down the hours spent without him at work. Count down the hours spent without him each Sunday dinner with my family. When I'm with him, I need to constantly touch him.

He stares at me for the longest time before closing his eyes.

A needle of panic injects into my heart.

But the panic doesn't have time to seep into my blood stream because Alex opens his eyes and presses a kiss to the tip of my nose. And then he smiles. And then he laughs. "I'm afraid I trump you. I don't think I love you. I know I love you."

Oh, but my chest fills so quick and so hard that for a moment I can't breathe.

Sunday 11th April 2004

Melody

I unlock my front door for the first time in thirteen days and rush upstairs.

"Oi," Alex calls after me. "You're supposed to let me blindfold you."

"After I've had a look," I call back, sniggering smuttily.

I fling the bathroom door open and my breath catches in my throat.

The last time I was in my bathroom, the new white suite had been installed but the walls were bare, the only features the lumps of plaster I'd pulled out with the tiles. The floor was still the original lino the house had come with, consisting of a pattern last fashionable when Madonna was still an ingenue.

Alex stands behind me.

The delay in completing my bathroom – and the reason why I've spent two weeks at his house rather than dividing our time between the two homes like we usually do – was, he told me, because the plaster he'd skimmed the walls with was taking longer than anticipated to dry.

He's put the black and white tiles I'd bought before we got

together up in the checked pattern exactly as promised. What he neglected to mention was the flooring. The skanky lino is gone. In its place is a mosaic floor filled with butterflies of all different colours and sizes.

I swallow hard.

There are times when it feels like Alex can read my mind, that he can see deep into the rooms I keep closed. Old childhood rooms that, so far, no situation or conversation has led me to open for him. It'll happen one day, I'm sure, but it hasn't happened yet.

And then I remember that I paint butterflies on most things so he's probably got a good idea of my love of them without having to be a telepathist.

"You lied to me."

"Sorry." He doesn't sound it.

I look at him and smile. "This is the most beautiful thing anyone has ever done for me."

Alex

The smile on Melody's face dazzles.

I'd wanted to do something like this in this bathroom first time around but never had the time. I worked full time, so renovating the house was done over weekends and evenings in order of priority. When the first lockdown of the Covid pandemic came, the house was pretty much how we both wanted it, and the weather so good that mosaicking the bathroom floor didn't even cross my mind. By the second lockdown, I was back at work.

Doing Melody's mosaic floor made me realise how much I used to love my work, made me feel more like the old me. Her reaction to my creations never failed to make me want to shake my peacock tailfeather.

After she's kissed my face off, she keeps her arms locked

around my neck and smiles again. "Something tells me you've picked up on my love of butterflies."

"There were a few giveaways," I say lightly, but there's a tightening in my chest as Lorna's words echo in my head.

You have to tell her. You know that, right?

I always thought if I got Mel back, I *would* tell her, but as the weeks and months roll on, broaching the subject gets harder and harder. Just as I'm not the Alex of old, this Melody is not my Melody of old. Not exactly. The old Melody couldn't wait to introduce me to her parents. This Melody has made me wait over three months even though I already know them in this world.

I don't know how she'll react to the truth, that's the nub of it. I don't dare risk it.

"I think you might be the most talented person in existence," she says.

"And I think you might be a bit biased."

"Never." She bites my chin and slides her hand to my crotch.

"We're supposed to be at your parents' in fifteen minutes," I remind her.

"Tell your cock that." She strokes the hard length and pulls her best seductive smile.

It totally works and Melody introduces her new boyfriend to her family thirty minutes later than planned.

The smiles on their faces when they recognise me almost makes the agony of getting to this point worth it.

Melody

I don't know which of my family is the most excited to see Alex. Honestly, they were already salivating about me bringing a man home (Martin, he of Alice's-teeth-in-the-arm fame was the last, and I didn't invite him, Dad did, and obviously Chris doesn't count), but for me to turn up with Alex on my arm had the same effect as if I'd turned up with tickets to Disneyland, first class air fares and unlimited spending money.

I've waited a long time to bring Alex home. Sundays have been spent apart with our respective families. This is the first time either of us have crossed the family barrier.

It was time, and not just because Alice has been guilt-tripping me about her not coming for a sleepover in so long. It's because I'm finally sure, not about his feelings for me or mine for him, but about us.

It's difficult to explain because we've lived in a selfish bubble of happiness since the night we fell into bed together, but there's been this faint feeling in the pit of my stomach that I can only describe as a sense of doom, like I've been waiting for something to come along and burst our bubble.

It's taken me all this time to understand the feeling is plain old fear. Alex has been a part of my world for so long and over the years I've run the gauntlet of practically every emotion in a thesaurus for him, so it was a struggle to believe this happiness belongs to me and that nothing was going to come along and snatch it away.

Alice, who practically wet herself when she saw Alex at the door, insists on sitting between the two of us while we eat, which means I can't hold his hand or touch him in any way for at least two hours (Sunday dinner here is a ritual that is always savoured). She bombards him with questions about Australia which are extremely narrow in scope.

"Did you ever sit on a redback?"

"No."

"Not ever?"

"No."

"Do you know anyone who sat on a redback?"

"Sorry. No."

"Did you even *see* a redback?"

"No." Then, to placate her, he says, "But I did once have a spider in my living room that was bigger than my hand."

"Was that a redback?"

"No."

Dad's had enough of spider talk and wants Alex's attention just as much as Alice does.

"What are you doing for work now you're back? Are you going to join the business again?"

Alex swallows his potato. "Uncle Jimmy closed the business two years ago. Took early retirement."

"Will you start it again?"

"I'll be honest with you, most of my clients were wan..." He darts a quick glance at Alice and adjusts his insult to, "Not very nice. If all my clients were like you, I would've started it up again, but as it is, me and my brother are going into business together. We're going to renovate old buildings."

Dad looks crestfallen. "So you won't be doing your mosaics anymore?"

"I will, in the renovations. That'll be one of our selling points. All being well, we should have bought our first property by the end of spring."

I beam with pride and delight. I'm looking forward to meeting Ollie. I've heard so much about him and all their business plans. I just hope they don't over-extend themselves in doing it. Alex insists the finances are in place but I still worry. I guess it comes with the territory of loving someone.

"You can always mosaic our patio while you wait for that to go through." Dad elbows Mum and exaggerates a wink. "Can't he, Pats?"

"One day," she says, winking far more subtly at me. "Another Yorkshire, Alex?"

"Please." He takes one from the bowl she passes to him and pours a load of gravy over it, saying, "If you want your garden doing, I'll do it. Gladly."

Dad's face falls. "Can't afford it at the moment, can we, Pats?"

"I wouldn't want payment," Alex says before Mum can answer.

They both stop eating. Two forks hover in the air as they stare at him, then their mouths open and they're protesting in unison at how they couldn't possibly ask that of him etc, etc.

"Honestly, it would be my pleasure," he insists. "You can pay me with food."

"We'd pay for the materials," Dad says.

I sense Alex wants to protest this too, but he says, "I'd get them at cost. My labour would be free. Have a think about it and let me know."

Dad nods vigorously. "We will, won't we Pats?"

Mum merely smiles indulgently and passes Alex the bowl of potatoes.

Sunday 26th September 2004

Alex

It's quite something watching Mel cook. There's a lot of head scratching and checking of the recipes her mum has written out for her.

"You sure I can't help?" I ask for the fourth time.

"This is your birthday meal," she snaps but with a twinkle in her eye that cancels the sting.

"And we'll celebrate again then, just the two of us." I slide my arms around her waist and nuzzle my nose into her hair.

She slaps my hand. "I'm trying to concentrate. This cooking malarkey is hard work."

I kiss the nape of her neck then pour her a glass of wine. "Maybe this will help?"

She abandons her recipes to take a huge sip, and giggles. "Excellent idea. If I get pissed, I can blame my drunkenness for the shit food."

I suspect our families will eat something before leaving their homes. Just in case. Even Roy looked like he was thinking of an excuse when Melody said she would cook for everyone. Only

BUTTERFLIES

Alice didn't look alarmed at having to eat Melody's cooking, but she's not even nine yet and doesn't know any better.

If only they knew how, in another life, Melody became a sublime cook. We learned together when we bought the house in Juniper Crescent and found we had much less disposable income for eating out and takeaways. We only learned the basics, enough to stop ourselves starving, but then the accident happened and within a year the kitchen was filled with recipe books and exotic spices.

That other life won't be repeated. The conditions that led to her giving up work and taking up cooking to stave off boredom will not happen again. I will not let it. We're out of the woods with Lorna, but the danger hasn't passed for Mel. Not yet. Four and a bit months to go and then I will be able to sleep easily at night.

I can't trust the butterfly effect to keep her from danger. I can only trust myself.

I love this new Melody who's my Melody but with subtle differences. She's still bonkers. Still funny. Still loving and kind. But seven and a half years living a different life to the one we first shared has made her more cautious, and it's this caution that's held me back from asking her the question that's played on my mind every day since New Year's Day.

I can't hold it back another minute.

I take the glass from her, put it on the counter and cup her face in my hands. "I love you, Melody Aldridge. Marry me. Please."

Just like the first time, my heart beats so hard and so fast while I wait for her answer that I fear it'll burst through my ribs.

But then the beaming smile spreads over her face and relief is bursting instead of my heart as she loops her arms tightly around my neck and says the magic words I've so longed to hear again.

"Yes." She kisses me. "Yes, yes, yes."

Melody

I'm floating so high on happiness that I can barely bring myself to care that I've cooked all the moisture out of the beef joint or that the potatoes and parsnips are black, or that my old primary school cook would have been ashamed to serve the cabbage that ended up on our dining table.

Thursday 30th September 2004

Melody

Alex has laid a path from his boot room to the gate that divides his land with the manor's grounds. After shouting another goodbye to him, I set off.

I overslept (surprise!) and so haven't had time for my first nicotine fix of the day. I dig for the cigarette packet in my handbag and pull one out. Instead of lighting it though, I find myself examining it like a forensic scientist.

What the hell am I doing to my body smoking these things?

For the first time since I started smoking at sixteen, the thought of putting a cigarette between my lips repulses me.

I put the cancer stick back in its packet and ram the packet back in my handbag.

My strides to the manor are more purposeful than my usual dawdle.

Saturday 13th November 2004

Melody

"Which one do you like the most?" I ask Lorna.

Honestly, I'm on the verge of losing my patience with her. I thought it was the bride who was supposed to be the monster when it came to choosing the dress, not the chief bridesmaid.

I chose my dress in the second wedding shop we visited. We've set a date for next June. It sounds a long way off but Mum assures me the time will fly by. We're now in our fifth shop and there's two dresses from this one short-listed along with four previous ones, and Lorna still can't decide which one she wants. I might just put my foot down and make her wear a baby-pink meringue out of spite.

"Let's get coffee and cake, and then I can look at the pictures with fresh eyes," she says.

I resist kicking her.

Alice has her karate lesson so her and Mum leave us to it. Unlike Little Miss Fussy, Alice, the actual child of us all, is happy to wear whatever dress we choose so long as she looks like a princess.

We find a table in a heaving coffee shop. I lay out the polaroids of the six shortlisted dresses.

"Make a choice," I say bossily.

She gives a put-upon sigh. "Okay... well I like the colour of that one but it makes me look fat, and that one fits nicely but the colour makes me look sallow, and that one's nice but way too expensive –"

"You're not paying for it," I interrupt.

"I know but it's a lot of money." Her eyes give the slightest flicker. "How are you paying for it all?"

"Alex. He's got savings put aside from when he sold his bar in Australia."

"Must be a lot of money saved."

"He made a lot from it."

"Is that what he told you?"

"Yes... No... Well, not in so many words."

I think of the rundown manse him and Ollie bought. My worries about Alex over-extending himself were worries that, so far, have come to nothing. The few times I've questioned him to make sure he's okay money-wise, he's kissed me and told me I have nothing to worry about. I believe him but...

God, I hate admitting this but I can't help feeling he's holding something back from me.

"You haven't asked him?"

I grit my teeth. "What are you implying?"

"Nothing."

"Doesn't sound like it. Don't you want me to marry him?"

"Of course I do."

"Then what's your problem?" I hate confrontation but this has been over a month in coming. "You've been off with me since we got engaged."

"I haven't."

"You have." I take a deep breath and ask in a gentler tone, "Is it to do with Carrie?"

"No!"

Well, that was pretty adamant.

"Then what is it? If you've got doubts about us, tell me."

Because I have doubts too. Not doubts about our love for each other, but there's something lurking out of reach and it frightens me.

Something has frightened me about Alex since the day he lunged at me in The Merry Thief all those years ago. That fear has taken many different forms, from fear of him to fear about my feelings for him. I have no fear of him anymore – I haven't for a long, long time – and I no longer fear my feelings for him either, not when they're so fully reciprocated, but something's there all the same, nestled in the pit of my stomach, a fear that wakes me in the night and has me pressing my hand to his chest to feel his heartbeat and assure myself that he's safe and really there. My fear only grows when I wake in the night and find his eyes open and staring at the ceiling.

I don't know if it's the money thing but Alex is holding something back from me.

He *is*. I can feel it.

I've just not wanted to admit it.

What that something is frightens me more than anything.

Lorna holds my stare for the longest time.

Does she know what that something is?

Or am I just being paranoid?

Please let it be paranoia.

Then she sighs. "I don't have doubts about you. You're made for each other and I'm happy for you, I promise. Maybe I'm just jealous?"

"Are you asking me or telling me?"

She grins. "Both?"

"You have nothing to be jealous of."

"I can't ever get married, can I?"

There's a pang in my chest for her. Lorna's never said anything about wanting to marry. Carrie's still her only real relationship.

"Aren't they looking to bring in civil partnerships?" I say, trying to think of a positive for her.

"It's not the same thing."

I take her hand and squeeze it. "Look at it this way, it wasn't so long ago that they got rid of Section 28. Now, how about we make a deal – you choose a bloody dress and I'll picket Downing Street with you until they give in and give full marriage equality for everyone?"

"It'll never happen."

"What? You choosing a dress or two women being allowed to marry?"

Now she does laugh, and picks up the polaroids. She flicks through them and then plucks one out.

"This one," she says.

It's the most bloody expensive one.

Monday 22nd November 2004

Alex

Someone's at the door. Judging by the length of time they keep their finger on the doorbell, that someone is determined to get my attention.

I look at my watch. It's only three thirty. Plenty of time before I leave to meet Mel when she finishes work.

My visitor is Lorna.

"What are you doing here?" I ask, stepping aside so she can come in out of the cold.

"Playing hooky from work."

"Something wrong?"

"You could say that."

"Don't keep me in suspense. What's on your mind."

"You."

"Me? What've I done?"

"It's what you haven't done."

Melody

The banging above Brocklehurst Manor's library, which I've seconded for use as my temporary office, has been so loud all day it's given me a banging headache. As soon as the workmen are done for the day, I call Jan and ask permission to finish early. We're closed for visitors until the Spring, which is when all the renovations will be complete and we can have our grand re-opening, but any hope I had of slacking off is long gone. The renovations have unveiled a treasure-trove of manuscripts and trinkets hidden in nooks, crannies and priest-holes for me to delight and pore over and catalogue. Also, someone has to supervise the work and that someone is me.

The sun's still out when I open the dividing gate between the manor's and Alex's grounds. As the days have gotten shorter, he's taken to meeting me so I don't have to navigate the grounds alone in the dark. My early finish will save him a trip.

Alex

"I'm serious. You have to tell her," Lorna says for the third time since she turned up. "You can't marry her on a lie. It's not right."

"There is no lie."

"There is, and you know it."

"I've done everything I can not to lie to her. Not outright lies."

"You're holding back a whole life from her."

I slam our coffees down on the table. "Lorna, listen to me," I say, trying my best to keep a lid on my anger. "Remember how you reacted when I told you? How do you think she'll react? What the fuck do you think it will do to her?"

If I had a cast iron guarantee that Melody would take it well then I would have told her a long time ago, but if I've learned anything in my two lifetimes it's that nothing is guaranteed. My

Melody of now is not my Melody of before, but being with her again has only reinforced that a life without either of my Melodys is no life at all. I will not risk losing her again, not for anything.

"What do you think it will do to her when she finds out another way?"

"Are you going to tell her?"

"Of course not, but sooner or later you're going to slip up."

"There's nothing to slip up about."

"You were together for nearly *thirty years*. Sooner or later those years are going to blur with the present. That's how I knew Carrie was cheating on me. She was reminiscing about our daytrip to Hunstanton in her Mazda." She grimaces. "We never went to Hunstanton. She went with Jonathan. She bought the Mazda while she was living with me. I never confronted her about it. I told myself she was talking about a time before she moved in, that she'd got her cars confused and her years muddled up. All the signs were there that she was seeing him again but I ignored them. I was terrified of losing her but when I think back, I'm sure it would have got to the stage where I couldn't ignore the signs anymore and would have had to confront her. Do you want that to happen with Mel? Can you honestly say you haven't slipped up along the way already and not even realised it?"

My chest has tightened.

I tripped up just two weeks ago. Mel mentioned something that happened when she was at university and I asked if she was talking about Cerys, one of the girls she used to share a house with. Mel's never mentioned her in this life but she didn't notice that slip.

She noticed the one before though, a month ago, when she decided to attempt making a meringue and I reminded her of the time her Aunt Allie had nearly set fire to her house making the same thing. She couldn't remember telling me about that. I felt like a gaslighting pile of shit for letting her think it was something she'd forgotten mentioning.

Past and present blur more strongly when we're in our

marital home. Memories live in its walls. I censor myself a lot there. Melody wants to rent it out when we marry. I have to bite my tongue to stop myself telling her to sell it.

"And what about your money?" Lorna's warming to her theme. "She has no idea what you're worth, but I tell you now, she's getting suspicious. I know Melody and I'm telling you, she knows something's off. The honeymoon period when love is blind is wearing off. All it will take is for her to go looking for something and stumble on a bank statement. How are you going to explain having millions in the bank? Anonymous donor, my arse."

"We've been back together nearly a year and she hasn't –"

"You're living on borrowed time!" she shouts. "She is going to find out. You have to tell her, Alex. You have to."

"Tell me what?"

Melody is standing in the doorway that connects the kitchen to the boot room, still bundled up from the cold.

Lorna and I both freeze.

"Tell me what?" Melody repeats.

Shit. Fuck. Bollocks.

"I heard something about the anonymous donor," Melody says. There's uncertainty in her stare as well as her voice when her gaze lands on me. "Is that you?"

I cannot tell her a barefaced lie. Not now. Not even when I sense deep in my bones that our lives have reached a pendulum and a swing the wrong direction will smash everything we have into pieces.

I take a deep breath and clear my constricted throat. "Yes."

Melody's face has always been an open book to her thoughts and feelings, and now is no different as I watch her process this. "But... how? Where did you...?" She shakes her head as if clearing water from her ears. "Why didn't you tell me?"

What the hell do I say? Where do I begin?

"Tell her," Lorna groans, burying her face in her hands. "Tell her everything."

Melody

The beats of my heart are racing in my throat. And in my ears.

Something is very, very wrong.

Perspiration breaks out on my forehead.

I've been living with the fear of something being wrong for so long that to suddenly realise I've been right to be fearful is terrifying in its own right.

A sense of doom pulses in me. Our happy bubble is about to burst.

A dozen possibilities flash through my mind: Alex is ill, Alex has a secret wife, Alex and Lorna once shagged, Alex is bankrupt, Alex has a genetic disorder that means he can only father Smurfs, Alex is cheating on me...

I immediately discount the last thought and manage to swallow a breath. Whatever it is, it's not that, and if it isn't that then it can't be too bad and I'll handle it and everything will be fine. And I have to discount bankruptcy too if he's the mysterious million-pound donor... unless it's the donation that's made him bankrupt, because how on earth did he get a huge sum of money like that? He lives in a huge house but that came from the sale of his bar in Australia, but then there's the manse he's bought with Ollie and the renovation costs, so maybe he *is* a secret millionaire, but then if he is, why didn't he tell me, and...

And my mind is racing because these two know whatever the truth is they're arguing about while I'm left speculating because I don't have a clue what's going on.

"Will one of you just tell me," I beg, unable to bear the suspense a second longer.

Alex just stares at me. There's no colour on his face.

Time ticks slowly, cruelly, on until Lorna lifts her head from her hands. She's on the verge of tears. "Alex was married to you before. You died. He came back in time to start his life with you again and save you."

What the hell is in that mug she's drinking from? Magic mushrooms tea?

"Very funny. What are you really arguing about?"

A tear rolls down her cheek. "It's true. Alex is from the future. We were arguing about whether or not to tell you."

I want to laugh. I mean, this is hilarious, right? I want to laugh, but my windpipe has frozen.

Alex bows his head and rubs his neck.

"Alex?" I croak.

"It's true."

"Bullshit."

He lifts his head and meets my eye. And then he opens his mouth and recites a story so ridiculous that by the end of it, I'm slumped on the bay windowsill, hugging myself tightly and wondering if I need to have the pair of them committed to a mental institution or if I need to check myself into one for falling in love with a psychotic, compulsive liar.

Alex

I can hardly breathe while I wait for Melody to respond. It doesn't have to be with words. Anything but sit as she is, staring into space like a catatonic patient in *The Awakenings*.

Lorna crouches in front of her and takes her hand. "Mel?"

She doesn't snatch her hand away. It's worse than that. She puts her other hand on Lorna's, slides the covered hand out of her hold, and pushes her. It's not a hard push but it doesn't need to be.

Without a word, she gets to her feet and leaves the kitchen. There's a dignity to her movements that takes me back decades, to the night we first realised we had something real and special. It was the moment when only the truth from me saved us from dying before we'd even really started. This time, I fear it's the truth that will kill us.

Assuming she needs a moment to compose herself, I stay put but less than a minute later the front door closes.

Shit.

I jump to my feet and follow her.

She's walking speedily up the driveway, shoulders hunched.

I catch up and fall into step. "I'm sorry. I should have told you sooner."

She doesn't answer, just keeps putting one foot in front of the other.

"I know it's a shock," I say. "I spent most of my first year back expecting to wake up in 2024."

Her only reaction is to up her pace even more.

"Look, the reason I didn't tell you is because when I told Lorna, I almost lost her friendship. I can't lose you again. I *can't*. I know how batshit crazy it sounds, but I can prove it."

She's almost at the gate.

"Your best friend at primary school was called Katie. She died of Leukaemia when she was eleven."

Not a drop in pace.

"Your favourite memory of her is the day your mums took you to Cotswold Wildlife Park. Traffic was bad so you stopped for a picnic on the way. You played in a meadow, and Katie made you a daisy-chain. It was the last thing she ever gave you and you kept it until it disintegrated."

She abruptly stops walking and rounds on me. Her face under the dark sky is ashen. "Who told you that?"

"You did."

"I did not. I've not spoken about Katie in years."

"Not in this life." I take a deep breath. "You love butterflies because they remind you of her. One sat on her shoulder that day and whenever one flies close to you, you wonder if it's her saying hello."

I'm the only person she's ever told the story of the butterfly to. It came years after our wedding when she painted butterflies on the kitchen tiles with such care and detail that I asked why butterflies were so special to her.

Her eyes are huge, her knuckles white where she's clinging to the strap of her handbag.

But she's listening to me.

"A few weeks before we met at the fishing lake, you went to the cinema with your friend Hayley to watch *Robin Hood*. You fell in love with the film and that Bryan Adams song. You bought the single and played it so much the tape broke and you had to buy a new copy. Every time you played it, you thought of me."

Something she only told me when we were planning our wedding; something she hasn't told me this time round yet.

"When we married, it was our wedding song."

I'm getting through to her. I'm sure of it.

"I always hated that song," I continue. "Thought it was sentimental tripe. Still do, I guess, but knowing you always thought of me when you played it made me love it too –"

"Stop."

She doesn't shout the word at me but the impact is the same.

"Alex," she whispers, "Do you have any idea how mad this sounds or how scary it is to know that someone has been snooping through the most private moments of my life?"

"I haven't been, I swear. These are things you told me. We were together for twenty-eight years."

"No, we weren't. I don't know where your sick obsession with me has come from, but it ends now."

I put my hands on her shoulders and will her to see the truth in my eyes. "Melody, *think*. How can I know any of these things if you hadn't told me?"

"There's no such thing as time travel."

"I'm living proof that there is, and I'm only here because of you, because you are so fucking special that even God or whoever it was that gave me the wine gum thing recognised it, but he didn't give me the chance for my sake, no way, the only good that came in my life came through you. It was for your sake."

"Because I'm going to die young?" she asks cynically.

"No, to stop you dying young a second time."

She clamps her lips together and breathes deeply, narrowing eyes not leaving mine. "You said it was a hit and run?"

"The knock-on effects from it."

"Okay, well thanks for the warning. I'll be extra-cautious crossing roads from now on, so consider your job done."

She shrugs my hands off her shoulders and pulls the gate open.

"Don't do this, Mel. Please don't do this."

She spins back round. Her eyes are filled with tears but they don't spill over. "The only thing I've done is fall in love with a liar and a fantasist."

"I never meant to lie to you. I didn't know how to tell you about the money without bringing up everything and running the risk of losing you again."

Her face contorts.

"And you know I'm not a fantasist. You know it. You and me, Mel. It's always been you and me and you know it in your heart. I know you're scared and I'm sorry, and I wish I could take this all back and do it again but I don't know how because none of this was ever in my control."

She shakes her head. "I don't want to hear anymore."

"Ask your sister!" God, I'm desperate. "Alice has known from the moment she saw me that you and I are meant to be together."

It's the wrong thing to say. Melody is fiercely protective of Alice. Her face is now a beacon of contempt.

"You need help, you lying creep. But I will say this – if you truly believe the shit you're spouting and love me like you say you do, then prove it by staying out of my life. I never want to see you again."

Melody

I lock my front door and slide the chain across it, then run around the house making sure all the windows are locked and all the curtains closed.

Only when I'm certain my home is secure do I climb into bed, pull a pillow over my head, and scream until my lungs burn.

Tuesday 23rd November 2004

Alex

A message pings in my phone.

I've put your things in a box on my doorstep. If they're not gone by the time I get home from work, I'll burn them and give the ring to a charity shop. Do what your like to my stuff. I don't want any of it.

Saturday 11th December 2004

Alex

Lorna and I are watching *Soccer AM*. We only like football when England are playing but this is mindless entertainment that occasionally makes one of us grunt, so it will do. It's the only thing we can agree to watch.

Lorna's babysitting me. She's roped Ollie into her rota. I'm letting her get on with it. It makes her feel better.

Melody's cut me off.

I'm beyond despair. The heaven I'd found again has been snatched away and all I feel is numb. I have no urge to drink myself into a stupor – medicating with alcohol doesn't work, only worries the people who love you – or hide myself away from friends or family, or escape back to Australia. I have no urge to do anything.

I keep asking myself if things would have been different if I'd made the donation as me rather than anonymously. Would a natural conversation have evolved where I explained how I'd come to amass the fortune from which I could cash-in a million quid's worth of investments on a whim?

Those investments were made and built up for her so we

could live the life we'd once dreamed of, so if Alice took a three-year contract in Chile I wouldn't have to take a job in Scotland to pay for flights to see her.

"Melody can never stay cross with anyone for long," Lorna pipes up. She's taken to saying this kind of thing. I think she's trying to convince herself. I'm not the only person Melody's cut off. The difference is, I don't think her silence with Lorna will last much longer.

"I'm the exception to that rule."

"No you're not. She got there in the end before, didn't she?"

"That time was different. And it took her five years to look at me without wanting to maim me."

"She loves you."

"She hates me."

"Doesn't mean she doesn't love you."

"She thinks I'm a psychopath."

I should have taken my chances and been honest with her from the start. Okay, maybe not *right* from the start, but definitely when Lorna first told me to, before I left for Australia. There were major world events about to happen I could have laid out as proof, like I did with Lorna. The Twin Towers. The war in Afghanistan. The war in Iraq. They've all happened since and now I can't think of anything important that's going to happen any time soon.

It's too late now.

I had my second chance of a life with Melody but my dishonesty and secrecy ruined it.

I have no one to blame but myself.

Saturday 18th December 2004

Melody

I can see from Lorna's face that she's not expecting Alice to be with me.

I arranged this meeting. A cup of coffee and a croque monsieur each in Brocklehurst's newest coffee shop. The same chain as the coffee we shared the day we were looking for bridesmaids' dresses and she tried hinting about Alex. Her hints should have been stronger.

I can't hate Lorna. I've tried but it's impossible. She was trying to be a friend to us both. What I will never understand is how she allowed herself to be suckered into his lies and fantasies.

And I will never understand why, when he was holding my shoulders and looking into my eyes and spouting his bullshit, I found myself believing him. *Wanting* to believe him, I correct myself. Desperately wanting to believe him.

I suppose that's why I forgive her. Because I had to fight myself not to get suckered into his lies too. And because I love her.

Alice is with me for protection, because I cannot guarantee my behaviour if Lorna utters his name.

I hate him.

I loathe him.

I despise him.

I want to make an effigy of him and stick pins in it.

I miss him desperately.

Alice knows we're not getting married. I've not given her or our parents any details, just said it didn't work out and that we realised we weren't right for each other. They all took it much worse than I anticipated. They'll get over it. They have to.

And so do I.

* * *

"Smelly?"

"Yes, Alice?"

"Why don't you love Alex anymore?"

It's a question she's asked me dozens of times. My answer never satisfies her.

I can't tell her the truth, that it's because he's a fantasist and a liar. She loves Alex. I could tell her he's an axe-murderer and she'd still want me to marry him.

"He's not right for me."

"He is." She's so damn certain of this. For a nine-year-old, she has convictions a nun would be proud of.

"On this, we have to agree to disagree." If nothing else, this is teaching Alice a valuable life lesson.

"He loves you." Her little face is fierce.

I stroke her hair and try to smile. "In his own way he does. Now go to sleep. It's late."

Rolling over, I turn the bedside light off.

Soon, her heavy breathing tells me Alice is asleep. She still likes to share a bed with me. When Alex and I were together, she'd sneak in and plonk herself between the two of us.

"There's Alex," she says, tugging at my hand.

We're on Watling Street looking at the display on the

jeweller's front window. I look to where she's pointing and see him on the other side of the road, heading towards the town hall.

"Alex!" she shouts, but all the traffic means he can't hear her. No, he can't hear *me*. It's me shouting his name. I'm behind him but my legs are weighted and can't run to catch him. I try to shout his name again but all that comes out is a hoarse croak, and now he's walking up the steps of the hall and panic is making me scream as loudly as I can but nothing's coming out of my throat and...

I sit bolt upright into the darkness of my room, panting. My chest is filled with ice. Tears are pouring down my face.

Sunday 16th January 2005

Melody

I sit Alice on my lap. She's nearly the same height as me but still likes to sit on my lap. I'll take it for as long as it lasts, even if it does mean my thighs and bum go numb.

"Remember, don't touch anything," I warn her.

"I know," she says impatiently.

Hands thoroughly cleaned and dried, I gently turn the pages of the sixteenth century manuscript found beneath a floorboard during the ongoing renovations.

I get to the page I was looking for and hover my finger over the name I've promised her is written there. "See? Alice Aldridge."

She bends her head but is careful not to allow even a strand of her hair touch the precious pages. Her nose wrinkles. "It doesn't say that."

"Does. It's just the way the letters are formed."

I carefully move the manuscript aside then pull out a notepad and pen from my top drawer. "Watch," I say, then slowly form her name in the same cursive that was written by a human hand over four hundred and fifty years ago. "A... L... I..."

"I see it!" Her eyes light up with glee. "I was here!"

"Told you." I finish copying her name onto the notepad then move her off my lap and pop out of the library to put the manuscript back in the box with the other recently found manuscripts.

"Alice Aldridge really came here with Henry the Eighth?" Alice asks when I return to the library. She's copying my copy of her name. I love the way she concentrates with her little pink tongue poking out of her mouth.

"Yep." I hoik her back onto my lap. "She was one of Jane Seymour's ladies and was part of her progress when she stayed here."

"She slept here?"

"Yep." Anticipating her next question – Alice always has lots of questions – I add, "I don't know where she slept, but she must have spent at least two nights here."

"How do you know?"

"There's lots of evidence but mostly because of all the food the owners bought for it. It's all dated and logged. The king and queen had a lot of courtiers and they were all greedy pigs."

She giggles. "*I* wasn't a greedy pig."

I tickle her belly. "I bet you were."

"What else did they do here?"

"I imagine they hunted. In those days, the manor was surrounded by acres and acres and acres of forests and land filled with deer – most of Brocklehurst! And I bet they danced too, in the evenings, and had music played for them. We still have a lute here that it's plausible, dates-wise, was used during the king's visit."

"What does plausible mean?"

"It means we have no actual proof but that there's enough evidence for us to think it could have happened..." The words have hardly left my mouth when a shiver coils up my spine and lifts the hair on my neck.

Unsettled, I shake the strange feeling off and check my watch. "Mum'll be here soon."

She jumps off my lap and puts the notepaper in her coat pocket.

Mum's waiting for us in the car park. Alice can't wait to tell her about her namesake, and starts rabbiting before she's even put her seatbelt on.

The road connecting the manor to Watling Street is a narrow, winding back lane that it's wise to drive along slowly. As happens every time, I hold my breath when we pass the turning to Alex's house. Alice is so busy jabbering on that, for once, the turning doesn't register and so I'm saved a bombardment of the Alex questions she normally subjects me to.

Mum indicates to turn right onto Watling Street. A blue car travelling from the left is indicating to turn in. It flashes mum. She pulls out. For the flash of a second my eyes connect with the driver's.

It's Alex.

Sunday 30th January 2005

Melody

The smallest of my spare rooms, the one not big enough to swing a cat, is piled high with the boxes I shoved in it when I moved in. Since that momentous date, I've added more junk to it. A lot more junk. I peer inside cautiously. One wrong move and I'll be flattened. I can imagine the obituary: *Spinster found crushed in hoarding tragedy*.

I've got four hours until my taxi (Dad) arrives, and I'm determined to make some headway with this room before he gets here. Chris and his boyfriend Tom are coming to stay next weekend, and I might have lied and told them I'd already turned this room from a hoardster's paradise into a proper spare room. For a teeny-weeny person. If I lied (I admit nothing), then it's only because they kept teasing me about it and asking when I was going to get a load of cats.

With music blaring from my bedroom, I fill five black bags with crap in the first hour, drag them through the garden – oof, it's *cold* – and dump them in the garage. Excellent progress.

Ooo, there's the fan I was looking for last summer. I'll put that under my bed.

Aha! There's my Daphne du Maurier's *Rebecca*. I'd better apologise to Lorna.

Two hours gone and all the random stuff has been cleared and I am shaking my tush to Spiller's 'Groovejet.' Just the boxes Mum dumped on me to go and then I will be done diddly done.

The first two boxes contain a load of stuff from primary school. I have a marvellous time reading through my childish projects on the Battle of Hastings and Helen Keller, and flipping through school reports ('talks too much' seems to be a common theme), and humming old primary school songs. At the bottom of the second box are all the class photos from reception, all the way to my final year. I study them closely. Me and Katie are sat or stood together in all of them. Apart from the last. She died two weeks before the final end-of-year photo was taken. It's the only photo in which my teeth aren't showing.

I wipe my eyes and take some deep breaths.

Strange, isn't it, how you can go for weeks and months barely giving someone a second thought and then, in an instant, you feel their absence so acutely that the pain is as fresh as it was the day you lost them.

Before Katie died, death had been an abstract thing to me. The only person I knew who'd died was our old next-door neighbour, Mrs Stewart, who used to let me pick apples from her tree. Mum and Dad sat me down and with very solemn faces told me she had gone to heaven. I think I was sad for about five minutes but I never *felt* her death, if you understand what I mean?

I learned what death really meant through Katie. It meant pain. Unbelievable pain. Her absence was as real to me as losing a limb would have been. For years I woke every morning hoping I'd dreamt her death and that I could run three houses along to hers, knock on the door, and run up to her bedroom and play.

There's photos of Katie's eleventh birthday party there too. She had a McDonald's party. Ronald himself entertained us. My memory can play tricks on me but I think that party was the day before we went to Cotswold Wildlife Park.

I don't remember knowing Katie was going to die. I knew she was very poorly. But I do remember my parents sitting me down with faces even more solemn than when they told me about old Mrs Stewart, and I remember screaming and screaming until Dad wrapped his arms around me and rocked me like I was a baby.

I flick through the boxes containing my secondary school stuff. There's not much I want to reminisce about in those. They can go in the garage and collect dust until the garage is so overloaded I'm forced to hire a skip.

Now there's only five boxes left. Four contain the junk I accumulated at university.

The final box...

I rest my hand on it. My heart is thumping again. I've deliberately left this one until last.

I need a cigarette. Should I go to the...?

No. I will not buy cigarettes. It has been exactly four months since I stopped smoking and I will not go back to that addicted life.

I take a humungous breath to smother the craving, then slice through the masking tape holding the box together.

I have to wipe more tears away to see the contents clearly. Four items. A video. A tape. A Walkman. A jumper.

I lift the jumper and hold it to my face. I breathe it in.

The only scent is *eau de musty cardboard* but I can smell him, and I breathe him deep into my lungs and breathe in all the memories of the night I fell in love.

I let it all come back. Every minute of it.

I fell in love so hard that night that nothing has compared to that feeling since. Nothing felt right after that. Not until I found my way back to him.

Alex was the missing piece of my puzzle.

I've tried so hard to forget him but I can't.

Since the night we met at the fishing lake, Alex Hammond has lived like a spectre in my thoughts and dreams, but since we got together, being without him is like living with a permanently battered and bruised heart. Not having him in my life is torture.

Oh, what am I *thinking*? That I'm going to run to his house and tell him I love him?

The man's delusional! A fantasist!

And loving. Sexy. Considerate. Really rather fucking wonderful, pardon my French.

Clinging to his jumper, I scramble to my feet and fling the bathroom door open and gaze at the floor he created with such love for me.

He knew about Katie.

I've never told anyone about my connecting butterflies to Katie because I know it sounds batshit crazy, something I've known since she died, so there's only one way he could know but it's impossible.

I gather my hair into bunches and pull hard in agonised frustration.

"GOD!" I shout at the top of my lungs. "IF YOU EXIST, IF YOU REALLY DID GIVE ALEX A WINE GUM THAT MADE HIM TRAVEL IN TIME, THEN GIVE ME A SIGN!"

Silence.

"GIVE ME A SIGN!"

Silence.

"GIVE ME A *SIGN*!"

A horn beeps outside.

Dad's here.

Thursday 3rd February 2005

Melody

It's long past closing time when I finish work for the day. Jan and Moira turned up wanting to talk about the gift shop and café that will be opening Easter weekend. For some reason, the Trustees think I'm an expert on the kind of stationary we should be selling and the kind of cakes our customers are most likely to want. Then, before I could beg a lift off one of them, the head of a primary school called to ask about the grand reopening and when she could bring a class of her kidlets along. Our publicity drive is definitely working, yay, but it's now gone six, it's dark, everyone's left and it's effing cold, boo. Worse, I have to walk. I mean, it's only two miles to my house from here, but still.

Bugger.

I keep tight to the verge and alert for cars as I walk my least favourite part of the route home, the narrow winding road to Watling Street. When I get to the turn for Alex's drive, I pause. And then I sigh.

Every time I've walked past his drive this week I've scurried past it like a frightened hamster.

I can't keep scurrying.

I open the gate.

Halfway up the drive, I see the house. All the lights are out. His car's not there.

I have no idea if the emotion flooding me is relief or disappointment.

It's not as if I'd planned to drop in on him is it? I mean, what would I have said if he'd been there?

'Hi, Alex. I love you and I'm not sleeping and I desperately want you back in my life, but any rational person would say that your claims to be a time traveller are irrational and delusional and that I should be making plans to admit you into a mental institution, not wondering how I'm going to cope spending the rest of my life without you because this missing you malarky is getting worse, so can you please provide me with some of that proof you said you had? Pretty please? Pretty please with a cherry on top?'

Too much?

I turn back and continue on my way, and soon I'm on Watling Street.

Effing hell, it is *freezing*. One of these days I'm going to remember to buy myself a pair of gloves.

Alex

She's coming. I see her, huddled into herself against the cold.

I step back and stand beside the old-fashioned red phone box, out of her eyeline. The crossing she'll take is directly in front of me.

Melody

I walk past a boutique that opened just before Christmas. It does posh evening wear. I only know this because Mum's going to have a look for a dress in it for Ladies Day at Ascot. I've walked or been driven past this boutique twice a day for over a month, and this is the first time I've noticed the butterflies stencilled on its glass shopfront.

I look at them a moment, remembering again what Alex said about Katie and the butterfly.

How had he *known* that? I've asked myself that so many times since God refused to give me a sign, and I'm still no closer to an answer that wouldn't have me certified insane alongside Alex.

But there is no other answer. None.

I reach the traffic lights I need to cross. The left lane is light with traffic for this time of day, especially compared with the busy right lane, and I briefly wonder if there's been an accident further up and the police have stopped cars. I press the button and go back to my Alex thoughts while I wait.

When is he ever *not* in my thoughts?

There are so many things he knows. Little things that meant nothing at the time but when you put them together and think of the meaning of plausible...

The pedestrian walk sign flashes green and a spark flashes in my brain with it.

Why am I waiting for a sign when I've already had a million signs over the years? He placed a butterfly on my shoulder in my parents bathroom mosaic for heaven's sake!

Dear God (sorry, God), he couldn't have signposted the truth any clearer.

I laugh. I'm going to have to be certified insane because I believe him –

A brick wall slams into me and throws me across the road.

Friday 4th February 2005

Melody

If not for his dark hair, Alex would be indistinguishable from the white bedsheets. I've pulled the visitor's chair as close as I can get without disturbing all the tubes and things keeping him alive. I hold his giant, unreceptive hand. I've never thought of him as vulnerable before. Not my Alex, not the man I've loved every day of my life since that magical night when I was sixteen.

The doctors are hopeful he'll pull through. I try hard to cling to that. Hope is all I have.

"Don't leave me," I say to him for the thousandth time. "I love you. Please don't leave me."

Don't die, Alex. Please don't die. Please, please, please don't die.

Alex

"Something smells good," I say as I stride into the kitchen.

Mum slaps my hand before I can dip my finger into the bowl of icing she's mixing. "It's coffee cake. It'll be ready soon. Go and wash your hands."

I hold them up for her to inspect. "They're clean."

She lifts her glasses to peer closer and gives the half-smiling, half-suspicious mum look that always makes me feel guilty even when I haven't done anything wrong. "They'll do."

Music's playing. It's a song I recognise but it's coming out muffled.

There's coffee on the table. We sit down.

Mum takes my hand. I feel the warm pressure of it but her face is blurring.

"You've turned into such a handsome man, Alex."

I try to put her features into clearer focus. "Do I still look like granddad?"

"Even more now. He sends his love."

"Am I dead?"

She shakes her head. She's fading. The music is becoming clearer.

"Oh. It's a dream?"

I sense more than see her smile. "I love you, Alex. Live well."

"*Everything I do...*"

"I love you, Mum."

My eyes snap open.

Mum has disappeared. The room's so bright my vision needs to adjust but the dark eyes looking at me now belong to Melody.

There's still a compression on my hand. It's Melody's hand covering mine.

Other things are coming into focus.

I'm in hospital. I'm not in any pain but my left leg feels weighty. There's something in my ear. It's where the music's coming from. I can hear it perfectly now.

I notice all this without taking my eyes from hers. I'm scared that if I look away or blink she'll disappear like Mum just did.

'*There's no love, like your love...*'

I swallow. The last time my throat was this dry I'd sunk two bottles of Jim. "Mel?"

She brings her face to mine. Anxiety is etched on it. There's a black lead running from her ear and down her neck and further down where I can't see, and now I realise she's listening to the music with me, one ear piece each.

"How long have you made me listen to this shite?" I croak.

Her pale face breaks into a grin. "An hour."

"An hour?"

She holds a Walkman up for me to see. "Alice brought it over. I don't think the batteries will last much longer."

"Thank God for that."

The song ends. Without letting go of my hand, she presses a button on the music player that even now, in 2005, is obsolete.

"What are you doing?"

"Rewinding it."

"You're not going to make me listen to it again are you?"

"One more for luck, and then I'll spare you until our wedding."

"We're getting married, are we?"

"That's what I've told all the staff here, so I've kind of committed us to it. Sorry."

I have to say, this is either the most excellent dream or I'm on some superb painkillers.

"Don't worry about it," I say nonchalantly. "I wouldn't want you getting into trouble with the staff. They can be scary."

"Terrifying. Oh, and you have to promise to never lie to me again. Omissions count as lies."

"I promise. I should have told you the truth from the start."

A tear trickles down her cheek but her smile doesn't dim. "I have to forgive you. After all, you saved my life."

"You may address me as Superman."

"Super-twat might be more appropriate." She's still smiling but her chin's wobbling. "You've broken your leg in about fifty places, smashed your pelvis and ruptured your spleen."

That explains the weighty feeling on my leg.

I tighten my fingers around hers. "What about you? Were you hurt?"

She brings my hand to her lips and kisses the tips of my fingers. "It was like being rugby tackled by my cousin Nikos, but other than a bruised shoulder from the impact, no damage at all."

I exhale my relief slowly and raise my hand to touch her face. I stare at her for a long, long time. The strange dream-like humour that's carried us to this point has vanished.

"I love you," I whisper.

Her chin wobbles again. "I love you too." She kisses my fingers again. Another tear falls. "You could have killed yourself."

I lift my head to get closer to her. "I made my choice a long time ago, Mel. A world without you in it is no world for me."

"What about *my* world?" she chokes.

I don't know what she's talking about.

"How am I supposed to live without *you*? I thought you were going to die." She takes a long breath through her nose as more tears fall. "I've never known terror like it. Saving me at your own expense would have killed me too." The tape's finished rewinding. "I would have turned into a living ghost and your effort would have been wasted."

"Mel..."

"It's you and me, Alex." She wipes her tears and attempts a smile. "It's always been you and me."

I squeeze her fingers. "Always."

She kisses me. I think it might be the softest, sweetest kiss I've ever tasted. "Thank you for saving my life."

"Thank you for saving mine."

She kisses me again, then gently nestles her face in my neck.

Neither of us speaks for the longest time, not until she lifts her head and strokes my hair. "What happens now? For us, I mean? Any more near-death experiences?"

"I don't have a clue."

"Seriously?"

Laughter wells up in me. "Seriously. Your accident was the last thing I set out to change and I've done it. From now on the butterfly effect's in charge."

"A blank canvas for both of us?"

"A ride neither of us knows the end of."

"As long as we ride it together, then that's good enough for me."

She presses play.

Bryan Adams starts crooning in my ear.

Sunday 1st June 2025

Alex

I'm in the kitchen propped on a stool, chopping salad. Melody's in the garden. I see her in the distance, zipping around on her ride-on lawnmower.

For someone who doesn't drive in this life, she's not averse to treating the mower like a bucking bronco, and I wince as she narrowly avoids mowing the geums that have only just overspilled their patch of the flowerbed. She doesn't notice the near miss. She's too busy beaming at the simple joy of a simple task and the slight element of danger that comes with it (for the flowers, at least).

Her long corkscrew hair billows behind her. It's streaked with white but she won't put any colour on it, not even when Alice teases her. And speaking of Alice, there she is, striding over the lawn and waving at her dinky older sister to stop.

Whatever Alice says makes Mel throw her head back and laugh, then lean out of the mower and swipe at Alice's backside.

"What are they up to?" Patty asks. I hadn't heard her join me.

"With those two, it could be anything."

She laughs. "Do you want me to do anything before I start on the potato salad?"

"We're pretty much good to go, thanks. Where's Roy?"

"In the shower."

Mel's parents are staying with us for a few weeks. When Alice went to university, Mel finally talked them into making some modest investments through me. Six years ago they upped sticks, bought themselves a small yacht and set off around the world. Whenever they come home, they stay with us. Alice moved in with us when she finished her history degree. Melody never believes me when I tell her that in her other life, the baby sister who followed in her footsteps and now works at the thriving Brocklehurst Manor with her was an astrophysicist, even though Alice can always be found outside on a clear night looking through her telescope.

Mel's half-standing astride the mower, waving and hollering. I crane my neck to see who's came straight round to the garden. It's Lorna, her wife Daisy and their young daughter – our goddaughter – Belle, who goes running straight to Mel. They moved in with us a month before the pandemic struck, when Belle was only two months old. We were prepared for it, you see, and so was anyone else who listened to us.

Chest freezers full of meat, bread and frozen milk, shelves of tinned goods, half the garden turned into a vegetable plot, a cellar full of wine, and enough toilet roll to have caused a riot if anyone had seen it, we had all the provisions needed for us and those we love to be hermits together until the vaccinations were approved. Being on the shielding list, I was one of the first to be jabbed.

Mel and I never did have kids. It wasn't through lack of trying or want, it just never happened. We don't know if my injuries were the cause. We never looked into it or went the treatment route. We just accepted it wasn't meant to be. Sometimes the butterfly effect works in your favour, sometimes it doesn't. Some things are just fated.

As Mel always says, make the most of what you've got for the time you've got it.

Live well.

THE END

Acknowledgments

There are many people I need to thank, most significantly, my brilliant son Zak, who will cry like a baby if he doesn't get top billing. And really, he deserves it, because if he hadn't asked a theoretical question over dinner during lockdown, Butterflies would never have been born. That question was, "If you could live your life again, would you do everything the same?" After establishing that we'd be allowed to travel back with all our memories intact, I said yes but my husband said no – he would want to use his future knowledge to future-proof our life. As I then pointed out, the Butterfly Effect would come into play and our lives would diverge so significantly that there would be a very real chance we'd never meet... to which he said, "I'd find you." Not only did I choose to believe he meant it, but by the time we'd finished eating, Butterflies had come fully to life in my head.

As Butterflies is so different to the category romances I usually write, I initially set out writing it only for me. However, the more I wrote of it, the more I fell in love with Melody and Alex and all their family and friends (even Matt the Twat), which is why I must extend thanks to Nicola Caws, my old editor at Harlequin Mills & Boon. Nic read an early draft of the book, and if she hadn't been so enthusiastic about it, there's a good chance it would still be nestled in my OneDrive doing nothing.

I also need to thank my greatest cheerleader, my stepmum Jan, who's always happy to proofread for me. Along with my dear friend, the historical author Michelle Styles, she cast her all-seeing eye over Butterflies, so any typos or other errors can be firmly blamed on them (ha!). Jan and Michelle – I couldn't have done this without you two.

To the romance authors Pippa Roscoe, Jennifer Hayward, Clare Connelly, and all the other wonderful authors who write for Modern/Presents and who've encouraged me and passed on their words of wisdom – thank you.

To the rest of my family (Zak, you've already been mentioned!), my gorgeous son Joe and my beautiful daughter-in-law Amelia and their flipping amazing son Mitchell (yes, I'm a grandmother. Blame the parents), my wonderful dad Brian, who very considerately married Jan for my benefit, my incredible mum Lucie and her always-supportive husband Ted, my fabulous sister Jennie, equally fabulous stepsister Joanne, just as equally fabulous sister-in-law Lulu and her partner John, my amazingly supportive in-laws Geoff and Jan, and all my funny and unique nieces and nephews (listed in alphabetical order so I can't be accused of favouritism!), Eliza, Lily, Luke, Riley and Tilly... Thank you all, for everything. Thanks must also be given to Nicky and Mark, the best friends anyone could wish for.

Last but certainly not least, the biggest thanks go to my husband Adam. If I could do it all again, I would.

About the Author

Michelle's love affair with books began as a baby when, according to her mum, she would throw her teddies out of the cot and cuddle books instead. This love for all things wordy has never left her. A voracious reader, her tastes cross all genres. Her first experience with romance was as a child devouring copious amounts of fairy tales. As her reading tastes evolved, she discovered something special—that a book has the capacity to make her heart beat as if falling in love for the first time.

When not reading or pretending to do the housework, Michelle loves nothing more than creating worlds of her own featuring handsome heroes and the sparkly, feisty women who refuse to take crap from them. She hopes her books can make her readers' hearts beat a little faster, too.

If you enjoyed reading Butterflies, please consider leaving a review.

For more books and updates:
http://www.michellesmart.co.uk